"Who are you?" Vincenzo whispered against her lips.

"It doesn't matter," she said through her swimming senses. "I'm not real."

"You are real now—in my arms."

"Only here," she whispered.

"The rest doesn't matter. Kiss me—kiss me."

Julia did as he wanted, finding that after the years alone she still knew how. It was an intoxicating discovery. Now she allowed her hands and mouth to do as they pleased, and the things that pleased them were sensual, outrageous, experienced. He was right. This alone was real, and everything in her wanted to yield to it.

All the sensuality she normally kept banked down was flaming in his arms now, inciting him to explore her further, wanting more. He didn't know her real name, but her name no longer mattered. This woman was coming back to life, and he knew that he, and no other, must be the man to make that happen.

Curl up and have a

Heart *to* **Heart**

with Harlequin Romance®!

Just like having a heart-to-heart
with your best friend, these stories
will take you from laughter to tears
and back again. So heartwarming and emotional
you'll want to have some tissue handy!

Look out for more stories

in **HEART TO HEART**

Husband by Request
by Rebecca Winters
On sale July 2005

A FAMILY FOR KEEPS

Lucy Gordon

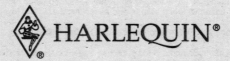

TORONTO • NEW YORK • LONDON
AMSTERDAM • PARIS • SYDNEY • HAMBURG
STOCKHOLM • ATHENS • TOKYO • MILAN • MADRID
PRAGUE • WARSAW • BUDAPEST • AUCKLAND

ISBN 0-373-18189-2

A FAMILY FOR KEEPS

First North American Publication 2005.

Copyright © 2005 by Lucy Gordon.

www.eHarlequin.com

Printed in U.S.A.

PROLOGUE

THIS would be a good place to die.

She didn't utter the words but they were there in her heart. They swam up from the depths of the black water. They lingered around the cold grey stones and whispered away into the darkness.

She hadn't thought about dying when she'd planned to come here. Only revenge. There had been a long time to think about that.

The passion for revenge had brought her to this corner of Venice. She'd envisaged no further, certain that the next step would reveal itself when the time came.

Instead—nothing.

But what had she thought was going to happen when she got here? That the first face she saw would be the one she was seeking?

Or rather, one of the two faces she was seeking. One face she might not recognise after so many years, but the other she would know anywhere, any time. It haunted her by day and lived in her nightmares.

It was cold. The wind whistled along the canals and down the little alleys, and there was no comfort in all the world.

'I can't sleep at night, yet now I could sleep for ever. For ever—and ever—and ever—

'Yes, this would be a good place...'

CHAPTER ONE

AT MIDNIGHT Venice was the quietest city in the world, and in winter it could be the most mournful.

No cars, only the occasional sound of a passing boat, footsteps echoing on the hard stones, or the soft lap of tiny waves. And even this would soon die away into silence.

Here, by the Rialto Bridge, shadow merged with stone and stone with water, so that it was hard to tell if the bundle of clothes in the corner contained a living being or not.

At first sight, Piero thought that it probably did not, so still did it lie. He approached the bundle and gave it a tentative prod. It groaned softly, but didn't move. He frowned. A woman from the sound of it.

'Hey!' He tapped again and she rolled a little way so that he could discern a face. It was pale and drawn, and in this light that was all he could make out.

'Come with me,' he said in Italian.

For a moment she stared at him out of blank

eyes, and he wondered if she had understood. Then she began to haul herself up, making no protest, asking no questions.

He half guided, half supported her away from the bridge, in to an alley, which turned into another alley and then into another, and another. To the casual eye they looked identical, all cold, narrow, gleaming with rain. But he found his way between them easily.

The woman with him barely noticed. Her heart was like a frozen stone in her body, numbing all feeling except despair.

Once she stumbled and he held her safe, muttering, 'Not much farther.'

She could see now that they had reached the rear entrance of a building. There was just enough light to reveal that it was palatial. There was a large set of ornate double doors, maybe twelve feet high. But he passed these and led her to a much smaller door.

At first it stuck, but when he put his shoulder to it, with a movement that was half a push, half a shake, it yielded. Inside there was a torch, which he used to find the rest of the way.

Their footsteps sounded hollow on the tiled floors, giving her the sense of a grandiose building. She had a brief impression of a sweeping staircase and a wall with pale spaces where there had once been pictures.

A palace, but a shabby, abandoned palace.

At last he led her into a small room, where there were an armchair and a couple of sofas. Gently he guided her to one.

'Thank you,' she whispered, speaking for the first time.

He regarded her with surprise.

'English?' he asked.

She made the effort. '*Sì. Sono inglese.*'

'There's no need for that,' he said in perfect English. 'I speak your language. Now you must have some food. My name is Piero, by the way.'

When she hesitated he said, 'Any name will do— Cynthia, Anastasia, Wilhemina, Julia—'

'Julia,' she said. It was as good a name as any.

In one corner stood a tall ceramic stove, white with gilt decoration. In the lower part was a pair of doors, which he opened and began to pile wood inside.

'The electricity is off,' he explained, 'so it's lucky that the old stove remains. This one has stood here nearly two hundred years, and it still works. The trouble is I'm out of paper to light it.'

'Here. I got a newspaper on the plane.'

He showed no surprise at someone who had managed to buy a plane ticket and then slept in the street. He simply struck a match and in a few moments they had the beginnings of a fire.

At last they considered each other.

She saw an old man, tall, very thin, with a shock of white hair. He wore an ancient overcoat, tied with string around the waist, and a threadbare woollen scarf wrapped around his throat. He seemed a mixture of scarecrow and clown. His face was almost cadaverous, making his bright blue eyes exceptionally vivid by contrast. Even more noticeable was his smile, brilliant as a beacon, which flashed on and off.

Piero saw a woman whose age he couldn't guess except to put her in the mid thirties. Perhaps older, perhaps younger.

She was tall, and her figure, dressed in serviceable jeans, sweater and jacket, was a little too slim to be ideal. Her long fair hair hung forward like a curtain, making it hard to see her properly. Perhaps she preferred it that way because she mostly let it hang. Just once she brushed it aside, revealing that suffering had left her with a weary, troubled face, large eyes, and an air of distrusting all the world.

Her face was too lean and almost haggard. There was beauty there, but it came from a fire that burned far back behind her eyes.

'Thank you for finding me,' she said at last, speaking in a soft voice.

'You'd have been dead by morning, lying in that freezing place.'

'Probably.' She didn't sound as though this were of much interest. 'Where are we?'

'This is the Palazzo di Montese, home of the Counts di Montese for nine centuries. It's empty because the present count can't afford to live here.'

'So you live here instead?'

'That's right. And nobody bothers me because they're afraid of the ghost,' he added with relish.

'What ghost?'

He reached behind the chair to where an old sheet lay on the floor. Draping it over his head, he threw up his arms and began to wail.

'That ghost,' he said, tossing the sheet away and speaking normally.

She gave a faint smile. 'That's very scary,' she said.

He cackled like a delighted child. 'If people didn't believe in the ghost to start with they wouldn't take any notice of me. But everyone around here has heard about Annina, so they tell themselves it's her.'

'Who was she really?'

'She lived seven hundred years ago. She was a Venetian girl with a vast fortune but no title, which mattered a lot in those days. She fell madly in love with Count Ruggiero di Montese but he only married her for her money. When she'd borne him a son he locked her away.

Eventually her body was found floating in the Grand Canal.

'Some said she was murdered, others that she had escaped in a small boat, which capsized. Now she's supposed to haunt this place. They say you can hear her voice calling up from the dungeons, begging to be released, crying to be allowed to see her child.'

He stopped because a faint sound had broken from her.

'Are you all right?' he asked, concerned.

'Yes,' she whispered.

'I haven't scared you, have I? Surely you don't believe in ghosts?'

'Not that kind of ghost,' Julia said softly.

He started the supper. By now the fire was burning merrily, so he fixed a grid over the burning wood, and used this to heat coffee.

'There's some sausages too,' he said. 'I cook them over the flames on forks. And I have rolls here. I have a friend with a restaurant, and he gives me yesterday's bread.'

When they were both settled and eating, she said, 'Why did you take me in? You know nothing about me.'

'I know that you needed help. What else is there to know?'

She understood. He had welcomed her into the

fellowship of the dispossessed where nothing had to be told. The past did not exist.

So now she was officially a down-and-out. It was not such a bad thing to be. After the way she'd spent the last few years it might even be a step up.

'Here,' she said, reaching into a bag and bringing out a very small plastic bottle, containing red wine. 'The man next to me on the plane left it behind, so I took it.'

'Would it be indelicate to ask if you obtained the plane ticket in the same way?'

She gave a real smile then.

'Believe it or not, I didn't steal it,' she said. 'If you go to the right airline you can get a ticket from England to Venice for almost nothing. But when you get off the plane—' She shrugged.

'You can find winter prices in the hotels now,' Piero pointed out.

'Even so, I'm not spending a penny that I don't have to,' she said in a voice that was suddenly hard and stubborn. 'But I'll pay my way here,' she added.

'Cheaper than a hotel,' he agreed, waving a sausage.

'And the surroundings are grand. You can tell it's the real thing.'

'Know a bit about palaces, do you?'

'I've worked in a few,' she said cautiously.

'I'm surprised someone hasn't bought this to turn it into a luxury hotel.'

'They keep trying,' Piero said. 'But the owner won't sell. He could be a rich man, but it's been in his family for centuries, and he won't let it go.'

She rose and walked over to the tall window from which came some illumination, even though it was night. She understood why when she looked out and saw that the room overlooked the Grand Canal.

Even in late November, past midnight, this thoroughfare was busy with life. *Vaporetti*, the passenger boats, still plied their trade along the length of the canal, and lights shone on both banks.

In the room where she stood, beams of dim light coming through the stained glass windows made patterns on the tiled floor. These and the glow from the stove were the only defence against the darkness.

She didn't mind. The gloom of this place pleased her, where bright light would have been a torment.

'Do you live here all the time?' she asked Piero, sitting down and accepting another coffee from his hands.

'Yes, it's a good place. The amenities have been turned off, of course. No heat or lighting.

But the pump outside still works, so we have fresh water. Let me show you.'

He led her down to the small stone outhouse where there was the pump and an earth closet.

'We even have a bathroom,' he declared with pride.

'Positively the lap of luxury,' she agreed solemnly.

When they went back inside she was suddenly swept by a weariness that almost knocked her off her feet. Piero looked at her with shrewd, kindly eyes.

'You're almost out of it, aren't you? You sleep on that sofa, and I'll have this one.'

He struck a theatrical attitude.

'Fair lady, do not fear to share a room with me. Be assured that I shall not molest you in your sleep. Or even out of it. That fire died years ago, and even in its better days it was never more than a modest flame.'

Julia could not help smiling at his droll manner.

'I wasn't afraid,' she assured him.

'No, I suppose certain things about me are fairly obvious,' said the gaunt scarecrow before her.

'I didn't mean that. I meant you've been kind and I know I can trust you.'

He gave a sigh.

'How I wish you were wrong!' he said mournfully. 'There are cushions over there, and here are some blankets. Sleep tight.'

She thanked him, curled up on the sofa in a blanket and was asleep in seconds. Piero was about to settle down for the night when a footstep outside alerted him, and a moment later a man entered, making him smile with pleasure.

'Vincenzo,' he said softly. 'It's good to see you again.'

The newcomer, who was in his late thirties with a lean, harsh face, asked, 'Why are we whispering?'

Piero pointed to the sofa, and Vincenzo nodded in understanding.

'Who is she?' he asked.

'She answers to Julia, and she's English. She's one of us.'

Vincenzo nodded, accepting the implication of 'us', and began to unpack two brown paper bags that he'd brought with him.

'A few leftovers from the restaurant,' he explained, bringing out some rolls, a carton of milk, and some slices of meat.

'Doesn't your boss mind you taking these?' Piero asked, claiming them with glee.

'Perks of the job. Besides, I can handle the boss.'

'That's very brave of you,' Piero said with a knowing wink. 'They say he's a terrible man.'

'So I've heard. Has anyone bothered you here?'

'Nobody ever does, although the owner is an even more terrible man. But if he tried to throw us out I expect you'd handle him too.'

Vincenzo grinned. 'I'd do my best.'

This was a game they played. Vincenzo was actually *il Conte di Montese*, the owner of the *palazzo* where they were standing, and also of the restaurant where he worked. Piero knew this. Vincenzo knew that he knew it, and Piero knew that Vincenzo knew he knew. But it suited them both for it to remain unspoken between them.

On the sofa Julia stirred and muttered. Vincenzo moved a little closer and sat down, watching her.

'How did you find her?' he asked quietly.

'Curled up in a corner of an alley, which is odd because she says she flew here.'

'She took so much trouble to come to Venice, only to collapse in the street?' Vincenzo mused. 'What the devil is driving her?'

'Perhaps she'll tell me the reason later,' Piero said. 'But not if I ask.'

Vincenzo nodded, understanding the code by which Piero and those like him lived. He was used to dropping into his empty home to find various squatters sheltering there.

He knew that a sensible man would have driven them out, but, despite his grim aspect, he lacked the heart. He looked in occasionally to keep an eye on the place, but he'd found that Piero was better than any caretaker, and the building was safe with him. Now his visits were as much to check on the old man's welfare as for any other reason.

Julia stirred again, settling into a position where more of her face was visible.

Moving quietly, Vincenzo dropped to his knees beside her and studied her. He supposed he shouldn't be doing that while she was unknowing and defenceless, but something about her drew him so that he could not turn away.

Her face spoke of mysteries and denied them in the same moment. She wasn't a girl, he thought, probably somewhere in her thirties, marked by grief and with a withdrawn look so intense that it was there even in sleep.

Her mouth was wide, generous, designed to be mobile and expressive. He had known women with lips like that. They laughed easily, talked well, and kissed urgently with warm, sweet breath.

But this woman looked as if she seldom smiled, except as a polite mask. And she had forgotten how to kiss. She had forgotten love and pleasure and happiness. This was a face from which tenderness had been driven by sheer force. Its owner was capable of anything.

But it hadn't always been true. She had started life differently. Traces of vulnerability were still there, although perhaps not for long. Something had brought her to the point where life would harden her quickly.

Then a strange feeling came over him, as though the very air had moved, and the ground beneath him had trembled. He blinked, shaking his head, and the feeling vanished. Quickly he moved away.

'What's the matter?' Piero asked, handing him a cup of coffee.

'Nothing. It's just that for a moment I felt I'd seen her before. But where—?' He sighed. 'I must be imagining it.'

He drank his coffee and turned to go. At the door he stopped and handed Piero some money.

'Look after her,' he said quietly.

When Vincenzo had gone Piero wrapped himself in a blanket and lay down on the other sofa. After a while he slept.

Doors clanged again and again. It was a dreadful, hollow sound, and it soon became agonising.

She flung herself against one of those iron doors, pounding and shrieking that she should not be here. But there was no response, no help. Only stony, cold indifference.

There were bars at the windows. She pulled herself up to them, looking through at the world from which she was shut out.

She could see a wedding. It did not seem strange to find such a scene in this dreary place, for she knew instinctively that they were connected.

There was the groom, young and handsome, smiling on his day of triumph. Was there something about his smile that wasn't quite right, as though he was far from being the man his bride thought?

She knew nothing of that. The poor little fool thought he loved her. She was young, innocent, and stupid.

Here she came, glowing with love triumphant. Julia gripped the bars in horror as that naïve girl threw back her veil, revealing the face beneath—

Her own face.

'Don't,' she said hoarsely. 'Don't do it. Don't marry him, *for pity's sake don't marry him.*'

The last words were a scream, and suddenly she was sitting up, tortured into wakefulness, tears streaming down her face, and Piero kneeling beside her, his arms about her, trying vainly to offer comfort for a wrong that could never be put right.

For breakfast next morning Piero laid on a feast.

'Where did these come from?' Julia asked, looking at the rolls stuffed with meat.

'From my friend from the restaurant who dropped in last night, the one I told you about.'

'He sounds like a really good friend. Is he one of us?'

'In what sense?'

'You know—stranded.'

'Well, he's got a roof over his head, but you might call him stranded in other ways. He's lost everyone he ever loved.'

Over breakfast she produced some money. 'It's only a little but it might help. You'll know where the bargains are.'

'Splendid. We'll go out together.'

She wrapped up thickly and followed him out into the day. He led her through a labyrinth of tiny *calles*, until her head was swimming. How could anyone find their way around this place?

Suddenly they were in the open, and the Rialto Bridge reared up over them, straight ahead. She'd been here the night before and gone to frozen sleep at one end, where the shore railings curved towards the water.

She'd come to this place searching for someone…

Now she looked around, but all the faces
seemed to converge, making her giddy. And perhaps *he* had never been here after all.

Venice was bustling with life. Barges made
their way through the canals, stopping to seize
the bags of rubbish that had been dumped by the
water's edge. More barges, filled with supplies,
arrived at the open air market at the base of the
Rialto.

Piero stocked up with fiendish efficiency, buying more produce with less money than she
would have thought possible.

'That's a good morning's work,' he said. 'Now
we—you're shivering. I guess you took a chill
from those stones last night. Let's get you into
the warm.'

She tried to smile but she was feeling worse
by the minute, and was glad to turn back.

When they reached home Piero tended her like
a mother, building up the stove and making her
some hot coffee.

'You've got a nasty cold there,' he said when
she started to cough.

'Yes,' she snuffled miserably.

'I've got to go out for a while. Stay close to
the stove while I'm gone.'

He left quickly, and she was alone in the rapidly darkening building. There was something blessed in the silence.

She went to the window overlooking the Grand Canal. Just outside was a tiny garden, bordered by tall wrought iron railings, right next to the water.

By craning her neck she could make out the Rialto Bridge, and the bank lined with outdoor tables on the far side of the canal. The cafés were filled with people, determined not to be put off by the time of year.

She wandered back to the stove and sat on the floor, beside it, dozing on and off.

Then something made her eyes open sharply. The last of the light had gone, and she could hear footsteps in the corridor. It didn't sound like Piero, but somebody younger.

The sound drew close and halted. Then the door handle turned. It was enough to make her leap up and hurry into the shadows where the intruder could not see her. Inwardly she was screaming, *Go away! Leave me alone!*

She stood still, her heart thumping wildly, as the door opened and a man came in. He set the bag he was carrying on the floor, and looked around as though expecting to see somebody.

She told herself not to be foolish. This was probably Piero's friend. But still she couldn't make herself move. Nobody was a friend to her.

The man came into a shaft of light from a large window. It was soft, almost gloomy light, but she could make out that he was tall, with a rangy build and a lean face that suggested a man in his thirties.

Suddenly he grew alert, as though realising that he was not alone. 'Who is it?' he called, looking around.

She tried to force herself to speak, but a frozen hand seemed to be grasping her throat.

'I know you're somewhere,' he said. 'There's no need to hide from me.'

Then he moved quickly, pulling back one of the long curtains that hung beside the window, revealing her, pressed against the wall, eyes wide with dread and hostility.

'*Dio Mio!*' he exclaimed. 'A ghost.'

He put out his hand and would have laid it on her shoulder, but she flinched away.

'Don't touch me,' she said hoarsely in English. His hand fell at once.

'I'm sorry,' he replied, also in English. 'Don't be afraid of me. Why are you hiding?'

'I'm—not—hiding,' she said with an effort, knowing she sounded crazy. 'I just—didn't know who you were.'

'My name is Vincenzo, a friend of Piero's. I was here last night but you were asleep.'

'He told me about you,' she said jerkily, 'but I wasn't sure—'

'I'm sorry if I startled you.'

He was talking gently, soothing her as he would have done a wild animal, and gradually she felt her irrational fear subside.

'I heard you coming,' she said, 'and—' A fit of coughing drowned the rest.

'Come into the warm,' Vincenzo said, beckoning her to the stove.

When she still hesitated he took hold of her hands. His own hands were warm and powerful, and they drew her forward irresistibly.

He eased her down onto the sofa, but instead of releasing her he slid his hands up her arms and grasped her, not roughly but with a strength that felt like protection.

'Piero says your name is Julia.'

She hesitated for a split second. 'Yes, that's right. Julia.'

'Why are you trembling?' he asked. 'It can't be that bad.'

Something in those words broke her control and she shuddered violently.

'It is that bad,' she said, in a hoarse voice. 'Everything is that bad. It always will be. It's like a maze. I keep thinking that there must be a way out, but there isn't. Not after all this time. It's too late, I know it's too late, and if I had any sense I'd go away and forget, but I *can't* forget.'

'Julia.' He gave her a little shake. *'Julia.'*

She didn't hear him. She was beyond anything he could say or do to reach her. Words poured out of her unstoppably, while tears slid down her face.

'You can't get rid of ghosts,' she wept, 'just by telling them to go, because they're everywhere, before you and behind you and most of all *inside* you.'

'Yes, I know,' he murmured grimly, but she rushed on, unheeding.

'I have to do it. I can't stop and I won't, and I can't help who gets hurt, don't you see that?'

'I'm afraid the person who gets hurt will be you,' he said.

For answer she grasped him back, digging her fingers into him painfully.

'It doesn't matter,' she said. 'Nobody can hurt me any more. When you've reached your limit, you're safe, so I don't have to worry, and there's nothing to stop me doing what I have to.'

Abruptly she released him and buried her face in her hands as the feverish energy that had briefly sustained her drained away, leaving her weak and shaking.

For a moment Vincenzo was nonplussed. Then he put his arms right around her and held her in a tight clasp. He didn't try to speak, knowing that there was nothing to say, but his grip was rough and fierce, silently telling her she was not alone.

After a long time he felt her relax, although even that had a strained quality, as though she had forced it to happen.

'I'm all right,' she said in a muffled voice.

He relaxed his grip and drew back slightly. 'Are you sure?'

'I'm all right,' she insisted fiercely. 'I'm all right, I'm all right.'

'I just want to help you.'

'I don't need anyone's help!'

Instantly he got to his feet and stepped back.

'I'm sorry,' she said, 'I didn't mean to be rude, it's just—'

'You don't have to explain. I know how it is.'

She looked up at him, and in the dim light he had an impression of a pale face, surrounded by long fair hair, like one of the other-worldly creatures that populated the pictures that had once filled this palace. He had grown up with the ghostly faces, accepting them as a normal part of his world. It startled him to meet one in reality.

'It's like that for you too?' she asked.

After a moment's pause he said, 'For everyone in one way or another. Some less—some more.'

He said the last words hoping she would tell

him about herself, but he could see her defences being hastily reassembled. The moment was already slipping away, and when he heard the sound of Piero approaching he knew it had gone.

CHAPTER TWO

PIERO pushed open the door, his face brightening when he saw the visitor.

'*Ciao,*' Vincenzo said, clapping him on the shoulder.

'*Ciao,*' Piero said, looking around. 'Ah, you two have met.'

'Yes, I'm afraid I gave the *signorina* a fright.'

'Why so formal? This isn't a *signorina*. It's Julia.'

'Or are you perhaps a *signora*?' Vincenzo queried. 'You understand, a *signora* is—?'

'Yes, thank you, I speak Italian,' she said edgily. 'A *signora* is a married woman. I'm a *signorina*.'

She wasn't sure why she insisted on parading her knowledge of Italian at that moment, unless it was pride. Vincenzo's understanding had made her defensive.

'So you speak my language,' Vincenzo said. 'I congratulate you. So often the English won't trouble to learn other languages. Do you speak it well?'

'I'm not sure. I haven't used it for a while. I'm out of practice. I can brush up on it here.'

'Not as easily as you think. In Venice we speak Venetian.'

After that he dived into the bags he'd brought, seeming to forget her, which was a relief. She took the chance to wander away to the window and stand with her back to them, watching the canal, but not seeing it.

Instead she saw Vincenzo in her mind's eye, trying to understand the darkness she sensed, in his looks and in the man himself. Everything about him was dark, from his black hair to his deep brown eyes. Even his wide mouth, with its tendency to quirk wryly, suggested that he was not really amused. Or, if so, that the humour was bleak and fit only for the gallows.

A man whose inner world was as grim and haunted as her own.

But still she tried to thrust him from her mind. He was dangerous because he saw too much, tricking her into blurting out thoughts that had been rioting in her head, but which she'd kept rigidly repressed.

I have to do it—I can't help who gets hurt.

Say nothing. Never let them suspect what you're planning. Smile, hate, and protect your secrets.

That was how she had lived.

And in one moment he had triggered an avalanche, luring her into a dangerous admission.

*Nobody can hurt me any more—so there's
nothing to stop me doing what I have to.*

She looked around, and saw to her relief that
Vincenzo had gone. She hadn't heard him leave.

Piero was beaming at her, waving a bread roll
in invitation.

'We feast like kings,' he announced grandilo-
quently. 'Sit down and let me serve you the
Choice of the Day. Trust me, I was once the head
chef at the Paris Ritz.'

She wasn't sure what to believe. Unlikely as
it sounded, it might just be true.

Her cold grew worse over the next few days.
Piero's care never failed her. From some store
room he managed to produce a bed. It was old,
shabby and needed propping up in one corner,
but it was more comfortable than her sofa, and
she fell onto it blissfully.

But he refused to let her thank him.

'It comes easily to me,' he assured her. 'I used
to be a top physician at Milan's largest hospital.'

'As well as being a great chef?' she teased
him.

He gave her a reproachful look. 'That was the
other night.'

'I'm sorry. I should have thought.'

She knew that Vincenzo sometimes came to

visit, but she always lay still, feigning sleep. She did not want to talk to him. He threatened secrets that she must keep.

But he too had painful secrets. He'd hinted as much.

Every second afternoon Piero would go out, returning three hours later. He never told her where he went, and she guessed that these occasions were connected with the events that had brought him to this limbo.

One afternoon he entered wearing his usual cheerful look, which became even brighter when he saw her.

'Did you find what you were looking for?' she ventured.

'Not today. She wasn't there, but she will be one day.'

'She?'

'Elena, my daughter. Ah, coffee! Splendid!'

She respected his desire to change the subject, but later, when the darkness had fallen, she asked gently,

'Where is Elena now?'

He was silent for so long she was afraid he was offended, but then he said, 'It's hard to explain. We sort of—mislaid each other. But she's worked abroad a great deal, and I've always been there to meet her when she returned. Always the same place, at San Zaccaria—that's the landing stage where the boats come in near St Mark's. If I'm not there she'll want to know why, so I mustn't let her down. I just have to be patient, you see.'

'Yes,' she said sadly. 'I see.'

She wrapped the blanket around her and settled down, hoping that soon her mind would start working properly again, and she would know what to do next.

Then she wondered if that would ever happen, for when she closed her eyes the old pictures began to play back, and there was only grief, misery, despair, followed by rage and bitterness, so that soon she was hammering on the door again, screaming for a release that would never come.

Sometimes she would surface from her fever to find Vincenzo there, then go back to sleep, curiously contented. This was becoming her new reality, and when she awoke once to find Vincenzo gone she knew an odd sense of disturbance. But then she saw Piero, and relaxed again.

He came over and felt her forehead, pursing his lips to show that he wasn't pleased with what he found.

'I got you something,' he said, dissolving a powder in hot water. 'It'll make you feel better.'

'Thanks, Piero,' she said hoarsely. 'Or do I mean Harlequin?'

'What's that?'

'Harlequin, Columbine, Pierrot, Pierrette,' she said vaguely. 'They're all characters from the Commedia dell'Arte. Pierrot's a clown, isn't he?'

His eyes were very bright. 'It's as good a name as any. Like Julia.'

'Yes,' she agreed.

The cold remedy drink made her feel better and she got to her feet, rubbing her eyes. Her throat and her forehead were still hot, but she was determined to get up, if only for a while.

It was mid-afternoon and since the light was good she went out of the little room into the great reception hall and began to look about her.

The pictures might be gone but the frescoes painted directly onto the walls were still here. She studied them, until she came to one that stopped her in her tracks as though it had spoken to her.

It was at the top of the stairs, and showed a woman with long fair hair flying wildly around her face like a mad halo. Her eyes were large and distraught as though with some ghastly vision. She had been to hell, and now she would never really escape.

'That's Annina,' said Piero, who had followed her.

'It's Annina if we want to be fanciful,' said Vincenzo's voice.

He had come in silently and watched them for a moment before speaking.

'What do you mean, "fanciful"?' she asked.

He came up the stairs, closer to her. She watched him with hostile eyes, angry with herself for being glad to see him.

'We don't know if that's what she really looked like,' he explained. 'This was done a couple of centuries later, by an artist who played up the drama for all it was worth.

'See, there are prison bars in one corner, and there's a child over here. And this man, with the demonic face, is Annina's husband. Count Francesco, his direct descendant, didn't like having the family scandal revived. He even wanted the artist to paint over it.'

Scandalised, Julia spoke without thinking. 'Paint over a Correggio?'

She could have cut her tongue out the next moment. Vincenzo's raised eyebrows showed that he fully appreciated what she'd revealed.

'Well done,' he said. 'It *is* Correggio. And of course he refused to cover it. Then people began to admire it, and Francesco, who was as big a philistine as Correggio said he was, realised that it must be good after all. So it's stayed here, and people take their view of the story from this very melodramatic picture. Naturally, the ghost looks just like her. Ask Piero.'

His smile showed that he knew exactly the trick the old man was playing to scare off intruders.

'I'm sure I don't know what she looks like,' Piero said loftily. 'I've never seen her.'

'But she's been heard often,' Vincenzo observed. He clapped Piero on the shoulder. 'I've left a few things for you. I may see you later.' He pointed a commanding finger at Julia. 'You— into the warm, right now.'

She returned to the little room with relief. Her brief expedition had lowered her strength, and when she had eaten something she curled up again and was soon asleep.

It was after midnight when Vincenzo reappeared. When he was settled he became sunk in thought. 'How many people,' he asked at last, 'could identify a Correggio at once?'

'Not many,' Piero conceded.

'That's what I thought.' He glanced at the sleeping Julia. 'Has she told you anything about herself?'

'No, but why should she? Our kind respect each other's privacy. You know that.'

'Yes, but there's something about her that

worries me. It could be risky to leave her too much alone.'

'But suppose she wants to be left alone?'

'I think she does,' Vincenzo mused, remembering the desperation with which she had cried, 'I don't need anyone's help.'

Nobody said it like that unless their need for help was terrible.

All his life he'd had an instinctive affinity with needy creatures. When his father had bought him a puppy he'd chosen the runt of the litter, the one who had held back timidly. His father had been displeased, but the boy, stubborn beneath his quiet manner, had said, 'This one,' and refused to budge.

After that there had been his sister, his twin, discounted by their parents as a mere girl, and therefore loved by him the more. They had been close all their lives until she had cruelly repaid his devotion by dying, and leaving him bereft.

He had loved a woman, refusing to see her grasping nature, until she'd callously abandoned him.

Now he would have said that his days of opening his heart to people were over. No man could afford to be like that, and he'd developed armour in self-defence.

He made an exception for Piero, whom he'd known in better days. There was something about the old man's gentle madness, his humour in the face of misfortune, that called to him despite his resolutions.

As for the awkward, half-hostile woman he'd found sleeping here, he couldn't imagine why he'd allowed her to stay. Perhaps because she wanted nothing from him, and seemed consumed by a bitterness that matched his own.

Suddenly a long sigh came from the bed. As they watched she threw back the blanket and eased her legs over the side.

Vincenzo tensed, about to speak to her, but then something in her demeanour alerted him and he stopped. She stood for a moment, staring into the distance with eyes that were vague. Slowly Vincenzo got to his feet and went to stand before her.

'Julia,' he said softly.

She made no response and he realised that she was still asleep. When he spoke her name she did not see or hear him. After a moment she turned away and began to walk slowly to the door.

She seemed to know her way as well in the darkness and in the light. Without stumbling she opened the door, and went out into the main hall.

At the foot of the stairs she stopped, remaining still for a long time. Moonlight, streaming through the windows, showed her shrouded in a soft blue glow, like a phantom. She raised her head so that her long hair fell back and they could both see that her eyes were fixed on the picture of Annina, at the top of the stairs.

'Can she see it?' Piero muttered.

'It's the only thing she *can* see,' Vincenzo told him. 'Nothing else exists for her.'

She began to move again, slowly setting one foot in front of the other, climbing the broad stairs.

'Stop her,' Piero said urgently.

Vincenzo shook his head. 'This is her decision. We can't interfere.'

Moving quietly, he began to follow her up the stairs until she came to a halt in front of the fresco showing the distraught Annina. It too lay in the path of the moonlight that entered through windows high up in the hall.

'Julia,' Vincenzo said again, speaking very quietly.

Silence. She was not aware of him.

'Dammit, that's not her real name,' Vincenzo said frantically. 'How can I reach her with it?'

'There's another name you might try,' Piero murmured.

Vincenzo shot him an uneasy glance. 'Don't talk like that, Piero. Enough of superstition.'

'Is it superstition?'

'You know as well as I do that the dead don't come back.'

'Then who is she?'

Vincenzo didn't reply. He couldn't.

A soft moan broke from her. She was reaching up to touch the picture, beginning to talk in soft, anguished tones.

'I loved him, and he shut me away—for years—until I died—I died—'

'Julia,' Vincenzo said, knowing it would be useless.

Instead of answering she began to thump the wall.

'I died—' she screamed. 'Just as he meant me to. *My baby—my baby—*'

Abruptly all the strength went out of her and she leaned against the wall. Vincenzo grasped her gently and drew her away.

'It's all right,' he said. 'I'm here. Don't give in. Stay strong whatever you do.'

She looked up at him out of despairing eyes, and he knew that she couldn't see him. For her, he didn't exist.

'Let's go,' he said.

She shook her head and tried to pull away. 'I must find him,' she said hoarsely. 'Don't you understand?'

'Of course, but not tonight. Get some rest, and later I'll help you find him.'

'You can't help me. Nobody can.'

'But I will,' he insisted. 'There has to be a way if there's a friend to help you. And you have a friend now.'

Whether she understood the words or whether it was his tone that reached her, she stopped struggling and stood passive.

It was the first time he'd seen her face turned towards him without suspicion or defensiveness. But he could still feel her trembling, and it made him do something on impulse.

Putting his hands on either side of her face, he kissed her softly again and again, her eyes, her cheeks, her mouth.

'It's all right,' he said again. 'I'm here.'

She did not reply, but her eyes closed. He wrapped his arms right around her, leading her carefully down the stairs. She held onto him, eyes still closed, but moving with confidence while he was there.

Step by step they made their way to the bottom of the stairs, then back into the little room, where Vincenzo guided her to the bed so that she could lie down again.

She murmured something that he could not catch, then seemed to relax all at once. Vincenzo pulled the blanket up and tucked it tenderly around her.

'Not a word of this, my friend,' he said, joining Piero. 'Not to anyone else and especially not to her.'

Piero nodded. 'We wait until she mentions it.'

'If she ever does.'

'You think she won't remember what happened tonight?'

'I don't think she even knows what happened tonight. She wasn't here.'

'Then where was she?'

'In some far place where nobody else is invited. It's dark and fearful, and it's from there that she draws her strength.'

'Her head must be very muddled if she thinks she's Annina.' Piero sighed. 'It was like meeting a ghost in the flesh.'

Vincenzo raised an eyebrow. 'Rid yourself of that idea, my friend. She is no ghost.'

'But you heard what she said. She was buried—she died—the child—she was speaking as Annina.'

'No,' Vincenzo said sombrely. 'What's really horrifying is that she was speaking as herself.'

At last Julia awoke to find everything clear. Her body was cool again and the inside of her head was orderly.

'Have you come back to us?'

Looking around, she saw Vincenzo sitting nearby, and wondered how long he'd been there.

'Yes, I think I have,' she said. 'More or less. I may even be in one piece.'

She swung her legs gingerly to the floor and began to ease herself up. He crossed the floor quickly and held out a hand.

'Steady,' he said as she clung to him. 'You haven't been eating enough to keep a mouse alive. No wonder you're weak.'

'I'm not weak. You can let me go.'

He did so and she promptly sat down again.

'OK, I'm weak.'

'Give yourself time. Don't rush it.'

He spoke in his normal way, but she had an odd sensation that something was different. He was looking at her curiously, with a question in his eyes.

'What's the matter?' she asked.

'How do you mean?'

'You're giving me a strange look.'

For once she seemed to have caught him off guard. 'I was just—wondering if you're really better. You certainly seem—' He seemed to be searching for the right words. 'You seem more like your normal self.'

'That's how I feel,' she said, wondering what he was implying.

'Good,' he said, sounding deflated. 'Stay there while I make you some soup.'

The hot soup was straight from heaven. When

she'd eaten she went down to the pump for a wash.

She returned to find Vincenzo still there. He was sitting by the window, sunk in his own thoughts, and didn't at first hear her. When she hailed him he seemed to come out of a dream.

'OK?'

'Yes. Who'd have thought washing in freezing water could feel so good? How long was I out of it?'

'Just over a week.'

'I slept for a week?'

'Not all the time. You kept recovering slightly, then you'd insist on getting up and walking around before you were ready. So you got worse again.'

'But to sleep for a week!'

'Or a hundred years,' he said ironically.

'Yes, now I know how the sleeping princess felt. I've even lost track of the date. Mind you, I often—'

She checked, as if about to reveal something, but then thinking better of it. Vincenzo's curiosity was heightened.

'You often forget the date?' he asked. 'How come?'

'Nothing. I didn't mean that.'

She met his gaze, defying him to disbelieve

her openly, although she knew he wasn't convinced. He backed down first.

'Well, anyway, it's December second,' he said.

'That's weird, to fall asleep in one month and awake in another. And no newspapers or television. It's strange how nice life can be without them.'

'To shut the world out!' he mused. 'Yes, that would be nice. What is it?'

He asked because she had suddenly stopped in the middle of the floor, and her eyes became vague, as though she were listening to distant voices.

'I don't know,' she said. 'It's just that—I had such dreams—such dreams—'

'Can you recall any of them?' Nobody could have told from Vincenzo's voice that the answer mattered to him.

'I think so—there was—there was—'

She closed her eyes, fighting desperately to summon back a memory that lay just beyond reach. It was disturbing, and yet in its heart lay a feeling of peace, the very one she was seeking.

'Try,' Vincenzo said, unable to keep a hint of urgency out of his voice.

But it was a fatal thing to say. The minute she reached out for the dream it vanished.

'It's gone,' she said with a sigh. 'I hope it comes back. I think it was lovely.'

He shrugged. 'If you can't remember it, how do you know it was lovely?'

'You know how it is with dreams. They leave you with a kind of feeling, even when you forget the details.'

'And what feeling did this one leave behind?'

'It was peaceful and—happy—' She said the last word in a tone of astonishment. 'Oh, heck, it was probably nothing at all.'

'Nothing at all,' Vincenzo agreed.

She looked around. 'Where's Piero?'

'He's gone to the landing stage.'

'Looking for Elena? Perhaps she'll come today.'

Vincenzo shook his head. 'She'll never come. She died several years ago.'

Julia sighed. 'I wondered about that. I can't make him out. How does he come to be living like this?'

'At one time he was a university professor. Elena, his daughter, was everything to him, especially after his wife died. Then she died too and everything finished for him.'

'He lost a child?' she murmured.

She felt something tearing at her at the thought of Piero and his lost child. There was no pain like it. How could anyone recover?

'She was drowned while out sailing. They found her body three days later. I was on the quay when they brought her home, and I saw Piero, staring out to sea as the boat came in. But when it landed he didn't seem to see it, just walked away. He didn't even go to her funeral because he refused to believe she was dead.

'He's never accepted it. I've tried to make him understand. I've even taken him to the cemetery at San Michele, to show him her grave, but he won't look at it.'

'Of course not. You shouldn't have done that.'

'Isn't it better for him to face reality?'

'Why?' she asked quickly. 'What's so marvellous about reality?'

'Nothing, I suppose.'

'Let him cling to his hope. Without it he'd go crazy.'

'But he's already a little crazy.'

'Then let him be crazy, if that's the only way to stop his heart breaking,' Julia said, almost pleading with him. 'How can you understand?'

'Perhaps I can,' he said wryly. 'Anyway, I know what you mean. Tell me—are you crazy?'

'Oh, yes,' she said, almost cheerfully. 'I'm as mad as a hatter.'

'Because of the ghosts inside you? That's what you said.'

'If I did, I was feverish. I don't remember.'

'I think you do. I think you remember what you want to remember.'

Her relaxed mood vanished and his probing made her nerves taut again.

'I don't know who you are,' she said in a low, angry voice, 'but I can't see why you come here.'

'Must there be a reason?'

'Well, you don't need a place to sleep, do you? And why else would you be here except to patronise us? No, I'm sorry—' She threw up her hand. 'I didn't mean to say that. But just don't start getting clever with me.'

'Not even to stop you hurting someone?'

'I'm not going to hurt anyone.'

'Except yourself.'

'That's my problem.'

'*Mio Dio*, it's like trying to argue with a hornet. I only said you picked your memories to suit yourself.'

She gave an edgy laugh.

'If I could do that I'd forget a lot of things. It's the ones I can't help remembering that are the problem. Piero's the wise one. He's found a way to choose what to remember.'

'Yes, I guess he has,' Vincenzo said wryly. 'And I think I hear him coming, so can we delay our hostilities for another time?'

She walked over to the window, annoyed with herself. For a brief moment she had been at ease

with him, regaining human feelings that she had
thought lost for ever. Then he had stepped over
an invisible line, actually daring to understand
her. And he had become an enemy again.

The door opened and Piero appeared.

'Not today?' Julia asked sympathetically.

'Not today,' he said brightly. 'Never mind.
Maybe next time.'

Abruptly Vincenzo remembered that he had to
be somewhere else, clapped Piero on the shoulder, and departed.

CHAPTER THREE

THE next afternoon, while Piero was out, Julia spent the time looking around the great building. The sight was both melancholy and magnificent.

The grandeur was still there. The Counts di Montese had lived like kings, secure in their wealth and authority. Now it was all gone. The rooms were silent and draughts whispered down the corridors.

The walls of the grand staircase were lined with frescoes, leading to a large one at the top, that she now knew was Annina. Watching it gave her a vague sensation of disturbance that grew with every moment. She wanted to run away, but she forced herself to keep climbing until she was facing the painted woman with her wild hair and her tormented eyes. Her heart raced faster and faster; she was suffocating—

And then it stopped. As suddenly as it had started the suffocating misery and terror ceased, leaving her with a feeling of calm release, almost as though someone had laid a comforting hand on her, and said, 'I'm here. I'll make it all right.'

The sensation was so clear that she looked around to see who had spoken. It was almost a surprise to find herself alone, the awareness of another presence was so intense.

She moved away from the picture. The disturbing currents that had flowed from it a moment ago had vanished. Now it was just a picture again.

Walking on through the building, she explored the rooms that were almost bare of furniture. She grew more fascinated as she went from room to room. She knew and understood places like this.

She took her time, studying the frescoes on the ceilings, some of which were very fine. Unlike the pictures, they were fixed, impossible to sell without tearing down the building. They gave her an idea of how magnificent this place must have been at its height.

At last she went into the great bedroom where the Count di Montese must have lived and held court. It was empty except for the huge bed and a few chairs, but the sense of grandeur lingered. She looked up at the ceiling frescoes. Then she tensed.

Was it her imagination, or was there a patch where the colours were darker? The afternoon light was fading fast, and she could not be sure.

Hurriedly she found a chair, pulled it out and

reached up. By standing on tiptoe she could just touch the patch and feel that it was damp.

And that meant it was recent, she thought. Somehow water was coming through that ceiling right now.

But where did it come from? She ran to the window and pushed it open, leaning out to look up. Just above her was a row of small windows, suggesting an attic.

She hurried out and down the corridor, urgently seeking a way of getting up to the next floor. At last she found a small, plain door that looked as if it might be the one. But it was locked.

There was no time to lose. She was assailed by a vision of water pouring down through ceilings, over walls, unstoppably ruining the beautiful building.

She rattled the door, which was old and shaky on its hinges. There was only one way to do this. Gathering all the strength she could muster, she gave a hard kick, and knew an unbelievable sense of satisfaction when the door gave way.

Oh, the blissful release of one violent action!

She sprinted up the stairs and found herself in the great attic at the top of the building.

It was long and low, and seemed to be used as a store room. There was some furniture here, and what looked like pictures, wrapped in heavy brown paper.

And there, by the wall, was a water tank, with a pipe leading from it across the floor. The pipe was old and broken, and water was pouring from it with terrible inevitability. If not stopped it would flood the floor, soaking down until the whole building was damaged.

Then she set her chin.

'Not if I have anything to do with it!' she breathed.

She needed something to wrap around the pipe! But what? Rags would do for now.

A frantic search around the attic revealed nothing of any use, and the water was pooling across the floor, threatening the wrapped pictures that were leaning against the wall.

Her handkerchief was too small. She would have to use her woollen sweater. Wrenching it off, she wound it frantically around the belching pipe, but already water was seeping through.

Something else! Her shirt. She managed to tear this into strips and tie them around the pipe, but the water just kept coming. Soon she would need a torch, as the light was fading every moment.

She must dash downstairs to find something more reliable, and put more clothes on, since with both her sweater and shirt gone she was freezing in her bra. She headed for the door, but stopped to rush back to the pipe and tighten the rough bandage. Then she raced back to the door, not looking where she was going, and colliding with someone.

At once two strong arms went around her and she fell to the floor with her assailant.

With everything in her she cursed him. It was hard when she was out of breath, but she did her best. She cursed him for delaying her, she cursed him for lying on top of her so that she couldn't escape the sensation of his big, powerful body against hers. She cursed him for his warm breath on her face and the smell of lemons and olives that came from him. Above all she cursed him for the feel of his loins against hers, and the sweet warmth that was beginning deep inside. She rejected it, she repudiated it, she wanted no part of it. But it was there, and it was all his fault.

'Get off me,' she snapped.

As he recognised her voice Vincenzo demanded, 'What the devil—?'

'Get off me.'

For a moment he didn't move. He might have been too thunderstruck to move, lying against her, gasping.

She too was gasping, she realised in outrage. The warmth was becoming heat, spreading through her.

'I said get off me.'

He did so, moving slowly, as if caught in a dream. In the gloom he pulled her to her feet, but didn't release her. Looking into his eyes she saw her own sensations mirrored and, perversely, it increased her rage at him.

'What are you doing up here?' he asked with difficulty.

'Trying to stop the place from being wrecked. There's a burst water pipe up here, and it's going to flood this building from the top down.'

He seemed dazed. 'What—what did you say?'

She ground her teeth. Was the house going to be ruined because he couldn't take in more than one idea at a time?

Then she saw that his gaze was riveted on her, and in the same moment she realised that her bra had become undone in the struggle, slipping down, revealing her full, generous breasts. Furiously she wrenched herself from his grasp, snapping, 'Can I have your attention please?'

'You've got that,' he said distractedly.

'Just you mind your manners.'

That seemed to pull him back to reality.

'I'm sorry, it must have happened when—it was an accident—'

'An accident that wouldn't have happened if you hadn't jumped me.'

'Well, I wasn't expecting to find you here in

a state of undress. *Mio Dio*, you haven't brought a man up here, have you?'

'There's going to be another accident if you don't watch it,' she threatened. 'One that may leave you unable to walk. Do I make myself clear?'

'Perfectly.'

She had been trying to hook up her bra at the back, but she was too angry to concentrate and it wasn't working.

'Can I help you?' he asked.

'No funny business.'

'That's a promise. I'll count myself lucky to get out of here alive.'

She turned and stood there while he hooked up the ends, his fingers brushing softly against her skin. She braced herself against the sensation on her skin that was already overheated from something that had nothing to do with the winter temperature.

When he'd finished he said meekly, 'Am I allowed to ask what you're doing here without being threatened with bodily violence?'

She remembered the broken pipe. In the last few minutes it had receded into unreality.

'You've got a burst pipe up here,' she said. 'It could soak the whole place.'

She led him across the floor to where he could

see better. As he realised the danger, a violent word, sounding like a curse, burst from him.

He stripped off his scarf and wound it around the pipe. But it too was instantly soaked.

'Hold it,' he told her tersely. 'I'm going to get something safer.'

He stopped just long enough to pull off his jacket and put it about her shoulders. Then he made a run for it.

Julia shrugged her arms into the jacket, which was blessedly warm. She was deeply shaken by the last few minutes.

She'd had it all sussed—or so she'd thought. No hopes, no pity, no sympathy, and above all no feelings, *of any kind*.

But some feelings were harder to suppress than others. They acted independently of thought and anger, and left a trail of problems.

She set her chin. Problems were made to be overcome.

In a few minutes Vincenzo was back, bearing a roll of heavy, sticky tape.

'This will hold it for a while,' he said, winding it around the pipe and the wadding. 'But we need a plumber.'

He took out his cell phone and dialled. There followed a curt conversation in Venetian.

'There'll be someone here in about half an

hour,' he said, switching off. 'Until then, it's a case of hanging on and hoping for the best.'

'Then we'd better move those pictures out of the way,' Julia said, indicating the wall.

Together they began lifting the pictures off the floor, balancing them on chairs so that they were clear of the water. Some of them were heavy, and after a while they were both breathing hard.

'Let's sit down,' he said.

As he spoke he returned to the pipe, settled beside it and began winding more tape. She went to sit on the other side.

'Are you all right?' he asked. 'It's hard work for someone who's been ill recently.'

'Yes, I'm fine. I've been feeling better ever since I kicked the door in.' She laughed. 'I think that's what I've really been needing all this time.'

'To kick a door in?' he asked, startled.

'Yes. It's one of the great healing experiences of life.' She gave a sigh of satisfaction.

'Well, it certainly seems to have done you some good,' he observed. 'You look more alive than I've ever seen you.'

'I feel it,' she said.

She was about to stretch luxuriously, but then she realised that this wasn't safe. Vincenzo was a big man and his jacket hung on her in a manner that revealed a lot, even with the darkness to help her.

And even the darkness didn't help very much. They were sitting by the window, and enough light came in to make life difficult.

'How did you come to be up here?' she asked quickly.

'I was going to ask you the same question,' he said, taking elaborate care not to look at her.

'You first.'

'I saw the door hanging from one hinge down below. I thought it must have been smashed in by a tank.'

'No, just little me,' she quipped lightly.

'I came up to see what was happening. If it's not a rude question, how do you come to be here?'

'I saw the water coming through in the room underneath. It's ruining the ceiling fresco. Honestly, the clown who owns this place ought to be shot for not looking after it properly.'

'Really,' he said with a dry irony that she missed.

'What a fool he must be,' she said indignantly, 'taking stupid risks with the water!'

'The water is cut off.'

'But nobody thought to drain that tank, did they? Or check the antiquated pipes.'

'No, you're right,' he said quietly.

'Well, there you are. He's an idiot.'

'Will you stop flailing your arms about like

that?' he demanded. 'At least, if you want me to behave like a gentleman.'

'What?' She looked down at herself and grabbed the edges of the jacket together again. 'Oh, that!'

'Yes, oh, that!' He was looking away from her. 'Can I turn back?'

'Sure. No problem. There's not a lot to me, anyway,' she declared hilariously.

His mouth twisted in mocking humour. 'Shouldn't I be the judge of that?'

Her answer was to pull the edges apart again and look right down, burying her head deep in the gap.

'Nope,' she said, emerging and drawing the edges together again. 'Nothing there worth looking at. Take my word for it.'

'If you say so.'

He stared at her, startled by the change that had come into her face. Her eyes were brilliant and she seemed to be almost in a state of exaltation, tossing her long hair back from her face so that Vincenzo had one of his rare chances to see it properly.

Where had the wraith of the last week gone? he wondered. This woman had an almost demonic energy.

'Anyway, why are you getting so worked up?' he asked. 'Why do you care so much?'

'Everyone should care about great beauty,' she said firmly. 'It can't defend itself. It has to be protected and cherished. It's not just ours. It belongs to all the people who come after us.'

'But why do *you* care so much?' he persisted. 'Are you an artist?'

'I'm—' The question seemed to bring her up short, like a shot from a gun.

'That's not important,' she resumed quickly. 'The Count di Montese should be ashamed of himself, and you can tell him I said so.'

'What makes you think I know him?'

'You know him well enough to summon a plumber to his house. Of course you might be the caretaker, in which case you're doing a rotten job. Still,' she added, tossing him an olive branch, 'maybe you couldn't be expected to know about that fresco.'

'Tell me about it.'

'It's a genuine Veronese, sixteenth century. I suppose the owner would have sold it off with the rest if it wasn't painted on the ceiling.'

'Very possibly,' he murmured wryly. 'By the way, the room below this is his bedroom. What shall I say if he asks why you were there?'

'Tell him he's lucky I was.'

Vincenzo grinned. 'I will.'

'I was just looking around. Snooping, I suppose you'd say.'

He grinned. 'Yes, I expect I would. If I tell the owner he'll kick you out.'

'Then I'll kick him back,' she said. 'Don't forget my kicking foot has had some practice today. I hope he doesn't dare to try to make me pay for that door.'

'He probably will,' Vincenzo assured her, his eyes dancing. 'He's a real stinge.'

She laughed, and her hair fell over her face.

'Oh, hang it,' she said, flicking it back over her shoulder. Looking around, she noticed a length of string lying on the floor, reached for it and used it to tie her hair back.

'That's better,' he observed. 'It's nice to be able to see your face.'

'Yes, people with my sort of forehead should never wear their hair long,' she agreed.

'What's wrong with your forehead?'

'It's low,' she said, showing him. 'Most people have foreheads that are high and curve backwards, so if they grow their hair it falls down the sides of their face. But mine's so low that long hair falls forward over my face.'

He assumed a mock serious air, making a play of inspecting her. 'Yes, I see what you—'

'What is it?' she asked when he fell silent abruptly.

'Nothing—that is—I don't know.'

Once more he'd been assailed by the odd feel-

ing he'd had the first night, that something about
her was mysteriously familiar.

There were sounds coming from outside,
voices from the stairs. The next moment Piero
appeared, and with him a man carrying a bag of
tools.

'At last,' Vincenzo said, getting to his feet.

'Mio Dio!' Piero exclaimed, looking around
him.

'Yes, it could have been a disaster but for
Julia. Take her downstairs, Piero, and get her
warmed up.'

Julia let herself be led away to the place where
there was warmth, and fresh clothes, and hot coffee. Piero laughed heartily at her story, especially
the tale of how she'd criticised 'the owner'.

'It's too bad of Vincenzo not to have told you
the truth,' he said. 'He *is* the owner. His full
name is *Vincenzo di Montese.*'

'*What?* You mean he's the count? But I
thought he was one of us?' she cried, almost in-
dignant.

'So he is. What do you think makes us as we
are? Is it simply not having a roof over our heads,
or is there more?'

'There's much more,' she said, thinking of the
last few years when she'd had a roof over her
head, and still been poorer than she was now.

'Exactly. Vincenzo has his ghosts and demons,

just like us. In his case it's virtually everyone or everything he's ever loved. They betray him, they die, or they're taken from him in some other way. As a boy he worshipped his father. He hadn't seen the truth about him then.'

'What truth?'

'Sheer brute selfishness. He was a gambler who cared about nothing and nobody as long as he got his thrill at the tables, no matter how huge his losses. People say he went to pieces after his wife died, and it's true he got worse then. But it was always there.

'The old count stripped this place of its valuables, so that now all Vincenzo owns is the shell. He lost the woman he loved. They were engaged, but the marriage fell through because her family said they didn't want to see her dowry gambled away, and who can blame them?'

'Didn't they put up a fight if they loved each other?'

'Vincenzo couldn't put up a fight. He felt that he had so little to offer that it wouldn't be fair. He's a Montese, which means he has the pride of the devil.'

'But didn't *she* fight?'

Piero shrugged. 'Not really. She may have loved him in her own way, but it wasn't a through-thick-and-thin kind of way.'

'What about him?' Julia wanted to know. 'Did

he love her in a through-thick-and-thin kind of way?'

'Oh, yes. He's an all-or-nothing person. When he gives it's everything. I remember their engagement party, in this very building. Gina was incredibly beautiful and knew how to show herself off. So she climbed those stairs and posed there for everyone to admire. And he stood below, looking up at her, almost worshipping. You never saw a man so radiantly happy.

'But that same night his father left the party and went to the casino. The amount of money he lost in an hour triggered the avalanche that followed, although I suppose it would have happened anyway.

'The count took his own life soon after. Having created the mess, he dumped it all on Vincenzo and made his escape. The final selfish betrayal.'

'Dear God!' she said, shocked. 'You must have known Vincenzo well if you were at the party?'

'I was there in my capacity as Europe's greatest chef.'

'Again?' she warned. 'You're repeating yourself.'

'Ah, yes, I've been a chef before, haven't I? Well, whatever. If you could have seen the look on Vincenzo's face that night—the last time he was ever happy. He loved that woman as few women are ever loved. And when she turned from him something in him died. That part of his life is over.'

'You mean he's given up women?' Julia asked with a touch of disbelief.

'Oh, no, quite the reverse. Far too many, all meaningless. He attracts them more easily than is good for him, and forgets them the same way.'

'Maybe he's the wise one,' Julia murmured.

'That's what he says, but it's sad to see a man bury the best of himself beneath bitterness. And it's got worse these last few months since he lost his sister, Bianca, the one person left that he could talk to. They were twins and they'd always been very close.

'She and her husband died in a car crash, only a few months ago, leaving him with her two children to care for. They're all the family he has left now. Everyone and everything gets taken away from him, and now he seems to feel more at home with down-and-outs.'

They heard Vincenzo and the plumber coming down the stairs, the plumber leaving, and Vincenzo approaching. Julia was standing by the window and he went straight to her, arms wide and eager. Then she was swallowed up in a huge hug.

'Thank you, thank you!' he said fiercely. 'You'll never know what you've done for me.'

'Piero's just told me who you are,' she said, struggling to breathe. 'You've got a nerve, keeping a thing like that to yourself.'

'I'm sorry,' he said unconvincingly. 'I just couldn't resist. Besides, think how much good you did me with that frank assessment of my character. Thank you for everything, Julia—or whoever.'

It was the first time he'd openly hinted that he doubted her name, and he backed off at once, saying hastily, 'I'm taking you both to supper tonight. Be ready in an hour.'

He vanished. Julia stood there, wondering at a tinge of embarrassment that had appeared in his manner.

Her clothes were all six years old, but she was thinner now and could get into them easily. She found a blue dress that was simple enough to look elegant.

She had almost nothing in the way of make-up, a touch of pink on her lips, and no more. But it had a transforming effect.

'That's better,' Piero said when he saw her. 'Let him see how nice you can look.'

'For heaven's sake, Piero!' she said, suddenly self-conscious. 'I'm not going on a date. What about you? Are you dressing up in your Sunday best?'

'Top hat and tails,' he said at once. 'What else?'

But when Vincenzo, smartly dressed in a suit, called for them Piero was still in his coat tied up with string.

'Are we going to your own restaurant?' he asked.

'We are.'

'Are you sure you should be taking me there, dressed like this?'

'Quite sure,' Vincenzo said, with the warmest smile she had ever seen from him. 'Now let's go.'

CHAPTER FOUR

VINCENZO'S restaurant was called *Il Pappagallo*, the parrot, and stood down a street so narrow that Julia could have touched both sides at once. The lights beamed out onto the wet stones, and through the windows she could see an inviting scene.

It was a small place with perhaps a dozen tables, lit by coloured lamps. A glance at the diners showed Julia why Piero had been reluctant to come here among those well-dressed people. But Vincenzo had overruled him for friendship's sake, and she liked him for it.

He led them inside and right through the restaurant to the rear door, which he opened, revealing more tables outside.

'Normally we couldn't eat outside at this time of year,' he said, 'but it's a mild night, and I think you'll enjoy the view of the Grand Canal.'

She had partly seen it before through the *palazzo* windows, but now she saw the whole wide expanse, busy with traffic. Behind the *vaporetti* and the gondolas rose the Rialto Bridge, floodlit blue against the night sky.

'Let me take your order,' Vincenzo said. 'I think we'll start with champagne because this is a celebration.'

She'd forgotten what champagne tasted like. She'd forgotten what a celebration was.

'We serve the finest food in Venice,' Vincenzo declared, and a glance at the menu proved it.

She returned it to him. 'Order for me, please.'

The champagne arrived and Vincenzo poured for them all in tall, fluted glasses.

'Thank you,' he said, raising his glass to her. 'Thank you—Julia?'

'Julia,' she said, meeting his eyes, refusing to give him the satisfaction of confirming or denying her name.

Piero was looking gleefully from one to the other. She guessed he was imagining a possible romance. She shrugged the thought away, but she supposed his mistake was understandable. Many women would find Vincenzo irresistible. It wasn't a matter of looks, because strictly speaking he wasn't handsome. His nose was a little too long and irregular for that.

It was hard to tell the shape of his mouth because it changed constantly, smiling, grimacing, always reflecting his mood, which wasn't always amiable. There was a touch of pride there, and more than a touch of defensiveness.

No, it wasn't features, she decided, but something else, an indescribable mixture of charm, bitter comedy and arrogance, something unmistakably Italian. It was there in his dark, slightly sunken eyes, with their gleam that was so hard to read. A woman could drive herself distracted trying to fathom that gleam, and doubtless many women had. There was a time when she herself might have been intrigued.

But the next moment, as if to tell her to be honest with herself, she was assailed by the memory of lying beneath him on the attic floor, so that the hot, sweet sensation began to rise up in her from the pit of her stomach, threatening to overcome her completely.

She drew a long, ragged breath against the threat, refusing to give in. She was stronger than that.

Piero provided a kind of distraction, rejoicing in the champagne, pronouncing it excellent.

'Only the best,' Vincenzo said.

'Yes, it is,' she agreed, for the sake of something to say.

Vincenzo nodded. 'I thought you'd know about that.'

She pulled herself together, refusing to let him

overcome her, even though he had no idea that he was doing so.

'Maybe I don't know,' she parried. 'Maybe I only said "Yes" to sound knowledgeable. Anyone can do that.'

'True. But not everyone would know about Correggio and Veronese.'

'I was guessing.'

'No, you weren't,' he said quietly.

She was getting her second wind and was able to say, 'Well, it's not your concern, and who are you to lecture me about people concealing their identity?'

'Can't you two go five minutes without bickering?' Piero asked plaintively.

'I'm not bickering,' Vincenzo said. 'She's bickering.'

'I'm not.'

'You are.'

'Stop it, the pair of you,' Piero commanded.

As one they turned on him.

'Why?' Julia asked. 'What's wrong with bickering? It's as good a way of communicating as any other.'

'That's what I always say,' Vincenzo agreed at once.

He met her eyes and she found herself reluctantly discovering that she was wrong. There *was* a better way of communicating. The look he was

giving her was wicked, and it contained the kind
of shared understanding she knew she would be
wiser to avoid.

Piero raised his glass.

'I foresee a very interesting evening,' he said
with relish.

'Can we eat the first course before we have to
fight another round?' Vincenzo asked.

It was her first experience of Venetian cuisine,
with its intriguing variety. A dish described simply as 'rice and peas' turned out also to contain
onions, veal, butter and broth.

They drank *Prosecco* from hand-blown pink,
opalescent glasses.

'They come from home,' Vincenzo said.
'There were some things I was damned if I was
going to sell.'

'They're beautiful,' she said, turning a glass
between her fingers. 'I can understand you wanting to keep them.'

'My father gave me the first wine I ever tasted
in one of these,' he remembered. 'I was only a
boy, and I felt like such a big man, sitting there
with him.'

You idolised him, she thought, remembering
Piero's words. *And he betrayed you.*

'Isn't it risky using them in a restaurant?' she
asked.

'These aren't for the ordinary customers. I keep them for special friends. Let's drink a toast.'

They solemnly raised their glasses. Somewhere inside her she could feel a knot of tension begin to unravel. There were still good times to be had.

'Are you warm enough out here?' Vincenzo asked her. 'Would you prefer a table inside?'

'No, this is nice.'

'We have the odd fine night, even in December. It's after Christmas that it gets really bad.'

When the rice and peas had been cleared away she saw Vincenzo look up and meet the eye of a very pretty waitress, who returned a questioning smile, to which he responded with a wink and a nod of the head.

'Do you mind doing your flirting elsewhere?' Piero asked severely.

'I'm not flirting,' Vincenzo defended himself. 'I was signalling to Celia to bring in the next course.'

'And you had to do that with a wink?' Julia enquired humorously.

'I'm trying to appeal to her. She's going to vanish next week, just when I'm going to need her most.'

'But I thought you didn't need too many staff at this time of year,' Julia said.

'It's true the summer rush is over, but in the run-up to Christmas there's a mini-rush. I shed staff in October and increase them in December. In January I shed them again, then increase them in February just before the Carnival. A lot of workers like it that way—a few weeks on, a few weeks off. But Celia's going off just when I need her on. I've begged and pleaded—'

'You've winked and smiled—' Julia supplied.

'Right. And all to no avail.'

'You mean that this young female is immune to your charm?' Piero asked, shocked.

'His what?' Julia asked.

'His charm. *Chaa-aarm*. You must have heard of it?'

'Yes, but nobody told me Vincenzo was supposed to have any.'

'Very funny, the pair of you,' Vincenzo said, eyeing them both balefully.

Celia appeared at the table bearing a large terracotta pot, in which was an eel, cooked in bay leaves.

'This is a speciality of Murano, the island where the glass-blowing is centred,' Vincenzo explained. 'It was once cooked over hot coals actually in the glass furnaces. I can't compete with that. I have to use modern ovens, but I think it'll taste all right.'

When Celia had finished serving the eel he

took her hand, gazing up into her eyes, pleading. His words were in Venetian but Julia got the gist of them without trouble, and even managed to decipher, 'My love, I implore you.'

Even if it was all play-acting, she thought, it had a kind of magic that a woman would do well to beware. Celia seemed in no danger. She giggled and departed.

'I guess I can't persuade Celia.' He sighed. 'Tonight's her last night. She's about to get married and go on her honeymoon. That's her fiancé over there. *Ciao*, Enrico.'

A burly man grinned at him from another table. Vincenzo grinned back in good fellowship. Julia concentrated on her food, trying not to be glad that Celia had a fiancé.

As they ate the eel, washed down with Soave, her feeling of well-being increased. She had forgotten many things about the real world: good food, fine wines, a man who had dark, intense eyes, and turned them on her, inviting her to understand their meaning.

She was too wise to accept that invitation, but the understanding was there, whether she wanted it or not. It tingled in her senses, it ached in her heart, so long starved of the joyous emotions. It told her that she must risk just this one evening.

After the eel came wild duck. While it was

being served she turned to look out over the canal.

'Have you ever been to Venice before?' Vincenzo asked.

'No. I always meant to, but somehow it never happened.'

'Not even when you were studying art? Please, Julia,' he added quickly as she looked up, 'let's not pretend about that, at least. You recognised a Correggio and a Veronese at the first glance, and you can't turn the clock back to before it happened. You're an artist.'

'An art restorer,' she conceded reluctantly. 'At one time I fancied myself as a great painter, but my only talent turned out to be for imitating other people's styles.'

'You must have studied in Italy. That's how you know the language, right?'

'I studied in Rome, and Florence,' she agreed.

'Then I'll enjoy showing you the whole house, although it's only a ghost of itself now. I wish you could have seen it in its glory days.'

'You've lost everything, haven't you?' she said gently.

'Just about.' He glanced at Piero and lowered his voice. 'Do I have any secrets left?'

'Not many.'

'Good, then I needn't bore you with the whole

story. Now let's eat. With duck we drink Amarone.'

He filled their glasses with the red wine that had just been brought to the table. Julia sipped it with relish and looked back at the canal.

'I should like to see Venice in summer,' she said, 'when it's bright and cheerful, not dark and menacing as it is now.' She glanced at him, smiling. 'I'm sorry, I don't mean to be rude about your city.'

'But you're right. It's true, Venice can be menacing, especially on quiet winter nights. Its history has been one of blood as well as romance, and even today there are times when an assassin seems to lurk around each corner, and peril haunts every shadow.

'In the summer the tourists arrive and say, "How pretty! How quaint!" but if Venice were only pretty and quaint it would soon grow dull.'

'Pretty and quaint are two words that never occurred to me,' she said wryly. 'That's what sleeping on the stones can do for you.'

His grin broadened into a laugh, and she realised how seldom there was real amusement in his face. It was there now, and it delighted her.

'You have all my sympathy,' he said. 'Nowhere else are the stones as hard as ours. Venice is the loveliest city in the world, but it can also be the most cruel. And that's why I wouldn't live anywhere else. Does that sound crazy?'

'No, I understand it. You can't study art for long without knowing that anything that's merely pretty grows tedious very soon.'

He nodded.

'In the same way, a woman who has only looks soon palls. Sadly, it takes a man time to understand that, and when he's found out it may be too late. The woman with the dark, dangerous heart may be already beyond his reach.'

She gave a wry smile.

'That's very nice talk, but aren't you deluding yourself?'

'Am I?'

'How many men truly want a woman with a dark, dangerous heart?'

'The discriminating ones, perhaps.'

'And how many men are discriminating? You don't need a dangerous heart to do the washing-up.'

'You mean that it would be an attribute of a mistress, rather than a wife?'

'I mean that you're spinning glittering fantasies in the air. They have no reality behind them.'

'I didn't realise that you knew me so well.'

The words were lightly spoken, but with a slight warning edge. In truth, she didn't know him at all.

'I like to choose my own fantasies,' he said lightly. 'And I decide what they mean.'

His eyes challenged her. She met the challenge and threw it back, but she could think of no words that weren't more perilous than silence.

She glanced at Piero, afraid that she would find him regarding them with gleeful interest; but he was engaged in a mad flirtation with Celia, who was laughing at his jokes, and giving him extra food and wine. He consumed everything with gusto, especially the wine, and it was clear that he was soon headed for blissful oblivion.

Seeing him so absorbed, she began to feel as though she were alone with Vincenzo, who didn't take his eyes from her.

'Why won't you tell me who you are?' he asked softly. 'And why you are here. I might be able to help.'

At one time she would have replied quickly that nobody could help her. Now she merely shook her head.

'You'll have to tell someone, some time. Why not me?'

'Because you get too close.'

'People who care should get too close. Don't keep yourself shut away. Why are you smiling like that?'

'Nothing,' she said. 'I wasn't really.'

'There you go again, hiding. You're like

someone who barely exists. I know only what you choose to tell, and, since that's almost nothing, it's like being able to see right through you. I don't know your name or what brought you here, or why you try so hard to conceal yourself in the dark.'

'The light frightens me,' she whispered.

'But why? You answer one question and a thousand others spring up. When will your mysteries end?'

'They won't. Vincenzo, please, it's better if you don't seek to know them.'

'Better for whom?'

'For both of us, but mostly for you.'

'Then you already know what's happening to me.'

'Don't. Don't say it. Don't think it. Don't let it happen.'

'Don't you want to be loved?'

'How can I tell? What is it like?'

'Are you saying that no man has ever loved you?'

'Please—'

'No man has wanted to take you in his arms and lie with you, demanded the right to claim and possess you in every way?'

'It doesn't matter what they've wanted,' she told him. 'Who cares what men say? Only fools believe them. No, I've never been loved. I might have thought so, but we all have these little self-delusions.'

'Until the truth breaks in at last,' he agreed. 'There's nothing you can tell me about self-delusion. But the biggest self-delusion of all is to tell ourselves that we can manage without love in future.'

'Look at my face,' she said, drawing the hair back. 'I'm an old woman.'

'No, you're not. There's suffering in your face, but not age. You're a young woman who's learned to feel old inside.'

She smiled in ironic acknowledgement. 'You see too much.'

His fingers brushed her hand, and she could feel in the light touch everything he was trying to say.

'Don't,' she warned him. 'Don't reach out to me.'

'Suppose I want to?'

'But I can't reach back. Can't you understand? I have nothing to give.'

His fingers possessed hers and he didn't look at her directly as he said, 'Perhaps I don't want you to give, but to take.'

'It makes no difference,' she said sadly. 'I no longer know how to do either. I forgot both long ago.'

'How long?'

She took a deep breath. 'Six years, two months and four days.'

The stark precision of the answer startled him.

'And what happened, six years, two months and four days ago?' he asked.

'I packed my feelings away in an iron chest marked, "No longer required". Then I buried that chest too deep to be found again. I've even forgotten where it is.'

'I don't believe that. You'll remember when you want to. Can't I help you do it?'

'I don't want to remember,' she whispered. 'It hurts too much. Tell me, Vincenzo, how deep is your iron chest buried?'

'Not as deep as I'd like. I find I can't do without those feelings, even if they hurt. Better be hurt than dead inside.'

'Meaning I'm a coward?' she demanded swiftly.

'I didn't say that.'

'You implied it.'

'Why are you trying to quarrel with me?' he asked quietly.

'Perhaps because I really am a coward,' she admitted after a moment. 'I have so little courage left, and I need all of it.'

'And I threaten it?'

'Yes,' she whispered. 'Yes, you do.'

She had said that she could not reach out, but

she knew how fatally easy it would be to seek warmth from this man who seemed to have so much to give. But it would deflect her from her true purpose, and nothing must be allowed to do that.

'You do,' she repeated.

'Don't be afraid of me.'

'I'm not afraid of you, *but I will not let you in*. Do you understand?'

'I told myself the same thing about you, but somehow you got in.'

'I wasn't trying to,' she said quickly.

'I know. Maybe that's how you managed it. You were there before I could put my defences in place.'

'You're forgetting that I don't really exist,' she said.

She tried to speak lightly, but it was hard, and he made it harder by coming back swiftly with, 'Sometimes I wish you didn't. You're trouble. I don't know how or why, but you're big trouble, and you're going to throw my life in turmoil.'

'Just ignore me.'

'That's a dishonest reply.' For a moment he was angry. 'You know it's too late for that.'

'Yes,' she murmured after a moment. 'Yes, it's too late. It's much too late.'

Hours had passed. Customers were leaving the restaurant, and lights were going off. Lost in her awareness of Vincenzo, Julia hardly realised it was happening.

A waiter approached them to say that Vincenzo was needed for some formality. When he'd gone Julia turned back to Piero, and found him, as she'd expected, deeply, blissfully asleep.

Vincenzo returned as the last customer was leaving, and smiled at the sight of their friend.

'He'd better stay here tonight,' he said. 'There's a little room behind the kitchen where I sometimes sleep when I'm working late.'

He summoned a waiter. Together they carried Piero through the kitchens into the tiny bedroom and laid him gently on the bed.

'You'd better stay here, too,' he told Julia. 'You can have the apartment upstairs that Celia has just vacated.'

He showed her up the narrow staircase into the tiny apartment. Celia had stripped the bed before leaving, and he helped her make it up.

'Thank you,' she said. 'But there was no need for you to take so much trouble. I could have gone back.'

'No,' he said at once. 'I don't want you sleeping in that huge, empty place alone. I couldn't feel easy about you.'

'You don't have to look after me,' she said with a little smile. Then she gave a little laugh. 'Except that you do, all the time, don't you? I just hate admitting it, which isn't very nice of me.'

Her voice fell softly on his ears and caused an ache inside him. She worked so hard to keep her gentler side hidden that when she allowed him a sudden glimpse it caught him off guard.

He came closer, looking at her with hot, dark eyes. He remembered another time when he'd looked at her like this. Then he'd held her in his arms, kissing her, and she had known nothing about it. She knew nothing now.

She had felt soft and good against his body, and her lips had been sweet against his. That sweetness had taken possession of him, making him long to kiss her more deeply, although he'd known he must not do so while she was asleep. Instead he had kissed her eyes and her tears.

But for her it hadn't happened. That thought was very bitter to him.

Unable to stop himself, he brushed her cheek with gentle fingers. She didn't draw away, only looked at him sadly, quite still.

'Vincenzo,' she said at last.

'Hush,' he begged. 'Say nothing.'

His fingers continued their way down her cheek and across the soft contours of her mouth. He was entranced, absorbed by her, lost in her. He touched her cheek and her mouth again with fingertips that barely brushed them, yet which seemed to burn her.

She tried to protest, but no words would come. She should stop him, but she lacked the will. This had been inevitable since a few hours ago, when she'd become aware of him as a man. She should have taken flight then, when there had still been time. Except that there had never been time.

He was going to kiss her, and she wanted it with an intensity that shocked her. It was against every plan she had made, but suddenly that no longer mattered. She could feel her hands tightening on him, pulling him forward until his lips touched hers.

They felt strangely familiar, as though they had kissed before in some other life. But in her other life there had been no kisses, no warmth or sweetness, or gentleness of lips teasing hers, part plea, part command, part exploration.

'Who are you?' he whispered against her lips.

'It doesn't matter,' she said through her swimming senses. 'I'm not real.'

'You're real now—in my arms.'

'Only here,' she whispered.

'The rest doesn't matter. Kiss me—kiss me.'

She did as he wanted, finding that after the years alone she still knew how to tease and incite a man. It was an intoxicating discovery and it sent her a little wild.

Now she allowed her hands and mouth to do as they pleased, and the things that pleased them were sensual, outrageous, experienced. He was right. This alone was real, and everything in her wanted to yield to it.

With every movement she made Vincenzo felt shock flowing along his nerves. He'd suspected the fires inside and it had tormented him, but now he knew for certain. He'd partly discovered the truth that afternoon when he'd discovered that her breasts were surprisingly generous, given her apparently boyish figure.

All the sensuality she normally kept banked down was flaming in his arms now, inciting him to explore her further, wanting more. He didn't know her real name, but her name no longer mattered. This woman was coming back to life, and he knew that he, and no other, must be the man to make it happen.

She kissed dreamily, but like a woman who understood a man's body, and every soft touch lured him on. Entranced, he dropped his lips to the base of her throat, moving them in soft, teasing movements and sensing her heated response. His own response was roaring out of control.

Only she could stop him now, and she made no attempt to do so. When he began to remove her clothes she trembled, but was removing his at the same time. It was she who drew him to the bed, and after that nothing could have stopped him.

CHAPTER FIVE

MY FIRST man in six years.

The thought came to Julia as the dawn crept in. The night had been hot and fervent, and it had left her feeling at ease in a way she had forgotten. The sheer sense of blinding, physical release had at first stunned, then invigorated her.

They had claimed each other again and again. After the first time it was she who had taken the initiative, voraciously demanding as she felt her body return to life. And he had responded with unflagging vigour.

Six years of cramped frustration, deprivation, ending in one night of blazing fulfilment.

Images came back to her: his body, hard, lean and strong, his love-making, a mingling of power and tenderness, with the power becoming predominant as he'd sensed her need.

My first in six years. And before that—ah, well!

Before that there had been passionate adoration given to the wrong man, who had betrayed it and left her with a smashed life to endure.

She sat up, careful not to awaken Vincenzo, who slept silently and heavily, as though exhausted. It was a tight fit in the narrow bed, especially as he stretched out in abandon.

He'd made love like that, she thought, with an abandon that had startled her, so different was it from the controlled surface he presented to the world.

She hadn't meant to take him to bed, so she told herself. Either that or she had meant it from the first moment. One of the two. Did it matter which?

Their aggressive encounter in the attic had awoken in her a physical hunger, long suppressed, and satisfying it had become urgent.

I didn't think I was like that, she thought wryly. But I suppose after so long…

He moved in his sleep and stretched out a hand, seeking until he encountered her skin. Then it stopped, lying gently against her as though nothing else in the world mattered.

Strangely, it was that gesture that alarmed her. If he'd grasped her robustly she would have cheerfully returned to the fray. But the touch against her body was tender. It spoke of emotion, and she knew that emotion must be kept out of this. Only that way could she feel safe.

After a moment she moved his hand away.

Vincenzo stirred and stretched, almost pushing

her out of the tiny bed. She laughed, clinging on for dear life, and he awoke to find her looking down at him. He grinned, remembering the night they had passed together.

Her passion had astounded him. More accustomed to her mental and emotional defensiveness, he'd been taken aback by her sensual abandon. She'd given everything with fierce generosity and demanded everything with an equally fierce appetite. When he had been satiated she had been ready to start again.

Now she looked fresh, light-hearted and mysteriously younger. There was even a teasing look in her eyes that had never been there before.

'That was fun,' she said.

The words brought him back down to earth. 'Fun' described a race through the canals, a brilliant costume for Carnival. It bore no relation to the experience that had just shaken him to his roots.

But he answered her in kind, speaking lightly.

'I'm glad you feel the night wasn't wasted.'

She was silent, but shook her head, teasing.

He reached out so that she could take his hand, then he would draw her closer for a kiss. But instead she laughed and got to her feet, looking around for something to throw over her nakedness. Finding his shirt on the floor, she seized that.

'Spoilsport,' he sighed.

She chuckled and left the room, heading for the kitchen. He followed at once, catching up, putting his arms about her from behind, and nuzzling her hair.

'All right?' he asked softly.

'Of course,' she said brightly. 'Everything's fine.'

He partly withdrew his hands, just as far as her shoulders. 'That's good,' he said quietly.

'Do you know how I make coffee in this kitchen?' she asked with a laugh.

'I'll make it.'

'Lovely. Then we'll go down and see if Piero's awake yet. He and I should be going soon.'

He dropped his hands.

'Whatever you say.'

She turned suddenly. 'There's something you should know. Don't expect too much from me just now. I'm not used to being in the land of the living. I've forgotten how things are done there.'

He frowned, alerted by a new note in her voice, but not understanding it. 'The land of the living? I don't understand.'

'For the last six years I've been in prison.'

Julia had told Vincenzo that kicking the door in had been one of the great healing experiences of life, and it was true. With that one blow she had put her lethargy behind her, and was ready for the task that had brought her here.

Walking home with Piero that morning, she bought a map, and studied it as soon as they were inside.

'Can I help?' he asked.

'I want to go to the island of Murano.'

'Take the waterbus. It's about a twenty-minute journey. I'll show you the exact place. Are you going to look at some of the glass-blowing factories?'

'No, I'm looking for a man. His name is Bruce Haydon. He has relatives there and they'll know where he is now.'

'Is he Italian?'

'No, he's English. He had some Italian family on his mother's side, but he's lived mostly in England.'

She knew he was hoping to hear more, and she was foolish to keep silent. She should simply say that Bruce Haydon had once been her husband; that he had betrayed her vilely and condemned her to hell. But just now she wasn't ready to say the words.

When she'd changed back into her jeans he led her to the San Zaccaria landing stage, and waited with her while the boat arrived. Passengers poured off, more passengers poured on. As she was about to turn away Piero tightened his grip on her arm.

'Come back safely,' he said.

'Yes, I will,' she promised him in a gentle voice.

As the boat drew away from the landing stage she looked back and saw Piero standing where she had left him. He remained motionless, growing smaller until she could no longer see him.

At last the boat reached the landing stage at Murano. It was a small island, constructed, like Venice, of canals and bridges, famous for its glass-blowing, but without the glamour of the main city.

With the aid of the map she was able to discover a row of houses beside a canal, and began to make her way along, searching for one front door.

Then it was there before her, the front door with a brass plaque proclaiming that here lived Signor and Signora Montressi, the name of Bruce's Italian relatives. Luck was with her.

She rang the bell and waited. But there was no reply.

She told herself she must be patient.

She found a café and ordered coffee and sandwiches. From her bag, she took a small photo album in which she kept pictures to show people who might have seen him. It wasn't very up to date. None of the photographs was less than six years old.

The first one was a wedding picture, showing a handsome man, grinning with delight. There was no sign of his bride. Julia had cut her out of the picture.

He had dark hair and eyes, but, although his Italian ancestry was visible, his face was slightly too fleshy for the kind of dramatic looks that Vincenzo had. He lacked Vincenzo's intensity too, parading instead an air of self-satisfaction.

She stopped and gave an exclamation of annoyance at herself. Forget Vincenzo! Comparing every other man with him was futile. For many reasons.

But there was no way to forget Vincenzo. Piero had said, 'He's an all or nothing person. When he gives it's everything.'

After last night she knew that it was true.

But Piero had also said Vincenzo had too many women, 'all meaningless'.

So he was like herself, she thought. Nature had shaped him one way, and hard lessons had shaped him differently.

In that hot, dark night he'd become his true self again, giving generously, endlessly, revealing himself to her with no defences, nothing held back.

And it shamed her that she'd only half responded, revelling in the physical pleasure that he gave so expertly, returning it with every skill at her command, but giving nothing else. Her heart was still safely hoarded in her own control.

She remembered the scene in the kitchen that morning. He'd been tender and affectionate, seeking to evoke the same in her. She'd disappointed him because she was unable to do anything else.

Blurting out that she'd been in prison had been an impulse, instantly regretted. After that she hadn't been able to get away from him fast enough, and he'd sensed it, and let her go, saying little.

She returned to the pictures, trying to concentrate on them and forget Vincenzo.

After the wedding snap came a selection of photographs taken over the next four years, during which the man put on a little weight, but continued to be good-looking and pleased with himself.

'Whatever did I see in you?' she asked the grinning head. 'Well, I paid a heavy price for it.'

He filled the first half of the book. In the second half there was a different set of pictures.

They showed a baby, starting with the day it was born. Then the child became gradually larger and prettier, with curly blonde hair and shining eyes. And always she was laughing.

Julia slammed the album shut, closing her eyes and fighting back the tears. For a moment she sat there, rigid, aching, while heartbreak tore her apart.

At last the storm passed, and she forced herself to return to reality and behave normally.

'Not much longer,' she promised herself. 'Not much longer.'

The weak moment was behind her.

Her second visit to the house was equally fruitless. It was dark before she returned a third time.

As she turned into the canal-side street she could see the lights in the windows. The door was opened by a pretty young girl.

'Signora Montressi?' Julia asked.

'Oh, no, she and her husband have gone until after Christmas. They're taking a Caribbean cruise. They left three days ago. I'm afraid that's all I know. I only come in to feed the cat. They'll be back in January.'

She almost ran away, needing to be alone to absorb the shock. To have got so close and then have the prize snatched out of reach.

She walked about aimlessly for a long time before catching the boat back across the lagoon. It was late but there were still plenty of travellers, and she stood looking over the rail at the black water. It would be a relief to get home.

Home. How strange that she should think of

the *palazzo* as home. Yet there would be a warm welcome for her there, and what else was home but that?

'Scusi—scusi—'

She moved as someone squeezed past her. At the same moment the boat ploughed into an extra high wave, causing it to lurch. As she grabbed the rail the strap of her bag began to slide down her arm. She twisted, trying to save it, and lost her grip.

As she watched the bag went sailing down into the water, carrying with it her precious album of pictures.

Vincenzo would have liked to get out of the dinner party at the Danieli Hotel, but he had promised and must keep his word. So he did his duty, sat next to an heiress who'd plainly heard of his circumstances, smiled, behaved with charm, concealed his boredom, and forgot her the moment the party was over.

From the hotel it was a short walk home, past San Zaccaria, and across St Mark's. Preoccupied with his thoughts, he'd actually walked past the landing stage before he realised what he'd seen. He turned sharply back.

'Piero,' he said. 'What are you doing here?'

'Waiting for her boat,' the old man said.

Vincenzo's heart sank. It was usually in the

afternoons that Piero came here on his fruitless mission. If he'd started coming so late at night, he must be getting worse.

'I don't think there are any more boats to-night,' he said, laying his hand on Piero's shoulder.

'There's one more,' Piero said calmly. 'She'll be on that.'

'Piero, please—' It tore him apart to see the frail old man standing in the cold wind, clinging onto futile hope.

'There it is,' Piero said suddenly.

In the distance they could see lights moving towards them. Sick at heart, Vincenzo watched as it made its slow journey.

'She went to Murano,' Piero said. 'I put her on the boat here this morning.'

'Her? You mean Julia?'

'Of course. Who did you think I meant?'

'Well—I was a bit confused. I probably had too much to drink. What's this about Murano?'

'She went there looking for someone called Bruce Haydon.'

After a moment they both saw her standing by the rail. As the boat drew nearer she seemed to notice them suddenly. A smile broke over her face and she waved.

The two men waved back, and Vincenzo saw that Piero's face wore a look of total happiness.

He wondered who the old man was seeing on the approaching boat.

At last it reached the landing stage and passengers came streaming off. Piero went forward, his arms outstretched, and Julia hugged him eagerly.

'You're back,' he said. 'You came home.'

'Home,' she said. 'Yes, that's what I was thinking.'

'Thank goodness you got back safely,' Vincenzo said. 'We were a bit concerned.'

She seemed to see him for the first time.

'There was no need,' she replied. 'I wasn't lost.'

'We didn't know that. Well, it doesn't matter. You're safe now.'

The three of them began to walk back across St Mark's Piazza and into the labyrinth of canals and little alleys that led home. Vincenzo kept firm hold of her arm, until she firmly disengaged herself.

She was angry with him again for knowing her secret—that she'd been in prison—even though she herself had disclosed it. And she was angry with herself for doing so.

'I'm all right,' she said. 'I don't need help.'

'Yes, you do. Even prickly, awkward you. And don't walk away from me when I'm trying to talk to you.'

'Don't talk to me when I'm trying to walk away.'

'If you aren't the most—'

'It's no use trying to reason with her,' Piero said. 'I've tried, but it's pointless.' He added in a deliberately provocative tone, 'After all, she's a woman.'

Julia turned and walked backwards, her eyes fixed on him.

'I'd stamp on your feet if I had the energy,' she teased.

Piero's answer to this was a little dance. 'You couldn't do it,' he asserted. 'I used to dance leading roles with the Royal Ballet in London.'

She began to imitate him, and they hopped back and forth while passers-by gave them a wide berth, and Vincenzo watched them, grinning.

Later, as the three of them sat by the stove Vincenzo said, 'Did things go well?'

'No,' she said robustly, 'things went just about as badly as they could. The people I went to see are on a cruise. I missed them by three days, and they won't be back until January. I had an album of pictures of the man I'm seeking, and on the way home it fell overboard. So now I don't even have that.'

Vincenzo frowned. 'For someone who's just lost everything you're astonishingly cheerful.'

'I'm not cheerful, just mad. Mad-angry, not mad-crazy. I've been acting like a wimp, but now I'm done with weakness. When the pictures went overboard I was devastated for a whole minute, but then something inside me said, "That's it! Time to fight back."'

'The man you're looking for,' Vincenzo said carefully, 'is he anything to do with—what you told me last night?'

'Anything to do with my being in prison? Yes, he put me there. He cheated and lied and managed to get me locked up for his crime.' She surveyed them both. 'He's my husband.'

Piero turned his head slowly. Vincenzo stirred.

'My name isn't Julia. It's Sophie Haydon. My husband was Bruce Haydon. My mother warned me against him, but I wouldn't listen. We were always a little uneasy with each other after that.'

'What about your father?' Piero asked.

'I barely knew him. He died when I was a baby. Bruce and I were married over nine years ago. We had a daughter the next year, a gorgeous little girl called Natalie. I loved her to bits. She— she's almost nine now.'

Her voice shook on the words, and she hurried on as though to prevent the others noticing.

'Bruce had a little business, import, export. It wasn't doing well and he hated it that I earned more than him. I was working as an art restorer, getting plenty of clients, starting to be employed by museums and great houses.

'And then there was a spate of art thefts, all from houses where I'd been working. Of course the police suspected me. I knew all about the keys and burglar alarms.'

She fell silent again, staring into space for a long time. Then she jumped to her feet and began to pace up and down, her feet making a hollow, desolate sound on the tiles.

'Go on,' Vincenzo said in a strained voice.

'I was charged and put on trial.' She gave a harsh laugh. 'Bruce made me a wonderful speech about fighting it together. And I believed him. We loved each other, you see.' She gave a brief, mirthless laugh. 'That's really funny.'

She fell silent. Neither of the other two moved or spoke, respecting her grief.

'In the last few days before the trial,' she went on at last, 'my mind seemed to be working on two levels at once. On one, I just couldn't believe that they could find me guilty. On the other, I knew exactly what was going to happen. I knew they were going to take me away from Bruce and Natalie, and I spent every moment I could with them. Bruce and I—'

She stopped. It was better not to remember those passionate nights, his declarations of undying love, lest she go mad.

'We took Natalie on a picnic. On the way back we stopped in a toy shop and she fell in love with a rabbit. So I bought it for her and she hugged it all the way home. When the trial began I'd say goodbye to her in the morning and she'd clutch that rabbit for comfort. When I came home she'd still be clutching him. The neighbour who was looking after her said she never let go of him all day.

'On the last day of the trial I got ready to leave home and Natalie began to cry. She'd never done that before, but this time it was as though she knew I wasn't coming back. She clung to me with her arms tight about my neck, crying ''No, Mummy. Mummy, don't go, please don't go—please, Mummy—''

She was shuddering, forcing herself to speak through the tears that coursed down her cheeks.

'In the end they had to force her arms away from around my neck, while she screamed and screamed. Then she curled up on the sofa, clutching her rabbit and sobbing into his fur. That was the last time I ever saw her. All she knew was that I went away and never came back. Wherever she is now, whatever she's doing, that's her last memory of me.'

She swung around suddenly and slammed her hand down on the back of a chair, clinging onto it and choking in her agony. Vincenzo rose quickly and went to her, but she straightened up before he could touch her.

'I'm all right. Where was I?'

'The trial,' he said gently.

'Oh, yes. They found me guilty. Bruce came to see me in prison a couple of times. He kept promising to bring Natalie ''next time'', but he never did. And then one day he didn't come. My mother told me he'd vanished, taking our little girl.

'I don't remember the next few days clearly. I know I became hysterical, and for a while I was on suicide watch. That was six years ago, and I haven't seen either of them since.

'It was him, you see. He'd copied my keys, picked my brains. He'd drive me to work and ask me to show him around, ''Because I'm so interested, darling.'' So he knew what to look for, how to get in, how to turn off the alarm. Sometimes there were security staff, but they trusted him because he was with me. And everything he learned he sold to a gang of art thieves.

'All the thefts happened over the same weekend, then they vanished abroad, leaving me to take the blame like a tethered goat. By the time I realised how Bruce was involved he'd vanished too.'

'But surely you told the police?' Piero asked.

'Of course, but even I could hear how hollow

it sounded—clutching at straws to clear myself. My sentence was longer because I'd been "uncooperative". I couldn't tell them anything, because I didn't know.

'And all the time I knew he had my little girl somewhere. I didn't know where and I couldn't find out. She was two and a half when I last saw her. Where has she been all that time? What has she been told about me? Does she have nightmares about our last moments, as I do?'

Her voice faded into a despairing whisper. After a moment she began speaking again.

'Then a couple of the pictures turned up at an auction house. The police managed to trace the trail right back to the mastermind, and he told them everything. He hadn't long to live and he wanted to "clear his conscience", as he put it. He said Bruce used to laugh about how I trusted him, and how easy I was to delude.'

'*Bastardo!*' Vincenzo said with soft venom.

'Yes,' she agreed, 'but I suppose I should be glad of it, because that story was what cleared me. It meant that Bruce and I hadn't colluded. My conviction was quashed and I was released.'

She paced a little more before stopping by the window.

'My lawyer's fighting for compensation, but my only use for money is to pay for a proper search for Bruce, if I haven't found him by then.'

'Aren't the police looking for him?' Vincenzo suggested.

'Not as hard as I am. To them he's just another wanted man. To me he's an enemy.'

'Yes, I see,' Vincenzo said, almost to himself.

Her voice mounted in urgency.

'He wrecked my life, left me to rot in prison and took my child. I want my daughter back, *and I don't care what else happens*.'

'Have you no family to help you?' Piero asked.

'My mother died of a broken heart while I was in prison. She left me a very little money, just enough to come here and start searching for Bruce.'

'So you came to Venice to find his relatives?' Piero asked.

'Yes. They're only distant, but they might know something that could help me. I had some good friends who visited me in prison, and they used to bring stories about how Bruce had been ''seen''. Some of them were wildly unlikely. He was in Arizona, in China, in Australia. But two people said they'd spotted him in Italy, once in Rome, and more recently in Venice, crossing the Rialto Bridge.

'That's why I went straight to the Rialto that first night. Don't ask me what I thought I was going to do then, because I couldn't tell you. The inside of my head was a nightmare. Luckily the Rialto is near this place and Piero found me on his way home. If my friend really did see Bruce it may mean nothing, or he may be living only a few minutes away. You might even have seen him.'

'It would help if you had some pictures of him,' Vincenzo observed.

'I know, but my pictures went to the bottom of the lagoon an hour ago.' She clutched her head. 'If only I'd shown them to you last week—'

'You were full of fever last week,' Piero said. 'You didn't know whether you were coming or going. It's just bad luck, but we probably wouldn't have recognised him anyway.'

She nodded. 'The Montressis are my best lead. They'll be back in January, and then I'll hunt him down and get my daughter back.'

'But will it be that simple?' Vincenzo asked. 'After six years she may want to stay where she is.'

She gave him a look that chilled his blood.

'I am her mother,' she said with slow, harsh emphasis. 'She belongs with me. If anyone tries to stop me, I'll—' She was breathing hard.

'Yes?' he asked uneasily.

She met his eyes. 'I'll do what I have to— whatever that might be—I don't know.'

But she did know. He could see it in her face and feel it in her determination to reveal no more. She wouldn't put her thoughts into words because they were too terrible to be spoken.

He didn't recognise this woman. She'd freely claimed to be 'as mad as a hatter', and there were times in her delirium and sleepwalking when she'd seemed to be treading some fine line between reality and delusion. But now he saw only grim purpose in her eyes, and he wondered which side of the line she had stepped.

And who could blame her, he wondered, if her tragedy had driven her to the wrong side?

CHAPTER SIX

'So,' VINCENZO said gently, 'when you find Bruce—'

'He's going to give her back to me. If he's reasonable I'll promise him twenty-four hours' start before I point the police in his direction.'

'But then he'll get away,' Piero pointed out.

Julia turned on him.

'You don't think I'm going to keep my word, do you?' she asked scornfully. 'As soon as I'm clear with Natalie I'll put them straight onto him. After what he did to me, I'll have no remorse about anything I do to him.

'I've had plenty of time to learn to be strong. I'm a different person now. Sophie was a fool. She thought feelings were wonderful because they made her happy.'

'She doesn't sound like a fool to me,' Vincenzo said quietly.

'Oh, she was worse than that,' Julia said with an edge of contempt for her old self. 'She needed people and she believed in them. She hadn't learned that that's the quickest way to hell. But

Sophie's dead and good riddance to her. Julia knows it's better to use people than trust them. She's grown wise.'

'Too wise to love?' Vincenzo asked. 'Too wise to need?'

'Too wise to feel. The one thing she learned in prison was not to feel anything.'

'Not even for her child?'

She took a sharp breath. 'That's different. She's part of me, flesh of my flesh. It's as though someone had torn my heart out and wouldn't give it back.'

'So that's why you said you had nothing to give,' he reminded her in a low voice.

'Yes, and it was true, so believe it.'

There was a flash of anger in his eyes. 'And suppose I choose not to believe it?'

'That's your risk, but remember that I warned you.'

He was silent for a moment. Then he nodded.

'I'll be going now. Walk a little way with me.'

She followed him quietly, and as they neared the outer door he said, 'It's a long time between now and mid-January. How are you going to spend that time?'

'Sharpening my sword,' she said with grim humour.

'Don't talk like that,' he said harshly.

'Why? Because you've got some fairy-tale

picture of me as sweetness and light? Maybe I was, then. Not now. Now I'm a monster who knows how to fight dirty. And I'll do it.'

He raised an eyebrow, dampening her agitation.

'I was only going to suggest a better way to pass the time. Come and work for me while Celia's away. Of course, for an artist, waitressing may seem like a comedown—'

'But for a gaolbird it's a step up,' she said lightly.

He refused to rise to the bait. 'Will you take the job?'

She hesitated. She had promised herself to beware of him. She made that promise often, and broke it constantly because he touched her heart, deny it as she might.

As if he could read her mind, Vincenzo said quietly, 'Never fear. I won't trouble you. In fact I ought to apologise.'

'For what?'

'Pressuring you. I guessed that something painful had happened, but I had no idea of anything like this.'

She smiled in mockery of herself. 'Now you know how I turned into an avenging witch. Not a pretty sight, am I?'

'I'm not judging you. What right do I have? But I can't believe that Sophie is dead. I think she's still there somewhere.'

'More fool you,' she sighed. 'You've been warned.'

'Let's leave that for the moment. You need peace and space, and I'll let you have them while you're working for me.'

'All right, I'll take the job.'

'Good. You can have the apartment over the restaurant.'

She shook her head.

'Thank you, but I'll stay here. I can't leave Piero alone now. I know he was alone before, but something's changed. I have a feeling that he needs me.'

'I thought you had no feelings.'

'This is family obligation.'

'And you two are family?'

'Not by blood, but in other ways.' She added quickly, 'And that's not an emotion either. It's survival.'

'And what about me? Am I part of the family?'

She didn't answer, and he knew he was excluded from the charmed circle.

It ought not to matter. He still had relatives with whom he would spend Christmas, leaving these two misfits to whatever comfort they could find with each other. And yet it hurt.

*   *   *

As the month moved towards Christmas, winking lights glinted everywhere, in shop windows, strung across the streets and over the bridges.

People called out of windows and across bridges, wishing each other, *'Buon Natale.'* Merry Christmas. Decorated trees appeared in the squares, and red-robed figures strode about the little city, waving cheerily and talking to children.

'Father Christmas,' Julia exclaimed, pleased.

'Babbo Natale,' Piero corrected her. 'That's what we call him. *Babbo* means "Father".'

'I thought that was *padre*?'

'Padre means "father" too,' Piero agreed. 'But it's more formal. *Babbo* is a kind of affectionate diminutive. Some children use it to their fathers, especially when they're very young.'

'Did Elena do that?' she asked.

'Oh, yes. I've always been *Babbo* to her, except for—well, there was a time when we argued a lot, and she started calling me *Papà*. But that's all over now, and when she comes back I'll be *Babbo* again. Hey, look over there! A whole collection of them!'

He pointed to the Grand Canal, where six red-garbed figures were rowing one gondola, accompanied by blaring Christmas music, and the subject of Elena was allowed to drop.

The week before Christmas she awoke to find

Venice under snow. Delighted, she and Piero went out and walked arm in arm through the city that had been totally transformed. Snow-covered gondolas bobbed in the water, snow-covered bridges glittered over tiny canals. A brilliant, freezing sun poured down blindingly on the white blanket, and she had to shield her eyes from the glare.

Now there were musicians wandering the alleys and the *piazzas*, wearing the traditional shepherds' garb of buckskins and woollen cloaks, and playing bagpipes. The sweet, reedy sound pursued them to St Mark's, where they threw snowballs, ducking and diving, laughing at each other like people who hadn't a care in the world.

Vincenzo had insisted on giving her a generous amount of money for saving his home from damage. 'Your caretaker's bonus,' he called it.

Julia had immediately passed it on to Piero. When he'd demurred she'd told him that this was only half the amount, and she was merely sharing with him. From his sceptical look she'd doubted that he'd been fooled, but he'd accepted the money.

'Get something warm to wear,' she told him.

But as the days went on there was no sign of new clothes. Evidently he had other priorities, which he was not prepared to discuss.

She was a huge success at *Il Pappagallo*.

Venice was filling up with Christmas tourists, and the restaurant was crowded every night. Some of the customers insisted on being served only by her.

She enjoyed this admiration, which made her laugh. Vincenzo, she was secretly pleased to note, didn't find it funny.

'You shouldn't let Antonnio monopolise you,' he said as they were walking through the dark *calles* one night. 'There are plenty of other customers.'

'He's the kind who always makes sure he's noticed,' Julia said lightly. Antonnio's persistent gallantry had done her ego a world of good.

'And you always make sure you serve him first,' Vincenzo growled.

'Only because he grabs that table near the kitchen.'

'Yes, so that he can grab your hand as you go past, and devour it,' he said, as close to ill tempered as she'd ever seen him. 'In future, I'll serve him.'

She chuckled. 'He'll love that.'

'*You're* loving it.'

'Well, he did promise me a very special tip,' she mused.

'Be careful. Antonnio's ''special tips'' are legendary and they don't involve money.'

She took his arm. 'Oh, stop being so pompous.

I'm just doing my job. And after six years shut up with women maybe I don't mind a little admiration.'

'A little admiration,' he scoffed. 'Another moment he'd have had you down on the floor.'

She didn't answer that with words, only with an ironic glance.

'I see,' he said grimly. 'Perhaps the woman who boasts of no feelings likes making me jealous?'

'The woman with no feelings says she doesn't belong to you, and you have no right to be jealous. What happened to your promise to back off and give me space?'

'I wouldn't be the first man to make a promise he can't keep.'

'Vincenzo, what are you hoping for?'

He shrugged. 'Maybe I'm waiting to meet Sophie.'

'She's gone. She died some time during my second year in gaol. She won't come back.'

'You're wrong. She never completely went away. That's why I can't free myself of you.'

They had come to a halt under a lamp that showed them to each other in bleached, unearthly hues. Her face, once too thin, had filled out a little, he realised, and lost some of its tormented look. She had fine, beautiful bone structure, and the slight extra flesh suited her, reclaiming some of her youth.

Tonight she had revelled, siren-like, in her customers' adulation, making him wonder at the different moods that turned her into so many people. Any of them, or none of them, could be the real woman, and all of them were driving him mad.

'You should try harder to free yourself from me,' she said. 'It's just a question of being strong-minded.'

'Maybe I don't want to be strong-minded.'

Snow began to fall, just a few flakes at first, then more and more. Through them she searched his face in the cold light. 'In the end I'll go away and leave you,' she whispered. 'Like everyone else.'

'I know,' he said sadly. 'But who knows when the end will be? Not tonight.'

As he spoke he gathered her into his arms, and she went into them easily, offering her lips to his kiss and returning it with passion.

She knew that very passion was her enemy. It threatened to distract her from her purpose, but she couldn't help it. He brought her back to life, and the feeling was sweet, wild, and frightening.

'No—no—' she whispered, more to herself than him.

He drew back to look at her with troubled eyes. 'Do you want me to stop?'

'*No,*' she said explosively, fastening her mouth on his.

She was kissing him with frantic desire, possessed by feelings that were almost too sweet to be borne. It was she who explored his mouth, almost attacking him in her urgency, teasing his lips, his tongue, feeling the deep satisfaction of his response.

'Stay with me tonight,' he murmured against her mouth.

But she shook her head. 'Not now—not tonight—'

'*Mio Dio!* How much do you think one man can stand? You're not being fair. *He* ill-used you and you revenge yourself on us all.'

'No, it's not that, I swear it. But I don't feel that I belong anywhere. The past is over and I can't tell about the future.'

'Your daughter is all that matters to you, I know that.' He sighed, resting his forehead against hers. 'But I can be patient and hope for my turn.'

'Even if it never comes?'

'Do you believe that one day you'll get your heart's desire?'

'I have to,' she whispered.

'So do I. Let's leave it there, and hope for better times.'

He slipped his arm about her shoulders, and

she leaned contentedly against him as they walked the rest of the way in the falling snow.

At midday on Christmas Eve a cannon was fired from the turrets of the Castel Sant'Angelo in Rome, and Christmas had officially begun.

She and Piero listened to it together on a battery-powered radio she'd bought. The restaurant had closed, Vincenzo had gone off to his family, and she had settled in for Christmas at the *palazzo*.

They had stocked up with seasonal goodies, including *panettone*, the traditional rich fruit cake.

'We're supposed to fast for twenty-four hours after the cannon,' Piero explained, 'but I don't believe in slavishly adhering to every tradition.'

'Neither do I,' she said. 'Let's have some cake.'

As they munched she said, 'I remember when I was a child, hanging my stocking up on Christmas Eve.'

'Children don't do that in Italy,' he explained. 'Stockings don't go up until Epiphany, January sixth.'

'I'm not waiting until then to give you your present.'

'You gave me those gloves, and the scarf, two weeks ago,' he reminded her.

'Well, I had to give them to you early before you froze to death. What happened to all that money you were supposed to be spending on yourself?'

'I gambled it away. I used to be notorious for breaking the bank at Monte Carlo.'

'All right, don't tell me. Anyway, here's some boots and warm socks. I had to guess the size.'

The size was perfect. He put them on and paraded splendidly before her. She smiled and applauded, feeling content.

'And this is yours,' he said, pulling out a small object, carefully wrapped in newspaper.

Opening it she found a china Pierrot figure in a black mask and a costume decorated with many colours. Now she knew what had become of his money. She had seen this in a shop and it cost a fortune.

'Pierrot,' she said.

'So that you don't forget me,' he said.

'Do you think I ever could? *Buon Natale*, Pierrot.'

'Buon Natale.'

Vincenzo's gift to her was a cell phone. He called her halfway through Christmas Day.

'It's a sad Christmas for you,' he said.

'Not really. I have my friends now, and I have hope. Is that your niece I can hear?' Behind him she could make out a little girl's laughter.

'Yes, that's Rosa.'

'It's a lovely sound,' she said wistfully.

'Your time will come. Cling onto that hope.'

'I will. *Buon Natale*.'

'*Buon Natale*—Sophie.'

She smiled and hung up without answering.

After the lull of Christmas there was an immediate flurry of business. As they were clearing up on the second night she said, 'Do you mind if I hurry away? I want to get back to Piero.'

'Isn't he all right?' Vincenzo asked quickly.

'He's got a bit of a cold. I'd just like to make a fuss of him.'

'I suppose he caught cold going to San Zaccaria.' Vincenzo groaned. 'I wish he wouldn't do that in this weather.'

'But he doesn't any more. He hasn't been there since—' She fell silent as the truth dawned on her. 'Since that day I went to Murano.'

'And we met your boat,' Vincenzo said. 'And you came ashore and hugged him.'

As Julia reached home she looked up, wondering if Piero would be there, looking out for her as he sometimes did. But there was no face at the window, and for some reason that made her start to run.

He was probably just asleep, but still—

When she entered their room she couldn't see

him at first. He was lying stretched out, breathing heavily. She moved quietly, not to awaken him, but then she realised that he was unlikely to have awoken, whatever she did.

His forehead was hot to the touch, and there was an ugly rasping sound to the breath, which seemed to tear his throat.

'Piero,' she said, giving him a little shake. 'Piero!'

He opened his eyes, but only a little way.

'Ciao, cara,' he croaked.

'Oh, my God,' she breathed. 'This is bad. Listen, I'm going to get help for you.'

'No need,' he gasped, and his feverish hand sought hers. 'Stay here,' he whispered. 'Stay with you—only you.'

'No,' she said fiercely. 'You've got to get well. I'm calling Vincenzo. He'll know what to do.' Then, before she could choke back the idiotic words she heard herself say, 'Don't go away.'

The ghost of hilarity flickered over his gaunt features. 'I won't.'

She found her cell phone and left the room. She didn't want him to hear her call. To her relief Vincenzo answered at once.

'It's Piero,' she said. 'He's very ill. I think it could be pneumonia.'

He made a sharp sound. 'All right, stay with him. I'll call an ambulance and be right there.'

She returned to find Piero sitting up, looking around him anxiously. As soon as he saw her he stretched out an arm.

'I wanted you—you weren't there…'

He held onto her like a child, his eyes fixed on her face.

'I called Vincenzo. He's sending for an ambulance.'

'Don't want—hospital—' came the painful rasping. 'Just you. Hold onto me.'

She settled him back on the sofa, and knelt beside him, one of his hot hands in hers. He kept his eyes on her, as though seeing her was all he asked. Her heart was heavy, for something told her that the end was very near.

He knew it too, she was sure, and wanted to spend his last few moments alone with her.

She heard a noise outside and went quickly to look out of the window. Down below, in the little garden that fronted onto the Grand Canal, she could see Vincenzo, opening the wrought-iron gate, and propping it so that it stayed open.

She returned to Piero, clasping him in her arms, and after a moment Vincenzo joined them.

'The ambulance is on its way,' he said.

As he got a better look at the old man his eyes signalled his shock, and he leaned over the back of the sofa, grasping Piero's arm warmly.

'Old friend, don't give us a fright like this.'

Piero managed a faint smile.

'Don't need—ambulance,' he croaked. He looked at Julia. 'I have—all I want—since she came back to me.'

Vincenzo frowned. Her eyes met his, reminding him of what they had realised earlier.

'He doesn't mean me,' she said softly.

Vincenzo nodded. He had understood.

'Of course I came back,' she said to Piero. 'You always knew I would, didn't you—*Babbo*?'

She hesitated only a moment before using the pet name that only his daughter had used. It was a risk, but worth it. She knew she'd guessed right when he turned a radiant face on her.

'Oh, yes,' he whispered. 'Always. I kept going to wait for you. People told me you were dead, but I knew—one day—you'd be on the boat.' A faint smile touched his lips. 'And you were.'

He gave a sigh and his eyes closed. Vincenzo's gaze met Julia's and she could see that he felt helpless.

Piero's eyes opened again and when he spoke his voice was faint.

'I was afraid—but when you saw me—you smiled—and I knew that I was forgiven.'

She drew in her breath. Suddenly her eyes were blinded with tears.

'There was nothing to forgive, *Babbo*,' she murmured.

'But there was—' he insisted weakly '—said such terrible things—you know my temper—always sorry afterwards but—this time—this time—'

His breathing came faster, more laboured. A frantic note crept into his voice. 'I didn't mean it, I didn't mean it—'

'Of course you didn't. I always knew that. I forgave you long ago.'

A smile broke over his face, and although the light was fading from him it was the most brilliant smile she had ever seen. Shining through it was the glow of happiness and peace.

Suddenly he seemed to become afraid. 'Elena—Elena—'

'I'm here—always. I love you, *Babbo*.'

'I love you, daughter.'

Vincenzo turned away, covering his eyes.

A few moments later there was the sound of footsteps outside, and a voice calling, 'Is anybody there?'

Hastily controlling himself, Vincenzo went out into the hall where two young men had arrived with the ambulance. He beckoned and they quickly followed him.

One of them gasped when he saw the room. 'What a way to have to live!' he said. 'The sooner we get him to hospital, the better.'

Julia spoke in a muffled voice. 'You're too late.'

They drew near to where the two figures clasped each other. Piero's eyes were closed and his rasping breathing had stopped. He lay quiet and peaceful.

'Poor old fellow,' said one of the young men sympathetically.

Julia laid her cheek tenderly against Piero's white hair.

'Don't feel sorry for him,' she said softly. 'He died as he wanted to, in his daughter's arms.'

The two young men took over, laying Piero gently on a trolley. Julia planted a last kiss on his forehead before he was wheeled away, down into the garden and into the ambulance boat tied up in the water.

Together they stood at the window as the ambulance pulled away down the Grand Canal, until its lights were no longer visible. When it had gone Vincenzo opened his arms and she went into them.

'I'm going to miss him so much,' she said.

'So am I. But you were right. He was happy at the end and that's what matters.' He took her face in his hands and looked down at her.

'You were wonderful,' he said tenderly.

He brushed the hair back from her face, then

drew her against him, with her head on his shoulder, and they stood like that in silence for a long time.

'I'm taking you away with me,' he said at last. 'You can't live here alone.'

'All right, I'll move. But not now.' She turned back into the room, suddenly so lonely. 'I want to spend one more night here.'

Piero's few pathetic possessions were still there, including the gifts she'd given him. She sat down on the bed, lifting his gloves, looking at them, stroking them.

'Who was he really?' she asked.

'Professor Alessandro Calfani, a philosopher. Once I thought I knew him well, but now I think I never knew him in any way that mattered. Did you understand what he meant about Elena forgiving him?'

'He told me she used to call him *Babbo*, but stopped after some kind of estrangement. It sounded as though they had a big row. I guess when he wanted to say sorry, it was too late.'

'But it was all right for him in the end.' Vincenzo sat down beside her, and slipped his arm around her shoulders.

Suddenly the sight of Piero's things hurt her unbearably, and she buried her face in her hands. She struggled to fight the tears, but it was useless, and at last she cried without trying to stop.

'I loved him so much,' she wept against Vincenzo's shoulder.

'So did I,' he said sombrely, holding her tightly as much for his sake as hers.

'Stay with me here tonight,' she said. 'I want to remember him with you.'

He drew her down onto the bed that was only just big enough for the two them, and drew blankets over them.

She was still weeping and he made no effort to stop her. Sometimes he kissed her tumbled hair. Once he drew it back and stroked her face with tender fingers before kissing her gently on the mouth. She looked at him quickly.

'It's all right,' he whispered. 'Go to sleep. I'm here.'

She closed her eyes and he felt her relax. At last her breathing told him that she was asleep. He rested his head against her and had begun to drift off when she stirred and began to mutter.

'Julia,' he whispered, but then, 'Sophie.'

She gave a gasp that was almost a cry, and awoke.

'What is it?' he asked.

'It's a dream—it keeps coming back—'

'What happens in your dream?'

'It's about Annina.'

'You identified with her, didn't you? I can see

why now. You loved your husband, and he shut you away for years—'

'And I died,' she said slowly. 'I died.'

'That's what you said, standing before her picture.'

She looked at him quickly.

'But how could you know that? It was only in my dream.'

'You were sleepwalking. You really went up there, and I came with you, just to see that you were all right.'

She searched his face. 'Yes, you did, didn't you?' she said. 'And you said you were my friend.'

'Do you remember anything else?' he asked anxiously.

'Yes.' She gave a faint smile. 'You kissed me.'

'That was the first time I ever kissed you, and you didn't know, not then or next day. I kept hoping you'd remember, but you looked through me.'

'Why didn't you tell me?'

'I couldn't. You needed to remember for yourself.' He grinned. 'I made good resolutions about waiting until the moment came.'

'You didn't keep them very long.'

'True. I'm not a patient man.'

'I'm glad of that.' She reached up and put her arms about his neck. 'I'm so glad of that.'

When he was sure he'd understood her properly he tightened his own arms about her.

'My love,' he said, 'let us drive the ghosts away. They have no place here now.'

'No,' she whispered, drawing him close. 'Not now.'

CHAPTER SEVEN

THE next day Julia left the *palazzo* for good, and moved into the little apartment over the restaurant. It consisted of one main room, and bedroom, with a tiny bathroom and even tinier kitchen.

New Year was almost on them, and she plunged into work, available at all hours, taking on any jobs, to keep her mind occupied.

'Don't overdo it,' Vincenzo advised one evening as she was just coming on for the late shift. 'You were here early, you helped with cleaning up all afternoon, and now you're starting work again.'

'I prefer to keep busy. The Montressis will be back soon. When New Year's over I'll try Murano again.'

'On your own?'

'Yes, but don't worry about me. If they're not there I won't fling myself melodramatically into the lagoon. I'll just keep trying until they are. I'll go as soon as Piero's funeral is over.'

It was Vincenzo who had paid for the funeral,

arranging for Piero to lie beside Elena on the island of San Michele.

When the day came they both boarded the black motor boat that would take them across the lagoon. They made the journey standing up behind the black-draped coffin. Inside, Piero lay wearing the gloves, scarf and boots she had given him.

Soon the island came in sight, the outer rim of cypresses encased by a terracotta wall, and a few minutes later they reached the landing stage. Pallbearers appeared and carried the coffin onto dry land.

At the inner gate they were met by an official who checked the details with Vincenzo.

They were the only mourners. During the service she kept her eyes fixed on the coffin, topped by flowers from herself and Vincenzo. She had known Piero only a few weeks, yet she felt she had lost a very dear friend.

It was time to take the coffin to its final resting place. As they moved out of the chapel she could see that some of the cemetery was conventional, with burials in the ground, and headstones.

But this place had been created for economy of space, and most coffins were placed in narrow vaults, piled on top of one another, as many as ten high. At the outer end was a marble plaque giving the details of who lay there, with a picture.

As there was also a holder for flowers a whole wall of these plaques was an impressive sight. Where two flowered walls faced each other the effect was of an enchanted bower.

Elena was on the fourth tier, her picture easily visible. She bore a marked resemblance to her father, having his sharp features and brilliant smile.

Slowly Piero's coffin was slid into the space beside her, and the end fitted into place.

'Goodbye,' she whispered. 'And thank you for everything.'

'I'd like to put some fresh flowers in my sister's urn,' Vincenzo said.

They walked along the long walls of flowers until Vincenzo stopped, pointing up at something above his head.

'That's Bianca,' he said. 'And the one beside her is her husband.'

Julia tilted her head back, but was unable to see the pictures clearly.

'How do you get up so high to change the flowers?' she wanted to know.

'There are some steps somewhere.'

He went searching around the corner and reappeared wheeling a set of steps high enough to reach the upper levels. Julia studied his sister's face and even from this distance she could see the family resemblance between them. There was a gentleness about Bianca that was instantly appealing.

'I didn't like him,' Vincenzo said, 'but she loved him. They only had four years together before they died.'

'Why didn't you like him?'

'He was too smooth a character. You can see it there in his face.'

She glanced up again, trying to get a better view of the man, whose face was partly obscured by flowers.

Suddenly she felt as though the very air about her had shuddered. She clutched the steps to avoid falling.

'What is it?' Vincenzo asked, concerned.

'I want to climb up.'

'Why? What's the matter?'

'I need to see more closely.'

Feeling as though she were moving through a nightmare, she began to climb the steps, her gaze fixed on the man's face as it grew closer. She took a deep breath, expecting it to change before her eyes. This must all be a terrifying mistake.

But there was no mistake. The face engraved in the marble was that of her husband.

She could hear Vincenzo's voice calling her from a great distance. Gradually the world stopped spinning and she realised that she was sitting on the steps, shivering violently.

'For God's sake, what's the matter?' he demanded, aghast. 'You nearly fainted up there.'

'It's him,' she said through chattering teeth.

'What do you mean?'

'My husband, Bruce. That's him up there.'

'Julia, you're overwrought.'

'I tell you, that's him.'

She forced herself to her feet. 'Let me see him again.'

'All right, and you'll find that it's just a chance resemblance.'

She climbed back to the top step and fixed her eyes on the man, almost hoping to find that it had been a mistake. But there was no doubt. It was the face she hated. Silently she went down and sat on the steps again, feeling as though she were turning to ice.

'That is Bruce,' she said slowly. 'How does he come to be here?'

'Julia, I think you're wrong. You haven't seen him for years and your memories are distorted by hatred.'

'I know what he looked like,' she said angrily. 'Oh, why was I stupid enough to lose his pictures overboard? If I still had them you could see for yourself. That's him.'

Vincenzo drew a sharp breath. If she was right

the implications were so monstrous that for the moment he couldn't accept them.

'I can't get my head around this,' he said slowly. 'I know him as James Cardew. He came here five years ago.'

'Was he alone?'

'Julia—'

She clutched his hand painfully. 'Was anyone with him? Tell me.'

'He had a little girl with him,' he said slowly.

'How old?'

'About three.'

'Blue eyes? Fair hair, slightly ginger?'

'Yes.'

'That's my daughter. Where is she?'

'*Mio Dio!*' he whispered, appalled. 'How can this have happened?'

'*Where is she?*'

'Since they died she lives with me.'

'I must see her.'

'Wait!' She'd half risen and he seized her arms. 'It isn't as simple as that.'

'She is my daughter. I am her mother. What could be simpler?'

'But you can't just go up to her and tell her who you are. She thinks you're dead.'

She shook her head wildly. 'No, I don't believe you.'

'James told us that he was a widower. The

child believed it. She's had years to get used to the idea. For her it's reality. Julia, please try to understand. You can't simply burst on her out of the blue.'

She leaned hopelessly against the side of the steps.

'I didn't believe I could hate him any more than I did,' she said. 'But he had one last trick up his sleeve.'

Other mourners were coming towards them along the tunnel of flowers. He helped her to her feet.

'Let's find somewhere else.'

They found a seat in the cloisters at the far end and sat quietly for a few minutes, both stunned by what had happened.

At last a harsh sound, part laugh, part sob, burst from her.

'I've dreamed of this for so long. It was going to be the happiest moment of my life. Now I feel as if I've been punched in the stomach. You've got to admit that's funny. Oh, heavens, isn't it hilarious?'

She began to laugh softly, trying to smother the sound with her hands.

'Don't,' Vincenzo begged, slipping his arm around her.

'What shall I do? Cry?'

When he didn't answer she looked up and saw

that he was looking back the way they had come, to where a middle-aged woman and a little girl had appeared before the plaques of Bianca and her husband. The woman was controlling a push-chair in which a child slept.

'Who are they?' she asked in a shaking voice.

'The woman is Gemma. I employ her as a nanny.'

'And the little girl?'

The world seemed to stop. He was looking at her with an expression of terrible sadness.

'Oh, my God,' she whispered. 'That's—?'

'Yes.' He was gripping her tightly now.

'Let go of me.'

'No. Julia, stop and think. She doesn't know you. She's grieving for the death of her parents.'

'They weren't her parents. Your sister wasn't her mother.'

'But she loved her as though she was. I'm sorry, I know this is painful for you, but for Rosa's sake you must listen.'

'Rosa? Her name is Natalie.'

'Not any longer. He told us her name was Rosa. She's forgotten Natalie.'

'Forgotten me, you mean?'

'I think he set himself to drive you out of her memory, yes.'

'And he succeeded.'

'It's been five years,' he said urgently. 'The

child believes what she's been taught to believe. Think what the truth would do to her now. Don't force any more burdens onto her.'

'You're saying I'm a burden to her?' she demanded, aghast.

'You would be *at this moment*. I beg you to leave it until we've both had time to think.'

'Time for you to spirit her away where I can't find her,' she flashed.

He didn't reply in words, but the white-faced look he gave her was so full of shock that she backed off.

'I'm sorry, I shouldn't have said that.'

'No, you shouldn't,' he said harshly. 'Is that the sort of man you think I am?'

'How do I know? Once I thought Bruce was wonderful. When people are fighting over a child they do things that you wouldn't have dreamed—'

'Are we fighting? Have we ever fought? I think I've deserved better from you than that kind of accusation. But since you lump me in with all the others, *here*.'

He pulled a small notebook from his pocket, scribbled something and tore off the page with a gesture that was almost violent.

'That's where I live now,' he snapped. 'Come any time and you'll find her there. But think very carefully about what you're going to say to her.'

Without giving her a chance to answer he stormed off in the direction of the woman and child. Julia sat, frozen with dismay, shocked at herself for having said such a thing to him, appalled at the discovery that had made them almost enemies.

She watched the little scene in the distance. The woman had drawn the steps up to the wall of plaques, climbing them, then taking out the flowers. She descended and indicated for the child to climb up, with the fresh flowers she was holding. She mounted and began to place flowers in the urns, first her father's, then Bianca's.

She was coming down now, sitting on the steps in exactly the same spot where Julia had sat only a few moments ago. She wasn't weeping, merely crouching there with the stillness of despair. The woman tried to comfort her, but to Julia it was hard to tell if the child even noticed.

She felt as though a band were tightening about her heart. How well she knew that feeling of desolation, so deep that the slightest movement didn't seem worth the effort.

Then it swept over her in a tide of anguish. This child was grieving for the loss of her parents, of her mother.

Her mother! Not Julia. Not the woman who'd yearned over her through heartbroken days and agonised nights. *Someone else!*

Then the little girl looked up, saw Vincenzo and, with a glad cry, began to run towards him. He opened his arms and she hurled herself into them, babbling in Italian. Julia could just hear the words.

'I looked for you—'

'I'm here now,' he soothed her. 'But what are you doing here?'

'You said you were coming to the funeral of your friend, so I asked Gemma to bring me to see *Mamma* and *Papà*. I knew you'd come to see them too.'

Julia began to move forward very slowly, staying close to the wall, making no disturbance, but getting close enough to see better. Then the little girl raised her head from Vincenzo's shoulder, and Julia gasped at the sight of her. If she'd had any doubts before, they were settled now, for it was her own mother's face that she saw. This was the child she had last seen years ago, at the start of the nightmare.

Vincenzo looked back and for a terrible moment Julia thought he would ignore her. Instead he said gently, 'Rosa, I have a friend for you to meet.'

The child looked straight at her. Julia held her breath, waiting for the burst of joyful recognition.

But it did not come.

Rosa regarded her mother politely but without recognition.

'*Buongiorno,*' she said.

'*Buongiorno,*' Julia replied mechanically. 'I am—'

She fell silent. No words would come. She could hear her own heart pounding.

'This is Signora Julia Baxter,' Vincenzo said.

'*Buongiorno, signora. Sono Rosa.*'

She offered her hand. Hardly knowing what she did, Julia took it. For a moment it lay in hers. Her daughter had shaken her hand like a stranger.

Vincenzo was introducing the nanny, who had a kind face. Julia greeted her mechanically. She was functioning on automatic while her brain struggled to cope.

'Julia came with me to Piero's funeral,' Vincenzo explained. 'He was a friend we were very fond of.'

'I promised Carlo he could come to see *Mamma* and *Papà* this time,' Rosa said. 'He was too young before.'

'Carlo?' Julia asked blankly.

She knew that she sounded vague, but that was because her mind was rejecting the monstrous idea that was growing. Surely it was impossible?

But nothing was impossible.

'He's my little brother,' Rosa said, indicating

the sleeping child in the pushchair. 'He's only two.'

She reached out eagerly to Vincenzo. 'Come with me.'

He took her hand and they went up the steps together. Julia heard her say, 'I didn't do the flowers properly.'

And Vincenzo's tender reply, 'Let's do them together.'

He helped her to arrange the leaves. When they had finished the child stood a moment looking at the pictures. Slowly she passed her fingertips over them as though seeking comfort from the cold marble, then leaned forward and kissed them, first her father, then her stepmother. Julia bent her head, unable to watch. But in the next moment she looked up again, unable not to watch.

She waited for her daughter to cry, but, as before, Rosa's face was blank. Whatever she was feeling was being kept bolted down and hidden from the world.

'Just like me,' Julia thought, appalled. 'I know exactly what's happening to her inside. But no child should feel like that, or have such a look of frozen misery. Dear God, what's happened to her?'

After a moment the little girl came down and

went to the pushchair, gently shaking the toddler.
He awoke with a gurgle, instantly smiling.

Like Bruce, Julia thought. He's got his face
and his charm.

The nanny started to help but Rosa shook her
head, polite but determined as she undid the
straps and helped him out. Hand in hand they
climbed the steps together.

'Look,' Julia heard her say. 'That's *Papà* and
that's *Mamma*.'

He beamed and stretched out his hands to the
faces of his parents, but when they encountered
only cold marble he flinched back. Puzzled, he
looked at his sister, and reached out again.

'Mamma,' he said. *'Mamma, Mamma!'*

He began to sob, pounding the marble with his
fists and screaming out his disillusion.

At once Rosa gathered the child into her arms,
murmuring soothing words.

'It's all right, little one. It's all right. We'll go
home now.'

She helped him down to the ground, put him
back into the pushchair and kissed him gently,
stroking him until he stopped crying.

'It would have been better to wait until he was
a little older,' Vincenzo told her.

Rosa nodded sadly. 'I'm sorry, Uncle
Vincenzo. I just didn't want him to forget them.
But I should have remembered he's only a baby.'

She turned politely to Julia.

'*Buongiorno, signora,*' she said, as politely as a little old lady. 'I'm afraid I must be going now. I hope that we will meet again.'

'So do I,' she said with an effort.

She watched as the little party walked away, the baby's hand extended to clutch Rosa's, as though there he could find safety.

'I didn't know they were coming here,' Vincenzo said. 'Rosa just spoke of the next few days.'

'That little boy—is he—?'

'Yes, he's Bianca's son, and James'. I wish it hadn't been sprung on you like that.'

'I suppose I should have thought of it.'

Suddenly the wind that blew down the corridor of flowers was bleak and desolate. She shivered.

'It's cold. I'm going home.'

The group had reached the end of the path and were about to turn out of sight. They stopped and looked back at Vincenzo.

'We need to talk,' he said, 'but—'

'But you have to go.' She smiled faintly. 'Your family needs you.'

'You'll come with us to the landing stage?'

'I think I'll wait and take the next boat. Go quickly before they get worried.'

'Yes.' He was uneasy, but there was no choice.

Julia didn't watch him catch up with the others. She turned away and walked in the opposite direction, wondering how this could have happened. After the years of yearning and hoping she had finally met her daughter again, and the moment that should have been so happy had brought her greater pain than anything in her life.

Vincenzo didn't appear at the restaurant that evening. Julia tried not to read anything into it, but she regretted hurling an accusation at him. He was her only friend and it was foolish to alienate him.

But she knew that this practical reason wasn't the only one. Bit by bit the sense of closeness they shared had become essential to her.

She thought of him as the man she might have loved if love were not impossible for her now. Deeper than that she didn't dare to look into her own heart.

When the restaurant closed she went wearily up the stairs and shut herself in. Her brain felt as though it were going around and around on a treadmill. She must go to bed and try to sleep, but she knew she would only lie awake.

The building was old-fashioned, with shutters on the windows. As she went to close them for the night her gaze was caught by something in the *calle* below. Pushing open the window, she leaned out and saw a man standing there.

'Come in,' she called.

She was at the door, waiting for him as he turned the corner of the stairs, ready to open her arms to him in her relief.

'I didn't think you'd come,' she said fervently.

He nodded almost curtly, but made no move toward her. 'I had to.'

'I thought you were angry with me after what I said.'

She stepped back to let him into the room, realising that there would be no embrace.

'No, I'm not angry any more,' he said. 'You were in a state of shock. Let's forget that it happened.'

This wasn't the joyful reunion she'd anticipated when she'd seen him in the street. He was here, but emotionally he was holding back from her in a way he'd never done before. When she laid a hand on his arm he smiled cautiously, but didn't take her into his arms.

'Perhaps you'd make me a coffee,' he said politely.

'Of course,' she replied, matching his tone.

As she was working in the kitchen he came and stood leaning against the doorway.

'I may even have deserved your suspicion,' he said. 'I wouldn't spirit her away, but for a moment I did wish I could turn the clock back, to before you appeared, and stop it happening. Rosa has been part of my family for five years. I love her. Do you think I wanted to admit that she's yours?'

'Does that mean that you're going to say that she isn't?' she asked sharply.

'I can't do that. I wish I could, but I did some checking on the internet tonight. I found several reports about the robbery, confirming everything you told me. One of them had a tiny picture of your husband, just good enough to show that he really was the same man as James Cardew.

'And the first time I ever saw you, that night Piero brought you home, there was something familiar about you. I didn't understand it, but actually I was looking at you and seeing Rosa.'

'But we're not alike.'

'Except for one thing—her forehead. She has exactly the same low forehead that you have. Usually her fringe hides it, but tonight I saw her brush the fringe back, and then everything became clear.'

They returned to the main room and he chose a single chair rather than the sofa where she might have sat beside him.

'I need to know more,' she said quietly. 'Everything you can tell me about him.'

'Does it really matter now?'

'I have six years of blanks to fill in. I won't like what you tell me, but I have to know.'

'Yes, I suppose you do,' he said at last. 'All right. I'll tell you everything I can.'

CHAPTER EIGHT

Vincenzo took a deep breath, and started.

'It seems as though your friends who thought they'd seen him in Venice and Rome were right. Bianca met him in Rome, where he was as an art dealer.'

'An art dealer?' Julia cried in disgust. 'But he knew nothing except what he learned from me.'

'He seems to have been a genius at presentation. Plus he had a lot of money and his premises were in the wealthy part of town.'

'That would be his cut from the robberies,' she guessed.

'Yes, it must have been enough to give the impression of success. When Bianca came home he followed her here. He said he was expanding, establishing a branch in Venice. The truth, as I later learned, was that he'd had to get out of Rome, fast. He'd sold some apparently priceless artefacts to a powerful family, who naturally wanted their money back when they turned out to be fakes.

'They sent people to Venice, who explained to

James that, if he didn't pay up, bad things would happen to him. So he did, having no choice.

'After that, what money he had left ran out quickly. He was extravagant. He bought useless rubbish for show, made bad investments. He was a rather stupid, shallow man.'

'Yes,' she said. 'That's exactly it.'

'But there was nothing to make me suspect him of worse than that. He had a passport in the name of James Cardew and hers said Rosa Cardew. He had a whole file of paperwork establishing that James Cardew was a successful art dealer with a list of grateful clients in several countries. Someone in the gang must have forged them for him before they parted company.'

'I don't think so,' Julia said. 'Otherwise the man who split on him could have given the police his new name. No, it must have been done later, by someone else. I dare say false documents are easy enough to get, if you have the money.'

'He certainly had money for a while. When it ran out he got desperate. He tried to get some out of me, although this was after the crash and the whole world knew that we had nothing. But he was sure I had some secret cache hidden from the creditors. He suggested that it was time I handed over Bianca's ''share''.'

'Yes, that was how his mind worked,' she remembered. 'He could never believe that things were exactly as they seemed, especially where cash was concerned. Did he think she had a secret fortune when they married?'

'He as good as admitted it. I don't think he married her entirely for love. Maybe not at all.'

It took her a moment to appreciate what he was saying, and then she turned on him.

'Is that supposed to delight me?' she demanded furiously. 'Do you think I care who he loved?'

'I don't know how you feel. You were once deeply in love with him.'

'That was in another life.'

He nodded wryly. 'I keep telling myself that things happened in another life. But it's odd how the lives overlap when you least expect it. Anyway, like a fool I borrowed against the restaurant for my sister's sake. She'd had a rough time. I didn't want things to get worse for her.'

'How long did it take him to come back for more?'

'Not long. This time we had a fight and he ended up in the canal.'

'Good,' she said simply.

'The one good thing I know of him is that he honestly seemed to love Rosa. In his way he was a good father.'

'A good father, after the way he separated her

from her mother, without a thought for either of them?'

'I only meant that he always showed her a lot of affection, and interest. If she tried to tell him something he'd stop what he was doing and listen, however long it took. Lots of parents can't do that, however much they love the child—'

'Yes, all right,' she interrupted him in a strained voice. 'You're right, he was a good father. I remember now how he loved being with her.'

'And she adored him. She also came to love Bianca. That's not easy for you to hear, but you have to know what you're dealing with.'

'Thank you,' she said in a colourless voice. 'I couldn't tell much from seeing her today.'

'No, she didn't cry or show any emotion, did she?' he said heavily. 'It's been four months, and still—'

Julia stared. 'You mean she's never cried?'

'Not once. Even on the first day, when the news came—' He broke off with a helpless shrug. 'She just closed in on herself. She won't let anyone in, not even me.' He looked at her. 'That's something you know all about.'

'Yes,' she breathed. 'Sometimes it's the only form of self-protection you have.'

'To pack your feelings away in an iron chest marked, ''No longer required''. Then bury that chest too deep to be found again,' he said, reminding her of her own words.

'But she's so young!'

'She's eight years old, but she's already lost three parents, and she can't talk to anyone about it. We all have our burdens but—'

'But hers are the worst,' Julia agreed sombrely.

'Normally she loves Carnival, but now she refuses to think of it.'

'Carnival?'

'In February. Everyone dresses up in masks and colourful costumes. Last year she had a wonderful time with James and Bianca. Maybe that's why she's not interested this year. I keep trying to entice her, telling her how excited she ought to be, but—' He shrugged.

'You can't get into someone's mind by force,' Julia said.

'No, I guess I know that.'

Suddenly she burst out. 'What am I going to do? Do you know how I've dreamed of the things I'd say to her when we met again? And now none of them will be right. What can I do?'

'You can trust me.'

'Can I?' she asked before she could stop herself.

He grimaced. 'I suppose you're bound to think that way.'

'How do I know what to think?'

He rose. 'Perhaps we shouldn't talk any more. We both have a lot riding on this, and we can't afford to quarrel.'

'In the meantime, I'm totally in your hands,' she said angrily. It was the kind of thing she'd resolved not to say, but she couldn't help herself. The strains of the day, the helpless sense of being so near and yet so far, filled her with tension that found relief in bitterness.

'I wish I could persuade you that you're safe in my hands,' he said.

'But you have my daughter and I don't,' she cried. 'How am I supposed to get past that?'

'Supposed to *forgive* that, you mean. Perhaps you never will. We'll talk another time.'

'When do I see her?'

'You have my address. All you have to do is turn up and bulldoze your way in.'

'You know I won't do that.'

'Right, because you're a good mother. That's what's holding you back. Not me.'

'And it'll always hold me back, won't it? It's what you're counting on.'

'Don't say any more, Julia. Don't say things that will make the future harder.'

She turned on him. 'Harder? How much harder than this can it get? Can't you understand what's happened? The last time I saw my child she clung to me and cried, ''Mummy, no!'' Today she—didn't even—recognise—me.'

The words came out in jerks. She was trembling violently, unable to prevent the sobs coming. They rose up in her, bursting out as gasping screams.

'Julia!' He came to her but she fended him off.

'No—no—keep away—I'm all right.'

'But you're not. At least let me help you.'

'How can you help me—when we're enemies?' she choked. 'That's true, isn't it?'

'No, we're not enemies. Perhaps we're on different sides, but you and I could never be enemies.'

'That's just words,' she flashed at him. 'If we're not enemies now, we will be in the end. Don't you know that?'

By his face she could tell that he did know it, however hard he might try to deny it.

'No,' he said, trying to sound convinced. 'There's too much between us.'

'There's nothing between us that matters,' she flashed. 'Nothing—nothing—'

She couldn't finish. The sobs were rising again, threatening to suffocate her. Vincenzo abandoned argument and did what he should have done at first, putting his arms around her and holding her tightly.

'Don't try to talk,' he murmured. 'Talking

doesn't help.' He sighed, resting his cheek against her hair. 'I don't really know what does help, but it isn't words.'

She couldn't answer. Waves of grief overwhelmed her. It was as if all the tears she had shed over the last few years were still there to be shed again.

From somewhere she heard him murmuring her name, and felt his head resting against hers. He was right. Words were useless. The only comfort lay in shared warmth, and it was only to be found in him.

'All these years,' she wept, 'thinking of her every day, longing for her, loving her, but not knowing what she looked like any more, dreaming of when I'd find her again, what we'd say to each other—'

'I know, I know,' he whispered.

'What did I think was going to happen? Deluding myself—she was bound to have a new life—but I wouldn't let myself see it—'

'Julia—Julia—'

'She doesn't want me.'

'It's too soon to say that.'

'No, it isn't. Don't you see I've been fooling myself all this time? I'm a stranger to her. She doesn't want me and she never will.'

She wept without restraint. She had come to the end of the journey and the ending was bitter and hopeless. He tried desperately to soothe her, turning her face up to him and kissing it repeatedly. Her wretchedness tore at him and for a moment he would have done anything in the world to make things right for her.

Anything but the one thing she wanted.

He'd seen her face like this once before, the night she'd walked in her sleep and he'd promised to help her. How far away it seemed now.

He kissed her tears, then her lips, gently at first, then fiercely as though trying to call her back from some distant region.

'You said there was nothing between us,' he said huskily. 'But you're wrong. There's this—and this—'

For a moment she almost yielded. The feeling was so sweet and welcome. But now the distress that fuelled her whole life had extended to him, and she would not weaken.

'Yes,' she said wistfully. 'But it's not enough. Please, Vincenzo—'

He sighed and released her.

'You're right,' he said. 'It's not enough. I'd better be going.'

She wanted to say something to keep him there. She wanted him to go.

She longed to think of the right thing to say, but the words wouldn't come to her, and he was equally silent.

'Goodnight,' he said at last.

'Goodnight.'

He left, closing the door quietly behind him. Julia could only stand, in violent despair, watching that closed door, wishing she could dash her head against it.

That night her dreams were haunted by a child screaming for the mother she was about to lose. She could feel the arms about her neck, desperately clinging on as she was torn away.

'No, Mummy, no!'

She awoke to find herself sitting up, staring into the darkness, clinging onto the wall as though to stop herself from falling.

After that she didn't dare go back to sleep. She got up and spent the rest of the night walking the silent *calles*.

She wondered what she would say to Vincenzo, but when she went to work there was no sign of him. Someone said he'd called to say he wouldn't be in today.

She made a decision.

'I'm due for a day off,' she told the head waiter, 'and I'd like to take it now. I'm sorry about the short notice—'

'It's OK, we're not too busy,' he said kindly.

She stormed out into the street and began to run in the direction of the Grand Canal. It was an unfamiliar route, but by now she was becoming a Venetian, and managed not to get lost more than once. When she reached the water she boarded a *traghetto*, one of the two-man gondola ferries that crossed the Grand Canal. Like the others she made the journey standing upright, huddling her jacket around her against the icy wind, and the snow that was falling again.

By studying a map she managed to identify the address Vincenzo had given her in the Fondamenta Soranzo. As she reached the shore she was already working out the rest of the way: down this *calle*, across that little bridge.

Suppose they weren't there? Suppose his disappearance meant that he'd taken her away? Wherever they had gone, she would find them.

There was the doorway, opposite her on the other side of a small canal. In another moment—

You're a good mother. That's what's holding you back. Not me.

The words seemed to leap out at her from the clear air. Only last night she'd said she would not 'bulldoze' her way in. And now she was doing it.

She watched the house for any sign of movement. Slowly, she began to retreat into the shadows until she turned the corner. Then she ran back the way she'd come and almost jumped into the returning *traghetto*.

On the other side she jumped out again and

headed straight for the nearest art shop. There she spent money in a fury, buying colours, pencils, brushes and pigments. She finished off with a large, canvas artist's bag, stuffed everything into it, and headed for the Palazzo di Montese.

As she came near she crossed her fingers, hoping that she could still get in. There was the little back door. She put her shoulder to it, giving it a push and a shake. It opened.

'Trust you to know how to do it,' she whispered to the unseen friend she still remembered.

Once inside she carefully closed the door and hurried on upstairs. In the upper corridor she stopped and looked up at the ceiling, where there were some frescoes that had taken her attention before. Now that the light was good she could see how really fine they were; also that they needed her attention.

'I should have done this before,' she muttered.

Unlike most of the ceilings in the *palazzo*, this one wasn't too high, and now she knew where to find a stepladder. She put it in place and shinned up, but was still not close enough.

A tall, empty bookshelf stood nearby. From the top of the stepladder she managed to scramble onto it. Lying on her back, she had just the view she wanted. The old, familiar excitement began to grow in her as she saw what time had done to the fresco, and knew what she could do to make it right.

So absorbed was she that she failed to hear the faint sounds coming from below. It was Vincenzo's voice that alerted her.

'Careful where you step. Take my hand.'

And then a child's voice, 'It's awfully big, Uncle Vincenzo. Did you and *Mamma* really used to live here?'

'We did once, when we were children. Did she ever tell you about it?'

'She did sometimes. She promised to bring me here, but *Papà* heard her and got angry. Why was that?'

'I don't know, *cara*. He had his own way of seeing things. Perhaps we shouldn't have come.'

'Oh, but you promised. I've been looking forward to it.'

'But it's a gloomy place, for you.'

'It wasn't always gloomy, though, was it?'

'No, my darling. Once it was full of lights and laughter. But that was a long time ago.'

Julia lay on top of the bookcase, unable not to eavesdrop, her heart beating fast at the sound of her daughter's voice. But Vincenzo's voice also caught her attention. There was no harshness in it now. It was gentle and tender as he spoke to the child.

They must just be on the stairs below, and she

could hear him very clearly, talking about the old days in this place. Sometimes the little girl laughed, and then he laughed with her. They were delightful together. Julia lay there, high up, listening, torn between sadness and aching delight.

But she couldn't stay here, waiting to be discovered. Slowly she began to inch to the edge of the bookcase, from where she could get to the stepladder.

Nearly there—nearly there—one hand on the ladder—a few more inches—

But the ladder moved as she touched it. Grasping frantically, she somehow lurched back against the bookcase, and the next moment the whole lot came crashing down to the floor, with her underneath.

For a moment she lay still, trapped beneath everything, more winded than hurt.

She heard Vincenzo call, 'Rosa, come back here—' and the next moment the child came flying around the corner.

'Uncle Vincenzo, come quickly.'

He appeared a moment later, frowning at the sight, then exclaiming violently as he recognised her.

'It's the lady from yesterday,' Rosa cried.

'Julia, what the devil? *Julia!*'

'I'm all right,' she gasped. 'If you could just get this stuff off me—'

Instantly the child reached out tiny hands to the bookcase.

'Get back,' Vincenzo told her sharply. 'You'll hurt yourself.'

When he was sure she was clear he removed the stepladder, then lifted the bookcase and swung it right away.

'Don't try to get up,' he ordered Julia as she began to move.

'I'm all right,' she said decidedly. 'No bones broken.'

'Your forehead's bleeding,' Rosa said.

She touched it and found the trickle of blood. Then Vincenzo's arms went about her and he was helping her to her feet.

'Can you walk?'

'Yes, of course I—hey.'

He'd lifted her and was carrying her to the room that had been the count's bedroom. Rosa ran ahead and opened the door so that he could go through and lay her on the great bed. He pulled off his jacket and put it under her head as a pillow. Then he sat beside her, glaring.

'If you aren't the most—what the devil were you doing?'

'Looking at your frescoes.'

'Why?'

'It's about time somebody did. It's my job.'

'You have to do it here and now?' he demanded, astounded and exasperated in equal measure. 'No—wait—that can come later. You need a doctor.'

'I just had a little fall and a few bruises. But I could do with something to drink.'

'I'll get you some water from the pump. Rosa, stay with her. Don't let her get up.'

He left the room, and at once the child came to the bed, as though standing guard.

'It's all right,' Julia said. 'I'm not going to run away.'

'Good, because Uncle Vincenzo says you mustn't.'

'Do people always do what Uncle Vincenzo says?'

Rosa considered this seriously. 'Sometimes.'

'Do you?'

She shook her head solemnly. Julia wondered if she was imagining a gleam of mischief in the childish eyes. She would have liked to believe it was there.

'You're the lady I met yesterday, aren't you?'

Julia nodded.

'Why are you here?'

'I'm an art restorer.'

'Is that the same as an artist?'

'No, I was never much good as an artist, so I

look after other people's pictures, and repair them.'

'Are you doing that for Uncle Vincenzo?'

'The truth is that I had no right to be here. I'm just nosy, I'm afraid.'

This admission seemed to strike a response in the child.

'Oh, yes, like when you're looking at a book of pictures and you've just got to keep turning over more and more pages.'

'That's it,' Julia said. 'The pictures are so beautiful that you can't get enough.'

'And you wish ever so much that you could make pictures like them,' Rosa said wistfully. 'But you just can't.'

Julia looked up quickly to see Vincenzo standing in the doorway. She hadn't heard him come in, and wondered how long he'd been there.

Rosa was full of eagerness.

'Uncle, this lady understands about pictures and wanting to look at them even though it's time to go to bed.'

Vincenzo grinned. 'We have constant battles about bedtime in our house.'

He brought a glass of water to the bed and offered it to Julia, who was hauling herself up painfully.

'Thank you,' she gasped, fumbling for the glass.

But it was Rosa who secured it, climbing onto the bed and directing Vincenzo to hold Julia up. He slipped his arms beneath her shoulders while the little girl held the glass to her lips.

'Can I have your hankie, please, Uncle?'

He handed over a clean handkerchief, and Rosa used it to dab at the blood on Julia's forehead. Her little face was concentrated, as though this were the most important job in the world. Her hands were gentle.

'There,' she said solemnly at last. 'That will do until the doctor sees it.'

'Thank you,' Julia said as Vincenzo laid her back on the jacket. She smiled at Rosa. 'That's very kind of you.'

'I'm going to be a nurse when I grow up,' the child told her. 'Or I may be an art restorer. If I can read all the books in time. But it's hard because Gemma keeps telling me to put the light out and go to sleep.'

'I used to get into trouble for that too. My mother couldn't understand that, to me, an art book was as good as a thriller.'

Rosa nodded again, this time vigorously. 'What did you do?' she asked.

Julia leaned nearer, like a conspirator, and whispered, 'I got smaller books and hid them under the bedclothes.'

She winked. Rosa gave a little gasp, which almost turned into a giggle. Almost.

'Now can I ask what you're doing here?' Vincenzo said. 'Why didn't you just tell me, instead of coming here alone and climbing about in that dangerous way?'

'I did it on impulse. I thought it would give me something to think about other than—well, things I didn't want to think about.'

Out of the corner of her eye she saw Rosa grow suddenly still. It was an alert stillness, as though someone had blown a trumpet, and she was waiting.

'I expect you have a lot of things that you don't want to think about,' Julia said carefully.

Rosa nodded.

'But you can't stop,' she said.

'I know. The more you don't want to think of them, the more you keep thinking of them, until it's like a great big stone crushing you. And you can't get out from under it.'

This time Rosa didn't nod, but a light came into her eyes, and she continued to watch Julia intently.

'I think I should get you back to your flat,' Vincenzo said. 'Then I'm sending for the doctor, and I want no argument. Nor are you coming in to work at the restaurant. You'll rest until Epiphany is over.'

'Then she can spend Epiphany with us,' Rosa breathed. 'Uncle Vincenzo, please say she can.'

Julia drew in her breath, waiting for Vincenzo to find some excuse.

'Will you feel well enough for that?' he asked.

'Yes, I know I will.'

'You'll come?' Rosa exclaimed. 'And stay with us all day?'

Julia glanced at Vincenzo. He was very pale, but he spoke steadily.

'Of course you will stay all day. So now you must rest properly, to make quite certain that nothing prevents you being our guest.'

'*My* guest,' Rosa said proudly.

CHAPTER NINE

IT SNOWED the night before Epiphany, but by the morning it had stopped, the sun was out, and Venice lay under a shining white blanket.

Vincenzo came to collect Julia and exclaimed, '*Mio Dio*, what are you carrying?'

'Gifts for Rosa. After all, it's her day, isn't it? Piero told me that Italian children hang up their stockings now, not at Christmas.'

'You'd better let me take some. There was no need to load yourself down like a donkey.'

'Six missing birthdays. Six missing Christmases. I'm making up for all those times I wasn't able to watch her face as she opened things. She won't know, but I will.'

As they walked through the snow she said, 'By the way, how did I become Signora Baxter?'

'It was the first name I could think of. Do you mind?'

'No, it'll do. I'm so happy today I'd agree to anything.'

She gave a little skip in the snow and he had to grab her to stop her slithering. They laughed together and now he could hear the different note in her voice. She had come back to life. The next moment she broke free and began to pelt him with snowballs. He dropped the parcels and pelted her back.

As it was a feast day there were no *traghetti* crossing the Grand Canal, so they walked over the Accademia Bridge. Halfway across Julia stopped and looked down the length of water to where it broadened out into the lagoon, flashing and gleaming like a million swords in the sunlight.

'If people knew Venice was as beautiful as this in winter, nobody would come in the summer,' she said.

'You're turning into a Venetian,' he teased.

'I reckon I am.'

She gazed ecstatically up into the sky, which was a brilliant blue.

'I can't believe this is happening,' she breathed. 'After all these years I've seen her again, I'm going to spend the day with her and she likes me. Not as a mother—it's too soon for that, I know. But she likes me, *she likes me*.'

'Steady,' he said, taking her shoulders. 'Try to keep your feet on the ground.'

'No, why should I?' she said, laughing. 'I don't want my feet on the ground. The ground's so hard. Believe me, I know. I've slept on it.'

He gave her a gentle shake. 'Julia, you're crazy.'

'Yes, I'm crazy,' she cried joyfully. 'I'm crazy with happiness, crazy, *crazy*!'

Some passers-by looked at her, but instead of scuttling past in alarm they grinned, falling in with her mood. This was Venice, where crazy people were the norm.

Just the same, Vincenzo took the precaution of kissing her firmly before she could say any more.

'Will you shut up?' he begged between kisses.

'Maybe. Persuade me.'

He kissed her again and again, feeling her young and glorious in his arms, wishing it could always be like this. He took her face between his hands, looking deep into her eyes. But although he saw his own reflection there he knew that was only on the surface. Behind that surface was something else that excluded him.

'Julia,' he said, trying to call her back to him. '*Sophie.*'

'Whatever. What does anything matter? I thought I'd never have even this much again, and I'm going to enjoy today. I'll worry about the rest later.'

Now he could see her as she'd been years ago, young and full of hope, before grief and despair had marked her. He grinned and told her something that would please her.

'You heard what Rosa said about your being *her* guest? Because she was the one who invited you. She's determined to do all the entertaining herself. She even wanted to cook the meal, but I drew the line at that. Gemma cooked it, but she'll be leaving as soon as we get there, to spend the day with her family.'

'You should have let her cook it,' Julia declared. 'It would have tasted glorious.'

'I've tasted Rosa's attempts at cooking,' he said darkly. 'Believe me, it would probably have poisoned you.'

'I wouldn't care. Isn't she a wonderful little person, Vincenzo? Did you notice what she did that day in the *palazzo*, when I had that fall?'

'You scared the life out of me.'

'But not out of her. She wasn't scared, although it must have sounded like a terrible crash down where you were, and I heard you tell her to come back, but she didn't take any notice—'

'The little monkey never takes any notice,' he said, unable to keep the fond pride out of his voice.

'She just dashed up bravely. It could have been anything making that racket, but all she cared about was finding out. She's one of those people who runs forward to life with her arms out. I'm so proud of her already, aren't you?'

'Yes, I am—'

'*She's wonderful,*' Julia carolled up to the sky.

He gave up trying to remonstrate, knowing that she was beyond reason. Nor did he really want to bring her down to earth. Something caught in his throat at the sight of her joy, and he wished it could last for ever.

'We should hurry,' he said. 'Gemma can't leave until we get there.'

'Then let's go,' she said, seizing his hand and pulling him off the bridge, determined to be delayed no longer. Soon they reached the Fondamenta Soranzo, where her eyes sought the windows of the house.

'Look, there's Rosa, watching for us,' she cried, and waved eagerly.

The little girl waved back, beaming. Vincenzo opened the front door into a large hallway, with a flight of steps leading up.

'We live up there,' he said.

'Uncle Vincenzo!' called a child's voice from upstairs, and the next minute Rosa came flying down to envelop him in a fierce embrace.

Then she turned her attention to Julia, too. But immediately she stood back and became the perfect hostess, polite and formal.

'*Buongiorno, Signora Baxter.* I am very pleased to welcome you to this house and I hope you will have a very happy day with us.'

'Thank you, I know that I will,' Julia said, charmed. 'But please call me Julia.'

'Signora Julia.'

'No, just Julia.'

Rosa cast a quick glance at Vincenzo, who shrugged and indicated Julia, saying, 'It's for our guest to decide.'

'*My* guest,' Rosa insisted. 'Because I invited you.'

'Yes, you did, and it was very kind of you,' Julia said, smiling.

The sun had come out. Her daughter was a charming child with generous, confiding ways, and she had reached out to her.

'Come with me.' Rosa seized her hand and drew her up the stairs, Vincenzo following.

The apartment was spacious and attractive. The main room contained furniture that looked antique and had probably come from the *palazzo*.

Rosa took her coat and ushered her to the sofa, then bustled busily away. Julia heard her speaking to someone in the next room, then Gemma emerged, wearing an outdoor coat, and bid everyone goodbye.

In the centre of the room was a low table on which stood several plates, bearing cakes and biscuits, some elegant glasses, and a bottle of *Prosecco*. Rosa reappeared and began to pour

some of the sparkling white wine for Julia and
Vincenzo and orange juice for herself.

'Please have a cake,' she said to Julia. 'Lunch
will be in an hour.'

'Perhaps I'd better look after the final stages,'
Vincenzo said. 'Why don't you show Julia your
presents?'

Rosa promptly became a child again, bouncing
to her feet and drawing Julia into the next room
where there was a decorated tree, and signs of
gifts opened with eager fingers. Rosa showed
them off proudly.

'I should really have waited for you to come
before I opened my presents.'

'Never mind,' Julia told her. 'When I was your
age I always got down to business very early,
usually about six o'clock on Christmas morning.
In England children hang up their stockings at
Christmas, not Epiphany.'

Rosa was wide-eyed. 'You don't have
Befana?'

'I'm afraid I don't know what that is.'

'Befana is a kindly witch. They say the three
kings invited her to visit the baby Jesus with
them, but she was busy and didn't go. Later she
changed her mind, but by then she'd missed the
star and lost her way. So now she flies around
on her broomstick and leaves presents in every

house where there are children, because she
doesn't know which house is the right one.'

'That sounds lovely. I'm glad you told me
about her. Now I know who it must have been.'

'Must have been?' Rosa queried.

'This old woman who whirled around my head
on her broomstick, and dropped something into
my bag. She said she hadn't delivered everything
to this house, and didn't have time to come back,
so would I bring a few things for her?'

As she said this Julia produced her gifts. She
had spent much time choosing them in an art
bookshop, asking for 'Something for a *very* in-
telligent eight-year-old.' The sight of Rosa's face
as she unwrapped everything told her that she'd
chosen well.

'You remembered,' Rosa breathed.

'Yes, I remembered what we said the other
day,' Julia agreed, 'but I also remembered myself
when I was your age. These are the kind of things
I loved to read.'

She fell silent, watching as Rosa examined one
book that she'd chosen with particular care. It
was almost entirely pictures, each one with a
large caption that was repeated twice, once in
Italian, once in English.

Rosa ran her fingers down one of the shiny
pages, letting them rest on the English. She was

frowning a little, but then she nodded and looked up, smiling.

Julia reached into her bag. 'And I brought this for Carlo. I didn't wrap it because I thought perhaps you should see it first and make sure it's all right.'

It was a magnetic fishing puzzle. There was a brightly coloured picture, showing jungle creatures against lush foliage. Each animal could be separated from the background by dint of dangling a magnet until it made contact.

Rosa let out a whoop. 'He'll love this.'

'I hope so. The shop said it was suitable for a two-year-old. It's supposed to develop his skills at—well, moving and co-ordination and that sort of thing. Oh, never mind that. It looks fun.'

'Oh, yes, it does. Carlo will love it.'

'I remembered how sad he seemed the other day, and I thought he needed cheering up.'

'You saw him at San Michele, didn't you? Uncle Vincenzo was right, I shouldn't have taken him. He thought he was going to see *Mamma* and *Papà* and when they weren't there he cried. But you see—' She hesitated.

'Please trust me,' Julia said. 'You can tell me anything. I won't repeat it.'

Rosa nodded. 'My mother died when I was the same age as Carlo, and I can't really remember her. And I hate that. It's like having a gap when there ought to be somebody. I didn't want that to happen to Carlo, but I got it wrong.

'He's too young to understand about people dying, you see. He only knows that there's something missing. So Uncle Vincenzo and I show him lots of extra love. Gemma does too, of course, but we're his family. And that's different.'

'Yes,' Julia said slowly. 'Family is different.'

'Do you have any family?'

'I—no.'

'None at all?'

'My parents are dead.'

'And you never got married?'

'Well, yes, I did, but he's dead too.'

'No little boys or girls?' When Julia didn't answer Rosa was immediately contrite. 'I'm sorry, I didn't mean to be rude. Please forgive me.'

'You weren't rude,' Julia said huskily. 'I did have a little girl but I—lost her several years ago. She would have been about your age now.'

Rosa didn't answer in words, but she got up from the floor where she was sitting and put her arms about Julia's neck. Julia hugged her back, overwhelmed by the feel of her child's warmth and her cheek pressed against her own.

'I'm sorry,' Rosa whispered.

She drew back and smiled directly into Julia's face.

'It would be nice to think she would have been like you,' Julia said.

A glint of mischief came into the child's face. 'You wouldn't like it really. Uncle Vincenzo says I'm a fiend.'

'Oh, does he? And are you?'

'Oh, yes. I'm the worst fiend who ever, ever lived.'

'Hmm. That sounds final enough. I guess you must be.'

As she spoke her eye was caught by a large photograph on the sideboard. It was a wedding picture, the bride in glorious white satin and lace. Vincenzo, looking younger, stood beside his sister.

Just behind it was another picture, showing the bride and groom with a little girl in front of them, and in another the bride stood alone, holding the child in her arms. They were regarding each other fondly.

Julia drew a sharp breath. For all her euphoric mood there would still be such moments to be faced. Rosa had been three when these pictures had been taken, and recognisable as the baby Julia had lost. Now she was nestling in the arms of another 'mother'. Unconsciously Julia tightened her own arms around her child, as though by doing so she could reclaim her.

'That was you,' she said softly.

'Oh, yes, when *Mamma* and *Papà* got married.'

Julia forced herself to let go. 'Do you have any more?'

'There's an album here,' Rosa said, diving down the side of the bookcase.

Vincenzo appeared in the doorway, saying, 'I'm just going to check on Carlo, see if he's awake yet.'

'I'd better come too,' Rosa said at once.

'I can be trusted to look after him,' he complained.

'Yes, but—he likes to see me when he wakes up,' Rosa said seriously, and hurried out of the room.

Vincenzo sighed. 'She's just like her mo— Like Bianca. She thinks nobody else can be trusted to do anything. We won't leave you alone for long.'

When they had gone Julia began to go through the album Rosa had given her. She knew the contents would hurt, but she had to learn all she could.

It was full of pictures of Bianca and Rosa: more wedding shots, then every milestone in the child's life, birthdays, Christmas, Epiphany.

There was the child in her father's arms, snuggling against him with an air of content. On this evidence he looked like a good father.

And he really did love her, she thought. That's why he took her with him instead of leaving her with my mother. What am I going to tell her when the time comes?

'Come along,' said Rosa's voice from the doorway.

She was holding Carlo by the hand, leading him forward until they were both standing before Julia. He was the image of his father.

'Say *"Buongiorno"*,' Rosa told him in a stage whisper.

But the little boy hid his face against her and shook his head vigorously.

'He's shy,' Rosa said. 'Look, little one, here's a present for you.'

But he only shook his head the more and began to grizzle, clinging onto his sister.

'I'm sorry,' Rosa said, lifting him in her arms. 'I'd better take him back. He'll be better later.'

She hurried out with the weeping child. Vincenzo, who had been watching, said in a low voice, 'While we have a moment, there's something I need to know, although I have a horrid feeling I know the answer. If your husband simply vanished I don't suppose there was ever a divorce?'

'Not that I heard of.'

'So he was still married to you when he married Bianca. *Bastardo!* And Carlo is illegitimate.

You've seen how it is with him and Rosa. He's one of the things that's holding her together.'

Something else linking her to her new life. Something else taking her away from her mother.

'Julia—'

'It's all right,' she said, shaking her head. 'I've got my breath now.'

She rose and went in search of Rosa. Hearing a murmur from behind a door across the hall, she followed the sound and found herself in a room with a bed and a cot. The two children were sitting on the floor.

'May I come in?' she asked tentatively.

Instead of hiding, the little boy giggled at her. Encouraged, Julia sat down on the edge of the bed.

'He doesn't mind me?' she asked.

'No, he's all right here,' Rosa explained, 'because this is our room. Befana brought him lots of presents this morning. Look.' She swept out a hand towards a merry pile. 'But this one is still his favourite, even though it's years old.'

She pointed to a blue furry rabbit that the boy was clutching, so old and shabby that much of its fur was gone. As Julia looked a strange feeling began to come over her, part ache, part joy. She had seen that rabbit before, long ago, in another life, when it was bright and new.

'Yes, it looks very old,' she said slowly. 'Who gave it to him?'

'I did,' Rosa said proudly. 'His name is Danny. He was my best friend when I was young.' She spoke as if she were a hundred. '*Mamma* said that when we met I was clutching him and I wouldn't let him go. *Papà* was ever so cross.'

'Wh—why?' Julia asked in a shaking voice.

'He didn't like Danny. He kept trying to throw him away.'

Of course he did. Because he knew I'd given you that toy just before we were parted, and he wanted to wipe me out of your mind.

'When you say he *kept* trying to throw him away—'

'He did it again and again. *Mamma* kept rescuing Danny and giving him back to me. It's funny that she understood when *Papà* didn't.'

'She sounds nice,' Julia said carefully.

'She was lovely. She used to get cross with *Papà* because he wouldn't write home to the family and try to get some pictures of my mother.'

'*She* did that?'

'Yes. She'd ask me if I remembered my real mother, but he stopped her. I heard them arguing. He said *she* was my mother, but she said a real mother was special and nobody could take her place.'

So Bianca had been generous and kind. Julia felt a moment's gratitude to her, mingled with pity that she too had come under Bruce's spell.

'I don't think *Papà* liked my mother very much,' Rosa went on. 'He didn't keep any pictures of her, and he wouldn't talk about her. If I asked him, he always started talking about something else.'

'You don't have any pictures of her at all?'

'No,' Rosa said wistfully. 'I don't even know what she looked like.'

'You can't remember anything?'

'Oh, yes, odd things. She used to hold me close against her, and she smelled lovely. And she laughed all the time. I remember her voice too, not the words because I didn't understand them, but the way she spoke. She loved me. I could hear it.

'But I can't see her face. That's why it would be nice to have some pictures of her and me together, and it would be real again. Because she was real, and yet she wasn't. Like a ghost really. If I saw her I wouldn't recognise her.'

'Yes,' Julia whispered. 'I know what you mean.'

Carlo made a small sound, demanding attention. Rosa took charge, arranging his arms more firmly around the elderly rabbit.

'Danny looks like a good friend,' Julia said.

'He's always been *my* good friend,' Rosa confirmed. 'But now he has to look after Carlo. I've explained that to Danny, so that he doesn't think I don't love him any more.'

'That was clever of you,' Julia said. 'Some things need to be explained in case people—or rabbits—misunderstand.'

Now she knew why Vincenzo had said the baby was keeping Rosa together. She had become his mother, responding to his needs and forgetting her own, feeding him, encouraging him.

She lost me at the same age, Julia thought. She knows exactly what to do for him.

And suddenly she saw herself, not as a mother alone, or a mother bereft, but as a mother in an eternal line of mothers, all loving a child more than themselves, whether or not it was their own child, and ready for all the sacrifices.

Whatever those sacrifices might mean.

CHAPTER TEN

WHEN it came to serving lunch Rosa was in her element, taking charge of the kitchen, blithely disregarding the fact that Vincenzo was a restaurateur, and reducing him to the status of a waiter. Julia watched in amusement as he meekly obeyed her orders.

As the guest of honour she was served first and received constant attention. The meal was excellent, and she solemnly thanked her hostess.

'I was there too,' Vincenzo said, aggrieved.

'Yes, you were very helpful,' Rosa told him kindly. Behind her hand she told Julia, 'Actually Uncle Vincenzo did quite a lot.'

'Thank you, ma'am,' he said, catching her eyes and grinning.

She grinned back. Carlo joined in the laughter, banging his spoon on the table, and Julia laughed from sheer happiness.

Afterwards Rosa put Carlo down for his nap while the others got on with the washing up.

'I must take my hat off for the way you're coping,' he said.

'I've had to take a few deep breaths, but I'll be blowed if I let anyone know that.'

'Except me. Or don't I count?'

'In a way you don't,' she mused, not unkindly, merely reflecting. 'You already know the worst of me.'

'I know the best, too.'

She turned to him eagerly. 'Vincenzo, listen, something wonderful happened. Do you remember that rabbit I told you about, the one I bought her a few days before we were separated?'

He nodded. 'It's Danny, isn't it? I thought so as soon as I knew who you were. I remember the first time I saw her. She was clutching it tight. Her father didn't like that.'

'Yes, she told me. She also said that your sister kept rescuing it. She seems to have defended my right to be part of my daughter's life, despite everything he did to blacken me.'

'He cast you in a bad light whenever he could. I suppose he had to, in order to explain why he had no contact with your family. But, as you say, Bianca defended you.'

He stopped quickly as Rosa came back to say that Carlo was sleeping. She spent the next hour going through the books Julia had bought her, showing them to Vincenzo and carefully explaining any points that he might find too difficult to understand. Julia watched him with fascination, liking the way he didn't talk down to the child.

After that Carlo woke up and they all played magnetic fishing. Carlo went at it with great energy and crowed with delight whether he succeeded or not. Vincenzo was unaccountably clumsy, while Julia and Rosa, both equally dextrous, went head to head in a hard-fought challenge.

'I think that's a draw,' Vincenzo said at last through his laughter as the two competitors solemnly shook hands.

The phone rang. Yawning, he answered it.

'Gemma! Are you having a good day? Oh, I see—yes, it's a tough situation—you'd better stay. Don't worry, I can manage. I'll just take my orders from Rosa. *Ciao.*'

He hung up. 'Gemma's elderly mother is feeling poorly and she wants to stay there tonight.'

'Lovely!' Rosa bounced with joy. 'Now Julia can stay with us. I'll make up the bed in Gemma's room.'

'Rosa,' Vincenzo said hastily, 'you're supposed to ask our guest what she wants to do, not just mow her down with a bulldozer.'

Rosa turned astonished eyes on Julia. 'But you do want to stay, don't you?' she asked in a puzzled voice. 'I mean, you don't really want to walk home alone in the cold and dark.'

'She wouldn't be alone,' Vincenzo said. 'I'd walk with her.'

'No way,' Julia said. 'You can't leave Rosa and Carlo here alone.'

'No, I can't, can I?' he realised.

'You see?' Rosa said triumphantly. 'And you don't want to do that walk alone, do you? Because it's terribly cold and terribly dark and you might fall into the water and you wouldn't like that.'

'I might even get lost and that would never do. It's very kind of you to ask me.'

'That's all right, then.' Rosa bustled away.

Julia choked with laughter, barely able to meet Vincenzo's eye.

'It looks like you're stuck with me,' she said.

'Oh, we've both been given our orders. She's a very assertive little character.'

'She always was,' Julia remembered. 'Even when she was Carlo's age she was strong-willed.'

'I wonder where she gets that from,' Vincenzo said wryly.

'No, you don't. You think you know.'

He grinned. 'It may have crossed my mind.'

'I'd better go and help Rosa.'

Together they put fresh linen on the bed in the snug little room. The look Rosa gave Julia was brim-full of delight.

We could be a family, she thought as they settled down for tea. I'm dreaming and if I pinch myself I'll wake up. But I don't want to.

Nothing happened to spoil it. A lull fell on the evening and they watched cartoons on television until it was bedtime.

Rosa departed with Carlo, then came back in her pyjamas.

'Carlo wants you to say goodnight to him,' she said, taking Julia's hand.

But they found him already asleep. Despite her efforts she felt her eyes blur as time shifted back to another dimly lit bedroom, another two-year-old, sleeping in perfect trust and confidence.

'Goodnight, my darling,' she whispered, leaning down to kiss his cheek. Suddenly she couldn't resist adding the words she had always said, all those years ago. 'Angels keep you.'

'What did you say?' Rosa asked quickly. 'It sounded like English.'

'Yes, it was English. I don't suppose you understand that, do you?'

'Not very well, but I've started English lessons at school. The teacher says I'm the best in the class.'

Of course you are, she thought, because English was your first language. At two and a half you knew three hundred words, and the last words you cried out to me were in English.

Rosa hopped into bed and held out her arms. Julia hugged her fiercely.

'Say it to me too,' Rosa begged as she lay down to be tucked in.

'Buonanotte, mia cara. Speroche gli angeli ti custodiscano.'

'No, like you did before, in English.'

'Goodnight, my darling. May the angels keep you.'

She kissed her child, and sat there holding her hand until Rosa went to sleep. Even then she sat there, brooding, full of joy and sadness.

At last she backed quietly out of the room, and closed the door.

As she returned to the main room she could hear the phone ringing again, and then Vincenzo speaking in an angry, impatient voice.

'Look, don't call me at home, and especially during Epiphany. Don't you people have any families? I've told you before, the answer's no, and it's going to stay no. Goodbye!'

He hung up firmly.

'Well, that's telling them,' Julia said, going in and settling herself comfortably on the sofa.

'Someone wanting to buy the *palazzo* for a hotel,' he growled. 'It's like trying to swat flies. Kill one and there's a dozen others.'

'Piero once told me that you were dead set against it.'

'That's putting it very mildly indeed.'

'It's a pity. It would make a wonderful hotel.'

'Are you out of your mind? Sell my home?'

'Of course not. *You* turn it into a hotel.'

'Using what for money?'

'You get investors. Why not? Look at the Danieli. It started its life as a *palazzo*, in the fourteenth century.'

'That's true.'

'Put yours to use. Bring it back to life. Isn't that better than letting it fall into ruin?'

'It's already doing that.'

'So put a stop to it now. There's still time to restore it before things get worse.'

'Ah, now I see. You're touting for business. Mind you—it's an idea.'

'I don't know why you've never thought of it before.'

'Because I'm the world's worst businessman. All I saw was fending off the sharks who thought I was desperate enough to sell at a knock-down price. I just wanted to make enough money from the restaurant to keep my head above water, but that's not enough, long term.'

'No, and the best way to beat the sharks is to steal their ideas. You'll have your home back, not as it was, but more than you have now.'

'People don't live like that any more,' he mused. 'Not in the modern world. They either go into business, or the place goes under.' He smiled. 'Maybe it floods when there's nobody there to protect it.'

She nodded, smiling back at him.

'I'm getting dangerously light-headed,' he mused. 'You're filling me with crazy ideas and they're beginning to sound sensible.'

'Of course. I'll be your first backer.'

'Have you got any money to invest?'

'Not money. These.' She held up her hands. 'I'll renovate the frescoes for nothing, and that will be my stake. You'll have to do the place up and get some suitable furniture. It might be best to open it a wing at a time, and move the restaurant in there almost at once.'

'And what about the pictures that were sold?' he demanded. 'Even with investment I couldn't buy them back. Or do we open with bare patches on the walls?'

'Of course not. You put up copies, which is what you'd have to do even if you had the originals. The insurance company would insist.'

'And you're going to knock me out some copies, are you?'

'Certainly. I do a mean Veronese, and my Rembrandt is even better, although I must admit my Michelangelo isn't so hot.'

'Your—?'

'But we can put those in a dark corner and

people won't notice. And don't forget you still own some pictures, stored upstairs. You can either hang them or use them to raise more cash.'

The words were pouring out now as the excitement of the idea gripped her. For a moment she was all artist and planner. Vincenzo regarded her with wry admiration.

'You've got everything worked out, haven't you?'

'Not at all. It came to me this minute, because of that phone call, but now it's all becoming clear.'

'Wait, I can't keep up with you.'

'You don't have to. Just say yes to anything I say, and leave the rest to me.' She added unnecessarily, 'I'm a very organised person.'

'So tell me what we're going to do.'

'We're probably not going to do anything,' she said regretfully, 'but if we were I'd say you ought to start making plans. It'll be Carnival soon—'

'In a few weeks. It'll take a year before we could open—'

'I know that, but you could have a big party there during *this* Carnival, and make a press announcement.'

'A party,' he mused. 'We used to have great Carnival parties there when I was a boy. Such costumes, such outrageous masks!' He gave a sudden grin, full of sensual reminiscence. 'If you only knew the things we did!'

'I think I can imagine. All behind the safety of the masks, of course.'

'Of course. That's what masks are for. When it all started, hundreds of years ago, masks were forbidden the rest of the year. But in the last few weeks before Carnival anyone could hide their face, become someone else, and do as they pleased. Then you had all of Lent to fast and be good, and generally make up for it. The tradition lasted.'

'And did you usually have much to make up for?' she teased.

'Well—' he said in a considering tone. 'A moderate amount.'

'Hmm!'

'Perhaps a bit more than that. When you're a young man—' He stopped with the air of someone choosing his words carefully.

'Go on,' she encouraged.

'Let's just say that self-restraint wasn't considered a virtue.'

'I suppose being a Montese helped.'

'Nonsense. With the mask on, nobody knew who I was.'

'Oh, yeah?' she said with hilarious cynicism.

'Well—maybe.' Again there was the grin, recalling days of delight, before the crushing burdens descended.

'I'll bet the girls were queuing up halfway across St Mark's Square.'

He looked offended. 'What do you mean, *halfway across*?'

He stared into his glass of red wine, seeing it all there, the whirling colours and wild faces, the dangerous freedom and the dangerous use he'd sometimes made of it.

He'd loved that sense of wonderful things about to happen, but it had gone from his life, fading away down the winding alleys, like his outrageous youth.

Only once, recently, had he recaptured that feeling: in the darkness of a hot, sweet night with a woman in his arms who had maddened and intrigued him from the first moment. She had made love to him with a fervour and abandon that had startled even while it had thrilled him.

Afterwards he had told himself that she was his, and it was the biggest mistake he had ever made. But for those few riotous hours he'd known that she belonged in Carnival, beautiful, secret, unpredictable.

'Your face gives you away,' Julia said, watching him.

That startled him. 'What am I thinking?'

'You're remembering your wild youth.'

'Well—yes, but there was a bit more to it than that.' He looked at her leaning back against the cushions, her eyes bright.

'I wish I'd known you then.'

'You might not have liked me. I was a bit of a hooligan, the way young men tend to be when they have too much money and are too much indulged. You know what happened to my family. The fact is that when the crash came I wasn't very well equipped to cope. Too spoiled. Too used to my own way.'

'What happened to your fiancée?' Julia asked, trying to sound less interested than she was.

'She married a man with pots of money. Our engagement party was a Carnival event, with everyone dressed up to look like somebody they weren't—which is ironic, if you think of it.'

'Do you still mind about her?'

He shrugged. 'It's so far away that I can't remember what it felt like to love her. I was another person. You know that feeling.'

She knew it well. Wisdom told her to drop the subject now, but for some reason she couldn't let it go.

'Piero told me how she came down the grand staircase, looking wonderful, and you stood there—'

'Probably with a fatuous expression on my face,' he said. 'I should have seen then that it was the staircase and the surroundings, plus the title, that she really wanted. She just had to marry me to get them. When they weren't on offer any more—' He shrugged.

He gave a brief laugh. 'I suppose in my heart I always knew the truth, but I wouldn't let myself believe it. When she dumped me so fast it was a surprise, and yet it wasn't, if you see what I mean.'

She nodded.

'I'd like you to see one of those Carnival parties,' he said.

'Well, maybe I will, if our idea comes off.'

'Oh, suddenly it's *our* idea?'

'But it's a *good* idea. Vincenzo, after what happened to you, you seem to have got your life back together, but actually you're treading water. It's time to go on to the next thing. Get your home back, and as soon as it's even partly habitable, you, Rosa and little Carlo can take up residence.'

'And what about you?'

'I'll be there, not in expensive rooms because we'll need them for paying customers. I'll just have a tiny place, and we'll meet for business discussions.'

'You mean you'll stay a ghost?' he challenged her. 'You came in the night, now you plan to haunt the fringes of my life?'

'Hardly the fringes, since we'll be living under the same roof. It's the best thing for Rosa. I'll be around when she needs me. She and I can see each other every day, but I won't be intrusive. You say I'll be a ghost, but maybe that's right for her. She's at ease with ghosts, haven't you noticed? She knows some of them are friendly.'

'And is that the best we can ever hope for?' he asked in a low voice.

'I don't know. You once said you'd like to turn time back until before we met. If you did that, I'd be wiped out too, wouldn't I?'

'I didn't mean that,' he growled. 'Do *you* understand your own feelings about everything? I wish I hadn't met you *like this*. It might have been so different, but who knows where the road leads from here?'

'Some day—'

'Some day—when one of us has turned the other's life upside down.'

'Yes, we can't get past that, can we?' She sighed. 'The rest is a happy dream, and dreams can only last so long.'

'But you know better than anyone how long dreams can last,' he said. 'As long as you have the courage to make them. Let's keep ours while we can, forget reality and think about us. I know, I know—' He silenced her with his fingertips across her lips. 'Who can tell if there'll ever be an ''us''? But can't we pretend, just for a little while?'

She tried to murmur, 'Yes,' but he silenced her again, this time with his lips. The touch of them answered all questions. For a few precious moments there was no other reality but the one to be found in his arms.

When he rose and held out his hand to her she went with him, smiling. As they passed through the dark hallways he held her close, burying his face against her neck, her hair, telling of his desire in whispered tones that made the hot eagerness spread through her like fire.

'Mummy!'

The sound ripped through the air, piercing them, driving them apart.

'Mummy, Mummy, no!'

It came from behind Rosa's door and it was followed by a long, despairing wail. Julia was through the door in a moment, putting on the light.

Rosa was sitting up, her eyes closed, her arms outstretched as if in a desperate plea, tears pouring down her face, lost in some terrifying nightmare. Julia sat on the bed and pulled her into her arms, hugging her tightly until the little girl awoke.

'There, darling, there, darling.' She was talking English although she didn't know it. She was aware of nothing except the need to soothe and comfort the child.

Rosa was awake now, sobbing violently, clinging onto her. Vincenzo went to Carlo, who'd been roused by the noise, and picked him up. His face was haggard.

At last Rosa's weeping subsided, and she lay with her head on Julia's shoulder, hiccupping slightly. Julia drew back and looked down into the tear-stained face, trying to believe what she had heard. The child's words had been so like that other time. Surely it wasn't possible—?

'What happened?' she asked, remembering to speak in Italian this time. 'Did you have a bad dream?'

'Yes—I think so—it was cold and dark and I was frightened.'

'Can you remember anything else?' she asked, trying not to let her voice shake.

Rosa frowned for a long time, but at last she shook her head.

'It's just dark, and I'm feeling scared and—so lonely and unhappy. It's like—the worst thing in the world is happening, but I don't know what it is.'

'Do you—remember what you called out?'

'I don't think I said anything. I just screamed and screamed.'

She searched Julia's face in sudden anxiety. 'Did I say anything?'

'No,' Vincenzo said in a tense voice. 'You didn't. You just made a lot of noise and scared us both to death, you little rascal.'

His voice had become teasing, telling her everything was all right, warning Julia to probe no further.

The warning was needless. Not for the world would she have pushed her child faster than she was ready to go. Tonight she'd been shown a ray of hope, and she would live on that.

'Do you want some hot milk?' he asked.

Rosa nodded contentedly, resting her head against Julia again.

'Can you get it, please, Uncle Vincenzo? I want Julia to stay.'

He laid Carlo back in his cot and went out to the kitchen.

'Do you get nightmares often?' Julia asked gently.

'Sometimes. Since my parents died. But they're all confused and muddled up and afterwards I can never tell what they were about…'

Her voice trailed off and after a moment Julia realised that she had gone to sleep again, contented now. She sat stroking the tousled hair, brooding over her child with fierce, protective joy.

After a while she laid her down, and Rosa half opened her eyes, whispering, 'Is Carlo holding Danny?'

'No, he's on the floor.'

'Can I have him?'

Julia picked up the shabby old rabbit and tucked Rosa's arms around him. The child gave a small grunt of pleasure, and was asleep instantly.

Julia slipped to her knees beside the bed and knelt there, holding one of Rosa's hands, watching her with loving eyes that missed nothing.

Vincenzo, coming in a moment later, found them like that, and went silently away without being observed.

CHAPTER ELEVEN

GEMMA returned next morning, and Vincenzo walked home with Julia. Rosa would have come with them, but Vincenzo gently discouraged her. This was their first chance for a private conversation since the events of the night before.

She had remained with Rosa a long time, emerging to find that Vincenzo had gone to his room. That had been a kind of relief. What would they have said to each other?

Now they walked in silence until Julia said, 'I feel as if I'd got to know Bianca, with Rosa's help. I'm glad. She's real now. And I have to deal with her.'

'Deal with her? How?'

'By accepting her. I suppose I had some idea of driving her out because she was usurping my place, but I can't do that. There has to be room for all of us. Rosa will only turn to me if she can bring Bianca with her.'

'Does that make you hate my sister?' Vincenzo asked in a low voice.

'No, I'm grateful to her. She did me no wrong.

She looked after my child, and made her happy. Rosa says that Bianca actually defended me when her father tried to wipe me out. She wouldn't let him do it.'

'She was the most generous woman alive,' Vincenzo said sadly.

'Yes, I know that now. She tried to do me justice, and I'll do her justice.'

'And in the end Rosa will turn to you,' Vincenzo said. 'And you'll take her away.'

'Are you saying you'd just stand back and let me?'

'I won't stop her being with her mother, if that's what you mean. It has to be her choice, but you're going to win. We both know that. The affinity is there. She feels it. Deep down inside that child knows who you are. She doesn't understand what she knows, but it's there, and sooner or later it will come to the surface.'

'It nearly happened last night,' Julia said. 'She was crying out in English.'

'How can you tell? No is the same in both languages.'

'But she cried ''Mummy'' not *''Mamma''*.'

'Yes,' he said heavily. 'She was reliving that moment, but when she woke up she didn't remember. Next time—'

'It's a lot for her to take in,' she said placatingly. 'It might be a while yet.'

She wondered at herself for denying the very thing she most longed for, but, intentionally or not, he'd reminded her that they were on opposite sides, and she wanted to comfort him for the loss he was facing.

As the restaurant came in sight, still closed up, they saw a young man standing outside, trying to peer through the windows.

'Hallo,' Vincenzo called.

The young man jumped. He was thin, fair-haired and awkward-looking.

'Hallo?' he said. 'I'm Terry Dale. I work for Simon and Son. I'm looking for Mrs Haydon.'

'That's me,' Julia said at once. To Vincenzo she added, 'They're my lawyers in England. I called them when I moved in here.'

'Let's go inside,' Vincenzo said, opening the door to the restaurant and ushering them both in.

'I came because I've got good news about your compensation,' Terry Dale said when he was inside.

'I thought it was far too soon for the compensation to be settled,' Julia said.

'Normally, yes, but now that the conviction's been quashed, they want this one off their plate fast. They've made a generous offer.' Conscious of Vincenzo's unmoving presence, he scribbled something on a scrap of paper and thrust it at her. 'How about that?'

Julia's eyes opened wide at the sum.

'Are you sure you didn't add on an extra nought by mistake?' she asked.

'Good, isn't it? But that's not all. Everyone knows you've been looking for your husband, and if you've got any leads—well—'

'It's been years,' Julia said carefully. 'He may not even be alive any more.'

'That doesn't matter. Even if he were dead the police could track back and find out who he's been associated with, interview anyone he's known, that kind of thing. It could be worth quite a bit more to you.'

'I didn't know it worked like that.'

'Officially it doesn't, but this kind of information can help—'

Terry Dale was scribbling more figures, showing them to her like a puppy appealing for a pat.

'I don't like this,' she said. 'It looks like some people still think I'm in cahoots with him.'

'Oh, no, but they know you're looking for your daughter, and when you find her it'll help us get onto his trail. Like I say, it could be worth a lot of money to you.'

'That's too bad, because there's no help I can give,' she said firmly. 'I can't point you in the direction of my husband, and you can take that as final. The lesser compensation will have to do.'

'Well, it's a pity because—'

Julia picked up the paper with the figures and tore it again and again.

'Goodbye, Mr Dale. Please thank your boss for his efforts and ask him to finalise matters.'

She saw him out and turned to find Vincenzo regarding her with a look that was half appreciation, half suspicion.

'I didn't see the figures,' he said now, 'but it must have been tempting.'

'Oh, yes? And have police swarming all over the place, upsetting Rosa? No way.'

Inwardly she was cursing Bruce. Was his malign influence going to spread over the whole of the rest of her life, blighting everything?

'I've made my decision,' she said, 'and now I know where I'm going from here.'

A light had come on inside her. Vincenzo was reminded of the night she'd returned from Murano, ablaze with confidence and decision.

'What are you going to do?'

'First, give up my job as soon as you can do without me.'

'Right now if you like. Celia's due back from honeymoon.'

'Can I stay in the apartment for a while?'

'Sure. She won't be moving back in. But what are you going to do?'

'Get in practice at my job. Hone my skills again before I start on your place.'

She thought for a moment before adding, 'There's one thing I'm grateful for, and that's that the Montressis were away. If they'd been there I might have stirred things up in a way I'd be regretting now.'

'He's lucky they never bumped into him,' Vincenzo observed. 'They might have recognised him.'

'Not really. I don't think he'd seen them for years. They were only very distant relatives, but I pinned everything on them because they were all I had. Well, I won't need to bother them now. I'm just going to get to work.'

In prison she'd done some drawing, and even taken an art class for other prisoners, but now she needed sustained work to bring herself back up to standard.

Taking sketch books and charcoal, she began to walk around Venice the next day, making rapid strokes, creating life on the paper.

At first she took in the showplaces, St Mark's, the Rialto Bridge, but then she turned away into the little canals, the *calles* with washing strung overhead, the empty boats bobbing in the water. The outlines were easy, but when she'd mastered them there was the more tantalising task of evoking the atmosphere of those mysterious little places.

Absorbed in this challenge, she took a while to realise that she wasn't alone. A small but determined ghost was flitting just behind her, always vanishing if she turned her head, but then emerging again in determined pursuit.

'All right,' she called at last. 'Come out where I can see you.'

A figure, swathed up to the eyebrows in scarves, and down to the ears in a thick woolly hat, emerged from around a corner and presented herself. Julia folded her arms, regarding her wryly. The figure immediately folded her own arms.

'Are you following me?' Julia asked.

A nod.

'Is anyone with you?'

A shake of the head.

'You've run away on your own?'

The eyes were as mischievous as the voice. 'I'm not on my own. I'm with you.'

Rosa pulled down the scarf, revealing a cheeky grin.

'Uncle Vincenzo let me come to the restaurant with him today. He said you were upstairs so I was going to go up, but then I saw you leaving by the side door. So I followed.'

'Does anyone know where you are?'

'Yes. You do.'

'I don't think that's quite enough,' Julia said, trying not to laugh, and pulling out her cell phone. In a moment she was through to the restaurant.

'Vincenzo? I've someone here who needs to talk to you.' She held out the phone to Rosa. 'Talk.'

Rosa giggled and began her persuasion.

'I ran after Julia, and she says I can spend the day with her—'

'I said no such thing.'

'But you were just going to, weren't you? I can, can't I, Uncle?'

'Give that to me before you land me in trouble,' Julia said, hastily seizing the phone. 'Vincenzo?'

'I'd only just discovered that you're both gone,' came his harassed voice.

'Vincenzo, if you're thinking what I think you are, I'll never forgive you.'

There was a silence.

'I wasn't thinking that.'

'Really?'

'I wasn't thinking that you'd run off with her,' he said tensely.

'You'd better be sure about that.'

'Is she all right?'

'Of course she is. She's having the time of her

life laughing at both of us. You'd better let her stay with me officially, otherwise she'll just creep after me at a distance. Don't worry, she's safe with me.'

She couldn't resist adding, 'Whether I'm safe with her is another matter.'

At this Rosa gave a giggle that clearly reached Vincenzo down the line.

'I'll say yes—having no choice. But you'd better put yourself in her hands. She knows Venice better than you do.'

Julia hung up and turned to her daughter. 'We're going to have a great time.'

Rosa gave a brilliant smile, took her hand, and they wandered on together.

'What did you think Uncle Vincenzo was thinking?' Rosa asked.

'It's a long, complicated story,' Julia said hastily. 'I'll tell you another time.'

After that the child said little, simply seeming to be content to be in Julia's company. And it was she who chose the next object to draw, pointing at an ornate bridge.

Julia promptly took out her sketch book, sat on a small flight of steps, and began to work rapidly. When she'd finished she showed the result to Rosa, who gave her an impish look, took the book, flipped over a page, and began to make a sketch of her own.

With disbelieving pleasure Julia looked at the result.

'You can draw,' she breathed.

Another page, another rapid sketch, drawn with an inexperienced but confident hand. Beneath a quiet surface Rosa was already a boldly confident artist. This was truly her daughter.

'*Papà* didn't like me drawing,' she confided. 'He said it was a waste of time. But *Mamma* said I should do it if I wanted to. It was our secret.'

'She was—' Julia checked herself and started again. '*Your mother* was right.'

The words were hard to say, but she felt she owed Bianca that much.

After that, wherever they stopped, they shared the drawing. Julia showed the little girl some new strokes, and had the delight of discovering a responsive pupil. It was a perfect day.

But then something happened that was like the sun going in.

As they moved closer to the glamorous heart of the city she noticed that almost every street had a shop that sold wild, colourful masks for the coming Carnival. Several times she would have stopped to look closely, but Rosa always pulled her on.

'Hey, stop a minute,' Julia begged at last.

Rosa stopped obediently and stood beside her, looking into the window. But she said nothing.

'They're for the Carnival, aren't they?' Julia said.

'That's right.' Just the two short words, almost snapped out.

'It's quite soon, isn't it?'

'Next month.'

'I've seen pictures, of course—people in those incredible costumes—it must be so exciting.'

'Yes, it is.'

Julia turned her head uneasily to look at the child, conscious of something strange in her replies. Her delight of only a few minutes ago had been abruptly quenched. Now she spoke like a robot, and her face was stiff.

Then Julia remembered Vincenzo saying, 'Last year she had a wonderful time at Carnival with James and Bianca, but this year she refuses to think of it.'

Silently calling herself a fool, she said, 'Why don't we go and have something to eat?'

Rosa nodded and followed her to a little café.

When they were seated with milk shakes she said, 'I'm sorry. I didn't think. It's your parents, isn't it?'

Rosa nodded. After a moment she said, 'I had a costume with lots and lots of colours last year, but this year I wanted a pink satin one. So

Mamma bought it for me last July. She said we'd keep it for the next Carnival. Only then—'

She stopped. She was controlling herself almost fiercely, but her lips trembled.

'And you don't want to go without her?' Julia asked gently.

'I won't ever go again,' Rosa said, calming herself at last. Now her voice was too controlled, too unyielding.

Julia took a risk.

'I think you're wrong,' she said. 'If *Mamma* bought that lovely pink dress for you, then she'd want you to wear it, for her sake.'

'But she won't be there.'

'No, but you can think about her, and you'll know that you're doing it for her.'

'But that won't bring her back, will it?'

'It'll bring her back in your heart, which is where it really matters.'

Rosa didn't answer this, but she shook her head stubbornly. The impish confidence was gone, replaced by a stark misery that was all the worse because she felt that nobody really understood.

'Let's go back,' Julia said gently. 'Vincenzo will be worrying about us.'

The sun had gone from the day and a dreary rain had begun to fall. They found Vincenzo at the door, looking for them.

'What is it?' he asked as soon as he saw Rosa's face.

In a quiet voice Julia explained. Instantly Vincenzo put his hands on the little girl's shoulders, searching her face tenderly.

'Hey there, *piccina*,' he said. 'Have you been crying?'

She shook her head. 'I just remembered what you said—about how everyone leaves you.'

'What?' he said, aghast. 'Rosa, I never said that.'

'Yes, you did. You said it to someone at *Mamma* and *Papà's* funeral. I overheard.'

'But I—' Vincenzo checked. What use was it to say that he hadn't known she was listening? '*Cara*, I was feeling terrible, and that's the sort of thing people say when—when—I didn't mean it.'

'Yes, you did,' she said quietly, looking him straight in the eye. 'And it's true. People leave you even when you plead and plead with them not to.'

Her voice faded. She was staring into the distance.

'Darling—' Julia put a hand on the child's shoulder, but Rosa didn't seem to notice. She was lost in an unhappy dream.

'Even if it's the most important thing in the whole world,' she said, 'and you're trying to make them understand and begging and begging them not to go—they still go—and they don't come back.'

Suddenly she looked straight at Julia, who drew in her breath. Did she imagine that those childish eyes contained a hint of accusation?

Then the moment was gone, and Rosa was looking bewildered.

'I think we should go straight up into the warm,' Julia said.

Upstairs they thawed out with the help of hot drinks sent up from the restaurant. Rosa began to seem more cheerful.

'Do you live here alone?'

'That's right.'

'Can I come and visit you?'

'Whenever you like.' She noticed Rosa's eyes closing. 'We walked a long way today. Why don't you take a nap?'

She tucked the child up in her own bed, where she fell asleep almost at once. Julia sat beside her for a while, free at last to watch over her with loving possessiveness.

You're mine, she thought. If only I could tell you.

Terry Dale called her a week later. Things were moving fast.

'The sooner you can get over here to sign the

papers, the sooner you'll have the money,'
he said.

'Fine, I'll be right there.'

'What about Rosa?' Vincenzo asked when she
told him. 'Have you thought that your going
away might worry her?'

'Yes, and I've got a plan. If I'm quick she
need not even know I've gone. She's back at
school now, and you said she has a good friend
who often invites her for sleepovers. If you can
get her invited for a couple of nights I can be
there and back before she knows it.'

A few days later he told her the plan was in
progress.

'She'll go home from school with Tanya tomorrow,' he said, 'and stay for two nights. Can
you be back by then?'

'I'll manage it.'

'I've promised her you'll have dinner with us
tonight.'

It was a good evening spent eating, laughing
and watching television. The shadow had gone
from Rosa's manner and she seemed free from
the ghost that had briefly haunted her.

Julia promised to come to dinner again when
Rosa returned from her visit, and the child went
to bed, content.

'And what about me?' Vincenzo asked as he

walked home with her. 'Do you promise me that you'll come back?'

'Don't be silly. You know I'm coming back.'

'Sure, you'll return for Rosa's sake. You heard what she said. Everyone leaves you in the end.'

'But that's what *you* believe,' she reminded him.

'Only because I've been proved right so often.'

'Trust me,' she said, echoing the words that he had said to her so many times.

'Shall I take you to the airport tomorrow?' Vincenzo asked.

'No, thank you. I have something else to do first.'

She refused to tell him any more. Next day she left, heading, not for the airport, but for San Michele. Before boarding the boat she bought flowers.

In the cemetery she went first to Piero's grave, and used half of the flowers to refill his urn.

Then she went to find Bianca. Pushing the steps into place, she climbed up, removed the wilting flowers from the urn, and replaced them with fresh ones. For a long time she looked at the sweet face of the woman her daughter called *Mamma*. Then she touched it gently.

'I just wanted to say thank you,' she said.

*   *   *

Julia's trip went well. She signed papers and received a cheque for the first part of her compensation, the rest to follow soon.

There were more questions about her husband, but she smiled and played dumb, and in the end her inquisitors gave up.

On the day of her return to Venice she was at the airport long before she needed to be, only to find it shrouded in fog. Passengers were allowed to board, pending an improvement in the weather, but it did not happen and they were requested to leave the aircraft.

Two hours later she called Vincenzo on her cell phone.

'I'm going to be late for dinner tonight,' she said. 'There's a thick fog and the planes are grounded.'

'There's no fog at this end,' he said, frowning.

'Well, it's a pea-souper over here.'

'How do I explain to Rosa? She doesn't know you're in England.'

'Make some excuse. Say I'm not well. Say anything—'

There was a whistling sound in her ear as the line went dead. The phone needed a top-up. While she was looking around for somewhere to do it a voice came over the tannoy.

'Will passengers for Venice please start boarding—?'

'Thank goodness,' she breathed. 'Oh, why did this have to happen?'

Vincenzo turned to see Rosa watching him, very pale.

'She's not coming, is she?'

'*Cara*—'

'I heard you say she was in England. She's gone right away and she's not coming home.'

'Yes, she is coming home, but her plane's been delayed by fog. She'll be here as soon as she can.'

'You didn't say she was going away to England.'

The sight of her rigid face shocked him. This wasn't simply childish disappointment. She was reliving an old nightmare.

He dropped down so that their eyes were on a level, trying desperately to find a way past her defences. It was like trying to communicate with someone behind bars.

He was assailed by a feeling of danger. If he couldn't reach her, and get her to reach out to him, she might be behind those bars for ever.

'Julia only went for a couple of days, to get things sorted out in England so that she can come here for good. We didn't tell you in case you were upset, and she's coming home quickly.'

Rosa shook her head. Her eyes were blank.

'No, she isn't,' she said.

He could have wept. If the child had been upset he'd have managed to cope, but her calm acceptance was ominous.

'You'd better talk to her yourself,' he said, hoping the noise he'd heard on Julia's phone didn't mean what he feared. But when he dialled he heard the same noise again and ground his teeth.

'She needs to top it up,' he said in despair.

'Perhaps she won't bother,' Rosa said.

'Of course she will. Why wouldn't she?'

She didn't reply, but her eyes revealed what she really believed: that Julia had blanked them out, and it was convenient for her phone not to work.

'She's probably boarding the plane right now,' he insisted. 'That's why she can't do anything about her phone. We'll hear from her when she lands.'

There was a touch of pity in the little girl's eyes. Why couldn't he face facts?

'Can we have dinner?' she asked. 'I'm hungry.'

'She'll be here,' he said, despairing.

'It's all right, Uncle. Honestly. You were right. People always leave you.'

'*Cara*, I wish you'd forget I ever said that.'

'But it's true.' Then, in a strange voice, she

said, 'I begged her not to go—but she did—and she never came back.'

It was as though a phantom had flitted past, chilling the air for a moment before it vanished.

'Who are you talking about?' he asked, barely able to speak.

'Let's have something to eat,' she repeated.

'Rosa, who were you—?'

But it was useless. The phantom had gone. He let the subject drop, fearful of doing damage if he persisted.

For the rest of that evening she behaved normally, even cheerfully. You had to know the truth, he thought, to recognise the storm she was suppressing. Nor could he help her, because she wouldn't let him.

He kept hoping that Julia would find a way to call them soon. But the evening passed with no word from her, and at last it was time to go to bed.

He was awoken in the morning by Gemma, shaking him urgently.

'I can't find Rosa,' she said.

He threw on his clothes and checked every room in the apartment, but it was a formality. In his heart he knew where she had gone.

'Has the phone rung?'

Gemma shook her head.

'All right, I'll be back soon.'

He called for a water taxi and reached the nearest landing stage just as it arrived.

'The airport, as fast as you can,' he said tersely.

He entered the terminal at a run and kept on running until he saw Rosa sitting, watching the arrival doors with terrible intensity.

She glanced at him as he sat beside her, and something in her face silenced all words of reproach.

'How long have you been here?' he asked quietly.

'A couple of hours.'

He looked up at the board. It showed two planes landed from England, but he didn't know if either of them was Julia's.

'She'll be here,' he said. 'She promised.'

There was no reply, but he felt a small hand creep into his and grip it so tightly that he winced with pain.

The doors slid open. Passengers were beginning to stream out. Rosa's gaze became fixed again, as if her whole life depended on this moment. Vincenzo too watched, trying to distinguish one figure from the many others.

But it was Rosa who saw her. Leaping up with a sudden shriek, she began to run.

'Mummy—Mummy—Mummy!'

Heads turned as the child darted through the

crowd to throw herself into a pair of open arms. With a heart overflowing with relief, Vincenzo followed her until he was a few feet away from Julia, and was in time to see Rosa draw back to look her radiantly in the face and say, *'You came back.'*

CHAPTER TWELVE

'YOU came back.'

'Yes, darling. I always meant to, it was just the fog.'

But Rosa shook her head, impatient that Julia hadn't understood.

'You didn't come back before,' she said.

Then the first inkling of the truth came to Julia and her startled eyes met Vincenzo's.

'Before?' she asked cautiously, hardly daring to hope.

'You went away before,' Rosa cried, 'and you never came back.'

Julia dropped to her knees, holding onto Rosa and searching her face.

'Do you remember that?' she whispered.

Rosa nodded. 'You gave me Danny, and then you went away. And I cried. I didn't want you to go, but you went.'

'Do you know—who I am?'

'I—think so,' Rosa said slowly. 'I think—you're Mummy.'

'Yes, darling. Yes, I am—I am, *I am*—'

She buried her face against Rosa and wept tears of joy, feeling them sweep away all the other tears she had cried through so many bitter, anguished nights.

'But I don't understand—' Rosa said.

'I know, *piccina*—this is your mummy,' Vincenzo said. 'There'll be time to understand later. Let's all go home.'

He took charge of Julia's trolley, and wheeled it out of the airport, glancing over his shoulder to see where they were following, walking slowly because they were hugging each other at the same time.

He helped the boatman with the suitcases, noticing that Julia had managed to acquire several new ones, and that they were heavy. By the time they caught up, everything was ready for departure.

He sat in the front, leaving them together in the back, just sitting, holding hands, not speaking through the roar of the engine, simply content in their discovery. As they sped across the water he wondered where the future led. He had only to glance at the faces of the mother and child in the back to know that each of them had all they wanted.

At last the boat came to a halt in the Fondamenta Soranzo.

'You need to be here tonight,' he said in answer to Julia's look of surprise.

While waiting for Julia's arrival he'd already called Gemma to say that Rosa was safe, so they arrived to find the apartment empty, Gemma having taken Carlo shopping.

Vincenzo assigned himself the role of cook and waiter, plying them with breakfast while they looked at each other in their new light.

'Why did you go away?' Rosa asked sadly. 'You left me, and you never wrote or sent cards, and *Papà* said you were dead—' Her voice shook.

Until this moment Julia had never quite decided how much she would tell Rosa when the time came. To speak of prison and her father's betrayal seemed terrible. But now she saw that the child was carrying a burden that crushed her, the belief that her mother had callously abandoned her.

'I had no choice, darling,' she said softly. 'They put me in prison for something I didn't do, and then your father took you away. I didn't know where you were, but I never stopped loving you, and as soon as I could I came looking for you.'

She knew she'd judged right when she saw the load lift from Rosa's face. Her mother had not, after all, walked away from her. Nothing really mattered beside that.

Rosa noticed Vincenzo carrying Julia's things upstairs.

'Are you coming to live with us now?' she asked, thrilled.

'I'll be here tonight, and we can talk all we want. After that—'

After that—what? She sought Vincenzo's face for some sign of what he was feeling, but his features revealed nothing.

'You can have my room,' he said.

'That's very kind of you, but you—'

'I'll be fine.' He almost snapped out the words. 'It's time I was getting to work. I've neglected it a bit recently.'

'I'm sorry about what I did,' Rosa told him. 'I mean, running off. But you see—'

'Yes, I do see,' he said, ruffling her hair. 'But we were very worried about you. I'm so glad you're safe. Now I must go.'

They didn't see him for the rest of the day. For Julia it was a happy time, spent with her daughter, exchanging memories, feeling the bonds assert themselves.

'I always knew there was something about you,' Rosa confided. 'I didn't know what, but I knew you weren't just anyone.'

Vincenzo telephoned to say that he'd contacted Rosa's school and arranged for her to have a few days off for them to be together. But he hung up before Julia could thank him.

Late that night she waited up for him to return. There were so many things that she wanted to say to him too, if only he would be here. She resisted the thought that there was something ominous in his choosing to be absent.

As the hours passed she went to bed and lay awake, listening, longing for him. Now her heart reached out to him as never before as she understood the full extent of his generosity. He'd known from the start that he would lose Rosa as he had lost almost everything else. But he had put no barriers between them. On the contrary he'd done all he could to help the two of them rediscover each other, whatever the cost to himself.

She wanted to see him, hold him, and pour out her feelings now that the road was clear for them at last.

Eventually she heard the front door, then his footsteps. Throwing on a dressing gown, she went out to see him, and found him making up the sofa.

'You can't sleep there,' she said aghast. 'It isn't long enough for you.'

'It'll do for tonight.'

'But tomorrow—' Surely there was some way

to say that his bed was big enough for two, if they squeezed in tightly. But why did it need saying?

'I've made arrangements for tomorrow. There's a tiny hotel just opposite. I've taken a room there.'

'A hotel?' she echoed, aghast.

'It's just on the other side of the canal. You can see it from here.'

'But when will I see you?'

'I'm not the one you need to see.'

'What about all the things we need to talk about?'

'Such as?'

There was no encouragement in his manner and so, instead of what she wanted to say, she blurted out, 'Money.'

His face seemed to close against her. 'Go ahead. Talk about money.'

'Now I've got my compensation I can invest some money in our hotel. And I've got the name of an Italian firm that goes in for this sort of thing. My lawyer in England has some international connections and he says these people are very good, completely trustworthy. Here.'

She handed him a scrap of paper, and he studied it before saying briefly, 'I've heard of them. They have a good reputation. Have you been in touch?'

'Certainly not. This is your show.'

'Really?'

'I only obtained their name,' she said indignantly. 'You said yourself that you're the world's worst businessman.'

'All right, all right.' He held up his hands as if fending off a swarm of bees.

It was going all wrong. Why didn't he take her into his arms and make everything perfect? Why couldn't he apparently see that now they were free to love each other? Unless he didn't want to see it.

'You'd better get back to bed,' he said. 'I'll sleep pretty well here. Goodnight.'

'Goodnight,' she said despondently, turning away to the door.

'Julia.'

'Yes?' She turned back, heart beating with hope.

'Thanks for all you've done—about the money and the hotel and everything. Goodnight.'

'Goodnight,' she said again, and closed the door behind her.

Vincenzo listened to her go into his room, cursing under his breath, wondering what was suddenly wrong with him.

Why should such an apparently simple thing have become so hard? She stirred his blood and his heart more than any woman had ever done, including his faithless fiancée. And what could be more natural than to ask her to be his wife?

But the words had frozen in him because he couldn't dismiss the picture of her face when she'd said it was better to use people than trust them. He closed his eyes, trying to blot out the memory, but it was replaced by another one: Julia saying, 'I'll do what I have to—whatever that might be.'

And if he could obliterate her voice and her expression, there was another memory that could never be dismissed because he could still feel it in his flesh: their first night together when she had loved him with wanton abandon, taking him on, challenging, demanding, giving, with a desire that was as fierce as it was dazzling.

Only afterwards, when he knew her story, had the niggling questions come.

Me? Or was I just the man in her bed when her need was great?

'Better to use people…' She had said it.

He wanted to shout a denial, to say she wasn't like that. But, as she'd so often told him, he knew nothing of her true self: as little, perhaps, as she did herself.

Today she had reclaimed her daughter's heart, but there were still matters to be sorted out. Not just living arrangements, but the child's attachment to himself and her baby brother.

For Julia, their marriage would make solid, practical sense. If he proposed now, she would say yes but he wouldn't know why. They would set up home with the children, the perfect picture of a happy family.

And he would never be quite certain of her or her love, as long as he lived.

The next day Vincenzo discovered the reason for Julia's numerous heavy suitcases. Somehow, in a mere two days, and in between dealing with lawyers, she'd found the time to buy up half the clothes shops in London.

Her hair had been cut short, brushed back and styled elegantly against her head. She no longer felt any need to hide her face from the world, or anybody in it.

She had drawn a line between her past and her future, and her transformation had rocked him onto the back foot. If he hadn't known what to say to her before, he was totally at sea now.

He concentrated on practical business, contacting the firm she'd mentioned. A posse of dark-suited men descended from their offices in Milan, looked the *palazzo* over and expressed enthusiasm. There were discussions with Julia. How much could she invest? What value did she put on her restoration work? Finally they declared that they already had investors on their books eager for just such an opportunity.

They agreed to the idea of a Carnival party to make the press announcement, after which serious work would begin, to have everything ready for the following year.

When they'd gone Vincenzo walked around the empty building, trying to come to terms with the way his life had been turned upside down yet again, but this time in a manner that offered him new hope.

'To come back,' he murmured. 'To see it come alive again.'

'It'll be wonderful,' Julia said. She had been keeping a little behind him, in the shadows.

He looked at her, thinking that here was something else to unsettle him. He was just about growing used to her changed appearance.

She might have stepped out of the pages of *Vogue*. She was elegant, groomed to perfection, wearing a white silk shirt and the very latest fashionable trouser suit in dark blue. The perfume that reached him was as clear and subtle as a spring flower.

She belonged in a palace, he realised. The lost soul he'd first met had been an aberration. Now she was mistress of the situation, mistress of her own life at last. She exuded confidence from every pore, every sleekly groomed line. He could almost feel her being carried away from him by an irresistible current.

'I'm going to start work down here,' she said, indicating the great hall.

'I thought this was where we were having the press party.'

'It is. This will give us a point of interest to show people.'

'I see. Good idea.'

Would they ever, he wondered, have anything else to talk about but business?

Julia watched him standing at the foot of the great staircase, looking up.

What did he see? Perhaps it was his fiancée, the woman he had loved more than all the world, slowly descending, receiving the tribute of his radiant expression? Was this why he had suddenly become unable to draw closer to her?

'I'd better be going,' she said. 'Rosa knows something's up, and she wants to be told *everything*.'

He grinned. 'I can just hear her saying it.'

'Will you be in for supper tonight?'

'I'm afraid not. The tourists are already beginning to arrive for Carnival, and the restaurant is busy. We'll have to move fast if this place is going to be ready for the big evening.'

An army of cleaners moved in the following

day. Julia took Rosa along to see them at work, and to keep a jealous eye on the frescoes.

'I'm going to set up work just here, behind the staircase,' she told her. 'I might even give a demonstration at the party.'

'Aren't you going to wear a beautiful dress?'

'If I'm going to paint, I'm probably better in jeans. But you can wear a beautiful dress. What about the one you told me about, the one your mother bought for you?'

'But aren't—you my mother?'

'Yes, darling, but she was too.'

Suddenly Julia remembered that Rosa had never wept for Bianca's death, and, perhaps, now she might feel that she never could. She hurried to say, 'You don't have to choose between us. It's all right to love us both.'

Rosa's eyes were wide with relief. 'Is it *really*?'

'Of course. You've got two mothers. She's *Mamma* and I'm Mummy. It's all very simple.'

She hugged the little girl and Rosa seemed happier, but Julia still had the feeling that something was being held back. Patience, she told herself.

The next moment Rosa startled her.

'When are you and Uncle Vincenzo going to get married?'

'I—what makes you think that we'll get married?'

'But you must. It would make everything perfect. He can't keep living in a hotel.'

How like a child, Julia thought, to see the matter in a sensible light. It was true that there were many realistic reasons for their marriage. And just as many reasons why it could never happen.

'It takes a little more than that,' she said carefully. 'People have to love each other as well.'

'But of course he loves you. Do you want me to ask him?'

'No!' Julia exploded before she could stop herself.

'All right,' Rosa said plaintively. 'I only thought—'

'Darling, do me a favour,' Julia begged. 'Stop thinking. Put it right out of your head.'

She thought she'd gained her point, but a moment later Rosa said, 'Is it Gina?'

'Who?'

'Gina, that he was going to marry. Everyone says he was dotty about her, but that was ages ago.'

'And everyone still talks about how she swept down that staircase and he looked at her adoringly,' Julia couldn't help saying. 'Even now, so long after.'

Rosa looked at her wisely.

'Perhaps you should make them talk about you,' she said.

For years afterwards, Julia wondered if she'd known, even then, what her daughter was planning. She denied it to herself, but sometimes even her own secrets were hidden from her.

Carnival started on February tenth, the first day of a two-and-a-half-week-long feast of gaiety and indulgence.

'Aaaa-aaah!' Julia greeted the day with a luxurious sigh up to the deep blue sky. 'This is gorgeous. I can't believe it's still so early in the year. Look at this weather.'

'The sun always comes out for Carnival,' Vincenzo told her, 'even if it goes in again afterwards.'

The festivities were everywhere. Outrageous costumes, topped by mysterious masks, could be seen whirling through the *piazzas* and peering around corners.

Harlequin and Columbine, Pantalone, Pulcinello, Pierrot, Pierrette: they all danced through the music-haunted streets, celebrating the wild liberty that came with anonymity.

Rosa seemed to have forgotten her resolve to play no part in the jollity, except that Julia sensed it was not so much forgotten as put aside for the moment. She now seemed determined to make

Julia take her responsibilities as hostess seriously.

The party was to be in eighteenth century dress, and brilliant costumes began to appear in Julia's room, to be pored over, then returned to the hire shop. Rosa was ruthless about discarding any that did not appeal to her.

'But I rather like that gold one,' Julia said.

'The white one is better,' Rosa said firmly.

It was truly a glorious dress, satin and brocade, with a tiny waist. In a few minutes Julia was surveying herself in the mirror, adding yet one more persona to the long list she'd acquired recently.

She wasn't quite certain who this mysterious creature might be, with her sequinned gown and mask. But she felt it might be fun to be her for a while.

When the cleaners had finished work at the *palazzo* they were able to move into a few rooms temporarily, and oversee the arrangements. Over five hundred people would be there. Some were press, others had bought costly tickets. Venice was alive with rumours and nobody wanted to miss this event.

Even baby Carlo was brought to sleep there for a couple of nights, for no Venetian was ever too young for Carnival.

Acting on Rosa's instructions, Julia had not

mentioned her costume to Vincenzo, who, as far as she knew, had made no plans to dress up.

'Shame on you,' she teased. 'You're the host of this party and you should be wearing satin knee breeches and lace.'

But she'd misjudged him. He was a Venetian, and satin and lace held no terrors for him. On the night he appeared before her in all his glory. Eighteenth-century garb suited him. The brocade of the black and gold coat and the lace at the neck had the strange effect of underlining his masculinity.

'Dressed like this,' he said, 'a rake could go out on the town and—' He broke off with a wistful, reminiscent sigh.

'Fine,' she told him. 'We'll go out on the town—but together.'

He might have answered, but Gemma looked in to say, 'Rosa has a surprise for you.' She vanished, leaving the door open.

After a moment Rosa appeared. She was wearing a pink satin carnival dress. It was grand and glorious, sweeping the floor, with sleeves like wings. On her head she wore a bonnet of pink satin and lace, and in her hand she held a pink, full-face mask on a stick.

Slowly she advanced towards them, the mask held up over her face, and sank down in an elegant curtsey. They all smiled and applauded, and she rose.

But she did not remove the mask, just stood there, her shoulders seeming to sag. It was Julia who reached out to draw the mask away, revealing that behind it the child was in tears.

She didn't try to hide them now, just stood there with them sliding down her cheeks.

'This is the dress you told me about?' she said. Rosa nodded.

'*Mamma* bought it for me, for Carnival,' she said huskily. 'But I wouldn't wear it because I was angry with her for going away. Now—' a sob shook her '—now I want to tell her that I'm sorry, *and it's too late.*'

At last she could hold back no longer, and when Julia opened her arms she went into them, weeping.

Julia held her close, torn between pain for her child and happiness that Rosa had opened her heart to her.

'It's not too late,' she said. 'There's still a couple of days of Carnival to go. Tomorrow we'll go to San Michele together.'

'Can we really?' Rosa was transformed.

'Tonight everyone can see how lovely you look. And tomorrow you can tell her all about it.'

'Can I wear my dress to San Michele, for *Mamma*?'

'Of course you can.' She dried the child's tears.

When Rosa had gone Julia glanced at Vincenzo who had remained silent and very still, watching them. She wished she could read the expression in his eyes, but his jewelled mask concealed them.

'Aren't you going to get dressed?' he asked. 'I don't even know what you're wearing yet.'

'Excellent. Then you won't know which one is me. I think I'll enjoy that.'

'You'll drive me too far.'

'I probably will in the end, but we aren't nearly there yet.' Her eyes dared him. 'It's going to be a fascinating journey.'

'Julia—'

'I think people are arriving. You'd better go and greet them.'

'What about you? This is as much your night as mine.'

'I'll be there.'

From the first moment the evening was a triumph. The knowledge that the Palazzo Montese was to live again had aroused interest all over Venice, throughout the hotel industry, and among those who passed their lives in one hotel after another.

Julia left the spotlight to Vincenzo, while she worked in the corner she had set apart for restoration, answering a stream of fascinated questions. She was dressed quietly and simply in velvet trousers and silk shirt.

Rosa was having the time of her life, but at last she came and fetched Julia determinedly, taking her hand and drawing her upstairs. Gemma was there, and the two of them helped her to dress.

'Time to go,' she said at last. 'This way.'

Brooking no argument, Rosa took her hand and led her down as far as the top of the main staircase.

'Darling, I don't think—'

'Go and stand in front of that picture, the one of Annina.'

Too dazed to do anything but obey, Julia went down to stand before the picture. Something drew her eyes up to the wild face of the woman who had once seemed so like herself in her misfortunes.

Not any more. It was time to do what Annina had never been able to do, to seize her fate and wrest it to her own will. An excitement was growing in her. She knew now why Rosa had done this.

Behind her she could hear the buzz of the crowd fall silent. Slowly she turned.

Vincenzo was standing at the foot of the steps, looking up at her. As she had always known he would be. As Rosa had always known he would be.

Slowly Julia began to descend, a vision in shimmering white, her face covered by a white lace mask. After a few steps she removed it, looking down on the man who never took his eyes from her.

His hand moved up to his own mask, seized it, tossed it away. Now she had a clear view of his face, and it was brilliant with love and happiness. It was the look she had longed to see.

He didn't take his eyes from her as she approached closer and closer. The masks were gone. Now there was only truth.

'Who—are you?' he asked uncertainly.

She was standing before him. Slowly she kissed him, then drew back at once.

'That's who I am,' she said. 'The woman who loves you.'

Once more she laid her lips on his, and kept them there while his hands settled on her waist, lifting her into the air, while not letting his mouth part from hers.

The crowd broke into applause, although none of them was really sure why. Somebody must have started it, but it could have been anyone. It might even have been a little girl, watching gleefully from above, determined to make this turn out right. A good organiser. Her mother's daughter.

There were still formalities to be gone through, guests to be greeted, smiles to give. But everything that happened now seemed part of a dream, and the only reality came at the end of the evening when Rosa led them to the side entrance, where a gondolier was waiting.

As they pulled away Vincenzo blew her a grateful kiss, before leaning back against the cushions, drawing Julia into his arms.

'I think it's all been taken out of our hands,' he said.

'Perhaps it's the only way it could happen,' she agreed. 'Why did everything suddenly become so hard?'

'A thousand times I came to the edge of telling you how much I love you, and want to marry you. But I became afraid in case you thought I was seizing you for fear of what I'd lose. I wanted you to trust me and I didn't think you ever would.'

'If you'd told me that you loved me, I'd have trusted and believed you,' she said fervently. 'And I could have said that I love you.'

'I wasn't sure that you did. You tried so often to warn me that you couldn't love me.'

'That was foolish of me. I love you with all my heart.'

'If you say that, I have nothing else to want. I know now that I was wrong. Not everyone leaves. I'm not going to *let* you leave me.'

He kissed her fiercely, letting his passion make the argument for him, feeling her response give him the answer that said more than speech.

'Are you sure it isn't a risk?' she murmured.

'Maybe. My risk.'

'*Our* risk.'

He nodded. 'Our risk. But love is always a risk, and I'll take it if you will.'

The gondola was leaving the centre of the city behind, leaving the music, the dancing and the wild figures, drifting into the semi darkness, where the little canals were illuminated only by tiny lamps and silence waited around every corner.

He took her hand in his, holding it tightly.

'If there is any safety in the world,' he said, looking at their clasped hands, 'it's here. But perhaps we shouldn't ask for safety, just a light showing the way to the next canal, and perhaps the one after that.'

She didn't answer in words, but when he released her hand and laid his lips on hers she gave herself up to him completely. All turmoil stilled. All questions answered.

Behind them the gondolier rowed silently, taking them towards the light that showed the way to the next canal, and the one after that, and then onward to wherever the future led.

HARLEQUIN®
INTRIGUE®

WE'LL LEAVE YOU BREATHLESS!

If you've been looking for thrilling tales of
contemporary passion and sensuous love stories
with taut, edge-of-the-seat suspense—then
you'll love Harlequin Intrigue!

Every month, you'll meet six new heroes
who are guaranteed to make your spine tingle
and your pulse pound. With them you'll enter
into the exciting world of Harlequin Intrigue—
where your life is on the line
and so is your heart!

THAT'S INTRIGUE—
ROMANTIC SUSPENSE
AT ITS BEST!

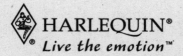

HARLEQUIN®
Live the emotion™

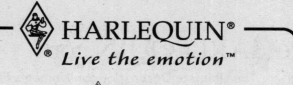

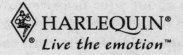

Praise for
A Guide to the Other Side

"*A Guide to the Other Side* is a
fun ride and a great concept. Chills galore."
—**James Patterson**, #1 *New York Times* bestselling
author of *Middle School: The Worst Years of My Life*

"Baylor's adventures will intrigue, excite,
and captivate young readers. . . . This series opener
is funny, mystical, and endearing."
—**Kirkus Reviews**

"A unique ghost story loaded with just the right blend
of laugh-out-loud humor and suspense. Anticipate high
demand for this series starter."
—**School Library Journal**

**Check out the next installment
of Baylor's adventures:**

Baylor's Guide to Dreadful Dreams

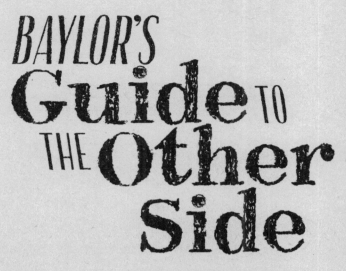

BAYLOR'S Guide TO THE Other Side

Previously titled
A Guide to the Other Side

ROBERT IMFELD

Aladdin

New York   London   Toronto   Sydney   New Delhi

ALADDIN
An imprint of Simon & Schuster Children's Publishing Division
1230 Avenue of the Americas, New York, New York 10020
First Aladdin hardcover edition October 2016
Text copyright © 2016 by Robert Imfeld
Previously titled *A Guide to the Other Side*
Cover illustration copyright © 2017 by Matt Saunders
Also available in an Aladdin hardcover edition.
All rights reserved, including the right of reproduction
in whole or in part in any form.
ALADDIN and related logo are registered trademarks of Simon & Schuster, Inc.
For information about special discounts for bulk purchases, please contact
Simon & Schuster Special Sales at 1-866-506-1949 or business@simonandschuster.com.
The Simon & Schuster Speakers Bureau can bring authors to your live event.
For more information or to book an event, contact the Simon & Schuster Speakers Bureau
at 1-866-248-3049 or visit our website at www.simonspeakers.com.
Cover designed by Karin Paprocki
Interior designed by Mike Rosamilia
The text of this book was set in Centaur MT Std.
Manufactured in the United States of America 0818 OFF
2 4 6 8 10 9 7 5 3
The Library of Congress has cataloged the hardcover edition as follows:
ISBN 978-1-4814-6636-3 (hc)
ISBN 978-1-4814-6637-0 (pbk)
ISBN 978-1-4814-6638-7 (eBook)

To Mom and Dad—
the first readers, the biggest fans,
and the best parents

BAYLOR'S Guide to THE Other Side

1

A good routine
is KEY.

MY DAY CAN'T BEGIN WITHOUT MY ROUTINE.

1. Wake up and light a candle. (I prefer a simple white candle, though I've been known to shake it up during the holidays and use a pine scent.) I breathe deeply and encircle myself with positive energy.

This first step is crucial to having a good day.

2. Check my dream journal to see if I scrawled any messages in the middle of the night. (There are a couple of lines on the page sometimes, but I'm pretty good at remembering my dreams, not to brag or anything.)

3. Check in with my twin, Kristina, and ask her how her night was.

4. Ask for only good vibes to emanate from the Beyond before I blow out my candle and start my day.

A chilly Thursday morning just two days before Halloween, the worst holiday ever created, I lit seven candles and placed them around me, creating a fiery barrier. I'd been doing the same thing at night, too, for the past week. Halloween may be fun for everyone else, but for someone who can communicate with ghosts, I can assure you it's not fun at all. Halloween is the one time of year where it can be tricky to control the malevolent spirits. So many of them try to break through, even if I ensure through my protections they can't communicate with me directly. It's all because of the morons who wear those grotesque, bloody masks and costumes without realizing the very real effect it has on my life.

Those costumes summon negative energy, and I can literally feel the forces floating around, circling me like sharks around a bloody seal. Kristina hates Halloween more than I do. I can forbid those spirits from entering my vision, but she can't, so while I'm walking down the street, choosing to be oblivious, she's turning left and right, looking at one horror after the next. I don't envy her.

It was on our walk to school that she mentioned how it was getting pretty bad already.

"Everyone must have tried on their costumes last night," she said. "You would not believe how many murderers and politicians we're passing."

"Are they saying anything to you?" I asked. My shoes crunched up the yellow leaves that covered the sidewalk.

"No, they're mostly grunting a lot. They know not to mess with us."

"I still don't get how they know that. Who would come rocketing over to this side to punish them?"

"I'm not entirely sure, but I know it would be bad," she said. "I think it's better not to know."

She was wrong. I wanted to know so bad. She always said stuff like that to me: "We're not permitted to know that yet," "We haven't learned enough to earn that knowledge." It was so frustrating that I couldn't grab her and shake more information out of her like I could with my little brother, Jack.

"Can you hear that?" she asked.

"Yeah." Some man was screaming about a lost dog, but I'd been awake for only twenty minutes and didn't want to deal with ghosts yet. "Does he expect me to knock on his wife's door and deliver a message for him? He knows that's not how this works."

"Give him a second," Kristina said lightly.

Three seconds later a door opened two houses ahead, and a woman walked out wearing a green bathrobe and pink slippers. Her arms were clenched across her chest, and she was looking around, confused.

"Why did I come out here again?" she mumbled.

Kristina raised an eyebrow at me, and I rolled my eyes and muttered, "It's too early for this," before I slouched my way up to the woman and said, "Excuse me, ma'am?" She turned my way and looked at me like I'd just personally caused her dog to run away.

"Yes, young man?"

"My name is Baylor Bosco, and I can communicate with people who have crossed over." I must have repeated that exact sentence more than two thousand times by now. "Your husband wanted me to let you know that your dog is with him on the other side now, and, well, it's time to move on, Trish. The animal shelter has a small brown terrier he thinks you might like."

I braced myself for her reaction. I might have done this more than two thousand times by now, but I was never sure how people would react. I got off easy this time, though. The woman's mouth dropped open, and her eyes filled with tears.

"How did you know that?" she asked. They always

ask that too, even though I've just told them I can communicate with dead people.

"I was born with a gift," I said, shrugging. "Oh, he also wants me to tell you that you need to change the curtains because they're hideous."

"That is just like him to say." She laughed so heartily that I found myself wishing everyone would react as well to weird messages like that. "Is he doing okay?"

I nodded. "Just fine."

Then I kept on walking. Normally, I would engage with the alive person more, but her husband was still shouting nonsense in our ears and I needed him to stop. It was 7:30 a.m., and no one, dead or alive, should have permission to scream that early. After I broke the connection, the shouting stopped, as it always did after I shared a healing message. It was Kristina's job to seal the ghosts on the other side and make sure they no longer disturbed us.

It might seem harsh, but some of them just don't get it. I'm here to relay the message, and it's not up to me whether the person on the receiving end listens or not. When I first started delivering messages, before Kristina helped me tune out most spirits, I'd have these horribly persistent ones poking me over and over to deliver the same message I'd just passed along.

"They didn't believe you, you need to go back over and try again," they'd say.

Later Kristina established a rule with the ghosts: If you're going to use Baylor to deliver a message, you've got only one shot to deliver it. They could come back with a different message, and that'd be fine, just as long as it wasn't the same one.

"He was loud," I grunted. I hadn't slept well last night because I kept getting ruffled by some ghost children who passed through my room.

"*You* think it's loud? Try being on this side of the fence. The man was practically screaming in my ear."

"Your nonexistent ghost ears?"

"Shut up, they hear better than yours do."

Oh, there's one important detail to know about Kristina—she's dead.

2

Imaginary friends and dead twin sisters aren't the same thing.

MOST PEOPLE DON'T BELIEVE ME WHEN I TELL them my sister's ghost accompanies me through life, but it's true. Well, I take that back. Most people don't believe me *at first.* The only reason I can see my sister in the first place is because I can talk to all dead people, so usually there's a talkative aunt or a doting grandma around who can help me deliver a persuasive message to the doubters. My sister, though, was never born. We were in the womb together, hanging out and growing cells, when one day her body fell apart.

I was born just fine, and early on I had no idea I didn't have a real, live sister. She was always beside me, talking to me and playing with me and even fighting with me. My parents thought I just had an extremely active imagination, complete with an extremely realistic imaginary friend.

When I was five years old, I mentioned something to my mom.

"Mommy," I said, "how come you never talk to Kristina?"

"Kristina's your imaginary friend, honey," my mom said for the hundredth time. "I can't see or speak to her."

"But she was in your belly with me," I said. "She told me she was. She said you cried for days after you lost her, but you didn't lose her, because she's right there."

I pointed to my smiling twin sitting in her chair at the kitchen table, rays of sun shooting through the wide window but not quite bouncing off her curly golden hair. I didn't realize the look on my mom's face was one of horror. It simply didn't register with me that she would be stunned to find out her son's imaginary friend was no friend at all, but rather her miscarried daughter.

"Baylor," she said slowly, "how do you know you

had a twin? Did you overhear Daddy or Grandma talking about it?"

"No, Mommy!" I said, so frustrated she wasn't getting it. "She *told* me."

"Baylor, tell her that the envelope she's missing fell between the desk and the filing cabinet," Kristina said, giggling.

"And," I said, "she told me to tell you that the missing envelope fell between the desk and the filing cabinet."

My mom's face transformed from horror to confusion to panic. She left me at the table and sprinted to the home office, then returned a moment later holding an insurance document she'd apparently misplaced weeks earlier.

I saw her hands shaking violently, but I didn't know what that meant. Now that I'm older—thirteen, in fact—I see those shaky hands a lot, and I try to be as empathetic as possible when relaying messages to people from their loved ones. People can't help but feel scared when confronted with this sort of supernatural activity.

After my mom found the letter, she sobbed for an hour, then finally pulled herself together and asked my dad to come home from work. She wouldn't say why, but since my mom was pregnant with my brother, he thought something bad had happened. When he burst through the door, he found my mom a blubbering mess at the table, and he found me sitting on the kitchen floor, pushing my fire truck along the tiles while Kristina made loud siren noises next to me.

They talked for a bit, and then my dad walked over to me in the funniest way, like I was a snake that had gotten loose in the house and he was trying to catch me. He crouched down slowly in front of me and took a big gulp.

"Hey, buddy. Mommy told me about your imaginary friend," he said. I'll never forget how his knees wavered as he talked to me, like he couldn't find his balance.

"Kristina's not my friend, she's my sister, Daddy," I said, barely looking over. I didn't get why they were making such a big deal out of it. I didn't get why they didn't just love her like they loved me. I had never noticed until a few days before that they never tucked her in, or set a plate for her at dinner, or hung her drawings up, or even had a bed for her. I thought that was pretty mean. "She's sitting right there."

I pointed to the space in front of the fridge, and of course my dad saw nothing. But to me, she was as fully formed and normal as any of my new kindergarten friends were. There was one difference, though, which I had spotted even back then as a little boy: The only way to know for sure if a person is a ghost is to watch his or her eyes.

Ghosts don't blink. They just stare at you like they're trying to break the record for the world's creepiest staring contest. You'd think there'd be more obvious ways to tell if people are dead or alive, but there's really not. They don't breathe, of course, but it's not like it's easy to tell if people are breathing when they're just standing there. And they're not transparent, either, as much as the movies like to think they are. They're as normal-looking as the next person . . . well, most of them, anyway.

My dad looked at the empty space and back at me and then back at the empty space.

"Baylor, buddy, you're telling me you see a little girl sitting right there right now?" he said, trying his best to laugh.

"He doesn't think I'm here," Kristina said sadly. At the time she also didn't totally grasp the fact that she wasn't alive.

"I know," I said, frowning at her. "I don't know why."

"Tell him Mommy's baby is another boy, so he doesn't have to worry about having a girl yet."

I told him what she'd said, and his mouth dropped open and his face kind of fell forward.

"Another boy?" my mom squeaked from the table. "Oh! Good!"

It would take another month for the doctor to be able to confirm that the baby was, in fact, a boy, and when they came home from the doctor's office that day, they were walking on eggshells around me.

Looking back, I now realize how scared they were.

At school Kristina tends to keep to herself. She follows me around, but she knows I can't sit there and talk to her. I don't try to hide my gift, and although most of the kids at school know what I can do, they don't really know about Kristina. It would just be too odd to have a full-on conversation with someone that nobody else can see or hear.

School that day was so slow. For a few periods I thought maybe some evil spirits were playing a trick on me and slowing the clock down. I even excused myself during one class, hid in a bathroom stall, and lit my emergency lighter while casting away all negative energy.

Kristina giggled from outside the stall.

"It's not funny, Kristina," I said, the flame still lit as I envisioned myself covered in light.

"Actually, it is," she said back. "Nobody's doing anything to you. It's just a boring day."

By lunchtime I was ready to fall asleep, and I still couldn't shake the feeling that a spirit was at fault. At the lunch table I put my head down on my arms and closed my eyes.

"You okay, man?" my friend Aiden asked. We'd been pals since fifth grade, when I joined the band in elementary school. I was a band geek by choice, and Aiden was a band geek by default. He played the flute, was pudgy, and had terrible acne, and I was almost positive his mom cut his hair, though I'd never asked. But he was my best and most loyal blinking friend, and he'd stuck by me even after finding out my other best friend was my dead twin sister.

"I've been feeling terrible all day," I said.

"Is it because Halloween's soon?" he asked, opening his red lunch box and unpacking a pepperoni sandwich. "I know all the poltergeists come out to play this time of year."

I shot him a look. "I'm actually sort of worried that might be the case."

"Oh, sorry, man," he said. He took a bite of his sandwich, and a glob of mustard oozed down his chin. "Kristina hasn't done anything to help you?"

"How can I help you when I'm too busy watching

this mess try to eat?" Kristina said from next to me on the bench. I chuckled, causing Aiden to furrow his eyebrows.

"What's so funny?"

"Nothing, nothing," I said. "She said it isn't a spirit, so maybe I'm just being paranoid."

We changed the subject when two other band members came to sit with us. Plus, I wanted to try to forget about my weird spirit problems, if only for a few minutes.

The rest of the day passed in a blur, and when the final bell rang, I texted Aiden and told him I was skipping band practice because I needed to get home and rest. I almost always walked to and from school—it's barely over a mile away from my house—but today I called my mom and asked her to pick me up.

"You're being such a baby, Baylor," Kristina said. "I know you're not sick."

"Then why do I feel so bad?" I leaned back against the brick wall of the admin building and curled myself into a ball.

"I'm not sure."

"Well, if you can't make it stop, then you're not allowed to have an opinion." Maybe I was imagining it, but even the sky seemed darker—a dull, lifeless gray.

My mom arrived a few minutes later, and I opened the front door of her black SUV to climb in.

"What's wrong, honey?" she said. "Is it a fever?" She held the back of her hand to my forehead and frowned, making almost the same face as Kristina, though I didn't tell her that. It was still weird that she didn't know what her own daughter looked like, despite talking to her every day.

"I don't think it's a fever," I said. "I'm not sure what it is. I just feel terrible."

"Let's get you home," she said. "Did you say hi to Ella yet?"

When I was eleven, my parents welcomed a wonderful little accident named Ella into the world. To me and Kristina, though, she was no accident at all, as I reminded them when they told me Mom was pregnant.

"Remember what I told Dad when I talked to you both about Kristina?" I said. "'He doesn't have to worry about having a girl *yet*.' I told you both about her six years ago!"

The look of shock on my dad's face grew exponentially worse after realizing it was going to be a girl. He had raised two boys so far. What the heck was he going to do with a little girl?

But it wasn't something he had to worry about,

because Ella soon had him wrapped around her little finger. And I have to admit, I was right there with him. She was the cutest little thing I'd ever seen.

Plus, there was the whole fact that she could see spirits. Actually, most babies can—Jack was one of the twitchiest babies ever because of it—but Ella's ability seemed to be amplified thanks to me and Kristina working so well as a team. She couldn't communicate with them, and her ability would fade away in a couple years, but for now she could interact with Kristina and see the same spirits I could.

"Hi, baby Ella," I said, looking at her through the rearview mirror. I was too exhausted to turn my body around. "Seen any scary spirits today?"

She smiled widely at me for a second before turning her attention back to the baby doll she was holding. She had the most squeezable cheeks of any one-and-a-half-year-old I'd ever met, and they were soon to be overtaken by her ultracurly hair. Now that she was out of her late-night crying phase of life, I loved Ella a ton.

"Did . . . did Kristina say anything about your being sick?" my mom asked. She always spoke in a hushed tone when it came to Kristina, who could hear just fine at any volume.

"Nope, doesn't know a thing," I said. "Really helpful."

Kristina was probably happy Mom had asked after her, but the thought of turning to look at her made me queasy.

When we got back home, I essentially crawled upstairs and found Kristina already in my room with her arms crossed.

"You're starting to worry me," she said. "It must be all the Halloween energy. What else could it be?"

"It's never affected me like this before, though," I said.

"Maybe things are changing." She almost sounded excited. "Maybe I need to have a talk with one of my spirit guides tonight while you sleep."

"Please do. I'll take all the help I can get."

Without another word I passed out.

I woke with a start hours later, but I couldn't see the clock. It was dark outside, but the light was still on from earlier.

"Kristina?" I called out.

No response. I thought that was weird but remembered she was going to talk to her guides. Feeling better about her absence, I reached over to turn the lamp off.

When the room went dark, a horrible chill passed through every pore of my body. I sat up in bed, shivering, and in the corner of my room, right in front of the window, stood a man with a white sheet draped over his head.

He seemed very tall, but that could have been because I was in bed. He was perfectly still, almost like a statue, and the edge of the sheet was precisely ruffled like a coiled snake near the floor. Most people would have screamed, but I've experienced some weird things in my day.

But then I noticed the eyes. They were two small holes in the sheet, just big enough for the pupils, and even through the dark all I saw was shiny black pools of menace staring right at me. I forgot how to use my lungs, and as I gasped for air, it felt like the world was closing in on me. The second I saw those eyes, I knew something was wrong.

An evil spirit had breached my barrier.

3

Do not panic.

"BE GONE, SPIRIT!" I SHOUTED, BUT IT DIDN'T move. The eyes gleamed like black sulfur, but it still made no motion. The sheet didn't sway an inch.

I reached out for my lamp and clicked it on, and as the light filled the room, the demon vanished. A final chill overtook my body, and I exhaled heavily. I looked down and saw my hands shaking.

"Baylor!" Kristina shouted as she materialized from nowhere. "What happened? I couldn't access your room. One second I was here, and the next I was trapped outside."

I turned to her, and I'm sure my face was as white as the sheet that had covered that man.

"Baylor, it's okay," she said as she sat on my bed. "It's over. Whatever happened, it's over. Tell me what you saw."

I looked at my hands, unable to quell the shaking.

"It was some sort of terrible spirit, Kristina," I finally said. "I turned the light off, and a person wearing a white sheet was standing in the corner. His eyes, Kristina . . . it was like the devil was looking at me."

"Then what happened?"

"I told him to leave, and when he wouldn't go, I turned the light back on and he disappeared, and then you came back, and now we're talking, and my hands won't stop shaking."

"Demon dung!" she said, her voice hushed. "I need to speak with my guides right away."

"No! Don't go. What if he comes back?"

"Light some candles," she said. "Place them all around the house and ask for more good spirits to stand guard."

I nodded. "Okay, I'll go get some from downstairs."

"That will keep whatever it was at bay for now." She paused for a moment, looking at my shaking hands. "Whatever it was, Baylor, it was really bad.

I'm surrounded by positive energy, just as you are, and I couldn't even share the same space as it. I've never encountered anything like it before."

"Forget the candles," I said, springing out of bed. "I'm lighting the fireplace, and the grill, and I'm going to find a freaking torch to carry around."

After I had secured the premises with the candles—placing a few extras in Ella's room—I dug through the china cabinet in the dining room. I found what I was looking for tucked away behind the plastic plates and rolled-up tablecloths: a four-wick candle. My mom kept a few candles like this for special occasions, and I was pretty sure tonight qualified as more special than her boring book club.

With all four wicks lit, I went back up to my room feeling like I was holding a nuclear bomb. *Try and get me now, Sheet Man!* Whatever that thing was, it wouldn't be back. Not tonight, anyway.

Even so, I couldn't shake the image of those black eyes. It was bad enough seeing an exaggerated version of the classic ghost—*oh, a sheet over your head, super original*—but to see it unmoving and unblinking and unspeaking, with those deadened, haunting eyes? I felt threatened. Someone or something was trying to intimidate me, in my own home no less, and I didn't like it.

* * *

"They have no idea how it happened," Kristina said the next morning, fresh from a powwow with her spirit guides. "The fact that I couldn't be around it made them all incredibly nervous. They're setting up extra protection around the house."

"Well, that's good," I said. "Except now I'm more freaked out than I was last night. Shouldn't your spirit guides know everything? Isn't that what they're there for?"

"They know everything about *us*," she said. "Not random evil spirits who make you wet your bed, Baylor."

"I didn't wet my bed, Kristina."

"I'm not convinced."

"You're dead. You can go back and relive that moment."

"But it's so much more fun this way."

I shook my head. "This isn't funny, you know. That thing could have sucked up my soul or unleashed demon spiders on me or something." I shuddered at the thought of demon spiders descending from the ceiling and crawling all over me.

"Listen, Baylor, I know you're nervous, but it was a onetime thing. You'll have so much energy surrounding you today, it'll be like you're wearing a suit of armor."

"Well, that sounds good, I guess."

"Just try not to pee in it if you get a little nervous."

I didn't learn a single thing at school that day. I just kept tossing around the possible intentions of the Sheet Man's visit.

Was he actually threatening me? Sure, his eyes were freaky, but other than that, was he really that scary? Physically, no. But the fact that his presence had obstructed Kristina from sharing the room was alarming at best, and a harbinger of my impending death at worst.

Maybe he was just keeping watch over me in a way Kristina couldn't? I had been building up my positive energy so much for Halloween that it was difficult for me to accept that any sort of bad spirit could have broken through. Who's to say that he wasn't merely a sentinel with a sheet?

It was also possible he was trying to send a message. What if he needed help? What if some corrupt company was selling a brand of sheets that would somehow strangle people in their sleep? What if a bunch of children overseas were locked in a factory and being forced to fabricate the sheets? What if it wasn't a sheet at all and he was just a fashionable ghost? Unlikely, but since I could talk to dead people, I didn't like to rule out unlikely things.

By the end of the day I had resolved to do a little investigating. Since I was fairly confident it had been a sheet and not some sort of ghostly burka, I decided to go straight to the source and take the bus to Bed Bath & Beyond. It was practically sheet heaven. I figured maybe I could find a similar white sheet, which might lead to a clue.

Riding a bus, or a plane or a train or, well, any kind of transportation where I'm trapped with strangers, can be a very unpredictable experience for me. Sometimes the passengers around me will be boring and, in turn, have boring loved ones who won't bother me.

Other times it's pure chaos.

The only thing I can compare it to is when you're walking along a street and a jackhammer is pounding into the pavement. That deafening, grating noise is all you can hear, and you can try to ignore it and talk over it, but it's just too loud.

Ghosts, especially the pesky ones, are my personal jackhammers pounding relentlessly into my brain. They will get in my face and yell at me until I deliver a message. Even when I try to tune them out, they'll scream from the other side, and eventually Kristina will get so annoyed with them that she'll force me to deliver the message just so she can break the connection and seal off the ghost.

It's really bad when there's more than one of these annoying ghosts, who always have the most inane messages. Stupid things like "She needs to remember to change the air conditioner filters more often" or "He needs to know that I'm okay with him throwing out all my socks." I could understand the urgency if the ghosts died tragically and they wished to tell a loved one that they were now at peace, or maybe they knew of a dark secret the person was keeping and they wished to give that person comfort. In those kinds of situations I'm almost always happy to help.

But when I have a small Venezuelan woman yammering in my ear that her granddaughter is using the incorrect arepa recipe and, thus, embarrassing her family's legacy, I'm not so pleased to relay the message.

Kristina, who's learned a lot alongside me over the years, once told me my purpose was to deliver healing messages, and if I didn't think a message was healing, I didn't need to deliver it. That's also why I'm able to tune out certain spirits.

But sometimes the ghosts are so strong and persistent that it's easier to give in.

"My name is Baylor Bosco, and I can communicate with people who have crossed over," I finally blurted out to the haggard-looking woman in the seat behind me. "I'm so sorry to have to tell you this, but your grandma will not stop pestering me. She says you're using the wrong kind of cornmeal in your arepas and that you're tarnishing her reputation every time you serve them to people and tell them that you used her recipe."

"Jor makin' me look bad, *chiquita*," the grandma lamented.

The woman blinked at me.

"Did you understand me?" I said slowly.

"Yes, I understood you," she said, shaking her head. "Shut up and turn around."

Ugh. A doubter.

"I'm not kidding, Ana."

Her eyebrows shot up.

"How'd you know my name?"

"Your grandma told me. She's standing right there." I pointed to the space just over her shoulder, where her grandma hovered, clucking her tongue as she examined her hair.

Her eyes followed my finger, but she saw nothing, of course. She looked around the bus, this time with a slight grin on her face. "Did Armando put you up to this?" She chuckled. "I'm gonna be on YouTube, aren't I?" She waved to the nonexistent hidden cameras while sticking out her tongue.

"No," I said, shaking my head. "It's just me, you, and your annoyed *abuela*."

"Do me a favah," the old woman said. "Tell Ana her hair looked bettah when it was dyed blue, not this nasty pink like it is now."

I repeated the message, and Ana's face collapsed into a frown.

"Oh." She looked out the window. "That sounds just like something she'd say. I got it done yesterday."

"She needs to go get her money back!"

I looked at the old woman. "I'm not saying that."

"What'd she say?" Ana asked, her head whipping back in my direction.

I sighed. "She said you should go get your money back."

"I thought people were supposed to get nicer after they died."

"Most of them do," I said.

Still frowning, her voice a bit terse, she asked, "What's the right cornmeal, then?"

"She says it's Masarepa flour, not masa harina, because that has lime in it and makes the arepas taste *malas*."

I can't speak Spanish, but that's a funny thing about communicating with ghosts. Even though I speak with them in English, whenever I relay a message to their loved ones, a part of their personality and soul can also come through.

I turned to Kristina and nodded. My work here was done, and a second later the woman had disappeared.

"Did she say anything else?" Ana asked. "Did she mention my fiancé? Does she like Armando?"

My lips pressed together awkwardly. "I'm not sure. She just left."

"Typical," she muttered, rolling her eyes. "Do me a favor: Next time keep my grandma's messages to yourself."

Inside Bed Bath & Beyond, I wandered around looking for the bedding department, bewildered by all the products I never knew existed. There were so many different kinds of pots and pans and baking sheets and knives and kitchen utensils. There was an entire wall of pillows, soaring up to the ceiling some twenty feet high. How were people supposed to see the pillows at the very top? Not everyone had a ghost sister who could drift up and give her opinion.

Once my shock wore away and I found the right section of the store, I realized it would be no easy task to find the correct white sheet, mostly because there were about two billion styles to choose from.

"Can you sense anything?" I asked Kristina. I was perusing the rows, one by one, touching every single package in the hope that some sort of message would be attached to one of them. Sometimes I can see a memory associated with an object. The problem is that there doesn't seem to be any real rhyme or reason to these visions, so I'll find myself randomly touching something and gasping in shock when a memory takes over. I've learned to avoid antique shops.

"Nothing," she said. "We're on a wild-goose chase here, Baylor. That sheet could have been purchased from anywhere, and that's if the sheet matters at all, which I can almost guarantee you it doesn't."

"There has to be something else that we're not getting, Kristina," I said. "It doesn't make any sense that he'd stand in the corner and not say a single word."

"He was probably trying to scare you," she said. "It's Halloween. Spirits like to have fun too. Especially the evil ones."

I shook my head. "I have a weird feeling about this. I don't know what the feeling is or why I think it's weird, I just know I have it."

A woman with auburn hair, who'd been examining a white comforter with red flowers on it, was glancing at me, her eyes filled with concern. When I was younger, I used to blush whenever people caught me speaking to Kristina, since I knew they thought I was crazy and speaking out loud to myself. But time heals everything, and I nodded as I passed her.

"Happy Halloween," I said. "Watch out for the evil spirits."

When I got back home, my mom asked where I'd been.

"Just doing some shopping," I said.

"For what? Are you actually going to dress up this year?" Her face had lit up from behind the counter, where she was dicing an onion. She was always so disappointed that I refused to participate in Halloween. All the other moms got cute pictures every year of their children dressed as ninjas and Bugs Bunny and clowns, and all she got was a kid who preferred to spend Halloween night wandering around a cemetery with his dead sister.

"Sorry to disappoint you," I said, "but no."

"Come on, Baylor!" she pleaded. "You're thirteen. This will probably be the last year you can get away with trick-or-treating. No one wants to give candy away to a guy who has to shave."

I sighed. "I don't care about Halloween, Mom, you know that."

"I know, I know," she said. She threw the onions into

the frying pan, and they hissed and smoked. "I just don't want you to regret anything when you're older."

A part of me wondered if she was right. I hadn't dressed up for Halloween since I was at least eight, and I couldn't remember ever having gone trick-or-treating, mostly because I couldn't imagine being on the street and not knowing who was alive and who was a ghost . . . or worse.

"Maybe I'll text Aiden and ask what he's doing tomorrow," I said. "If only so you can have one picture of me, Jack, and Ella dressed up for Halloween."

My mom dropped the spoon she was using, and her eyes welled up.

"Would you really do that for me?"

Oh no. I hadn't really been serious, but now that the thought of a single photograph had made her cry, how could I backtrack?

"Uh, yeah, of course," I said.

Sitting on the couch in the family room, I texted Aiden.

BAYLOR: Got any plans for tomorrow?

AIDEN: Me, bobby and j are gonna trick or treat around my neighborhood

BAYLOR: Care if I come?

AIDEN: You serious? I didn't tell you about it only cuz you reject me every year

BAYLOR: I changed my mind this year

AIDEN: YES. Meet at my house at 7

All I had to do was find a costume.

Beware: Halloween is more tricks than treats.

I KNEW IF I COULDN'T AVOID THE MASSES on Halloween night, I'd need to pick a costume that increased my protection by its very nature. No bloody masks or devil horns for me. I racked my brain for ideas and even asked Kristina what she thought.

"An angel, of course," she said.

"I can't go as an angel! I'll look ridiculous, and not in a good way!"

"No spirits would bother you, though."

"I'm not dressing as an angel. Any other ideas?"

I rejected going as a priest, a nun, a Greek god

(too cold for togas), a (friendly) clown, and a doctor before I finally settled on something that was both funny and positive: a baby.

The next day I went to Wal-Mart and found giant pink footed pajamas, which were perfect for the cold night ahead, as well as adult diapers to put over them.

But just walking through Wal-Mart gave me some second thoughts about trick-or-treating. Though I had lit all my candles that morning, it was clear the negative Halloween energy was starting to infringe on my positive energy, because I could see some dark spirits floating around me. They didn't disturb me, since they knew they couldn't touch me, but they stuck close to the people they'd attached themselves to. I asked Kristina to show me the auras of those people, one of her handy tricks.

"Brace yourself," she said grimly.

An aura is the outward reflection of a living person's soul, and these people were in dire straits. Their bodies glowed nearly black—but in the radioactive, toxic-waste sense of the word "glow." Their souls were tarnished from those dark spirits, and it made me shudder to think of some of the even more evil spirits lurking around me that hadn't yet attached themselves to people.

Spirits can be really different from ghosts. Ghosts

are the souls of dead people wandering about, while a spirit can be any sort of nonliving supernatural entity. It's like that miserable square-and-rectangle math rule: All ghosts are spirits, but not all spirits are ghosts. You'll never hear me say an evil ghost is lurking around. As Kristina used to say, "Ghosts are good, but spirits need speculation!"

A ghost would never leech on to a living person's aura, but an evil spirit would. And the longer it leeched, the more powerful it became. One woman in particular had such a dark aura that I couldn't even see her face properly. She was shrouded in darkness, and it was obvious why. An Ashen, the name for a newly formed demon, was sucking away her energy. Just based on the darkness of her aura, I'd bet a hundred bucks this Ashen had used her to transform from a regular old evil spirit to a demon, the evil version of a caterpillar becoming a butterfly. A disgusting, wretched butterfly.

I felt the need to help her, so I found the candle aisle, grabbed a few small white ones, and tracked her down near the checkout line. When the Ashen noticed me, its face went rigid. The demon's lower half was as billowy and misshapen as smoke, giving way to a solid top half that was shrouded in loose black material. Its face was, in so many words, pointy and deformed. The chin was a sharp triangle, so sharp that poking it with my finger would draw blood. Its cheeks were scaly and sunken, and the forehead was big enough that you could sell advertising space on it for a nice profit.

And those awful eyes—unblinking furnaces of burning green. They'd turn red one day.

"Ma'am," I whispered, looking at the demon, trying in vain to block it out. She turned to me, looking confused, since my eyes weren't focused on her.

"You talking to me, kid?"

"You need to buy these candles, light the wicks, and imagine the light of the flames surrounding your body." The demon roared with anger upon hearing my words, and I backed up a few feet.

"Baylor, it can't hurt you," Kristina reminded me. She was standing between me and the Ashen, her arms crossed and her eyes also scanning the creature. I wondered for a second if it could hurt her.

The woman narrowed her eyes at me. "What are you talking about, kid? I'm gonna call security on you if you don't get away from me."

I was still staring at the demon, which almost appeared to smirk, but that's nonsense, since demons don't smirk. As quickly as I could move, I pulled out my lighter, lit a candle, and sent the light her way.

Like a rope cut by a white-hot sword, the demon detached with a terrible hiss as the light enveloped the woman.

Now that the demon was no longer attached to a person, I could easily block it from my view with Kristina's help.

"Much better," I said, sighing with relief. I raised my eyebrows at Kristina and did a little jig with my feet. Nothing like banishing a demon to really get your day going.

"What did you just do to me?" the woman asked. She wasn't mad, though. In fact, whereas she had been hunched over just a moment ago, she now stood nearly a foot higher. "I haven't felt this great in years!"

"That does not surprise me." I blew out the candle and handed the armful over. "Buy the candles. Do what I told you. You'll need it." Demons always find a way back into people's lives. It's up to them whether they choose to fight the demons or let them wreak havoc.

She took the candles, thanked me, and walked off. Kristina nodded her approval.

"Nice one," she said. "You're making excellent progress."

"What does that mean?" I asked.

"Oh, nothing," she said casually.

* * *

Back at home I finished the costume with one of Ella's bibs and an old rattle.

When I checked myself in the mirror, I smiled. It was perfect.

"You have never looked this dumb," Kristina said crossly, her hands on her hips. "I know you're supposed to be a baby, but you're not a cute baby. You're an overgrown monster of a baby, and I think it's only going to attract negative energy."

"I think you're jealous," I said, turning to admire the way my butt looked in that diaper. "This costume can't bring me anything but good vibes."

She shook her head. "At least Mom'll be happy."

And she was right. When my mom saw the costume, she actually started jumping.

"Stay right there!" she yelled. "I need to get my nice camera." She ran away for a moment, returning with her massive DSLR camera, and she proceeded to take a hundred pictures of me standing there, dressed as a giant pink baby.

"You look so good! I need to get Jack and Ella ready so they can jump in too."

A couple of hours later my mom was getting the pictures she'd dreamed about for years in front of our sparsely decorated house.

We live in a nice neighborhood in Keene, a boring city in New Hampshire. All the houses on our street are old and give off that classic New England feel, with slatted wood, pillars, and stoops galore. Around Halloween most of our neighbors go crazy with their decorations. They put cobwebs and little white, cartoony ghosts in their trees. They hang big, hairy spiders around their doorways and plant bloody zombie hands in the soil. Witches on brooms seem to be very popular, and there's always a few that feature the witch smashed headfirst into the side of the house—exactly what witches deserve, if you ask me.

Not our house. Except for a small orange sign that says HAPPY HALLOWEEN! and the occasional jack-o'-lantern (carved only with happy faces), you'll never know it's the season of goblins and ghouls at the Bosco residence. I forbade my parents from hanging up any decorations long ago, much to my mom's displeasure. She used to love Halloween, but now that she had a child who could see those ghouls people usually only joked about, she'd had to stifle her affection for the holiday.

"Jack, smile for this next picture!" Mom said as we shivered in front of the house. Keene isn't exactly known for its warmth and sun in the winter, but with highs in the thirties, it was unseasonably cold even for our frigid little town.

"I can't feel my face!" he said. "Maybe I should put on last year's costume. That one had a mask." He was dressed up as a soldier from one of his favorite movies. Last year he'd been a dinosaur.

Ella was a princess, and a very cute one at that, with a pink tiara, a gold dress, and little pink shoes. Kristina was staring off into the distance near an almost bare tree, a few scattered leaves still clinging to the branches.

"You look good!" my mom said. "You'll just have to run from house to house to stay warm!"

"Dad's gonna love that," I said, tickling baby Ella to make her laugh. My dad goes around with Jack every year while my mom stays home and passes out candy.

I usually go to the cemetery. It's the most peaceful place to be on Halloween night, and the one place where spirits almost never hang around. Ghosts couldn't care less about their bodies once they've died; they only care to be around the people they loved or hated.

This was the first time in years I wouldn't be going to the cemetery, and it felt really strange. It had become a tradition to go down there, explore the different sections, read all the headstones, and hide from the evil spirits roaming through the night. It was my sanctuary, in a way. But not tonight.

After the photo shoot I headed to Aiden's. I normally walk over, but since it was so cold, my dad gave me a lift on his way to meet Jack's friends. He was just as surprised as my mom that I was going out that night.

"This is a big step for you, buddy," he said. "I'm proud of you."

"I'm dressed as a giant baby to go trick-or-treating, Dad," I said. "I'm not sure this is the best time for you to be proud of me."

He laughed. "Well, you know what I mean."

My dad had worked as a CPA for forever, but after his dad died a few years ago (a traumatic time for the two of us for *very* different reasons), he decided he wanted to be a teacher. Now he teaches math at the local high school. The very same one I'll be attending next year.

"Have a good night, buddy!" he said as I got out of the car in front of Aiden's house.

"Stay away from the scary costumes!" I warned Jack, totally serious. "You don't know who or what will be near them."

Jack's expression melted into a grimace as they

drove away. Ghosts had always scared him, and having me as his big brother was probably his enduring nightmare.

I knocked on the door of Aiden's house and was greeted by his mother, Mrs. Kirkwood. She is the friendliest woman I've ever met but also one of the largest. She took up the entire width of the doorway, and she shrieked when she saw me.

"Aiden told me you were joining in on the fun tonight!" she squealed, wrapping me in a giant hug and pressing me into her soft yet still somehow very firm body. Hugging her fascinated me because it was like hugging a rubbery boulder. When she finally released me, she pushed me back and held me at arm's length so she could look me over. "And that costume, Baylor! So funny! Oh, you four are going to have such a great time tonight! I'm just so excited for you all!"

"Thanks, Mrs. Kirkwood," I said. Kristina laughed next to me, but I didn't acknowledge her. Mrs. Kirkwood could get a little too excited by my gift, so I'd found it was best to pretend like it didn't exist whenever I was around her. "Is everyone here already?"

"You're the first to arrive!" she said giddily, closing the door and leading me to the kitchen, where she

had set out bowls of M&M'S, chips and salsa, and a
gourmet cheese and cracker plate.

Aiden, dressed as a very wide skeleton, was hovering over the bowl of salsa, a handful of chips in his hand.

"Dude, you actually came!" he said. "I know you said you would, but I didn't believe it till right now."

"Yeah, I decided to mix it up this year," I said, grabbing some M&M'S. I looked over his costume and decided it was okay. I hadn't told him not to dress as anything negative, and I didn't think a skeleton was too bad. I had one inside of me, after all. It was really a scientific diagram, I justified to myself. It totally wasn't a deteriorated corpse. Nope. Nothing to be afraid of.

"Well, this is going to be awesome," he said. "You got a bag?"

I frowned because I didn't know what he meant, and then I slapped my forehead. A bag for the candy! I hadn't been trick-or-treating in so long that I'd forgotten I needed something for my loot.

"Shoot!" I said. "Totally forgot. Do you have one I could borrow?"

"Oh, don't worry, Baylor, all the kids use pillowcases," Mrs. Kirkwood said as she wandered out of the kitchen. "I'll grab you one."

"So you're okay, man?" Aiden asked. "Finally gonna face the ghosts out and about tonight?"

"Yeah," I said. "It was time."

"What changed your mind?" He threw a handful of M&M'S into his mouth.

"My mom said something about how this might be the last chance I ever get to trick-or-treat, since we're getting so old."

Mrs. Kirkwood came back in at that moment and wore an expression like I'd just slapped her in the face.

"The last chance?" she said, her lips quivering. "Oh dear. I . . . I didn't even think about—I guess you wouldn't want to trick-or-treat next year as high schoolers. You'll probably have some cool party to go to instead."

"Cool? She knows she's talking to you and Aiden, right?" Kristina chimed in. She was sitting at the kitchen table, looking out the big picture window into the dark woods behind the house.

"Yeah, probably," Aiden said. "We'll barely be able to get away with it tonight."

Kristina snorted. "You're an overgrown toddler, Aiden. You'll be able to trick-or-treat until you're forty!"

The doorbell rang, and Mrs. Kirkwood let in J and Bobby. Bobby, who was dressed as a girl, is one of our really good friends. He's also in band, except he plays the drums. He's one of those guys you can't help but like, and I had a theory that Kristina secretly had a crush on him, not that she could do anything about it. When I looked over at her, she was fixing her hair.

"J" is short for "Janet," and she's one of the scariest people I've ever met. Not scary like a bully, but more like she will look at you and tell you her exact opinion on anything and why she's correct. She'll be going to Harvard or Yale one day; I think it just depends on which one offers her more money. She's not in band with us, but we became friends after Aiden got to know her in Debate Club last year.

"Looking dapper," J said to me as she gave me a hug. She was dressed up as a nurse, but she wasn't wearing a skimpy outfit or even blue scrubs. She had on a long white dress and a floppy white cap, both emblazoned with giant red crosses. Her thick, purple cheetah-print glasses, though, gave her away as a thirteen-year-old girl and not an actual Civil War nurse pestering me to deliver a message.

Aiden was ogling her, and I was trying to catch his eye so he'd remember to close his mouth. He'd harbored a crush on her from the day they met, but he was, in his words, "too fat and goofy" to do anything about it. Instead, he just hung out with her all the time and did everything he could to make her happy, while very much not being her boyfriend. It was depressing to witness.

"Doesn't he realize that she likes him, too?" Kristina said. "I don't understand the logic of blinkers sometimes."

I shrugged but didn't say anything. It was pretty standard communication for the two of us when we were in front of people. She'd make a comment, and I'd find some way to respond. She'd told me that we might be able to communicate with our thoughts one day, but I didn't like the sound of it. What if she accidentally caught some of my private thoughts? There'd be no coming back from that.

"Did they run out of the cute nurse costumes at the store, J?" I asked.

"What are you talking about? I'm Clara Barton."

I blinked, not sure if I was supposed to know what that meant.

"The founder of the American Red Cross," she said, as though it were immensely obvious. Then she pointed at Bobby. "Can you believe this idiot?" He was posing like a Cali girl in his short jean skirt and red top, complete with a stuffed bra, bright-blond wig, and atrocious makeup.

"I thought he was your patient, actually," I joked, and I turned to glare at Aiden. He still hadn't recovered from seeing his crush in her costume, and he needed to get it together. He caught my eye and jumped.

"You guys look great," he managed to choke out. I shook my head while Kristina scoffed from her perch at the table.

"The haul's going to be great this year," Bobby said, his mouth doubled from its normal size thanks to the smeared lipstick covering it. "All the parents who usually hang out on the streets are going to be home, since it's so cold, which means more houses to go to, which means"—he shook his hips excitedly—"more candy for us."

"It's not going to be good candy, though," J said. "They're just going to give us whatever they had lying around, since they didn't have time to run to the store."

"Where," Bobby said, turning to her dramatically, "is your optimism?"

She laughed, and Aiden turned back and forth between them, smiling with a vague look of panic beaming from his eyes.

"Oh, wow, this is like watching a train wreck," Kristina said, exasperated. "Pull it together, Aiden!"

I chuckled, but I didn't know what to do. I had

already given Aiden as much advice as I could. I had dropped hints on his behalf to J. I wasn't sure how to help them, and now it looked like a lost cause. He had wanted to ask her to the Back-to-School Bash in September, but she had been very vocal about wanting to go with a group of friends. When I told him to ask her to the Fall Ball coming up in November, the look on his face suggested that I'd just described a murder scene in gory detail.

"Let's take a picture," J said. She whipped out her cell phone and handed it to Mrs. Kirkwood, who'd been leaning against the fridge the whole time and grinning like a madwoman.

"You all are just so cute," she said under her breath as she squinted at the screen and tapped it aimlessly, while we all pressed together in front of the table. I had specifically positioned myself between Bobby and J so that Aiden was on her other side. "There! I think it worked! I'm not sure, though."

J took back the phone, giggled, and said, "I'm gonna post it right now." She showed it to us, and even though we all looked like fools, the main thing I noticed was a strange light in the corner. Kristina had managed to find her way into the picture in her own special ghost way, and I winked at her. She smiled and nodded.

I wondered, sometimes, what it was like to have only one person to talk to. To be invisible your whole life—could you call what she was experiencing a "life," even?—at the mercy of someone else. I had never asked her, but I wondered why she was the one who'd had to die and I was the one who'd gotten to live. And I wondered if she ever got sad about it. Whether or not she did, on nights like these, when I got to hang out with family and friends and she had to hang out in the corner, silent and unnoticed and effectively non-existent, I felt sad for her.

"This candy sucks!" Bobby yelled as we walked to the next house. "Dum Dums and Tootsie Rolls? I mean, come on, they may as well have opened the door, flipped us off, and spit in our faces."

"I actually like Tootsie Rolls!" J said, her floppy cap bopping up and down with every step she took.

"Me too!" Aiden said quickly, close behind.

"Whatever, you freaks can have them, then," Bobby said. "I'll trade you for the good stuff."

We'd been going for nearly an hour, walking as fast as we could between the houses, since it was only getting colder. Our bags were bulging, and I could tell I had gotten some decent treats. Three houses so far had given out king-size candy bars, which was akin to finding the Holy Grail three separate times.

"Okay, let's turn left down Acorn Road, since that's a good cul-de-sac," Bobby said. "We can hit a bunch of houses really fast."

"Perfect!" said J. "Then maybe we can think about heading back to Aiden's? My legs have only got twenty more minutes, max, before they're going to be classified as medically worthless."

"Are you kidding, J?" Bobby asked. "It's barely been an hour!"

"But we've gone to so many houses!" she said. "How much candy do you need?"

"All of it, J," he crooned. "I want as much as I can get."

She shook her head. "Twenty minutes, then I'm done."

"I'll go back with you, J," Aiden said quietly as Bobby ran ahead. "Don't worry."

J looked up at him and smiled. She couldn't see his face, since it was covered by a black-and-white skeleton mask, but I would have bet an even $1,000 that he was bright red.

When we turned onto Acorn Road, we passed a group of kids in the grade below us. Bobby nodded to them and kept walking, but when I got a look at their costumes, it was like a lightning bolt had hit my spine.

One had on a zombie mask with ripped flesh and bloody eyes. Another was dressed in a white shirt covered with blood and tire marks. And still another wore a hockey mask and carried a fake machete.

I had been doing fine all night, focused on hanging with my friends and running from house to house and ignoring everything else, and I had barely noticed a spirit around. But when I saw those costumes, it was so jarring and unexpected that I lost my concentration and an invisible wall crumbled. I was immediately surrounded by spirits, good and demonic alike, and the deafening chatter of a thousand ghosts.

I gasped, and all of a sudden Kristina was in front of me, reminding me to breathe, to shut my eyes and imagine only the good, and to let that image become my reality.

But then she was gone, and my friends were too, and I was all alone on Acorn Road. I looked around at the houses, where all the lights had gone out, yet the decorations glowed an eerie red.

Then, from the gaps in between the houses, a hundred men wearing sheets filed out and charged right at me. They weren't moving their legs; they were floating, their feet angled toward the road like they'd just been hanged.

And there were a hundred pairs of those awful eyes, beady pools of black evil, all illuminated a malicious red from the strange glow, boring into my soul, daggering into my skin.

I turned and ran.

TIP

5

Make sure you can run fast . . . or else.

I RACED DOWN ACORN ROAD, CUT A LEFT, and sprinted like I was competing in the Olympics.

I glanced back and saw the Sheet Men zipping toward me, like I was the magnet and they were pieces of iron, like I was the matador with a giant red cape and they were the angry bulls.

No one else was around. No one was there to help.

If these demons caught up to me and somehow attacked, I'd be all on my own.

I looked ahead. I summoned up all the strength I had and willed my legs to compete with the speed of light. They blurred into pink nothings, moving so fast I couldn't even feel them.

I turned out of Aiden's neighborhood and sprinted down the main road. Not a single car was anywhere in sight.

I looked back again to see how close they were, and immediately I wished I hadn't.

The Sheet Men had taken on a V formation, like a deranged flock of murderous geese, and the leader was mere feet behind me, the white sheet not flapping an inch.

I wasn't fast enough. He'd catch up to me at any second. I could feel the energy around me changing, and everything becoming hazy. I could sense that he was about to take over my soul and enlist me into his sheet-wearing army. I knew it was over.

Then, with an almighty bang, Kristina materialized in front of me, shimmering into my view as sparks of blue rained down around her. That red glow suddenly vanished, and after I skidded to a stop, I turned to see all the Sheet Men had gone too.

Except now I was in the middle of a busy road, and a truck was speeding right for me.

"Look out!" Kristina cried. She lunged for me, blasting me to the side of the road in another tornado of blue sparks. I rolled into a cold, muddy ditch, tumbling several feet down into a swampy crevasse.

Once I stopped rolling, I lay there for a second, panting hard and shallow, my pink pajamas now covered in mud and bits of grass.

"Baylor," Kristina said, "are you okay? Are you hurt?"

I didn't respond because I hadn't attempted to move any part of my body. The shock of the last couple minutes was still too great. I couldn't feel anything.

"Baylor, say something!"

I squeezed my eyelids together, then looked over at her figure, which was still glowing blue, and said, "Did you see how fast I ran?"

"Baylor! You almost just got killed!"

"I guess you're not a very good guardian angel, then," I said, closing my eyes again, digging my head deeper into the mud.

"You disappeared from my sight! I had no idea where you'd gone, or how. It's never happened before."

"Well, that's comforting," I mumbled.

"I had to cross to the Beyond and get one of my guides to help me break whatever trance you were under."

"That explains the blue," I said, waving my hand in a figure-eight pattern over her body. The shimmer had nearly faded away.

"Yes," she said stiffly. "I don't have that sort of power yet."

"One day," I said. I raised my torso, resting on my elbows to look around. No one had pulled over to check on me. My friends were probably still on Acorn Road, wondering how I'd vanished. I didn't have the energy to find them and make up some lie. "Let's go to the cemetery."

She cocked her head at me, but she nodded. Slowly I rose from the ground and tried to brush myself off, but a thick layer of mud and leaves stuck to my hand. I shook it off and started walking.

As we made our way down the road, I couldn't quite keep the spirits tuned out. It was just like listening to the radio and having static come in and disrupt a song. Every few seconds I'd suddenly see ghosts speeding down the highway at sixty miles an hour, surrounding the cars, and then they'd disappear.

The cemetery was only a ten-minute walk, but in my current state it took double that time. We walked in silence. Once we'd reached Woodland Cemetery, I threw myself over the fence that divided it from the road, and landed on the soft grass with a gentle thud.

I let out a big breath as a feeling of relief washed over me. I was in my sanctuary, and I felt safe. It didn't matter that the spirits kept flickering in and out. I was now in the one place where none of them would be.

I walked aimlessly for a little bit, passing by several unfamiliar stones, until I finally spotted the big spruce tree next to the little road that cut through the cemetery.

From there I followed the road for a bit, looking for the tombstone topped by a cherubic angel with a chipped wing. Turning left, I counted seven markers until I got to the one I wanted.

When I was eleven, one of my classmates died in a horrific car accident, the kind where they had to bring in dental records to identify the bodies. His name was Tommy Thorne, and though he wasn't a good friend of mine, he was still someone I had seen nearly every day for almost my entire life.

I got to know him better after he died, after passing on a couple of messages to Tommy's father, from both his son and his wife. Since then, whenever I visited the cemetery, I always found myself back at his grave.

The dark-gray stone was etched with his name, the words BELOVED SON underneath. I had traced my fingers through those letters so many times. It was fascinating to me that he had been in the physical world, eating a bowl of cereal for breakfast and then picking out his favorite shirt to wear for the trip to the mall with his mom, not suspecting a thing, totally unaware that his life was going to end. One second he was here, and the next he was there, on the other side, in the place where only I could still see him.

Tonight I wasn't going to say hi. I didn't want to talk to anyone except for Kristina. But I made sure to send over some positive vibes through the mental barrier that separated my sanity from all the roaming souls and spirits, just to let him know I was thinking of him.

I had other things on my mind, though. Bigger, scarier things.

Namely, the fact that my sister kept being forced away by a silent, creepy man covered in a white sheet who had apparently recruited many more demons to help him . . . help him what? Kill me? Attack me? Scare me? Send me a message?

I had no idea why any of it was happening. A simple note or a few quick words would have been a tremendous help, but I got nothing. So I sat there in my dirty Halloween costume, my back against Tommy's grave, and wondered aloud to Kristina all those thoughts.

"It's so random," I said. "I have nothing to go on. It's like I'm being attacked for no reason."

Kristina nodded. "It doesn't make sense."

"Didn't you say my 'protection' had been amped up? What happened?"

"If there was really a hundred of them chasing after you, the extra protection probably didn't help much. These are evil beings, Baylor. They're infiltrating our defenses in ways I can't understand, and it definitely doesn't help that I can't get a look at them see what we're dealing with."

"Then I need to fight back, Kristina," I said. "What can I do?"

She stared at me for several seconds and began to pace.

"First things first, you need to begin surrounding yourself with light every hour. Twice a day clearly isn't enough. Carry a candle and set an alarm to remember to light it. We'll keep several candles lit at night, too."

"Great. More candles. Got it," I said, picking at the grass. "I'm not going to lie, Kristina, I'm getting a lit bit tired of having to rely on freaking candles. There's got to be a more powerful weapon I can use, maybe something that's actually a weapon and not what kids blow out on their birthdays after making a wish that won't come true."

She stopped moving and shot me a look. "Candles are fine for now," she said tersely.

"So there is something else!" My eyes narrowed into slits. "You've been keeping it from me!"

"You know the drill, Baylor," she said, pacing again. "We're not ready yet."

I rolled my eyes. Of course.

"Plus, I want to see if the disturbances will continue once Halloween is over."

It was a good point. In just a few hours the costumes would be peeled off and tossed away by everyone in the city, and the negative energy would begin to fade—not all at once, of course, but it wouldn't be maxing out at its current wattage.

"So we'll wait," I said. "I'll layer myself with plenty of light, and we'll hope that the visits stop now that this terrible day is ending."

"I think that'll do for now," she said, nodding. "And if it doesn't, we'll come up with a plan."

I smiled grimly. "Tiki torches?"

A bit later I called my mom and asked her to come pick me up at the cemetery. When she arrived, she got out of her car and ran over to me, looking frantic. She squeezed my face and then sort of attempted a hug, but after she saw how dirty I was, it turned into more of a pat on the back.

"What happened to you?" she asked, shaking mud off her hand.

"It's kind of a long story," I said. "I'll tell you

back at the house so Dad can hear it too."

I spent most of the ride home deflecting concerned texts from Aiden. He wasn't mad or anything, just really confused, since I'd dropped my bag of candy and then disappeared without anyone noticing. He said he'd bring the candy to me on Monday, but he couldn't guarantee there'd be much left, because Mrs. Kirkwood thoroughly enjoyed the spoils of Halloween.

Mom and Dad were not happy once I relayed all the events of the last couple of days.

"That thing was in our house and you didn't bother to mention it until now?" my mom shrieked. She had begun chopping random vegetables midway through the story, even though it was nearly eleven o'clock at night. She'd plowed through two onions, a red bell pepper, and a lumpy sweet potato by the time I finished.

"I didn't know the Sheet Man was going to return," I said. "I thought it was a one-time visitation."

"One-time visitation," she scoffed under her breath. "Till the thing came back with a hundred of his dead little demon friends and made you almost get hit by a semitruck."

My dad sat across from me at the table, his chin

pushed back into his neck, creating four additional chins. He was looking at his hands, and I wasn't sure if he'd heard a word I'd said.

"It was either the truck or a hundred Sheet Men getting their wispy hands on you," Kristina said from her spot at the head of the table. She'd been reminding me of details to add in.

"That's true," I mumbled.

"What'd she say?" Dad asked, looking up suddenly.

"She said it was better to nearly get hit by a truck than to have a hundred of those things finally catch up to me."

My mom threw down her knife, which clanged violently onto the counter, and marched over to me.

"Kristina, I don't know where you are, but you need to do something, okay?" my mom sputtered. "You need to make sure this can't happen again." She looked at me, then quickly turned to stare out the window into the blackness, but not so quickly that I couldn't see the tears welling up. "I've already lost you," she said, her voice cracking. "I can't lose another one."

Kristina's mouth hung open slightly. I had never seen her speechless before. She rose from the table and walked over to Mom. She tried to hug her, but as always, her body just sort of sank in, making them look like Siamese twins.

My mom shivered violently and her shoulders jerked back. "I've never gotten the chills that bad before!"

"Kristina just hugged you," I said.

She shot me a strange look, a mixture of sadness and panic, then hurried back to her cutting board and resumed her violent chopping.

"Well, this has been a stranger night than usual," I said after another minute of silence. Part of me wondered if I should have just kept all this to myself. The stress of hearing this story would do no favors for my dad's rapidly graying hair.

My dad nodded, throwing his hands open. "I don't know what to say, Baylor. I feel so helpless. If those guys wearing sheets were real people, I'd say forget the police and just hunt them down myself. But in this situation . . . I don't know what to do."

"We light candles," I said, smiling sarcastically at Kristina, who stuck her tongue out at me. "And we stay positive."

He attempted to smile, but it resembled that same sort of pained, teeth-baring grimace that he'd worn after finishing his first marathon a couple of years ago. He stood, walked to the hall closet, and pulled out the duffel bag of candles we had stockpiled inside.

"Let's get to work."

We finished protecting the house in less than ten minutes, and afterward I went up to bed while my mom was throwing all the ingredients into a pot to make some veggie chili.

"Might as well," she said. "I won't be sleeping tonight anyway."

In the bathroom I finally peeled off my dirty pink costume and looked at myself in the mirror. Man, I was gross. My entire face was flecked with mud and grass, and everything else ached from the extensive tumbling I'd done off the side of the road.

I took what must have been a thirty-minute shower and then collapsed into my bed.

"Good night, Baylor," said Kristina, who was lit up by the glow of the ten massive candles I'd placed around my room earlier.

"Good night, Kristina," I said, yawning. "Thanks for your help tonight."

"Of course," she said. She hesitated a moment. "I just wanted to say, before I go for the night, that I'm sorry I didn't protect you better."

"It's not your fault," I said, my eyes closed. I secretly wished she'd go.

"I know," she said. "But I still feel like I let you down."

"You didn't," I said lightly, peeking my eyes open. "You did your best."

She looked odd, though, and if I hadn't been so tired, I would have pressed her on the subject. But before I knew it, she'd vanished, and I passed out not five seconds later.

Tubas may cause bodily harm. Proceed with caution.

I SPENT ALL SUNDAY IN BED, MY BODY POSI-tively on fire from the tumble the night before, but between the frequent bowls of veggie chili delivered by my mother and the hours of TV that I mindlessly watched, I began to feel somewhat better.

Monday, however, was dreadful. I could barely walk, and I'd completely forgotten about a science quiz I needed to study for.

"What kind of a ridiculous jerk gives a quiz the Monday after Halloween weekend?" I mumbled to Kristina on my way to the next class. "And you wouldn't even help me out with any of the answers. I bombed that so bad."

"You know I can't help you, Baylor!" Kristina said. "We've been over this maybe a million times."

"It wouldn't hurt anyone to help me out a little bit."

"That's what you think," she said ominously.

I ignored her comment and marched on, somehow getting through the day and looking forward to band practice. I thought about skipping it, but since I'd missed Thursday, I felt like I had to go.

I'd started playing the tuba on a whim a few years ago. I had tried out for soccer because I liked how much I got to run, but I quit during my first game. There were far too many ghosts on the field, and I could barely tell who was a player and who was dead. Twenty minutes in I stomped off the field and told my parents I couldn't play anymore.

Playing the tuba, on the other hand, has become my saving grace. Whereas running around in soccer allowed my mind to be too receptive to all the spirits around me, playing the tuba forces me to concentrate on the music. The sound helps block out all the chatter. After a few minutes of staring at sheet music, I almost transform into someone who can't talk to dead people. I'd never admit this to Kristina, but it's nice to feel truly alone, even if it's only for a little bit.

Four years later, and I'm still playing the tuba. I've learned to play the guitar and the piano, too, but I prefer the tuba. There's something about wrapping that instrument around my body and blasting music out of it that makes me feel like I'm in my own little world with no one to bother me.

The band instructor, Mr. Gilbert, was a short man with long, curly red hair. He wore a tie every single day, and today it was decked out in little Snoopy drawings.

"Looking good, Mr. G.," I said as I limped into the giant room. There were a bunch of skylights that lined the ceiling, casting a dull, wintry light over the room, and flimsy blue soundproofing material covered every wall.

"Glad to see you're feeling better, Baylor," he said, "though that limp doesn't look too great."

"Took a nasty spill on Halloween," I said. "Collecting free candy is hard work."

He raised an eyebrow at me. "Children," he said, shaking his head and smiling.

I got my tuba from the instrument closet and said hey to Aiden before taking my place in the semicircle of chairs. He'd given me the surprisingly full bag of Halloween candy at lunch.

"I had to hide it from my mom in my dirty-clothes

hamper," he'd said. "You know how she gets." I'd searched for some Twix while trying not to think about my candy languishing next to Aiden's filthy underwear for two days.

As he unpacked another pepperoni-and-mustard sandwich, he'd asked, "So where'd you disappear to, anyway? Why'd you drop all your candy?"

I'd sort of frowned at him and said, "Believe me, Aiden, you do *not* want to know." He'd widened his eyes and didn't ask anything else about it.

Today we were prepping for the parade that would take place downtown on Main Street the weekend before Thanksgiving. We'd be near the end of the parade, and Mr. G. felt confident that tackling a Christmas medley would set the mood for the holiday season.

"A classic medley!" he said. "Something we've never done before but that's been done to death by everyone else in America."

"Then why are we doing it, if it's been done before?" asked one of the saxophonists.

"Because we live in Keene, New Hampshire," he said slowly. "Our town loves anything festive."

It was true. Our town was infamous for its huge pumpkin festival, trying to break a Guinness world record for the most jack-o'-lanterns lit at once, and at Christmastime the downtown square transformed into a majestic, brightly lit wonderland.

Mr. G. passed out the sheet music and asked us to play through everything once so he could gauge what needed the most work. We started with a rough rendition of "Jingle Bells," followed by "The Little Drummer Boy," and finally finished with an interesting mash-up of "Silent Night" and "All I Want for Christmas Is You."

We sounded so bad I wasn't sure what Mr. G. would think needed the most fine-tuning, and he looked just as perplexed. He'd winced with every wrong note and disharmonious chord, which meant his flowing hair had whipped around nearly nonstop for ten minutes.

He decided to start with the mash-up: If it wasn't going to work, he wanted to know fairly early so that we could practice something entirely different.

After running through it four times, I started to get a little bored. Considering "Silent Night" was a peaceful, almost relaxing song, the tuba didn't have much of a place. I began to sing the lyrics in my head, closing my eyes and letting the positive energy of the Christmas music overcome me. Christmas was the one time of year when I never had any trouble with ghosts.

Silent night! Holy night!
All is calm, all is bright
Round yon Virgin Mother and Child.
Holy Infant, so tender and mild,
Sleep in heavenly peace,
Sleep in heavenly peace.

When we had to stop and do it a fifth time, I sighed and looked at Aiden, who was visibly sweating. He was in the opposite situation from me: The flute was prominently featured.

By now even I could tell the mash-up wasn't going to work. How on earth would Mariah Carey lyrics fit in there?

"One, two, three . . . ," Mr. G. called out, and I reclined back, closed my eyes, and began to recite the lyrics in my head once more.

Silent night! Holy night!
All is calm . . .

The music stopped all at once. I opened my eyes to see what had happened, but I was alone in the room.

Except I wasn't alone—he was there.

The Sheet Man was standing in the middle of the semicircle, staring at me. He hadn't brought his cronies this time. It was just him and me, and by this point I'd had enough.

"What do you want?" I said, standing up with my tuba. "Say something or stop bothering me."

He didn't say a word, but the sheet, which had remained so still before, began to whip violently, like a tornado had just entered the room. It raised higher a bit, and for the first time I caught a good glimpse of his shoes: some kind of brown leather with an odd, shiny buckle on top.

I couldn't see them for more than a second or two, though, because once that nonexistent wind started blowing, I began to feel light-headed. So light-headed that I began to question how I was still standing, how I had gotten to this room, how I was still alive even.

It felt like he was sucking all the energy out of me.

"Stop," I said, clasping my tuba for support, forgetting I was the one supporting it in the first place. "Stop!"

It did stop, and I found myself swaying back in the middle of the band room full of my friends, all of whom had stopped playing and were turned my way, their mouths agape in horror. But it was too late. It felt like all the blood had left my body, and before I could do anything else, I went crashing to the floor.

Ghosts, just like living people, can be quite rude.

DURING THOSE FIRST CONFUSED SECONDS after I came to, I had no idea where I was, what the time was, why there was a huge crowd of people around me, and why my head hurt so much.

"Finally, he's up," said a squat woman to my left. She had brown hair that was twisted into a bun on her head, and she looked at me like she was scolding a naughty child. "We've been waiting for hours."

"What took so long?" said a gruff bald man in a black biker vest, tattoos covering his bare arms. "It was just a tuba."

"Move over!" a familiar voice said. "Get out of the way!"

Kristina emerged from behind a large, frowning woman who was wearing a muumuu.

"Baylor!" she said. "How's your head?"

"Not good," I said, trying to lift my arm from the stiff hospital bed but getting caught in a jungle of wires.

"Your head is covered with electrodes," she said. "Monitoring for a concussion."

"Great," I moaned. "Where are Mom and Dad?"

"Outside talking to the doctor."

"Never mind your parents, they're fine," said the first woman. "I need you to tell my daughter that her husband is a scumbag. She's right down the hall."

"Enough with this demon dung!" Kristina said, enraged. She turned and pointed her finger at the woman.

"Oh no," the woman said as a blue wave of light surrounded her body before she vanished.

"Wow," I said. "I didn't know you could do that."

"Neither did we," said the bald biker guy, taking a step back.

"I've been developing some new tricks with my spirit guides the last few days," Kristina said, flexing her fingers. "That felt weird."

"How so?" I asked. It was funny to hear Kristina describe things because she couldn't actually touch anything in the physical world and had no true reference.

"It felt hot, like whenever you get into the car in the summer and all you do is shift around and complain about how it takes forever to cool down."

"I don't do that!"

"My goal is to find this Sheet Man who keeps making an appearance and zap him into the next universe," she said, ignoring my denial.

"Did you just zap that woman into some weird universe?" I asked.

"No, I just made her go away," she said, shrugging. "She was being rude."

"Does this mean he's not going to deliver messages right now?" asked the woman in the muumuu.

"Obviously," Kristina snapped. "How could he? He's confined to his bed."

"He could call a nurse and have her deliver the messages room to room."

The crowd chimed in with their approval.

"That works!"

"He's not doing anything else!"

"My son needs to know he's dating a thief!"

"No!" Kristina said firmly. "The only reason

he can see you right now is because he can't focus enough to tune you out. Just because he's in the hospital doesn't mean he's your slave."

"It would be a nice thing, helping us," said the tattooed man.

"You know what would be really nice?" Kristina said, her voice seeped with venom. "It would be so nice if all of you would leave the room and come back at a more appropriate time. Our parents are coming back in a few seconds anyway."

"This isn't fair."

"Our families need to hear these things. That's what he's here for."

"He's seriously dating a thief! She steals raw meats from the grocery store! Who does that?"

"I never said I wouldn't help you," I said as they all backed out of the room in one smooth motion, like a vacuum was sucking them out. I wasn't sure if that was part of Kristina's new powers or if it was of their own accord. "I'm just not going to right now."

As the last spirits groaned their way out of the room, I noticed a doctor standing near the door, my parents next to him. He was probably in his late thirties, and he didn't look happy at all.

"You can't be serious," he said, turning to my parents. "I'm supposed to listen to him talk to an empty room for minutes on end and accept that nothing is wrong with his brain? You are both out of your minds."

"He does this all the time," my dad said in the same light, singsong voice he used with Ella. "It's perfectly normal."

"Talks to ghosts," the doctor mumbled, writing something on my chart. "Outrageous. The kid is hallucinating."

I shot a look at Kristina, and a moment later two old women were standing next to her.

"Thank you for letting us back in," the first one said. She was tall and had that long silver hair only a few old ladies can really pull off, though I wasn't so sure she was one of them.

"Dean's going through a hard time right now," the second one said. Her hair was the correct length, and she had a huge, gleaming smile that would have made me smile if the nerves in my face hadn't been screaming in agony right then. "His brother, Dillon, has a rare form of lung cancer. He only started smoking after he saw Dean do it when they were younger, but Dillon could never kick the habit after Dean did."

"He needs to let go of his guilt!" the one with long hair said. "Dillon is a grown man and made his choices. Dean didn't force a cigarette into his brother's mouth the first time he tried it, and he didn't force-feed every single one to him for twenty years, either."

I nodded to each of them and said, "Thank you," which made the doctor scoff and throw up his hands.

"This is ridiculous," he said.

"Uh, Dean? Can I call you Dean?" I asked, not leaving him any time to answer. "It's what your grandmas called you."

His eyes widened. "My grandmas?"

"They know you're in a bad place because of Dillon's cancer, but they want you to let go of the guilt associated with it."

He dropped the chart. "Who did you hear talking about this? Was it Marta? I'm going to have her fired. I knew I couldn't trust her."

"No! Don't fire Marta, I don't even know who that is," I said. "Your grandmas are standing right there." I pointed to the space to my left, next to a silver cart. He looked over, but of course he saw nothing.

"He was always so stubborn," the short-haired grandma said, laughing.

"I'll keep trying," I said under my breath. "Dean, Dillon may have lung cancer, but you didn't give it to him. You're not responsible for it."

"Why are you playing this trick on me?" the doctor

said. I'm sure his aura was bloodred with fury. "This is a very personal subject."

"I'm not tricking you at all. One of your grandmas has long hair and talks with a very proper accent, almost like she's British, but I know she's not. The other one has short hair and doesn't stop smiling. She's also way shorter than the other one."

Dean's hands started shaking as he searched the empty space where they stood beaming at him.

"Mention the little Easter chick he got as a child that lasted maybe five minutes before the dog got it," the long-haired grandma said. "That should do the trick."

Once I repeated that back to Dean, he left the room, still looking incredibly annoyed, and said he would return in a few minutes. The grandmas followed him out.

"Well, that was awkward," my mom said, plopping into the armchair next to my bed. "We mentioned to him that you might do that, just so he wouldn't think there was anything wrong with you if you started, you know, communicating with . . . them."

My dad wasn't looking at me because he was wiping away tears from his eyes. Ever since his father crossed over, he became emotional whenever he witnessed me delivering a message of any kind.

"What happened, Baylor?" my mom said, massaging

my right hand. "You've never passed out like that before. Were you feeling sick?" She spoke in a cheerful voice that was so obviously fake I couldn't let her continue for a second longer.

"It was the Sheet Man," I said. "He made an appearance during band practice, and this time I stood up to him. Except that after I stood up, I lost all my energy and the tuba fell on me. I knew I should have taken up the flute."

I grimaced at the memory.

"Oh my God," she said, her smile melting, the cheerful tone eliminated. "I knew it."

"The candles didn't work?" Dad asked.

"I guess not," I said. "Kristina is even learning some new powers, and with all that, he still got through to me."

"Isn't there a ghost police or something that can help you?" Mom's voice was raised, exasperated. "This guy needs to leave you alone! Oh God, I don't ever want to die, it's just chaos over there, Baylor."

"Calm down," I said. "If he wanted to hurt me, he would have already."

"Baylor, do you not see where you are right now?" she asked, her voice going up to an unsustainable octave. "You're lying in a hospital bed with your head all wrapped up!"

"Okay, maybe that wasn't the best choice of words," I said, "but I sort of caused this on my own."

"It's working," she said, panicked, turning to my dad. "That thing, it's working its evil powers on him already. He's getting Stockholm syndrome, but for ghosts! Stocksoul syndrome!" She turned back to me, her eyes moving like crazy over my face. "Snap out of it, Baylor!" She snapped both of her hands in my face. "That thing is dangerous! It wants to hurt you."

Kristina started laughing hysterically, and even I had to focus really hard to keep my mouth from twitching.

"Mom, you're overreacting," I said. "I promise you, I don't have Stocksoul syndrome. I'm just trying to figure out what's going on."

The concern remained in her eyes.

"I'll be watching you like a hawk, Baylor Bosco," she said. "Any sign of any of the sheet craziness, and I'm getting the holy water out."

8

Not all healing messages are created equal.

DOCTOR DEAN EVENTUALLY RECOVERED and came back into the room. He made no mention of my messages, but he didn't keep calling me crazy, either, so I guessed he believed me. He told me I had to stay overnight for observation, but that I was most likely fine. I just got my "bell rung" really good, as he said, causing my father to interject with, "More like he got his tuba blown." No one laughed.

I managed to persuade my mom not to spend the night. At first she flat-out refused to listen to me, saying the evil spirits were making me say that and it was all the more reason for her to stay, but I managed to turn that thinking around on her, saying that the hospital was filled with spirits that would play tricks on her, keep her up all night, and make her think she was going insane.

I knew I'd hit the nail on the head when I said the word "insane," because her eyes got really wide and it was clear she was starting to feel that way. She'd been pacing around the room nonstop and blurting out nonsensical things about sheets, and I made a pact with myself not to mention the Sheet Man to her anymore. The fewer details, the better.

It took a while, but she finally agreed to leave with my dad, which was exactly what I wanted, because Kristina and I needed time to talk.

"Kristina, he was wearing shoes," I said once they'd left. I'd decided to leave out that detail earlier in case my mom ran home and lit all our shoes on fire. "He showed them to me in the band room. They looked nice. Brown, leather, had some sort of fancy buckle on top of each one."

"It had shoes on?" she said incredulously. "Wow. I've never heard of a demon that wears brown loafers."

"That's the thing, Kristina: How do we know it's a demon? What if it's something else? What if it's someone who needs help?"

"Baylor," she said slowly, as if I were the dumbest person on Earth. "I understand that you think seeing shoes is a good thing in this situation, but let me remind you that neither I nor my spirit guides can control this thing. We can't be in the same space as it. I don't care if it was wearing gold shoes and dancing to jazz music, if I can't be in the same space as it, that's bad. Very bad."

I swallowed. "All right. They're evil shoes, then."

She nodded. "Good twin."

But in the back of my mind I still thought I was right.

"Aiden was here with his mom, by the way," Kristina said. "You were still passed out, so Mom and Dad told them to go home, because they didn't know how long it would be before you woke up." She eyed me with a sly grin. "Though I think the real reason was that Mrs. Kirkwood was sobbing uncontrollably and making everyone feel uncomfortable."

I chuckled and grabbed my phone. Twenty-seven texts from Aiden, three from J, one from Bobby, and a few more from some other friends. Aiden's were mainly a steady stream of panicked thoughts.

AIDEN: ARE YOU OK!?!?!?!?!?!?!?!?!

AIDEN: That tuba was SO heavy!

AIDEN: FREAKING OUT DUDE!!!!!

**AIDEN: Mom's baking everything for you.
Jack's not allergic to peanuts anymore, right?**

**AIDEN: Can't wait to reenact Mr. G's reaction to
your fall!**

I texted back.

**BAYLOR: Finally awake. Have to spend night
at hospital. Getting monitored for a concussion.
Hopefully my tuba career isn't over.**

Aiden responded almost immediately, first with a
million exclamation points, then with

**AIDEN: Glad you're alive!! Eating mom's cookies,
really good!**

"Should we go deliver some messages?" I asked, setting my phone down. "Might as well. If there's one
place to offer some healing guidance, I guess it's here."

"Okay, but you're not telling that guy that his girl-
friend is a thief."

"She is, though!" that same earnest voice echoed

yet again. The man who'd said it materialized before us. He had a case of male-pattern baldness so severe that even a trip to the Beyond couldn't fix it. "He's thinking about marrying her, but it's only a matter of time before that klepto gets caught with five pounds of raw chicken stuffed in her underwear."

I frowned. "Well, okay, maybe I'll just talk to him first and feel out the situation."

Kristina shook her head. "That isn't a healing message, Baylor, you don't need to pass it on."

"Kristina, we're in a hospital filled with hundreds of sick people and all their dead relatives, and I can't tune them out right now. If I get picky about which messages to deliver, we're going to have a bunch of annoying ghosts on our hands, and you're going to be zapping them away all night with your new blue magic."

"I wish I could sigh," she said, shaking her head. "This would have been the perfect time for one."

The next couple of hours were the most hectic I'd ever experienced. Ghosts swarmed me: I was a flame, and they were moths.

I had to stop saying my introductory sentence to people because I had too many messages to deliver. Floor after floor, room after room, person after person, I was chased by loved ones and spouted off as many messages as I could breathe, each one as nonsensical as the next, but filled with meaning for the receiver.

"Ma'am, don't go visit her, your husband says she's not worth your time, especially since you're in the hospital and it could be limited."

"She was right about the first one, sir. I don't know who the 'she' is or what the 'one' is, though—sorry, that's all your sister told me to say."

"You need to make the trip. Huh? Oh, sorry, you need to make the trip soon, like tomorrow. I know you're in the hospital. Sorry, I'm just delivering the message from your mom."

"I'm supposed to mention a green duck to you. That's all they want me to say. I know it's weird, but your grandparents are the ones who said it, not me."

Toward the end of my time walking the halls, the messages were thinning out, so I was able to stop and chat a little bit more. As I passed by one room, I noticed a little boy staring intensely at the woman resting on the hospital bed.

I walked in slowly and knelt down next to him.

"Hey there, buddy," I said. "My name's Baylor, and if you want to say something to your grandma, I can help you out."

He turned to me, his eyes full of concern. "How'd you know she's my grandma?"

That was a tough question for me to answer. The ghosts don't need to tell me. Sort of like how Kristina can show me auras, I can sense the energy running between the loved ones. I can tell right away what sort of relationship people shared, and continue to share.

"What's your name?" I asked.

"Louie."

"Well, Louie, I guess I just know certain things," I said.

"Can I help you with something?" the woman in the bed asked. She had a shock of tidy white hair, which didn't move an inch as she leaned over the side of her bed to watch me.

"Hi there," I said, standing up. "My name is Baylor Bosco, and I can communicate with people who've crossed over."

"You *what*?" Her voice quivered.

"Um, I can talk to dead people."

She shook her head, her mouth slightly open. "My drugs are really messing with my head right now." She shut her eyes tight, clenching her face together like she was bracing for a punch. Then she opened them again, looking disappointed to see me still standing there.

"Grandma's funny," Louie said, smiling sadly.

I smiled at him and looked back at his grandma, whose face had contorted into a pained expression. "I'm too afraid to ask why you keep looking down at that one spot."

"What's your name, ma'am?"

"Elmira," she said. "Elmira Ashworth."

"Elmira, your grandson Louie is here." He'd walked to the bed and peered over the foot of it, his eyes just barely peeking over the edge. "He's wearing a blue baseball hat and uniform. All that's missing is a glove."

She didn't say anything. She just looked at me, terrified.

"Louie, do you want me to tell your grandma anything?"

He seemed just as upset as his grandma was. I bent down again to talk to him quietly.

"Hey, buddy, it's okay," I said. "You don't have to say anything if you don't want to."

Elmira clenched her covers. "He doesn't want to talk to me," she said in a small, tense voice. "He's mad at me."

Louie nodded.

"Uhh," I said awkwardly. "Yeah, he's nodding."

She reached for the tissue box on the Formica

table next to her bed, speaking in a calm, controlled voice that made me think she was seconds away from totally losing it. "It's my fault he's dead. I'm such a careful driver. I always check the road three times to make sure everything's clear before I go at a green light. And that day . . . this guy came out of nowhere."

"That's not why I'm mad," Louie said quickly.

"He's not mad about that," I said just as quickly, hoping to staunch her crying.

"He's not?" she asked, horrified. "What else is there?"

"Tell her I'm mad that she stopped going to the park. I'm mad that she stopped playing cards with her friends and going dancing. I'm mad that a nice old man asked her to dinner last month and she said no." He turned to me, his eyes bulging. "I'm mad that she's using me as an excuse to stop living."

I paused for a moment, trying to figure out if there was a way to deliver his message that wouldn't totally crush her soul. Maybe if I just sounded casual enough . . .

If I thought I was phrasing my words gently, Elmira's reaction immediately tipped me off that I didn't do a good enough job. She wailed, profusely, for ten minutes, doing her best impression of a hungry newborn baby. Four times I had to turn the nurses away with some vague excuse.

"This is the worst message I've ever given," I said to Kristina out of the corner of my mouth.

"Just wait," Kristina said.

Louie's anger had reconstituted itself as concern after he saw his grandma's reaction, and he'd climbed into bed next to her. Several times she'd massaged the spot on her arm where his head was touching.

Finally, once her sobs had sputtered out, she caught her breath and looked at me.

"Where is he?" she said. "I want to look at him for a moment. Or I want him to look right at me."

"He's right next to you," I said. "He's the reason why your arm's been tingling."

She gasped. "Is that so?"

She looked down at the nothing beside her, the nothing that used to be her everything, and she smiled.

"Louie, I'm sorry," she said. "You're right. I've been dishonoring your memory by sulking at home for the last year. This guilt, though, it's just . . . so unlike anything I've felt. I can't escape it."

"Tell her it wasn't her fault. She was taking me to get ice cream at the park that day. She's the best grandma ever."

When I repeated his words, Elmira smiled, still trying to spot her grandson next to her. "It was going to be such a good day. You and your orangesicles."

"You need to have more of those good days, Grandma! Don't think of me and be sad. Think of me and be happy about all the memories we made."

As I said that to her, she seemed in danger of howling again, but she held it together.

"I love you," Louie said. And with his message delivered, he faded away.

"He's gone," I said. "But the last thing he said was 'I love you.'"

"I know," she said. "I could feel it."

"Well, that was intense," I said. "Sorry, I didn't mean to upset you. That happens sometimes with these messages."

"No, no, are you kidding?" she said. "Come here and give me a hug, Baylor Bosco."

As I hugged Elmira, a horrible sensation came over me and, like I'd touched a hot pan, I shot away from her, a distant hiss penetrating my ears.

"Did you hear that?" I asked Kristina.

Eyebrows raised, she shook her head no.

"Hear what?" Elmira asked.

"I just heard and felt something . . . odd," I said. "Odd" was far too positive a word, but I didn't want to upset her again. "It was just a whisper, though. It said, 'You left me,' and it made me want to vomit."

That was all it took for the color and joy she'd just gained to drain from her face. She started fidgeting with a ring on her right middle finger.

"Do you know who that was?" I asked.

"I think you'd better go," she said icily, staring at the beige curtain.

"Elmira, who was that?"

"Someone . . . from a long time ago."

"Someone bad?"

She stiffened but didn't say anything else, so I apologized and left the room.

"What was that?" I asked, walking quickly back to my room.

"I didn't hear or feel anything, Baylor," Kristina said. She sounded worried, and when Kristina worries, I panic.

"Kristina, whatever it was, it was bad. How did an evil spirit just communicate with me?"

"I don't know."

"The Sheet Man just stares at me with his weird black eyes, but he never says anything, and he never actually touched me. But whatever just happened, that was new. And it's not good, especially since Halloween's over." We entered my room and I shut the door. "It's not just the Sheet Man anymore. They're all starting to break the barrier, aren't they?"

She pursed her lips. "That's the last straw. Tonight I'm bringing in reinforcements."

Not all ghosts
stick around. ☹

AS IF I WEREN'T ALREADY FREAKED OUT enough, the next morning I woke up to discover two horrible things.

First, I didn't have a candle. Candles weren't allowed in hospitals, according to some nurse with an attitude problem, because they were a fire hazard.

"Not having a candle is a hazard to my life," I replied. "Do you want me to die? You need to find me a candle right now."

"You're not getting a candle," she said flatly, and walked out.

Second, Kristina was nowhere to be found. When I go to bed, she goes somewhere in the Beyond to learn, to update her spirit guides, to ask for advice, to socialize (I assume), and essentially to become a better ghost, all while loosely monitoring my dreams and making sure no one's attacking me in my sleep.

When I wake up, she's always there. It was completely and incontrovertibly unlike her to be absent.

Except for that brief period when she was gone for a while.

Just before I turned eight, I woke up early one day to find my grandpa sitting at the kitchen table. He lived out of town, and my parents hadn't told me he was visiting from Ohio. I ran over to him in my Ninja Turtle pajamas and gave him the biggest hug I knew how.

At least, I tried to hug him. Ghosts may not be transparent, but they're definitely not solid.

"Hey there, Baylor, my buddy boy," he said, kneeling down. "Things are a bit different now, huh?"

I backed away, not sure what to do or how to react. I looked at Kristina, who seemed just as confused. Until then I'd never interacted with anyone on the other side except for Kristina, and as far as I knew, Kristina hadn't either.

Grandpa smiled, but in a strained way that looked more like a frown.

"You don't need to be sad or scared, Baylor. It's just me."

In my head I definitely wasn't sad or scared. I'd been putting things together. Grandpa had lived far away when he was alive, but now he was dead. And I could communicate with ghosts. So that meant I'd get to see him all the time now. This was great news!

I told him so and then said, "I'm hungry. Want to watch me eat breakfast?"

Grandpa definitely wasn't reacting the way I'd expected. He looked heartbroken. "I . . . I came to say good-bye, kiddo," he said. "I just want you to know how much I love you. And your parents and brother, too."

"Huh?"

"And there's something else, too." He reached out to Kristina, beaming. "My granddaughter. My beautiful granddaughter." He stroked her face like it was the first time he'd seen her. . . . It *was* the first time. "You get to come with me for a little while."

"I do?"

"You do," he said, nodding. "It's time for you to learn some things in the Beyond. You just needed someone to show you how to get there."

Kristina shot me a look of panic, and I shot her the exact same one back, and before I knew it, he took her hand and held tight.

"She'll be back soon, Baylor," he said. "I promise."

And with that, both of them walked forward and disappeared. They were gone. It was just me standing alone in the empty kitchen, stunned.

That's when I started crying. I ran to my parents' room, and I sobbed to them about how Grandpa had taken Kristina to somewhere else and I couldn't see them anymore.

The kicker, of course, was that my dad didn't know his father had passed away yet. Both of them shot up in bed and looked at me, each distinctly terrified of the answer to their next question.

"Which grandpa was it, Baylor?"

"Grandpa Bosco," I whimpered, and I watched my dad fall apart in bed. I didn't get why he was so upset, and frankly, I was more upset that he was crying harder than I was and getting all the attention from my mom.

"He said to tell you he loves me and you and Mom and Jack," I said, trying to return the focus to my problem, but it only seemed to make him feel worse. "Then he grabbed Kristina, and they both left!"

"Honey, I'm sorry they're gone, but your father is *very* sad right now," my mom said with quiet exasperation, clutching my dad's head during his heaving.

"Mom, I'm sad too!" I cried. "What am I going to do without Kristina?"

That was a tough year for everyone. Just as my father mourned his father, I mourned the loss of my sister. Strangely enough, it was the first time I began to understand death.

The questions. The permanency. The heartache.

It took her 367 days to come back. I had never felt so lonely, and now that she was gone for the first time in years, a small but very distinct part of me began to panic.

Kristina had apparently learned a lot about her role in my life during our year apart. Whenever we mention that year, she always laughs because it didn't feel that long to her. To her it seemed like a long day of classes.

But she always emphasizes the *long* part. She's told me only bits and pieces—what she's allowed to tell me so far—but one thing she learned is that she was never meant to be alive. Kristina was always meant to be my companion in life, just as I was always meant to be able to communicate with dead people. We were slotted to be a two-person team from the very beginning, and maybe even before then. I was to be the message giver, and she was to be a sort of spirit manager—a buffer between the physical world and the Beyond.

Before she disappeared for that year, I could see ghosts, but I never communicated with them, nor could I block them out. Even during that year she was gone, the ghosts kept their distance, though I could still see and hear them. When she got back from the Beyond, she seemed different—older and more confident—and she told me it was time to start relaying messages to allow people to heal.

Then the floodgates opened. The ghosts that had always hovered nearby suddenly swarmed me, drowning me with their nonstop chatter, desperate pleas, and sometimes scary images.

Kristina helped me out immensely. Whenever I had a problem, she was there. She was the one who came up with my daily routine. Once I started lighting my candle every morning to surround myself with light and positivity, talking to spirits became a bit easier.

At first my mom refused to buy me a candle and my own lighter. I was much too young to be playing with fire, she'd say. But after my dad reminded her that I was also too young to deal with talking to dead people, she gave in.

But then she wouldn't let me keep the candle in my room, or let me light it. She didn't understand why it was so important. But who could expect her to? How was she supposed to know that, without that positive energy, I could see menacing phantoms with creepy, glowing green eyes circling the house? How was she supposed to know that the light kept away the negative spirits who had left unfinished business on Earth? Heck, how was I supposed to know that, without Kristina guiding me?

When I tried explaining it to my mom, she threw me into the car and drove to the community church, where she made the reverend bless me with some sort of spiritual protection prayer. It actually helped a little bit, but Kristina told me that any prayers from any person of any faith were always good.

Afterward Mom explained my gift to Reverend Henry, and he became the first person outside of my family to know what I could do. I think my mom had expected him to deny it, to refute her claim, but he didn't. Instead he knelt down beside me and whispered, "You have a very special gift, Baylor. Use it wisely. I'm always here if you need help."

After that my mom started asking me every day how Kristina was doing.

"Is she . . . is she happy?" she'd ask, usually while

fidgeting with my lunch box before school. I'd look over at Kristina, who would nod ferociously in her delight over our mom's change of heart.

"She's nodding yes," I'd say.

My mom would sigh, her shoulders sinking low. "Good, good. I'm glad to hear that."

But if my mom asked about her today, what would I say? That she had been ghostnapped? That she wasn't by my side for the first time in more than four years and I was trying not to panic?

Unlike with a missing breathing person, no one could help me find a missing ghost. It was just me, with absolutely no resources except to ask other random ghosts if they'd seen the girl version of me walking around.

Of course, they all said no.

My mind jumped to all sorts of conclusions, ranging from *She got lost on the way back from the Beyond and is in some undiscovered universe* to *The Sheet Man is holding her hostage, and it's up to me to track them down.*

The only consolation of that morning was that I was so distracted by the poking doctors and prodding nurses and pestering parents that forgetting to panic wasn't so hard. By the time I was discharged, when my dad had already left for work and my mom was waiting with Ella to take me home, I had a plan.

"We need to make a pit stop before home," I said gravely.

"We do?" my mom asked.

"Don't worry. You'll appreciate this particular stop."

Demon shoes are never in style.

FIFTEEN MINUTES LATER WE WERE AT THE community church. I needed some sort of higher-power blessing this morning, and if I didn't have Kristina or my candles, Reverend Henry was the next-best thing. Plus, it had been a while since he had done any protections on me, and I secretly hoped that the barrier between me and the spirits had become more malleable because his auxiliary protections had lapsed.

Leaving my mom in a pew with Ella, I found Reverend Henry back in his office, talking to some-one on the phone.

He grinned when he saw me and held up his finger.

"Yes, I know that's how you're feeling right now, but you'll soon see that it's worth it. I promise you."

He made a funny face and tapped his thumb rapidly against his fingers, the universal sign for *Yada, yada, yada, this broad won't shut up.*

A couple of minutes later he hung up the phone and widened his eyes to ghost size.

"Women, I tell ya!" he said jokingly. "My daughter, calling from her dorm room and panicked that she picked the wrong college to attend."

"She's somewhere in Texas, right?"

"Yep. In Austin. She thinks it's too far away, she misses home and family and proper seasons, she thinks she should transfer, and so on and so forth. You know, normal teenager stuff." He leaned back in his seat. "But enough about my daughter. What brings you here, Baylor? Shouldn't you be in school right now?"

"Things aren't too great, Rev," I said, before launching into the events of the previous few days.

"And I just left the hospital and came directly here," I finished. "Help me."

"That is some story, Baylor," he said slowly. "Wow. Well, first things first, you didn't get to do your routine today, so let's light some candles."

Four candles and a hundred deep breaths later I felt the calmest I'd felt all morning.

"Now," he said, returning to his chair, "maybe you'll have some peace of mind to think. I'm sure Kristina will return soon too. I guess the good thing about her being dead already is that you don't have to involve police."

"Except that when she goes missing, there's no one to help me at all."

"True," he said, lifting his legs up and crossing his feet on his desk. "But as you said, she's probably in the Beyond learning some more ways to protect you. It's likely just taking a while, since you both have never faced anything like this before."

He kept talking, but I'd stopped paying attention because I'd noticed his shoes, and a deep chill ran down my back.

"Reverend," I said, interrupting him, my eyes fixated on his feet. "Where did you get those shoes?"

"These?" He laughed. "Believe it or not, they're actually from a big donation we got from some out-of-towners. I needed a new pair, and I saw they were sort of run-down, but they seemed like a nice brand, nothing I could ever afford, so I thought, *Hey, why not?* Owning some secondhand name-brand shoes for once won't kill me." He paused for a moment and seemed perplexed. "I think it won't kill me, at least. Why do you ask? Can you tell they're old?"

"No," I said. "They're the same shoes the Sheet Man was wearing."

His face fell. "Are you telling me I'm wearing demon shoes?"

"I don't know what I'm telling you," I said, leaning forward to examine the silver buckles. "I just know they look like the ones I saw before the tuba fell on me. When did they arrive?"

"Uh, last week at some point. Thursday, probably."

"Thursday was the first day the Sheet Man visited!" I nearly yelped with excitement. "Who made the donation?"

"I honestly couldn't tell you," he said, taking his legs off the desk and slipping the shoes off. "But now I think I'm going to burn them."

"That's not the worst idea, but let me see them first."

He set them on the edge of the desk. I hesitated for a moment because I was worried what I was going to see by touching the shoes. There was a big chance any memories attached to them were brutal.

But when I picked one up, nothing happened. I turned it all over in my hands, running my fingers along the seams on the side and tracing the edge of the buckle, as if trying to massage a memory out of it, but it was just a normal shoe. The leather was so soft that I felt bad for telling Reverend Henry that they were probably cursed—I could tell they were comfortable.

On the inside, just under the shoe's tongue, I saw something written in black marker. I squinted, but it was blurry, like it had been written a hundred years ago.

"There's something written there," I said, getting my phone out to shine some light on it. "Can you make it out? I think the first letter is an *A*."

The reverend took the shoe and peered inside. "Sort of looks like it says 'APARKER.'" He tilted his hand and moved the shoe an inch away from his face. "I think it says that, at least."

"What's an aparker?" He handed back the shoe and I looked again. It did sort of look like that.

"It's probably a name, like A. Parker, with the *A* being an initial."

"What kind of man writes his name on his shoes? Especially a pair this nice."

"I can't say. Could be any reason."

"I wonder if I could track him down online. At least I have something to work with." I held out the shoe, smiling. "You can have this back now."

He threw his hands up. "I don't want to touch that thing again."

"Oh, come on," I said. "You've been wearing them for a few days now. I think they're fine. I didn't feel anything negative when I touched them."

He still looked hesitant. "I'll wear them for today because I'll be barefoot otherwise," he said. "But tonight they're going straight into the fire."

I told my mom the news in the car, but she didn't share in my excitement.

"You didn't tell me you saw that thing wearing shoes! And the reverend was wearing the same shoes?!" She gasped. "Oh my God, I hope you incinerated them on the spot!"

"I don't think they're cursed," I said. "They didn't have a bad energy."

"Well, it can't be a good energy, Baylor!" she said.

"They're just shoes," I said. "They're fine."

"Well, you're a boy, so you don't get it, but if I found out my shoes belonged to a dead lady who was haunting me, I wouldn't be very happy. I'd probably even demand a refund."

Mom agreed to let me take the rest of the day off instead of going back to school. At home there was a gigantic package of baked goods sitting on the kitchen table, courtesy of Aiden's mom. She really *had* baked a lot: There were cookies, brownies, blondies, seven-layer bars, and a small lemon cake. I grabbed a cookie, ran upstairs, lit a candle, and hopped onto my computer. Just as I was about to start searching the web for some more clues about the Sheet Man, my computer started to fritz. The screen blurred for a few seconds, then turned blue.

Then, letter by letter, a message appeared on the screen.

Don't worry about me. Be back soon. K.

Then it disappeared.

"Well, that's just great," I mumbled to myself. At least she wasn't in danger. Still, she could have given me some idea of when she'd return. I told my grandma that I'd see her soon all the time, even though I had no idea when the next time would be. It could be a year, for all I knew.

"Soon" was what you said to comfort someone. I didn't want to be comforted. I wanted my sister back to help me solve this problem.

Think logically. You're being followed by something Kristina thinks is really bad. She wouldn't leave you for a long time, since she knows you need her help. She will be back soon, and by "soon" she means shortly.

Feeling a bit better after rationalizing away my paranoia, I took to the Internet to dig up information on A. Parker.

First I typed in "A. Parker shoes." Nothing.

Next I tried "A. Parker sheets." Still nothing.

Then I typed in "A. Parker, Keene, New Hampshire."

It turned up some results, but nothing too specific. I tried to think of what else I knew that would be helpful, and then I smacked my hand to my forehead.

"Of course!" I added one word to the search bar: "obituary."

Jackpot. It turned out an Alfred Parker had died some three years earlier in Winchester, a nearby town. He'd been seventy-two when he died, been divorced, and had a son and a daughter. Seemed he was a late starter with having kids—both of them were only in their midtwenties when he died. It looked like he'd remarried, too. It didn't state what he'd done for work, just that he'd "pursued many successful entrepreneurial endeavors."

He seemed relatively normal. Nothing screamed that he would transform into a creepy demon stalker.

I read it once more and stopped at the line about the children, Isabella and William.

I had a feeling they would be my best bet, so I searched for them next. The results were limited, though, with just a few viable entries before everything devolved into sign-ups for online yellow pages. But I did find some pertinent information, like some old articles about Alfred and their mom, Rosalie T. Parker, and even some old photos. I managed to figure out Isabella was in California working as a teacher, and William was going to school in Boston.

William seemed the most promising, since Boston was only a couple of hours away from Keene.

The only problem was figuring out how to get there.

"Absolutely not," my mom said when I told her about my discoveries. She was sitting on the floor of the family room playing with Ella, and I was shoving down a brownie. "I am not driving you to Boston so you can attempt to meet up with the son of the dead guy who put you in the hospital. End of discussion."

"But, Mom," I said, my mouth filled with chocolate, "what if he needs my help?"

"Baylor, haven't you mentioned several times now that Kristina can't confront him because he's evil? Maybe he should have thought about getting help before he died and had to face the consequences of his poor life decisions." She looked at Ella and cooed, "Isn't that right, Ella-Bella? You make good choices in life! Good choices!"

"Good!" Ella screamed, throwing a block into the air.

"That's right!" My mom laughed. "Good girl. Don't be bad, or else your brother will have to deal with you from the Beyond, and we don't want that."

"So that's it?" I asked, annoyed. "What if I ask Dad?"

"Don't bother. Even if he were up for it, I am forbidding you to go."

"Forbidding? Mom, I can talk to dead people because I'm supposed to pass along healing messages. You're preventing me from doing my life's duty. You realize that, right?"

"I've grown to appreciate your gift and think it's wonderful that you can help people who need it," she said as she scooped up Ella and headed to the kitchen. "But when you wind up in the hospital because of it, guess what? I get to put my foot down. And if someone on the other side has a problem with it, you tell them I would be *more* than happy to discuss that with them." She kissed me on the cheek. "Got it?"

11

Consider developing your whittling skills.

THE NEXT DAY AT SCHOOL EVERY TIME MY classmates saw me, they would stare awkwardly or say something like, "Feeling okay, Baylor?" Apparently, news had traveled to everyone about my collision with a tuba.

To make matters worse, Kristina still hadn't reappeared. I lit five candles that morning and asked her to come back, but when I got done with my shower and looked in the mirror, there was a message written in the fog.

Stop being a baby.

It freaked me out she had been there without even saying hi. I just hoped she couldn't see me in the shower. The mere thought made me shudder.

At lunchtime I told Aiden that it seemed like everyone was making a bigger deal out of the incident than they should be.

"Well," he said, unpacking his usual pepperoni sandwich, "they're not talking about your accident as much as they are the fact that you screamed like a banshee and had the scariest face any of us have ever seen outside of a movie."

"What?"

"Yeah, people think you're haunted or something," he said, shrugging. "Not everyone gets what you can do."

"That sucks!" I said, slamming the table. "Being in band is bad enough for my reputation. I don't need that rumor on top of it."

"You should know that what people think of you doesn't matter," he said pointedly.

He was right. How many times had I passed on messages from ghosts saying they wished they had lived their lives the way they wanted instead of the way others wanted? Too many to count.

But still . . . junior high is hard enough without ghosts yammering in your ear, and I needed all the help I could get.

"How's that head, Baylor?" J asked, stopping at our table on the way to her next class. She wasn't in our lunch period, thankfully; otherwise, Aiden would be in danger of choking to death every day.

"A bit sore," I said. "Too bad people think I'm haunted."

She smiled. "Well, better to be haunted than stupid." Aiden was grinning like an idiot at his sandwich the whole time. "Uh, are *you* okay, Aiden?"

"Yeah, yeah, fine, fine," he said, looking up at her. "Just pretty happy about this pepperoni, is all."

I turned my head and closed my eyes. It was so painful to watch *and* hear.

"Well, enjoy," she said, shaking her head. "Let's hang out this week? Maybe head to the Patty Joint on Friday night?"

"Sounds good," I said as she walked away.

I let a moment pass before turning to him. "Seriously? You're going to die alone."

"I know," he said, taking a bite of his sandwich. "I know."

After school I had an injury-free band practice, although my ego was still slightly tarnished. Mr. G., in an effort to be nice, had placed pillows around my chair in case I collapsed again. My cheeks were on fire as I thanked him, but all he'd really done was inadvertently remind everyone that I was the crazy guy who'd had to go to the hospital.

But all the embarrassment melted away when I walked through the door of my bedroom and saw Kristina waiting for me on my bed.

She wasn't alone, though.

Standing beside her and gazing politely around my room was the ghost of a man dressed to the nines as an eighteenth-century British soldier, complete with leather kneecaps, a tricorn hat, and a vivid red coat.

"Is it . . . is it Halloween again?" I asked, looking the man up and down while he studied the picture of a Florida sunset that was hanging on my wall.

"There you are," Kristina said, rising. "Baylor, I'd like you to meet one of our spirit guides, Colonel Fleetwood."

The man turned and bowed slightly to me. "How do you do, Baylor?"

"I'm very well, thanks," I said. "How do you guys do?"

"Ugh, stop being awkward, Baylor," Kristina said. "Colonel Fleetwood is here to help us with the Sheet Man."

"Oh, good. Are you going to be able to capture him and compel his exit?" I asked.

"In a way, yes," he said. He had a pleasant face,

although his cryptic grin confused me: I couldn't tell if he was annoyed or amused to be here. Even odder was that he seemed way too young to be a soldier. I'd guess he was sixteen when he crossed over.

"So," I said, "how?"

"I hope you've kept up with your whittling skills," he said as Kristina smiled mischievously next to him.

A few hours later, in the dark of the night, I found myself wandering through the woods near my house and wondering what it would be like to be normal, to not have to talk to ghosts and construct talismans to ward off evil spirits.

"Tonight is the full moon," Kristina had said earlier, "so it's the perfect time to build it."

"You know I have homework, right? I need to write an English essay and try to understand the math lesson I missed yesterday. I don't have time for this."

"It must be done tonight, young lad!" Colonel Fleetwood said. "No other night will offer the protection that a full moon can."

"First off, 'young lad'? You're, like, two years older than me. Secondly, why can't I do it during the day, when the big ball of fire called the sun is shining? Doesn't that offer some protection?"

"The sun knows only light," the colonel said. "The moon, however, sees through the dark."

"Uh, okay," I said. "Did you get that from a fortune cookie?"

"A fortune cookie? I don't know what that is, but it sounds delightful!"

Kristina scoffed. "Stop, Baylor. The full moon offers the best protection because it illuminates even the darkest of nights. Isn't that obvious?"

It did make sense to me, in a way, but I couldn't figure out why they hadn't just brought over some high-powered ghost zapper from the Beyond to blow the Sheet Man up. Surely, *someone* over there had to be capable of stopping him.

Alas, they wouldn't hear of it. This situation was one I had to deal with head-on.

"I learned a bit more while I was gone," Kristina said, "and I think you were right, Baylor. Even though there's something seriously wrong here, I don't think the Sheet Man is purely evil."

"You learned a bit more? Who teaches you these things? Were you and the colonel sitting in a classroom taking notes from Buddha or something?"

"Shut up, Baylor. There's something bizarre going on, and we need to figure out how to help."

"And this talisman is going to stop him?" I asked.

"Oh, yes," Colonel Fleetwood said. "It's quite effective."

Before heading into the woods, I had been sort of excited, like we were going on a mystical adventure, just me, my ghost twin, and our British soldier spirit guide. But when they finally told me what I was looking for, my spirits fell, pun absolutely intended.

"I'm looking for a big piece of wood and a stone," I said. "You can't be serious." I had been expecting them to say we needed something really weird, like thirteen roses and the blood of a newborn deer.

But no. I needed some wood and a stone—the tools a caveman would use to crush bugs into paste. Not what I viewed as the ideal tools to keep a spirit from stalking me.

We trekked through the woods for a while, and an eerie silence seemed to permeate the air. My flashlight, in addition to the full moon, provided ample light, and yet there were no trees rustling, no birds chirping, no squirrels running amok, and heck, not even an earthworm wriggling around. I suspected the two energies walking alongside me had something to do with it.

I shone my flashlight on more than a hundred pieces of wood before finally finding one that Colonel Fleetwood deemed suitable. It was a part of a fallen branch, the snapped end just wide enough that I could hollow it out to fit a stone inside.

Then we went to a babbling brook nearby and searched for some stones. This hunt proved to be easier in terms of finding the perfect stone, since the only requirement was that it be as spherical as possible, yet getting it was infinitely more challenging because the water was probably forty degrees. It had to come from the water, though, because of some dumb rule about purity. All I know is that by the time we had found the perfect one, I could no longer feel my hand.

"Welcome to our world," Kristina said as the colonel nodded. "We don't feel a thing."

I rolled my eyes. Of course I wouldn't get any sympathy from the dead people.

Back home I found the jack-o'-lantern carving knives, which hadn't seen the inside of a pumpkin in a long time, and headed up to my room. Under the guidance of the colonel I sawed off the long, scraggly end of the branch, leaving me with a hunk of wood that resembled a thick hockey puck. Then I began whittling away at the wood bit by bit to create a deep enough space. I slowly carved for hours while I listened to the ghosts chat casually like they were old friends. Well, they probably were old friends, but it was still weird to hear Kristina chatting with some-one who wasn't me.

"It felt quite strange, greeting my mother once she crossed over," the colonel said to Kristina as he leaned against the wall. "So I can only imagine how utterly unreal it will feel to you when you must do the same for yours."

"Your mom at least knew what you looked like," Kristina said. "Mine doesn't even know what color my hair is."

"She does too," I said. "I've told her a million times."

"Yeah, but she doesn't really know," Kristina said. "You didn't do that good of a job describing it."

"I repeated to her exactly what you told me to say!"

"Yeah, and it still wasn't very good."

"That side seems ready, lad," Colonel Fleetwood said, looking over my shoulder. "One more side to go and you'll have a good space there."

I nodded. "Got it."

He turned back to Kristina and said, "Did you hear from Lincoln what Selene said about the moon tonight? She was apparently in a bad mood and wanted to cover the sky with clouds, but he put a stop to that for us."

"As he should have," she said. "Everyone's too riled up for her to go doing something like that."

"Hopefully, it'll all be sorted out soon. This talisman should do the trick, and then I'll be able to be on my way."

"You're staying?" I asked, whipping my head around.

"Of course he is," Kristina said. "I told you I was bringing reinforcements."

"Oh. I didn't realize you meant *him*." I jerked my head toward the colonel. "I thought you meant someone like, I don't know, Jesus or Vishnu or someone like that."

Kristina and Fleetwood looked at each other for a loaded second before throwing their heads back in laughter.

"What! Why is that so funny?"

"I can't . . . I can't . . . s-speak!" Kristina sputtered.

After a few minutes she finally regained her composure, while I sat there, jaw clenched, whittling away like Mister Geppetto.

"Sorry, Baylor, I don't mean to laugh so hard," she said. "It's just that, well, this issue isn't really *that* serious. To put it in a way you might understand, it would be like dropping a nuclear bomb to kill a spider, rather than just using a rolled-up newspaper."

"He kills spiders?" the colonel asked, suddenly perturbed.

"I tell him not to," Kristina said, her voice going high. "He doesn't listen."

"Lad, you shouldn't do that!" he said. "Bad karma."

"Weren't you a soldier, Fleetwood?" I asked, totally aware of how annoyed I sounded. "Didn't you kill people when you were alive? How is killing a spider worse than that?"

"I was duty-bound to serve in a war," he said, nodding. "It was something I had no control over and believed to be justified."

"Well, I feel justified in killing spiders when they sneak up on me out of nowhere," I said. "They have double the legs of most animals. It's creepy. Why do they need that many legs? They're clearly monstrous animals, and I treat them as such."

He raised his eyebrows at Kristina, who slowly shook her head, but I didn't care because I felt like I had won the argument.

After I was done whittling, they instructed me to crack an egg downstairs and bring the shell back to my room.

"This is the stupidest thing I've ever done," I mumbled to myself, walking from the kitchen, egg-shell in hand, and thinking of Fleetwood and his dumb accent. Why was Kristina even bothering to hang around him? There had to be better spirit guides in the Beyond besides that clown.

"Here we go," I said, presenting the shell to them. "One eggshell, at your service."

"Wonderful," Fleetwood said. "We're nearly there!"

"All you have to do now," Kristina said, "is put the stone inside the eggshell, close the shell up, and then place it in the center of the wooden bowl."

I furrowed my eyebrows. "Okay," I said slowly as I did as they instructed.

"And here we are," Fleetwood whispered, admiring the talisman. "Excellent work, Baylor. Now, if you'll kindly turn off your lights and light a candle for us."

I nodded, grabbing a fresh one from my nightstand and switching off the light before walking back. Illuminated by the glow of my computer's screen saver, I struck a match and lit the wick, which crackled violently.

"We're ready," the colonel said. He and Kristina positioned themselves around me, forming a small circle. "Baylor, place the talisman on the ground and keep hold of your candle. Good. Now, what I need you to do is very simple: Imagine the light of your candle enveloping the talisman with positive energy, and all the while think the words, 'With this tool I will only do good.'"

I shut my eyes and imagined the flame spreading out from its home on the wick and encircling the talisman.

With this tool I will only do good.
With this tool I will only do good.
With this tool I will only do good.

I opened my eyes and nearly dropped the candle. A thin golden ribbon was slowly slicing through the air, like a river on fire, heading right for the talisman, where it began to shoot around the way an asteroid would orbit Earth, quickly, blindingly, securing the wooden bowl into its web of flames.

I watched with awe, longing to touch it just to see what would happen.

"Uh, Kristina? You never told me I could do this."

"Not now, Baylor," Kristina murmured. She extended her hands, palms down, over the talisman and calmly said, "Spread your light." And from her hands emerged that same blue light that she had used to send away the meddlesome spirit at the hospital. It pulsed out of her in feeble waves, eventually joining the candlelight and turning the sphere electric blue.

Colonel Fleetwood mimicked Kristina's hand position and said, "Find your purpose." The waves of light that emitted from his hands were shockingly white, hitting the blue and gold with a sharp hiss and causing the whole thing to swell and burn white, like a small supernova.

After several seconds of staring at the inferno, both amazed by what was happening and worried that my retinas were burning, a fierce, powerful sensation boomed from within me, like I was made of fire, and I found myself saying, "Love conquers all," in unison with Kristina and the colonel, both of whom seemed completely unsurprised.

And then, as soon as the last word escaped our mouths, the ribbons of energy dissipated, the lights in my room turned themselves back on, and the wooden bowl on the ground was . . . still a wooden bowl.

I bent down to pick it up and noticed it looked exactly the same, except for one small change.

"The shell isn't broken anymore," I gasped, as if that were really the most amazing thing that had happened in the last two minutes. I jerked the bowl around and noticed the egg wasn't rolling around either, like it was glued to the wood.

"The stone is sealed inside," Colonel Fleetwood said. "The next time you are visited by the Sheet Man, crack the egg open and throw the stone at him. You'll find your troubles will end there."

12

NEVER eat at
Italian restaurants.

I HAD TO CARRY THE TALISMAN WITH ME everywhere, just in case the Sheet Man appeared at a random time. That meant putting this strange wooden bowl into my backpack at school and trying to hide it from my classmates. The last thing I wanted was for people to know that the haunted band geek carried around a goofy-looking wooden bowl with an egg in it.

At school the next day, I had the pleasure of having both Kristina and Fleetwood following me around. My very own ghost entourage. Kristina was having the time of her life. She usually had to sit in silence and learn all the things she already knew, but today she and Fleetwood were basically having a party. They were going on and on in my English class about something hysterical Shakespeare had said to Hemingway, until finally I glared at Kristina, and she and the colonel went to wait outside.

"Sorry, Baylor," she said as I walked out after the bell rang. "I forgot that you actually have to concentrate in class."

"It's fine," I said. "It's not like the ending of *Julius Caesar* is a big surprise."

"It was to him," Fleetwood said gravely. "He's still a touch bitter about it, even after all these years."

After band practice I found my mom waiting for me outside. I was surprised to see her, since I'd planned for Aiden's mom to give me a ride home.

"What are you doing here?" I asked. "Hey, Jack. Hi, Ella." Ella smiled at me with sheer delight while Jack waved feebly.

"It's your great-aunt's birthday, remember?" my mom said. "You forgot, didn't you?"

"I was in the hospital three days ago for a possible concussion, remember?" I said. "You forgot, didn't you?"

"Don't be smart with me, Baylor Bosco," she said. "I've told you since the beginning of October about this dinner."

"How old is she, anyway?"

"The woman's turning eighty-eight!"

"Why are we having this dinner? That's such a random number. If she were ninety, I'd understand."

"Baylor, when you get to be eighty-eight years old, every year that you don't die is an accomplishment. I know that concept may be difficult for someone like you to grasp, but for the rest of us it's a big deal."

"I guess I get it," I said. "Where are we going?"

"Carrino's!" Jack said from the backseat.

I glanced at Jack, then turned my head slowly to my mom; she had her lips pursed, and her eyes were focused squarely in front of her, pretending like she didn't notice my glare.

"You have got to be kidding me," I hissed. "If you had mentioned the name of the restaurant, I wouldn't have forgotten about the dinner. You are a sneaky, sneaky woman."

"I'm sorry, Baylor, but it's her favorite restaurant, and it's *her* birthday. She's eighty-eight! What can I do?"

I shook my head, furious about the way this night was unfolding.

"Is there a problem with this establishment?" the colonel asked Kristina in the back.

"Baylor can't tune spirits out in Italian restaurants," she said. "We don't know why. He thinks it's the garlic. I think it's because Italians are known for their personable energy. Whatever the reason, whenever we go to an Italian place, it's usually a disaster."

"Dis-aws-ta," Ella squeaked, banging her doll on the window.

"Oh, how precious!" Fleetwood said, waving at Ella. "The child understands us."

"Come to think of it," Kristina said slowly, "Ella's never been to an Italian restaurant. I wonder how she's going to react."

My great-aunt Hilda had been married a long time ago, sometime in her thirties, but had never had children. Her husband had been a rich man, but no one seemed to talk about him much. I always got the impression he'd had ties to the mob, a suspicion that his early, mysterious demise seemed to confirm.

She had lived alone for the better of forty years, and since she had no other family, she nearly always joined our holiday celebrations, as well as any meaningful milestones, unfortunately for me.

The problem was that, despite being an agreeable

lady in most other facets of her life, Aunt Hilda was a firm nonbeliever in my gift. It's not just that she didn't believe I could communicate with the dead, but that she was very vocal to anyone who would listen that her grandnephew was a charlatan who played on people's emotions and gave them a false sense of hope about whatever comes after death.

It didn't bother me that she didn't believe me, but it did bother me that she openly called me a liar in front of strangers and family alike. We eventually learned never to bring up my gift in front of her, and if she even hinted around to it, we would change the subject faster than you could blink.

When we arrived at Carrino's that night, I was not in a good mood. I had Colonel British McBad-Teeth clinging to my twin, I knew I wasn't going to be able to tune out any of the spirits inside, and I would have to act like none of it was bothering me, all because my crazy great-aunt had decided to live another year.

Carrino's had big glass doors for the entryway, and from the outside I couldn't see or hear any spirits. It was one of the best Italian spots in town, though, so I knew it was going to be busy even on a random Thursday night. I walked up to the doors, took one final breath, and shot one last nasty glance at my mom, who was following me with Ella in her arms and a worried frown on her face.

With my eyes closed, I opened the doors and was immediately overcome by the noise. It was a small restaurant, and everything was amplified by the picture-frame-covered walls.

When I opened my eyes, I couldn't even see the tables anymore. It was like leaving the stadium after a Patriots game and getting caught in the middle of a million people taking half steps toward the exit, hoping not to get trampled by the crowd.

The difference was that I could tune out the ghosts at stadiums. At the restaurant it was so packed I couldn't tell who was dead or alive. I motioned for my mom to pass me so I could follow her lead. Otherwise, I'd be running into people I thought were dead, and I'd be awkwardly scooting around and saying "Excuse me" to people I could walk right through.

But she wouldn't go, because as soon as she walked by me with Ella, the baby began to scream one of those deep-from-the-gut, almost primal screams. The kind where you know something is really wrong.

"Ella!" my mom said. "What's wrong, Ella-Bella? You were fine just a second ago."

"It's packed, Mom," I said. "It's packed, and it's loud."

My mom tilted her head and frowned, walking back outside as a high-pitched voice chirped from behind me.

"Um, we're actually not packed at all," the tiny hostess said from her stand as a man with a thick black mustache leaned over and tried to smell her. She didn't mind, though, since he was dead. "We have plenty of available tables for your party if you'd like to sit."

"I, uh, that's not actually what I meant," I said, fumbling for words, trying to catch the spirit's eye over her shoulder so he'd know I could see him. "We actually have reservations for a birthday dinner."

"Oh, are you with Renee O'Brien's party?"

"Yeah, that's my grandma," I said, still focusing on the area just to the left of the hostess, where the man was now rubbing the girl's shoulder with his hands. She frowned at me, but then I saw her shiver. She could sense the man's presence but had no idea what was going on.

Luckily, Kristina turned her attention away from the colonel to realize what was happening, and she zapped him with her blue energy.

"It was just getting good!" he wailed as he faded into nothing.

"Ugh!" Kristina groaned.

"Follow me," said the hostess, and once she turned her back, I grimaced at Kristina, who, along with the colonel, smiled encouragingly.

"I daresay you've got this under control, lad," the colonel said. "At least you're not charging onto a battlefield on a cold, wintry morning, knowing that it will soon be smeared with your blood, and the blood of all the fine gentlemen you're leading."

"You are not helping right now, Fleetwood," I muttered as we passed a group of people I could only assume were alive. They turned and stared, and I raised my eyebrows at them awkwardly, not wanting to respond in case they were really dead. It would only make the people sitting at the next table feel uncomfortable.

"You're right here," the hostess said, sitting us down at the eight-seat table. We were the first ones to arrive, thankfully, so I took my seat at the end, and Jack sat right across from me. It was the sort of restaurant that put white paper on top of the tables to serve as both a tablecloth and a canvas for kids to draw on. The hostess set down crayons, and Jack went right to work.

As he was writing his name in awkward cursive letters, he leaned forward and whispered, "See anyone?"

"Yeah," I whispered back. "Lots."

He drew a sharp breath. "This isn't going to be very fun."

"Nope."

My mom got to the table a few minutes later. She'd managed to calm Ella down, but the girl was fidgeting, and it was obvious that she was like a leaky gas pipe just one spark away from an explosion.

"There are my sweet grandchildren!" Grandma said, barreling through a group of ghosts.

"Grandma!" Jack said, throwing down his crayon and jumping up to hug her.

"Hi, Wacky Jacky," she said. "Did you have a good day at school?"

"Yeah, I played four square today and only lost twice."

"I'm so impressed!" She turned to me and hesitated for a moment, knowing exactly what I was thinking. "Sorry, Baylor, but she insisted."

I got up and hugged her. "It's all right. It's just for a couple of hours. Honestly, Ella's the one you're going to have to worry about. She can see them everywhere."

She looked at Ella, and her jaw dropped upon seeing her granddaughter squirming in her seat, her head twisting around every few seconds as she looked at all the passing spirits.

"Oh my . . . ," she said. "Maybe I should have tried a little harder to make my dear sister change her mind."

Speak of the devil, Aunt Hilda crossed through the group of ghosts she would never believe I could see, gently led by Grandpa By (his longtime nickname since being cruelly christened Byron O'Brien).

I was the first one she saw, and if she was already annoyed with me, it wasn't apparent.

"Baylor, come help your ancient auntie get into her chair, will ya?" she said.

I grabbed on to her other arm and pulled the chair out for her. She plopped into it, reaching up to grab my neck and pull me down for a kiss. "It's good to see ya, kid. Can you believe this broad is eighty-eight?"

"You don't look a day over one hundred, Aunt Hilda," I said.

She threw her head back, clutching the half-heart necklace she always wore, the laughter croaking out of her mouth like an ad campaign against smoking, and said, "You slay me. Jacky boy, come here and give me a kiss."

As Jack clambered up from his seat again, Grandpa By pulled me aside and said, "You doing okay?"

I nodded. "They're everywhere. And they're loud. Ella sees them too."

"I told Renee not to come here. I said to her, 'Renee, you remember what happened last time we went to an Italian joint?' And she says to me—get this—she says, 'Yeah, By, but Hilda's eighty-eight years old, how many more chances is she gonna have to eat some Italian food?'" He threw his hands up. "If tonight goes poorly, let me tell you, it's gonna be her last time, I'll say that much. I'll say that much." He crossed his arms over his chest. "And you with the hospital visit this week, and the weird appearances from things I don't like to imagine too much, and the bad Halloween experience. How could it not go poorly?"

I shook my head. "You're reading my mind, Grandpa."

"Don't say that, kid," he said. "With you it could come true. I'll tell you, it's going to be a fiasco. But the lady is eighty-eight, and we're here, so we will deal with it, grandson, we will *deal* with it as all O'Brien men do. I know your last name is that Bosco non-sense, but I like to pretend it's O'Brien sometimes, you know?"

My dad arrived shortly after, and dinner finally got under way.

Right from the start everything went wrong. A ghost pretending to be the waiter came right up to me, introduced himself as Charlie, and asked what I'd like to drink.

"Uh, do you have hot chocolate?" I said, looking up at him and not realizing anything was wrong. "I'm sort of cold."

"Oh my word, he's already starting it," Aunt Hilda groaned. I looked at her and then looked back at the ghost, who was now lit up with blue and fading away. Kristina had zapped him, but the damage was already done.

"Oh, ha, ha, I was just, uh, practicing my Italian for when the waiter comes, Aunt Hilda," I said. "You didn't give me a chance to finish."

Everyone at the table was staring at me expectantly.

"Make something up," Kristina whispered. "Just say some gibberish, she'll never know."

"*Fl-flomargo deechay en la . . . en la dulce,*" I said, doing my best Mario and Luigi impression. My mom put her hand up to her forehead and shut her eyes, while my dad laughed silently behind his napkin. "*Encardo la noche de dudo! Bravo!*"

A brutal moment of silence passed, until finally Grandpa spoke up.

"Well, that was just amazing," he said sincerely. "I didn't know you've been learning Italian."

"Yeah," I said, looking down, my cheeks probably

the color of the tomato sauce I'd be eating soon. "Getting pretty good at it."

"I bet," he said, his lips threatening to smile.

I shook my head and glared at Kristina, who said, "Sorry! I wasn't paying attention."

After that she and Colonel Fleetwood stood guard around my seat, making sure no other spirits could goof with me.

I stayed mostly silent for dinner, only giving short answers whenever someone asked me a question. I stole a blue crayon from Jack and kept drawing the shape of a candle flame, over and over again, until I realized I had created what sort of looked like a massive thunderstorm, the blue flames doubling as raindrops. I chuckled to myself as my food came out, and for that moment I felt pretty good about my spaghetti and meatballs.

Then I just had to ruin everything by going for the cheese.

I picked up the little jar of Parmesan cheese sitting in the middle of the table, unaware as usual that there was a memory attached to it. I was sucked into a vision of a man arguing with his wife at our same table. The vision was just a split second, but once it ended, I gasped and dropped the jar of cheese, causing it to plume all over my shirt and the table.

"I'm sorry," I said, still breathing heavily, "I'm sorry, I'm so clumsy."

Grandma noticed right away that something was wrong. I'd bet money that my face was as white as the ruined Parmesan.

"Baylor, why don't you get cleaned up in the bathroom," she said helpfully.

Except the second I stood up, I realized it wasn't helpful at all. Navigating through a minefield would have been easier than navigating through all the people in the restaurant. I shot a look at Kristina, and she nodded, leading the way for me.

Kristina made sure the ghosts didn't disturb me while I was sitting with our family, but as far as they were concerned, I was fair game while walking to the bathroom.

"Finally, you're up!" a twentysomething shouted at me excitedly. "I need you to tell my mom that I didn't kill myself! It was an accident, through and through. Look at me, I'm too good-looking to have wanted to die that young."

I glared at him, and he smirked. "What, are you a mute now? I know you can speak English, and some really bad fake Italian, too. Go tell her, she's right there." He pointed to his right at a woman with short black hair.

I shook my head and tried to communicate with my eyes, but it didn't work.

"You can't leave me here," he said, his voice faltering. "I'm not comfortable going to the Beyond until I know that she knows that."

Kristina and I exchanged glances. I was given this gift for this exact reason, but at the same time I was only five feet from my table, and if Aunt Hilda overheard me, she was going to say that I ruined her birthday by parading around the restaurant and that I couldn't even give her one special night.

Kristina bit her lip, clearly thinking the exact same thing.

Finally Colonel Fleetwood stepped in. "Perhaps you could use your energy to direct your mother toward the back of the establishment, so they could engage in a conversation in private?"

The ghost looked at him, then back at me.

"Are you kidding me with this guy?" he asked. "Really?"

I didn't respond, but he shrugged. "Whatever." And then he turned to his mom, bent over, and whispered in her ear. Midconversation, as her friends watched in confusion, the woman got up from the table and nearly ran to the bathrooms at the back of the restaurant, down a narrow hallway. I followed her path, listening to her son describe the sordid details of his death while sidestepping all the dead people, and cornered her before she went inside.

"Ma'am!" I hissed. "Ma'am, stop!"

She turned around. "Are you talking to me?"

"My name is Baylor Bosco, and I can communicate with people who have crossed over," I said. "Listen, Terri, what I'm going to say won't be easy to hear, but you need to hear it. Chad didn't kill himself. He needs you to know that it was an accident, that he would never have taken all those pills if he'd known it was going to kill him."

She recoiled in shock, then looked around the hallway and clutched the walls. Her mouth was moving, but no sound came out. Her hands shot to her chest and she stared at me in panic.

"Oh man, this is bad," Chad said.

"What's wrong with her?" I asked.

"She's having an asthma attack," he said. "You need to go get her inhaler from her purse."

My eyes bulged out. "What? No! I can't just go rummage through her purse!"

"Just say you found her back here like this and you saw where she got up from!" Kristina said.

"Oh my God," I said, turning around and sprinting to her table the same way I'd just come. An old woman was walking toward the bathroom, and I ran right for her, thinking I'd pass through her just fine.

It was like a rhino colliding with a bowling pin. The whole restaurant went silent as we tumbled to the floor, our limbs flying in every direction.

"Dear Lord!" my dad yelled, running over to help us as a few others from random tables did the same.

"I'm sorry, I'm sorry!" I said, overwhelmed by all the people around me, confused that no one was speaking and that the only thing I could hear was a loud man singing about pizza pies and *amore*. "There's a woman by the bathroom! She collapsed and needs her inhaler!"

A man turned, peeked around the corner to see the other woman on the floor, and yelled at the top of his lungs, "He's right! That woman needs an inhaler!"

As my dad pulled me up from the ground to brush me off and examine the cut on my elbow, another man ran toward the bathroom, presumably with the inhaler in his hands.

I honestly didn't think things could get worse, until they did.

The woman I had stampeded over wasn't responding, so they had to call 911. Then a couple of patrons got into an argument about whether I ran into her on purpose, with one of them swearing I had been looking right at her and had known exactly what I was doing, and the other saying that I had panicked trying to help the woman who was having an asthma attack and simply hadn't seen her.

Once Terri recovered from her asthma attack, she started spouting off that I had caused her attack by telling her I could talk to dead people and that I'd told her that her son didn't commit suicide. She wasn't saying it in an accusatory way, though. Rather, she was thrilled, saying she had heard of me before and wondered if she'd ever get the chance to meet me.

This revelation caused nearly all the ghosts and patrons in the restaurant to talk at once, and all I could do was stare as the people and sounds blurred together into one, while a couple of paramedics worked on the still-unconscious lady on the ground.

Moments away from passing out, I looked at Kristina, who pointed to the table next to her and said, "Spread the light." I looked at the candle for a second, forgetting what it could do for me, and then I stumbled over, picked it up, and imagined the white light surrounding me. Suddenly my mind cleared.

Feeling rejuvenated, I stood on a chair and shouted, "Everyone, shut up!"

For the next ten minutes I acted as the conductor of a symphony of healing messages, one after the other, pointing at person after person and delivering messages rapid-fire.

"You," I said, pointing at a woman in a purple dress, "your husband says buy the green house, not the blue one."

"But I like the blue one more!"

"You," I said, pointing at the man with extra-large ears, "your brother says thank you for taking care of his children after he died."

He nodded, a strong blush blazing across his face.

"You," I said to the man with too much hair gel, "your mother says lay off the hair gel."

"But it's in style!"

"You," I said to the teenage girl who had been weeping for the last few minutes, "your father says you won't believe this is really him, and that the only way you'll believe it is if he brings up the giraffe tattoo you got on your back in memory of him, and he wants you to know that he hates it, and that if you get another one, he's not going to be able to rest in peace."

And so on and so forth until everyone in the restaurant was stunned into silence.

Everyone except for one person.

"He's a *fraud*," Aunt Hilda croaked from her seat, refusing to look at me and studying her necklace with great interest. "He's nothing more than a para-site feeding off your sadness. He made it all up, you fools."

Everyone looked at her for a few seconds, no one saying a word. Then the weeping girl walked over, lifted up the back of her shirt to reveal a tattoo of a giraffe with the word "Dad" scrawled between the spots, and silently walked away.

13

Even ghosts can lose their tempers.

THE AFTERMATH OF THE DINNER WASN'T pretty. Even though nearly everyone in the restaurant was satisfied with their messages, and the woman whom I'd plowed to the ground woke up and got a message from her husband, and a journalist showed up to write an article about the event, my mom was still mortified.

"You turned her birthday into a sideshow for your gift, Baylor," my mom ranted on the drive home. "Aunt Hilda will always look back on her eighty-eighth birthday and remember your . . . your . . . *shenanigans.*"

"Shenanigans?" I said incredulously. "It's not like I stood on the table naked and danced, Mom. You're the one who forced me to go to that Italian restaurant, so if you didn't want that to happen, we shouldn't have gone there in the first place."

"Never in my wildest dreams," she said, side-eyeing me while keeping her face forward, "did I imagine you would hijack an entire restaurant and do a group healing session."

"Well, spirits can make you go crazy sometimes," I said.

"Is that all you have to say for yourself?" she scoffed. "Your aunt Hilda is so upset."

"Who cares? Even after I delivered messages to more than a hundred people, she still called me a parasite, like I'm some nasty tapeworm that lives in your stomach. I couldn't care less that she's upset."

"Well, that's really too bad," she said, "because your father is going to take you to visit her this weekend so you can apologize in person."

"That's ridiculous," I said. "I'm not sorry. The best I can do for you is write her an e-mail and tell her that I'm sorry she's so offended by me."

She gripped the wheel, her fingers flying up and down in waves, while she took a deep breath. "Baylor Douglas Bosco," she growled, "you will visit your aunt Hilda and you will apologize sincerely to her, or else you will not get your driver's license till you're eighteen."

She had me in a death grip.

"Fine," I said. "Fine, I'll do it, but if you ever make me go to an Italian place again, you better believe it's going to be a hundred times worse than tonight was."

That night I asked Colonel Fleetwood to give me a moment alone with Kristina, and she got an earful.

"Your job is to protect me, Kristina, from all those crazy spirits," I said, my voice firm and tense. She was sitting in my desk chair, staring guiltily, while I paced in front of her. "And you and Colonel Fleetwood were so busy joking with each other that you couldn't even do the one thing you're supposed to. You might as well not have even been there. You might as well have been one of the ghosts crowding around the tables and making noise and distracting me." I shot her a look. "Oh, wait, you *were* one of those ghosts crowding around and distracting me."

"Baylor, I know, I'm sorry," she said. "You just have to understand, it was such a nice change for me to have a friend on this side for once."

"I'm your friend, Kristina. Talk to me."

"Oh, stop, you know what I mean," she said. "A friend who can talk to me instead of having to make weird faces at me."

"Well, that's the way it is!" I said. "There's a reason someone like Colonel Fleetwood isn't usually around, and tonight made it very clear why. You totally failed me. You should have been paying attention to me the entire time instead of letting me down."

"Oh, Baylor," she said, gazing at her feet, "shut up."

I stopped pacing. "What?"

"You heard me. Shut up. Just stop talking." She stood up, walked over to where I was staring at her, dumbfounded, and got in my face. "It must be so hard for you to be alive, and to be surrounded by your family, who can touch you and love you and hug you and kiss you, and it must be such a *challenge* for you not to be able to eat in one certain kind of restaurant, and to talk to anyone you want whenever you want, and to feel the sun in your face and the cold on your skin, and to be able to cry when you're upset and *feel* things."

She paused, her eyes searing into mine. "I am so sorry that you feel so put upon. I apologize for not banishing that creepy guy at the restaurant fast enough, and sure, maybe I shouldn't have let that ghost trick you into thinking he was the waiter, but if that's really the worst I've ever screwed up, then you know what, Baylor? You should just *shut up*."

And she turned around and disappeared.

I had never gotten into a real fight with Kristina before, and I was fuming. Absolutely fuming. Who did she think she was to talk to me like that? She was the one who'd screwed up, not me. I should have been the one to march away and end the conversation, not her.

It ticked me off big-time, and it was all I could think about at school the next day, especially since Kristina was being petty and didn't make an appearance that morning.

And it was all I could think about that evening, too, which was problematic, since I had plans to go to the Patty Joint downtown with Aiden and J.

Even a trip to the Patty Joint—a rustic restaurant with license plates covering the bare wooden walls, and the home of the best cheeseburgers in New Hampshire—couldn't invigorate my mood.

"What's up with you, Baylor?" J asked between bites of a mozzarella stick. "You've barely said a word all night, and from the looks of it, you seem to have a personal vendetta against that Rhode Island license plate you keep glaring at."

Stupid Rhode Island, with its stupid license plate

covered in blue waves and anchors and the words "Ocean State," as if people really thought of Rhode Island when they thought of oceans.

I shook my head and sighed.

"Sorry, I'm just a little out of it," I said. "Lots on my mind."

"Hmm." She pushed her glasses—tonight's were covered in dark-blue stripes—up the bridge of her nose. "Does this have anything to do with the article?"

"The what?"

She looked down at the mozzarella stick basket. "The article about the boy medium at Carrino's? It's online."

I looked over at Aiden, who seemed very interested in swirling ranch around his plate with his mozzarella stick.

"I haven't read it yet. What'd it say?"

"Oh, it was nothing bad," she said brightly. "If anything, it sounded like it would've been amazing to witness it."

I felt awkward because I'd never really broached the whole ghost subject with J.

I nodded. "Yeah, it was actually kinda cool, minus the old lady I nearly killed, and minus the fact that my mom hates me for ruining my aunt Hilda's birthday dinner."

Aiden choked. "Aunt Hilda? Oh, yikes."

"I know," I said. "Nightmare."

"I'm sure your mom doesn't hate you," J said, whispering. My mom and Mrs. Kirkwood were having a mom date at another table. I'm sure my mom was talking nonstop about last night's escapades.

"I know," I said. "There's just . . . there's some other stuff going on too, and she said she's not going to help me with it, and after last night she's *definitely* not going to help."

"Like what?"

"I need to go to Boston for something."

"What's in Boston?" Aiden asked.

"Just some, uh, ghost stuff I'm trying to figure out." J didn't know about the Sheet Man or my fight with Kristina, and as far as I was concerned, she didn't need to. Things were so out of control that I wanted to keep only a few people in the know, which would hopefully keep everyone else out of danger.

Our burgers arrived, and as I loaded mine with mustard and ketchup, J was staring over my shoulder. I'd seen that look before—the wheels were spinning in her brain.

"Baylor," she said quietly, leaning in, "what if we all took the bus to Boston?"

"Wouldn't it take, like, three hours on the bus?" I

frowned. "Besides, buses aren't exactly my style. Last time I was on one, a tiny Venezuelan woman kept yelling at me about recipes."

"But we'll be there to distract you!" she said, touching Aiden's arm. He immediately started coughing, pulling his hands away and grabbing his napkin to cover his mouth. It usually took him several seconds to recover from unexpected contact with J.

"Totally," he said, his cheeks completely red. "Let's do it."

I looked at them both across from me, their eyes wide and eager, and I smiled.

The next morning I left a note on the kitchen counter, telling my parents I was working on a project with J and to call if they needed me. I was even more proud of the fact that nothing on the note was a lie. It's not like I said I was going to her house, and we *were* working on a project, just one of the ghost variety.

Wearing my backpack, which contained the handy-dandy talisman—just in case—I biked to the bus stop downtown, where J and Aiden were waiting for me already. As I chained my bike, I eavesdropped on their thrilling conversation.

"Dinner was pretty good, huh?" Aiden said.

"So good. I love that place," J said. "Your mom was so sweet to give me a ride."

"Yeah, my mom's great."

"She is. I loved how, uh, excited she got when Baylor delivered that message to the waiter as we were leaving."

I felt like I could hear the blood rushing to Aiden's face. "Uh, yeah, she sure can scream, huh?"

It was like the Italian restaurant fiasco, part two, except not nearly as dramatic. She'd squealed so loud that the everyone in the Patty Joint turned to stare at her. There was no question which side of the family Aiden got his blushing skills from.

"It was cute," J said, her voice gentle and reassuring.

"You guys ready?" I asked as I approached them.

"You bet!" J said, handing me a ticket. "Eight thirty-five bus to Boston. We'll get there at eleven, do some investigating, and get our tickets home on either the three or five p.m. bus."

"Perfect," I said. The bus pulled up a few minutes later, and we were on our way.

The bus ride wasn't that bad, mostly because it was nearly empty. There was only one ghost asking me to pass on a message, and I waited until we arrived in Boston to deliver it.

The worst part of the ride was the very beginning, when we had to pick seats. I sat in a window seat without thinking, realizing too late that I should've arranged for J and Aiden to sit together. Instead I got to watch in horror as Aiden and J stammered to figure out who should sit next to me and who should sit alone.

Ultimately, J sat next to me, and Aiden sat across the aisle, all alone. He made sure to glare at me whenever J wasn't looking.

We took the T to the stop nearest the coffee shop where William Parker apparently worked. I had done some serious online stalking to find the place, a little café called Cup-o'-Soul. He worked there on the weekends, while attending grad school at Boston University. I'd found a research paper he'd written on the criminology department's website.

"We'll be right across the street if you need us," J said, pointing to the other coffee shop.

"Good luck, dude," Aiden said. I nodded to them, thinking about Colonel Fleetwood's comment about running toward death on the battlefield, and marched inside.

14

Things don't always go as planned.

THE CAFÉ WAS PACKED WITH BOLD-COLORED couches and round tables, and the wall behind the baristas was made of exposed brick. Rhythmic New Age music played from hidden speakers. It all felt very cool.

I approached the counter, fully aware that I had no idea what to do.

"Welcome to Cup-o'-Soul," said the frizzy-haired girl behind the cash register. She was short and perky, with teeth so white that she must have used bleach straight from the bottle to brush them. "What can I serve you today?"

"I, uh, I will have a . . . let's go with . . . how about . . ." The barista frowned. "I'll have a macchiato."

"It's mah-*KEE*-ato, not mah-*chee*-ato."

"Totally," I said, nodding. "I'm also looking for someone. William Parker? Does he work here?"

"Will? Yeah, he's on break in the back," she said. "I can get him for you. . . ."

"Please." I nodded.

She disappeared into the back room, and a few moments later she was followed out by a tall, lanky guy with shaggy blond hair. His nose was far too big for his face, and his acne scars resembled the craters of the moon, but just like the girl, he was smiling kindly.

"Can I help you, little dude?"

"Yeah, uh, hi," I said, really wishing for some reason that Kristina were there. "I was wondering if I could speak to you for a few minutes?"

"About what?" he said. His smile never faltered, but his eyes had drooped.

"I really think you should be sitting down for this part," I said, jerking my head to an empty couch near the window.

I grabbed my coffee, which was in a tiny glass, as he circled around the counter, and we sat down on plush purple sofas.

"I'm Baylor Bosco," I said. "And I know you're Will Parker. I took the bus from Keene this morning to see you. You're Alfred's son, right?"

He frowned. "Did you know my dad?"

"Okay, Will, I'm going to be honest with you, and I just need you to hear me out with an open mind."

He didn't say anything, much less react, so I kept going.

"I can communicate with people who've crossed over, so I—"

"Are you trying to tell me you can talk to dead people?"

"That's exactly what I'm telling you."

He rolled his eyes. "You've gotta be kidding me. Do you know how many loons have come out here and tried to tell me my dad left them a message telling me to invest in their company? At least a dozen. So who are you? What are you going to try to sell me on? It's not going to work, but I'm just curious, since you're the youngest one who's tried to do it so far. How old are you? Ten?"

"I'm almost fourteen! And listen, I'm not after your money," I said, spinning the small cup around with my fingers. "I swear. I'm here because I think your dad is in trouble." I took a sip and immediately regretted it. The bitter taste seeped down my throat like Drano.

"How could my dad be in trouble?" Will asked, his voice like acid as he watched me convulse from the coffee. "He's been dead for three years."

"I know that," I said. "But last week he visited me. He was wrapped in a sheet and couldn't speak. All he did was stare at me with these horrible black eyes."

Will stared at me the way most people stare at roadkill. "My dad didn't have black eyes. And if he was in a sheet, how'd you know it was him?"

"He visited a couple more times, and then he finally showed me his shoes. It had to be his way of communicating with me, because I found the exact same pair the next day, and they had his name in them, and then I searched online and found you and your sister."

He scoffed, looking at the frizzy-haired barista and shaking his head. "This is so stupid."

"I know it sounds crazy, but it can't be a coincidence that I just happened to find the exact same pair of shoes that the spirit was wearing, and they just happened to have 'A. Parker' written in them."

"What shoes?" he said, narrowing his eyes.

"They're brown with golden stitching on the sides, and there's a silver buckle on top."

He hesitated. "Those are the shoes he was buried in."

I bit my lip. "I don't mean to sound awkward, but

he wasn't buried in those shoes. Not unless he had two pairs."

He shook his head. "He was buried in those shoes." There was no point in arguing, even if he was totally wrong. We sat in silence for a few seconds, then he pointed at the little cup of brown sewage. "That might taste better if you put some more milk in it. It's on the counter."

I filled it up to the brim with milk and stirred it. It looked sort of like chocolate milk now, so maybe I'd be able to trick myself into thinking it tasted like it too.

When I sat down, Will was mindlessly scratching his upper arm, and I could see a tattoo hidden below the sleeve.

"What's the tattoo?" I asked before taking a sip of the drink.

Nope. Definitely not chocolate milk. I tried not to spit it out.

"Oh, this?" He pushed up his sleeve to reveal three stick figures: one boy and two girls. "It's me, my sister, and my mom."

His father seemed to hang in the air again as we stared at each other awkwardly. There were sugar packets on the table between us, and I thought I'd give the macchiato one last try with some sweetener.

I skimmed my fingers through the packets, looking for one that just said SUGAR, when I felt myself pulled into a memory attached to a packet of SuperSweetz.

It was a quick one: A woman was reaching for a packet of sugar when a red minivan crashed violently into a truck outside the window, and people rushed out of the café to help.

I lurched back to reality, knocking the packets all over the table. "Dang it," I said, gathering them up as he stared at me. "My bad. There was a memory attached to one of the sugars."

"A memory?"

"Yeah," I mumbled. "It happens sometimes, I have no idea how to control it."

"What was it?"

"A minivan hit a truck, and then a bunch of people rushed out to help. Whoever left the memory must have been really shocked. That's usually how it works, some kind of strong feeling behind it."

He blinked at me, bewildered. "That just happened a couple of days ago. It was the loudest bang I've ever heard. Everyone was freaked out."

"Oh," I said, nodding. "Hope no one was hurt."

"Everyone was fine," he said slowly, like he . . . like he didn't know what to think anymore. He was clearly confused that I knew about the accident, and I realized this was my shot to get him talking.

"Would you mind telling me about your dad?" I asked quietly, trying not to sound too desperate. "I'm just trying to figure out what he wants. I'm trying to figure out what he did when he was alive that was so bad."

He was looking at his hands, which were clenched tightly together, and I thought he was going to tell me to shut up. Miraculously, he started talking.

"The man was a machine, Baylor. Super successful. Good shape. Then he married some chick named Angela, got dementia, and left her all his money, and now my sister and I are broke, and there's nothing we can do about it." He looked up at me. "So if it is him, maybe he feels guilty for marrying some greedy, gold-digging monster who dismantled our inheritance, stole it for herself, and left his kids out to dry. Does that answer your question?"

"I'm sorry," I said. "I didn't mean to make you mad."

"It's not your fault, kid," he said, standing up. "I've dealt with it, it's whatever. I've moved on. My sister got out of Dodge, my mom stayed in Winchester, and God knows where Angela went. She didn't even show up to his funeral."

He said her name with an exaggerated Spanish accent, so it sounded like "An-hell-a."

"Maybe that's why he's visiting me?" I suggested, also standing. "Maybe he wants to make it right somehow."

"Do you really think we haven't tried?" he laughed. "We tried, many times. The legal documents were rock solid."

Part of me was panicking. What if the Sheet Man was going to stay with me forever? Will was my best chance at making this whole thing stop. "There has to be something we can do."

"We?" he said. "There's no 'we' here, Baylor. You're just a kid. You're not going to be able to do anything we haven't already tried."

I stood there frowning.

He sighed. "I wish you luck, Baylor," he said. "I really do. I'd love it if you found a way, but I know you won't be able to, so I'm not bothering to offer my help." He turned away and started to walk to the counter. "Cool trick with the sugar, kid."

I lunged over the sofa and grabbed his arm. "Can I at least get your number in case something comes up?"

He sighed. "Fine." He grabbed a napkin, bent over the counter, and scribbled his number. "Here."

"Thanks!" I said. "I'll leave you mine, too, just in case."

"Great," he said, although I strongly suspected he didn't think it was great at all. After he marched away, I went back to the counter, where the barista had been watching us.

"Did you enjoy your macchiato?" she asked.

"Not even a little bit," I said, setting down the still-full glass on the counter and wondering if that awful taste would ever go away. "Could I get a water and maybe some mouthwash if you've got it?"

Across the street Aiden and J were sitting at a table, chatting merrily about Debate Club. J was the president of the club, and Aiden was the worst-performing member. When I sat down, they were debating about what the next topic for the club should be, and Aiden was finishing an impassioned speech about sandwiches.

"I'm telling you, it's the perfect subject," he said, his arms flailing. "Everyone has their own very specific favorite sandwich, with a million different variables, and it's the sign of the truly skilled debater to convince someone why theirs is the best."

J was giggling and shaking her head as she turned to me.

"So how'd it go, Baylor?"

I frowned. I didn't know what I had expected. Maybe

a tearful, grateful son, sharing all his knowledge about his father with me? Maybe an angry person with a clear story as to why his father was most certainly at home in the evil part of the other side?

But what I got from Will wasn't helpful. Leaving your kids no money is pretty bad, but it doesn't make you evil. I still had no real answer for what was happening with his father.

It seemed safer to keep them both in the dark as much as possible about the Sheet Man, so I just told them the practical facts of what Will had told me, and how none of it was very useful.

"Well, that's annoying," J said. "But at least you learned the ex-wife lives in Winchester? Maybe you can visit her next."

I hadn't even thought of that. "Brilliant, J!" I said. "You are *brilliant.*"

"She *is* brilliant," Aiden said dreamily. We both turned to him, and a look of horror dawned on his face that he'd apparently uttered those words aloud.

"Uh, time to go, guys, right?" he said, hopping up. "Let's get a move on."

I'd never seen Aiden move that fast in my life unless a pepperoni sandwich was at stake.

"Wait a second!" J said, looking at her watch. "The next bus to Keene isn't for an hour and a half."

Aiden turned around, slow-motion style, emanating a silent but very real distress signal out to the world, his eyes begging for help from me, from the barista, from a hole in the ground that would swallow him up and take him far away from here.

"What are we going to do for an hour and a half?" he croaked.

"We could do some sightseeing?" I suggested. "Anything close to here?"

"It's Boston!" J said, her eyes bulging with excitement. "The birthplace of the American Revolution. There's *so* much to see. We could walk part of the Freedom Trail and visit the key sites of the Revolution! The Boston Massacre, the Old State House, Paul Revere's house, and oh, I think Paul Revere's grave is on the trail too. You might like that, Baylor!"

"Uh," I said, horrified by my mistake. "I think the river's nearby. Can we just go look at that?"

"Look at the river?" She looked bewildered, turning her head back and forth from me to Aiden. "But all the stuff I just . . . oh, come on, guys, you at least have to see the Boston Tea Party ships!" She smiled eagerly at Aiden, but he didn't notice, since he was still mentally berating himself.

"Sure," I said. "Is it on the river, right over there, steps away?"

She frowned. "No."

"Darn," I said, picking up my bag. "To the river!"

We crossed Storrow Drive and wound up on an embankment along the river. It was freezing—the wind was blasting like a high-speed train over the river, apparently arriving fresh from the Arctic Circle.

"Isn't this great?" I said, teeth clattering, to J, who was clutching her arms over her chest. "What a view." The river was a dark, choppy mess; the sky was gray and bleak.

"Yeah, Baylor," J said sarcastically, "this was your best idea ever."

Aiden, still too afraid to say anything, stood motionless, looking like he wanted nothing more than for the wind to pick him up and carry him swiftly away.

"Let's just go," J said. "We'll get to the bus station early and have some hot chocolate."

I set my backpack down and took a step closer to the concrete balustrade on the edge of the river. "You want to leave already? We just got here."

"You've got thirty more seconds until I kick you into the river," she said between shivers.

I looked out at the gray sky; there was such a thick layer of clouds blocking the sun that it felt like a miracle the light was making its way through at all. I remembered the nonsense that Kristina and the colonel said when we made the talisman, about the sun knowing only light, so the moon's light in the darkness was more special. I scoffed. What did they know? Look at the sun now, doing its best to shove its rays through the nearly impenetrable Boston sky.

A prickle of chills lightly spread on the back of my neck, a different sort of cold than what we'd been experiencing.

"Baylor, let's go!" J said defiantly. "I've had enough."

"One second," I said, leaning far over the railing, the concrete hard against my stomach. There was something there, some kind of presence. I could feel it.

Any color that had been in the sky seemed to disappear.

I turned to look at J and Aiden, but they were gone. The chill in my neck now pulsated throughout my body, and I swung back around to face the river.

Over the violent waters the Sheet Man was gliding right toward me.

15

Seriously,
DO NOT PANIC.

THE EYES WERE FOCUSED ON ME, UNBLINK-ing, little black holes soaking up light and energy. The sheet was perfectly still despite its quick movement through the fierce wind and thrashing waves.

The talisman! It was in my bag steps away.

I crawled off the railing, dismayed to see I was totally alone. J, Aiden, all the other pedestrians that had been walking by—were they really gone, or was Alfred transporting me to some other realm, some sort of perpetual limbo where only he existed?

I lunged for my bag, but before I had the chance

to unzip it, the Sheet Man was there, so close I could reach out and touch him. My breathing became shallow and I felt light-headed. This was it. He'd finally gotten me. I noticed the shoes were gone, so his bare feet hung there, the toenails yellow and shriveled.

And the eyes. I looked back at the feet because the eyes were scarier than I remembered, especially this close up, like ash was smeared around them.

"Can I help you, Alfred?" I asked, clutching the bag, sneakily attempting to open it, trying to keep my voice from shaking.

No response.

"I met your son today. William? He was disappointed in you."

Still nothing. He just floated there like a casual ghost friend of mine. He didn't seem to notice my hand inching into the bag.

"He said you didn't leave him or your daughter any inheritance. You left all your money to your new wife."

I'd struck a nerve. A strange scream erupted from somewhere inside of him, and then, like he was giving birth to another evil Sheet Man, a spirit hurtled out from under the sheet. It was tangled in the fabric, the arms tied up like they were handcuffed. The spirit unraveled itself, and I gasped.

"Kristina!" I yelled, dropping the bag. "What the . . . how the . . ."

"Baylor!" she yelled. "The wife! Talk to the—"

And then they disappeared.

At the same moment Aiden and J came back into focus, screaming my name over the railing by the river.

"I'm here," I shouted behind them. I noticed they were no longer alone; people had stopped to help them.

"How did you do that?" J yelled, running over to me, Aiden hot on her heels, tears streaming down their faces. "You disappeared"—she snapped her fingers—"like that."

I was barely paying attention to them. How could I? Kristina was caught in whatever limbo the Sheet Man existed, and there was nothing I could do about it.

"It was like an alien beamed you up," Aiden said, bending over, huffing loudly.

"It was him," I said, my voice hoarse. "The father of the guy I visited today. And he somehow took Kr—another ghost hostage." I swallowed, the lump in my throat huge, the tears seconds away. I was too afraid to say her name out loud. What if it somehow affected her? "I . . . I don't know what to do. This situation is absurd. They're all dead. There's no one I can call. There's no one I can turn to." I looked at their tearstained faces, and I wondered if they were somehow in danger just being around me.

Where was Colonel Fleetwood? Surely, he had to be aware of Kristina's absence. Unless he had been kidnapped too?

"I need to go home," I said. "I need to light a million candles."

Before I knew what was happening, a gruff pair of hands turned me around.

"You gave your friends quite a scare there, son." A police officer was looking me up and down. He'd walked over from the river, and I noticed an ambulance was pulling up behind him. "They thought you'd fallen into the river."

I turned to Aiden. "You called nine-one-one?"

Aiden raised his hands limply. "We didn't know what to do, Baylor. We thought you were drowning."

"Luckily, I was nearby and could offer my help," the officer said, puffing out his chest. "Your parents around, son?"

I gulped. A chill entirely unrelated to the Sheet Man or the cold entered the pit of my stomach. "We live in Keene."

"You kids are in Boston alone?"

"We took the bus," J said.

"I see," he said. "Looks like I'm going to have to give them a call."

"That won't be necessary, Officer," I said, brushing myself off and gathering up my bag. "Really, I'm fine, and we have a bus to catch."

"You three are minors alone in Boston who just had to call nine-one-one because one of you nearly went tumbling over the river's edge." He smiled kindly but spoke firmly. "What's your parents' phone number, son?"

My mom spoke to the officer at length, and when he handed the phone to me, she tersely said two sentences before hanging up: "Take the bus home. I'll pick you up at the station."

J, Aiden, and I didn't say a word to one another the entire ride home. They knew I was furious with them for calling the cops, but they also felt completely justified in trying to save my life.

When we got to the bus station, my mom was there with a nervous-looking Mrs. Kirkwood.

"J, Mrs. Kirkwood is going to take you home," my mom said, not looking at me. She turned to Aiden's mom. "I'll call you later, Karen." She marched to the car, and I looked one last time at Aiden and J. It was obvious I was a dead man walking; their smiles, meant to be encouraging, looked more like Ella's when we tried to feed her pureed peas.

"Not a word," my mom said, her voice a dangerous whisper. "Not one word until we're home." Of course. She and Dad had to yell at me together.

My mom may have wanted to make sure my dad was present to yell at me, but she took care of the bulk of it herself.

"I forbade you, Baylor," she said, chopping away at a bunch of carrots. I could imagine her hanging up the phone with the officer and heading straight to the store to stock up in preparation of this exact moment. "I literally said, 'I am forbidding you to go.' Let that word soak in for a second. Forbid."

She chopped as I sat at the kitchen table in silence. My dad sat next to me. He didn't seem angry as much as he was abysmally confused.

"*Forbid.* And why did I forbid it, Baylor? Do you remember?"

I didn't say anything. If there was one thing I knew about my mom, it was that it was best to let her get it all out, no matter how long it took, like a balloon slowly, painfully deflating its air.

"Because you told me you wanted to meet the son

of that dead thing that put you in the hospital. Now, that's just crazy, isn't it? Isn't it, Douglas?"

My dad grunted.

"I thought it sounded like a bad idea, Baylor, because you could get hurt, maybe wind up in the hospital again, something awful." She heaved a pile of diced carrots into a Tupperware container. "And then today I get a *phone call* from a *police officer* in *Boston* about my son, who was there alone with friends and seemed to go missing, and guess what, Baylor. *You proved that it was a bad idea.*"

It went on like that for a while, until they sent me to my room to begin my punishment of being grounded for forever, and then when they died and crossed over, they were still going to make sure I was grounded. I never gave them a straight answer about what led Aiden and J to call the police, nor did I tell them the Sheet Man made another appearance, this time with Kristina in tow. I didn't ever plan to tell them, since my mom would go berserk.

Seriously, what was I going to do? Whenever I had a question, I turned to Kristina. Kristina was the one who was supposed to stick with me. She was the one who was supposed to protect me from the evil spirits, especially the demons, like the Insymbios, who could sneak in unnoticed, take over my body, and make me go insane; or even worse, the Bru—I stopped and took a deep breath, vanquishing the thought from my brain. Even thinking about them could make me vulnerable.

What could I do to protect her? I couldn't bounce between realms. I couldn't simply walk over to the Beyond and ask for help. Even if I could go to the Beyond, which I obviously couldn't access since I wasn't dead, I wouldn't know what to say. The Sheet Man seemed to exist in his own weird, lifeless limbo, and it wasn't like I'd be able to cough up directions on how to reach him.

My mom was right. It was chaos on the other side.

With candles lit, I demanded Colonel Fleetwood get his butt back over here so we could come up with a plan.

Nothing. Not even a creak in the floor. Not even a flicker of the lights. Not any sort of small sign that anyone or anything was listening to me.

If Kristina was my buffer to the other side, it was horrifyingly possible that with her taken out of the loop, I'd lost my "in" with the Beyond. Could that really be?

My little séance obviously wasn't working, so I hopped on my computer and searched for Alfred's wife. Kristina's one clue was my only solid lead. But Angela was nowhere to be found.

Then I remembered that the ex-wife lived in Winchester, and J had suggested I find her next. She could be easy to track down, and maybe she knew something.

Sure enough, Rosalie Parker's address was listed online; she was located just outside of Winchester's little downtown area.

I jotted the address onto a piece of paper and ran downstairs.

"Dad, we're going into Winchester tomorrow, right? I need to apologize to Aunt Hilda and every-thing."

He and my mom both turned to me with shocked expressions.

"Baylor Bosco, what do you have planned?" my mom asked, her eyes narrowing.

"Nothing!" I said. "I just feel really bad about everything."

"Fine by me," my dad said with a shrug. "I want to stop at that fishing store on Main Street too."

"Well, be sure to call Aunt Hilda before you head down there," Mom said scathingly. "We don't want you to surprise her and give her a heart attack."

After a sleepless night, the next morning couldn't come fast enough. Luckily, my dad was an early riser because of his job, so we both got ready and drove the thirty minutes to Winchester. We ate breakfast at a café on Main Street, where he tried to talk to me about my fiascos in Boston and at Aunt Hilda's birthday dinner.

"Between you and me, I think it's crazy your mom is making you apologize to her," he said between bites of his ham-and-cheese omelet. "I walked into that place knowing something was going to happen. Everyone knows you can't function properly in Italian restaurants."

"*Thank you,*" I said, finally feeling vindicated. "Agreed. There were just so many people inside one little space. I sort of lost my mind."

"That being said, it was wrong of you to go to Boston after she *forbade* you from going." It sounded like he'd rehearsed this. "You're going to be paying for that one for a while."

"I know. Again, I'm very sorry."

He sipped his juice and sighed. "I do not envy you, son. The ghosts and the crazy stuff and all." He smiled at me. "Oh, and don't tell your mom I said any of that stuff about Aunt Hilda."

Afterward we browsed the tackle shop. My dad was looking for fall sales to stock up for spring, and he bought a couple of snagless sinkers as well as a few spools of line. But when we called Aunt Hilda at ten to let her know we wanted to come over, she was nowhere near ready.

"Now what?" my dad asked. He looked around at the other shops. "I guess we can get some Christmas shopping done. My mom would probably like something from one of those antique shops."

I shuddered. Antique stores are the worst place for objects with memories attached to them.

"Hey, Dad, you know what? One of my teachers lives just around the corner," I said. "Would you mind driving me over so I could stop by and say hi?"

"You want to visit a teacher on a Sunday at ten a.m.? Isn't that a little weird?" he asked.

"Uh, I don't know, we were almost like friends, this teacher and I."

"Which teacher is it?"

"Mrs. Parker. Remember her? She's divorced now."

He scrunched his face together as he thought. "I don't think so?"

"Come on, it'll only take a few minutes."

"But you're grounded." I could see the wheels spinning in his head, calculating whether or not visiting a teacher really fell into grounded territory. "Why not? I don't mind catching up with my students, I'm sure she won't mind either."

And a few minutes later I was walking up the brick pathway to a tiny brick cottage. I had told my dad to stay in the car, but that he could come say hi at the end if he wanted, which was another bald-faced lie, but whatever.

The house had a nice front porch, with white iron lattice railings around the perimeter. The garden was kept up nicely, which is the universal sign that the homeowners care about their house, and I felt satisfied Rosalie wouldn't answer the door drunk and covered in weeks-old bits of food.

I rang the doorbell and heard a couple of dogs barking. They sounded like big dogs, and I wondered how they liked being cooped up in such a small house.

The door opened, revealing a woman wearing a red bathrobe. Her graying brunette hair was tied up in a ponytail, and she was already wearing makeup. She was pretty and seemed delicate, and I could easily see my mom looking similar to her in twenty years.

"Can I help you?" she asked, her brow furrowed.

"I'm Baylor Bosco, and I can communicate with people who have crossed over," I said. "I was hoping I could speak with you for a few moments about your ex-husband, Alfred."

She shook her head in her surprise, blinking vigorously.

"Is this a joke?"

"I'm sorry," I said. "I know Alfred has been dead for several years, but I've just started receiving very strange visits from him. He won't speak with me, though, so I don't know how to help him."

Her face sort of collapsed. One second she looked normal, the next second everything was wrinkled and twisted.

"You need to go," she said, reaching to close the door.

"No!" I growled, slamming it back open and surprising myself with my sudden fury. "I know he didn't leave your children any money, and now I need to know how to fix it so he'll leave me alone. Where can I find Angela?"

Rosalie was stronger than she looked. She managed to begin closing the door, while staring at me like she wanted to reach down my throat, pull out my intestines, and use them to decorate her Christmas tree. "I don't like to talk about my ex-husband," she said in a voice that wasn't her own. "Get off my property."

The door clicked shut, followed by a massive deadbolt clunk. I stared, stunned. Then I spun around and walked down the path, just as my dad was getting out of the car.

"What happened, Baylor?" He looked shocked.

"Did you make her mad somehow? Bring up the divorce or something?"

"No," I said, "she just didn't remember me. Guess we weren't as close as I thought."

I was so distracted by everything that had happened in the last twenty-four hours—talking to Will, discovering Kristina got ghostnapped, and meeting Rosalie—that I could barely remember why I was at Aunt Hilda's place.

"Sorry I ruined your birthday," I said flatly. "I didn't mean to ruin it. I know you only turn eighty-eight once, and since it was probably your last birthday, I feel bad it didn't go the way you wanted it to."

"Baylor!" my dad exclaimed, trying to force a laugh, while Aunt Hilda's eyes widened to the size of half-dollar coins. "Why don't you try that again?"

"Try what again?"

"Your apology," he said through gritted teeth. "One more time."

"Uh, I'm sorry you don't believe I have the ability to talk to ghosts, even though your friend Marjorie is standing behind you and telling you she's sorry she never paid you the forty bucks you won playing Bunco with her."

"I always thought she cheated," Marjorie said,

shrugging, her voice low and gravelly from what must have been decades of chain-smoking. "Who's that good at Bunco?"

"Marjorie?" Aunt Hilda said. "I just saw Marjorie last night. She can't be dead."

My dad's jaw dropped, and I pressed my lips together.

"Oh, sorry, kid," Marjorie said, laughing. "Forgot to mention I'm fresh as of early this morning."

"Thanks a lot, Marge," I snapped, looking at the troublemaking ghost over Aunt Hilda's shoulder before turning my attention back to her. "Sorry, Aunt Hilda, looks like Marjorie crossed over this morning."

Aunt Hilda looked at me with indecipherable eyes, and then she caustically spit, "I don't believe you."

"She's in for a nasty surprise if no one finds me before my cats run out of food," Marjorie said.

I grimaced, but before I could say anything, my dad grabbed my shoulder and steered me out of the apartment. "Sorry, Aunt Hilda. I'll have Connie call you later."

16

Always keep
chocolate handy.

NEEDLESS TO SAY, MY MOM WAS NOT HAPPY
with me.

"Less than a day after your Boston escapades, you
go over to Aunt Hilda's to apologize," she said, her
voice low and emotionless, "and you wind up not
only telling her that she's not going to have another
birthday, but that one of her best friends just died?"

"How was I supposed to know Marjorie had just
died?" I said, throwing my hands up. "It's not like the
ghosts walk around with a little calendar tied around
their neck telling me when they crossed over."

"And not only did you scar your great-aunt, your father seems equally traumatized."

My dad had burrowed himself into a bunch of blankets on the sofa because the experience with Marjorie and Aunt Hilda had resurfaced the memory of me telling him about his father.

"This is not my fault," I said. "None of it is! Be mad at the universe, or God, or Buddha, or Zeus, or whoever you want to be mad at for giving me this gift, but don't be mad at me. I can't help it."

She shook her head, looking sad and defeated. "Can't Kristina help you more? Can't she help you just, I don't know, somehow make them stop? Set up some healing hours and say that you're available to heal only on Saturdays between eleven and three?"

My jaw tensed. "I'll see what she can do."

That night I cracked open my Halloween candy and hunted for anything with chocolate. All the sweet, sugary stuff, like Smarties and Starburst and Skittles, got tossed aside. It was an old habit based on something Kristina said to me once. She had been watching me eat chocolate one day, and in a pathetic, puppy-dog way she said, "The one food I wish I could eat is chocolate. It's brown and strange-looking, but people get so happy when they eat it."

"People get happy eating anything when they're really hungry," I said.

"But chocolate is different. Chocolate is what people get for special occasions. People go out of their way to eat it, even if they're not hungry. Whenever people die suddenly, they never cross over and say, 'I'm so thrilled I decided to eat that stalk of celery.' It's always, 'I'm just happy I decided to eat that last piece of chocolate cake.'"

Since then I've always savored my chocolate, because even though I'm pretty sure I'm not going to die for a while, there's always a chance it could be my last time eating it.

As I chewed on a fun-size Milky Way, I wondered where Kristina was. I wondered whether she was uncomfortable being tied up with the Sheet Man, or if it even bothered her at all. It was probably just a minor inconvenience. It probably felt like only a couple of hours had passed. I was worried for her, of course, but I couldn't help but feel defeated by the fact that she was already dead. In books, TV shows, and movies the main drama always seems to involve death somehow, and how terrible it is.

Death was the least of my concerns. What more could the Sheet Man do to her, really? He could keep her trapped in that weird dimension he existed in. He could replace her eyes with black buttons to make her look like him. He could convert her to the Sheet Woman and make Sheet Babies. I shuddered. That was a terrifying thought.

I wanted to panic about her being gone, but all I could think about was how her absence affected *me*. Her duty was to assist me, and now that she was missing, it meant that a very important piece of my daily life was gone.

I swallowed the candy and reached for another as it dawned on me that this sort of thinking was the reason she had snapped at me that night after the Italian dinner. I was so worried about myself and how she could help me that I rarely thought about her.

But . . . she was dead! There was really nothing I could do to help her, and if she'd been having ghostly feelings about loneliness and missing out on the human experience, then she should have mentioned them rather than lashing out.

Right? That was a reasonable request. It was just hard to imagine her as a real person with feelings, but maybe I needed to do that nowadays. Her world was just so different from mine. Sure, we spent the majority of my waking hours together, but when I slept, Kristina was off in the Beyond living her secretive ghost life. I had no idea what happened over there except for the half hints and clues she gave me.

I sighed and grabbed yet another Milky Way. None of this would matter if she never got out of Sheet Man limbo. But I would get her out. I had the talisman. The Sheet Man would visit me again, and I would stop him and get Kristina back.

My phone rang suddenly, interrupting my thoughts. I didn't recognize the area code, but I picked up anyway, secretly hoping Kristina had somehow used her energy to communicate via the phone.

"Hello?"

"Hi, is this Baylor?"

"Uh, yes, hi. Who's this?"

"My name is Isabella Parker."

I shot up and jumped to my desk.

"Isabella!" I said. "I didn't expect to hear from you."

"Will told me about your meeting yesterday," she said. "It sounded pretty awkward."

"Yeah, he didn't seem too eager to speak with me."

"You probably caught him off guard," she said. "To be honest, I was caught off guard too. But then I searched for you online and came across all sorts of information. Did you know you have fans, Baylor? There are a couple of websites devoted to you. One group calls themselves the Baylievers."

I was thankful she couldn't see me blush. "That's

embarrassing. I really don't Google myself too often."

"And I found an article about you from just the other day. Apparently, you knocked over a lady and then held an impromptu reading at an Italian restaurant?"

"That . . . that, yes, that happened, but it was all an accident."

"Whatever it was, it's amazing to read about, and I called you the instant I read the last word."

"Well, thanks, I guess. It'll be helpful to learn more about your father."

"Will told me Dad's visiting you and wears a sheet on his head the whole time? That's very unlike him. He was a social creature and wouldn't hide himself like that."

"Could he have been involved with some bad deeds in his life?" I asked. "Maybe some dark stuff you don't know about?"

"I doubt it," she said, speaking a little faster. "He was a great guy. Even toward the end, when he had his memory problems, he was so sweet and felt so bad when he forgot one of us."

"Isabella, his presence is shrouded in evil," I said. "Something's wrong with this picture."

"It's got to be something with Angela." She said the

name in the same exaggerated accent as her brother. "That woman! She was evil, Baylor. She probably did something to my dad, and the residue of it is affecting his afterlife."

"What could she have done that was so bad?"

"Well, for starters, she only married the man for his money!" she said exuberantly, and I could picture her shaking her fist on the other end of the phone. "She was less than half his age when they got married, and they had dated for only a few months. It was so obvious! And then when he died, to find out that he'd left her all the money and didn't leave a dime for us? I don't buy it. She knew exactly what she was doing."

"It still doesn't explain the sheet," I said. "I can communicate just fine with people who've done far worse things."

"I don't think she was treating him right," she said. "Toward the end, whenever we visited them at their home, something felt . . . off. And I'm not just saying that because I don't like her."

"I don't know," I said. "It still doesn't seem serious enough for him to deserve this sort of fate."

"Then Angela must have done something worse, and we don't know about it," she said.

"Do you know where I could find her? To ask her some questions?"

"No idea," she said. "Once my dad died, she disappeared. She recently had the estate sale, so I bet she's gearing up to sell the house and run off with even more money."

"I hope not," I said. "That sort of bad karma catches up with everyone eventually."

"God, Baylor, this all makes sense in a weird way," she said. "I've never felt my dad's presence in the years since he died. Not once, not even so much as a nightmare with him in it. It's like a void."

"Well, hopefully, we'll be able to fix that soon."

"I hope so," she said. "I really do."

We ended the chat with the promise to call each other should we learn anything more. I hung up and looked at the notes I had written down on my notepad.

Nothing. It was nice of her to call, but I got nothing concrete from her.

I sighed and lay back down on my bed. I was no closer to finding Kristina than before.

When we were kids, we'd get into such trouble sometimes. Well, I'd get into trouble, and she'd giggle on the other side. Having a clued-in dead sister as an accomplice was not good for my behavior. One time at school Kristina told me the code to get into the teachers' lounge, and I sneaked in and took some sodas. I did it a couple of times more, and then I got cocky and brought some friends with me. As we were raiding the fridge, a teacher caught us and marched us straight down to the principal's office, where all my friends promptly turned me in as the ringleader.

Imagine explaining to your principal that your invisible sister gave you the code and you didn't realize it would get you in trouble. That led to a couple of awkward meetings with my parents, and afterward they gave me the strict instructions never to mention my gift to anyone.

This was all before Kristina went away and learned more about her soul's purpose. After that she rarely goofed around at all. But I still thought of us as partners in crime, and the fact that I didn't know how to help her like she'd helped me a million times before was the only thing on my mind as I tossed and turned that night.

17

Try not to miss the obvious.

I DREAMED I WAS WALKING THROUGH THE cemetery and saw Tommy Thorne. He was standing under the giant tree, guarding his tombstone, his bright red hoodie shrouded in mist. When he saw me, he tilted his head, his jet-black hair sweeping to the side.

"You know where to find peace," he said.

Then I woke with a start, unsure of when I'd fallen asleep in the first place.

It was seven forty-five on Monday morning, and I'd overslept big-time. I sprinted to the shower, rinsed off, brushed my teeth, and got dressed all in about three minutes.

Downstairs my mom was bouncing Ella on her hip.

"You're still here?" she said. "I thought you left twenty minutes ago."

"Obviously not," I said, grabbing a banana and heading out the door.

"Stay out of trouble," she called as I shut the door.

It was too late for that. The street was swarmed with spirits. Did Kristina really block that many out for me? There hadn't been that many out yesterday, though, so that couldn't be it. I walked down the block toward school, pulling my hoodie over my head and keeping my eyes to the ground.

It's always disconcerting to see demons floating around that early in the morning, and I felt strangely vulnerable without Kristina there to act as my buffer and, as much as I hated to admit it, my security blanket. Even though the spirits weren't bothering me that morning, all I wanted was to go straight to the cemetery. Tommy clearly had a message for me, and I needed to hear it. Maybe it would help me get a step closer to finding Kristina.

Once I got to school, I realized I hadn't done my routine. I was so zonked out from thinking about Kristina and Tommy and rushing for school that I completely forgot to surround myself with positive energy. I ruffled through my bag, pulled out my emergency lighter, sparked the flame, and enveloped myself with light, immediately feeling better . . . until someone screamed my name.

"Baylor Bosco!"

I turned around to look for the source of anger and saw my vice-principal standing near the entranceway, glaring at me. Mr. Connell was a very thin man who wore clothes that were always too baggy for his body, like dress shirts that were trying to swallow him whole. His voice also happened to sound just like Kermit the Frog's.

"What do you think you're doing with that lighter? Come here, young man."

I imagined a small amphibian scolding me, and I laughed as I walked up to him.

"Oh, you think it's funny, do you?"

"No, Mr. Connell, I'm sorry, it's all a misunderstanding."

"I don't think so," he said. "I saw you hold your lighter close to your face. You know there's no smoking allowed on school property, not to mention the fact that you're only thirteen! I'm going to have to search your belongings."

I thought about my mom's words as I'd left the

house: *Stay out of trouble.* Clearly, she was still mad at me, and the last thing I needed was for the school to call her and get me into more trouble.

"Mr. Connell, you read the newspaper, right?"

"What?"

"Did you happen to see that article about me the other day?"

His whole body reacted to my words. His face scrunched, his arms stiffened, and his feet shuffled several times.

"I don't like all that funny business," he said. "Go to class and don't let me catch you doing anything like that again."

I pressed my lips together to smile unpleasantly at him and then slipped past the doors, thankful it hadn't escalated into something further. It always amused me to see how people reacted to my gift. Even after hearing all the rumors and reading the occasional article on it, some people couldn't help but feel skeptical.

As I was walking between first and second periods with one of my band friends, my arm got pulled backward, and I swung around to see J holding on to me with a death grip.

"Hey," I said, rubbing my shoulder. "Everything all right?"

"No, everything's not all right," she said. "Do you know who Andrew Vallario is?"

The name brought a blurry image of a preppy-looking guy who looked like he brushed his hair a thousand times every night before going to bed.

"I think I've heard of him," I said. "Isn't he almost as smart as you?"

"Yes," she said. "And do you know what he did this morning? He asked me to go to the Fall Ball with him."

My eyes widened for a second as I thought of Aiden's unrequited love for J, then I realized I wasn't playing it cool and regained my composure. But it was too late.

"I knew it!" she said, bouncing on her toes. "Your eyes just gave it all away! Aiden wants to ask me, right?"

"I—I—I can't say," I stuttered.

"You're his best friend! Of course you can!"

"I think it could possibly be something he might have thought about considering?"

"Oh, really helpful, Baylor," she said. "I know Aiden wants to go with me. We spent so much time with each other this weekend, and I don't know how many more hints I can drop before I wind up accidentally asking him myself."

For a second I wondered whether she should just ask him herself. It would save Aiden a lot of awkwardness, and he wouldn't have to panic anymore about whether or not she liked him. But J obviously wasn't going to do that. She might be scarily smart, but she was still a girl who wanted to get asked on a date to the dance.

"Listen, I'll say something to him," I said. "Things are just sort of crazy right now."

"I know, I know," she said. "And I feel bad about even mentioning this to you after what happened on Saturday." She looked at me sadly. "I just don't want to hurt Aiden."

She walked away, her short hair bobbing up and down with every step.

When I recounted the story to Aiden at lunch, he looked like he was about to cry.

"Baylor," he whispered, his voice hoarse and his face a sickly pallor. "I did something really stupid."

"What is it?" I said, thrilled to have something other than Kristina to think about.

"Well, so, after your accident in the band room, Cassie could see I was pretty shaken up about the whole thing. She talked with me for a while after you'd gone to the hospital."

"Cassie who plays the clarinet? Okay. Why does that matter?"

"Well, we kept talking, and we started texting, and

I mean, it was stupid stuff, I thought we were just being friendly. . . ."

"Oh, no, Aiden, please don't say what you're about to say," I said, my hands squeezing my skull.

"She brought the dance up first! And I said it would be fun to go, but I didn't mean with her, I was thinking of J the entire time. But then she must have thought I meant *with her*, and she said yes and that she couldn't wait to go with me, and it all happened before I knew what was even happening!"

"And you didn't immediately tell me?"

"It just happened yesterday," he said, looking forlornly at his sandwich. "I'm still processing it."

"I don't know what to say," I said. "Clarinet Cassie? What were you thinking?"

"I wasn't!" Tears were actually welling up in his eyes. "I think I'm going to be sick."

"Well, you've got to get out of it," I said. "Tell her your phone was stolen and some jerk's been pranking her."

"I can't do that," he said. "I saw her this morning. She was skipping, Baylor. Skipping. You can't reject a girl after you made her so happy that she skips."

"Demon dung," I said, shaking my head. "You're right."

"What'd you just say?" His eyes narrowed in confusion.

"Nothing!" I sputtered, alarmed I'd said Kristina's favorite phrase so casually. "I just feel bad for you." He shrugged, and I could tell he was genuinely distraught. He hadn't even touched his pepperoni sandwich.

"What am I going to do? Once J finds out about Cassie, she's going to hate me and say yes to Andrew and my life will officially be over."

"We'll figure it out," I said. "Don't panic yet. There's got to be a way out of this."

I wished Kristina were there to help. She would've been the perfect person—uh, ghost—to construct a plan.

Aiden spent the rest of the school day texting me stressed messages.

> AIDEN: How could I have been so dumb?

> AIDEN: What if j finds out?

> AIDEN: I ruined my 1 shot at love!!!! :'(

I felt bad for the kid, but no good ideas had sprung to mind, and all my mental energy was focused on finding some way to rescue Kristina.

After band practice I walked the thirty minutes to Woodland Cemetery and went straight to Tommy's grave. I leaned against it, staring at the swaying spruce overhead.

"Tommy?" I called out. "Are you around?"

"Right here," said a voice to my left. He was leaning against his mom's tombstone, his hair brushing the stone, and staring at the spruce just like I was. "Nice of you to let me through this time."

Someone was a little bitter about being blocked on Halloween.

"Sorry about that," I said. "I was a little freaked out that night."

"It's okay," he said. "I know." Tommy mainly spent his time in the Beyond, but he came back every now and then to deliver a message or just to talk to me.

"Thanks for visiting me last night," I said. "I guess you knew I needed it."

"I could sense your angst. I thought maybe Kristina hadn't been around to help you for a few days."

"She got taken, Tommy," I said. "The Sheet Man who attacked me on Halloween night somehow took her. I've been trying to figure out how to get her back, but I have no idea how. She's trapped in some sort of weird limbo dimension."

"That explains why I haven't seen her," he said.

"You guys see each other?"

"Usually, yeah," he said. "Whenever she's in the Beyond."

"What have the ghosts been saying in the Beyond?" I asked, trying not to sound too anxious. "Why haven't they come back to this side to help me out?"

"They might be worried the same thing that happened to her could happen to them."

"But you cross back and forth just fine."

"I'm not one of your spirit guides, though," he said. "Just a friend."

"So the spirit guides have some kind of target on their backs?"

"It's possible, Baylor, but then again, you and Kristina are a special duo. Kristina may be dead, but she's not exactly your average ghost, either."

"What do you mean?" I asked. "She's just . . . a ghost."

"I'm not permitted to say too much," he said, pushing his hair out of his face. Was that some kind of phrase all ghosts were required to learn? "But come on, haven't you ever noticed that Kristina ages with you, while the other ghosts stay the age they died?"

It felt like he'd slapped me. How could I have missed something so obvious? The ghost children running through my dreams that stayed children. The dead grandparents that always stayed grandparents. And even Tommy, the skinny ghost with the cool hair, was still the permanent epitome of cool at age eleven.

But Kristina had been a baby with me, then a toddler, then a walking and talking little kid, and now a teenager. How had I never thought to ask about that?

"You should see your face right now," Tommy said.

"I can't believe I never realized it," I said. "It just seemed . . . natural."

"Of course it did," he said, shrugging.

"So Kristina's special in the Beyond just like I'm special in the physical world?"

He nodded.

"And because of that I'm on my own now?"

"You're never on your own, Baylor," he said, chuckling. "You just can't see or hear how you're being helped like you usually can, which means you're just like everyone else in the physical world."

"Well, I don't like it."

"Maybe you should try something different, then."

"What do you mean?"

"Well, you can't cross into the Beyond because you're still alive, but it seems like you can enter whatever dimension the Sheet Man exists in, right?"

"Right?"

"Well, then . . . enter it."

"You're making it sound so easy, Tommy. How can I get there?"

"Visit another one of your kind and have them help you."

"You think another gifted person could help me?"

He shrugged. "Why not?"

I didn't think Tommy's advice was bad, but I wasn't exactly friends with any other gifted people around town. To be honest, I wasn't sure if there *were* any other legit ones. Kristina had never spoken of any, so I didn't know whether or not to believe in them.

I searched the Internet for a few suggestions, and nearly all the results for Keene turned up with my name somewhere in them. My cheeks burned as I skipped past the Baylievers' fan boards ("Has boy wonder Baylor Bosco helped you somehow? Share your story here!").

But there were a few businesses listed in the area—in Keene, Winchester, some of the surrounding towns, and the mother ship in Boston—and as I perused the websites featuring shiny crystal balls and bloody tarot cards and floating feathers, I couldn't help but understand why people didn't believe in my ability. These people seemed ridiculous. I didn't need any special items to communicate. Sure, a candle helped me with my focus, but I didn't *need* it for my gift to work.

I wrote down the addresses for the two closest shops, both located in downtown Keene, and stuffed the paper into my backpack, next to my talisman. A flash of panic hit me about how I was going to get there. My parents would eviscerate me if they found out I'd gone to visit these shops. I'd just have to skip band practice tomorrow, and as long as I was home in time for dinner, and as long as I evaded any run-ins with the hospital or the police, they'd never need to know.

TIP

18

Grandpa
knows best.

THE NEXT DAY SCHOOL PASSED BY IN A flurry of awkward exchanges and glances.

J pointedly glared at me as she walked down the hall with her would-be date, Andrew. He was taller than I remembered, but every bit as preppy. He was wearing a pink button-down and a blue winter vest, and based on his hair, he most likely owned several hundred shares of stock in his favorite pomade company.

Mr. Connell seemed to be following me around the halls, looking for any trace of another lighter.

The third time I spotted him staring at me, I waved at him, and he turned the other direction and marched away like nothing had happened.

Aiden looked like a toddler lost in the mall. First I saw him staring helplessly at me while Cassie chatted merrily to him, and then during lunch he picked at his sandwich and formed sad pepperoni faces with the globs of mustard.

"What happened to the pepperoni?" Bobby asked as he sat down. "They know they're about to be in your stomach or something? Oh, maybe they're thinking about what happens next."

Aiden scowled. "These pepperoni slices are going through a hard time, Bobby."

Bobby blinked at him. "I'm sorry to hear that."

When school ended, I grabbed Aiden and told him to cover for me in band practice, since I needed to sneak off to downtown.

"Is it for a plan to kill Cassie or something?"

"No, Aiden!" I said, gasping. "Don't say things like that! An evil spirit could latch on to you when you put out that kind of bad energy!"

"Sorry, sorry, I take it back," he said. "But is it?"

"No, it's not," I said, launching into my plan to find another gifted person to help me get to wherever the Sheet Man resided.

"Wow," he said, shaking his head. "If I don't hear from you by ten tonight, I'm going to assume your soul is lost forever in some other dimension, and no, I'm not going to be the one to tell your mom."

Entering the city center of Keene was like traveling into the eighteenth century. Tall trees lined every road, and the buildings were mostly original brick construction occupied by small businesses that sported signs like YE GOODIE SHOPPE or WALPOLE CREAMERY ICE CREAM PARLOUR. A couple of church steeples soared into the sky, the only things in the city taller than the tree line.

I locked my bike up at Central Square and tuned in the spirits I'd been desperately attempting to block out during my ride so I wouldn't crash. I immediately spotted some Plegians casually hanging around the giant structure that held up all the jack-o'-lanterns during the annual pumpkin festival, comfortably reclining on it. Plegians are at once the most innocuous and the most terrifyingly destructive of demons: They don't latch onto people the way other kinds do, but they still cause needless harm. Whenever a freak accident happens—a building collapses, a car's brakes stop working, a sinkhole swallows a house— the Plegians are usually at play.

I veered far away from the structure, in case they decided to send it toppling down on me, and headed to the first address, just behind the square on Winter Street, less than two minutes away.

Downtown was looking very pleasant this time of year. The tree branches were grasping to the last stubborn, colorful leaves, and the occasional crisp breeze would sail through and wrest the leaves from the trees' grip, sending them tumbling through the air, spinning and spiraling in all directions. Lights were already strung around some of the trees, and it made the whole square look charming and welcoming.

I turned onto Winter Street and stopped dead in my tracks, inching back to hide behind the corner. Someone was exiting the tarot card shop, followed closely by a winged creature called a Bruton.

I'd seen that kind of demon only a couple of times before, but its image was seared into my brain. The face of a Bruton isn't well defined; when it moves, it blurs, so you're never sure exactly where it is or what it looks like. The wings seem too barbaric and jagged to actually fly, but they can expand as wide as a house and are extremely powerful. But the worst part, as usual, is the eyes—they're made of fire, and not the good kind of fire that I flock to, but the menacing kind that burns down houses and destroys forests.

Brutons latch onto people like other demons do, but in a more sinister way. Instead of sucking away a person's energy, they use their own negative energy to manipulate and deceive. People occasionally tell me that they have nightmares featuring scary creatures with flames for eyes and batlike wings, and I immediately hand them a candle, tell them to close their mind to negative energy, and then run far away from them. If a Bruton is passing through your dreams, you're in trouble.

The human and the demon didn't seem to notice me as they walked away, and I stayed hidden behind the corner until they were out of sight. I debated whether I should even enter the shop. If it was where Brutons regularly hung out, I didn't want to mix with that energy. But after I decided it'd be highly unlikely to have two Brutons in a small tarot card shop, I sucked up my courage and walked toward the door.

When I entered, annoying wind chimes sounded from above. "Oh, did you forget something, Miss Ti—" The clerk looked up from papers on the counter and realized I wasn't the customer who'd just left. "I'm sorry. How can I help you?"

He was a guy, probably in his early thirties, with

limbs as thin as ski poles. He'd been shuffling papers together, and I was amazed he had the strength to lift even a few pieces of them.

"Who was just in here?"

"I'm afraid my customer information is confidential."

"Well, whoever it was is in grave danger." I studied the object hanging around his neck: a pentagram, the symbol of a Wiccan.

"I see," he said curtly. "Can I help you with something?"

I hadn't asked Tommy what I should be on the lookout for. I assumed I'd know it when I saw it. "I'm not a hundred percent sure. Do you have anything that deals with, uh, other spiritual dimensions?"

"You're interested in the occult?" His eyebrows shot up. "Reaching another realm besides the physical one?"

"Sure," I said, feeling certain that if we were to nail down the specifics on what exactly he meant by that, we'd have very different opinions.

"You're just a kid," he said, rummaging around on his desk, "so I'm not going to get too into it with you, but I'd feel comfortable giving you this, at least."

He handed me a pamphlet with the words "Introduction to the Far Shadow" boldly printed on the cover.

"What's the Far Shadow?"

"Everything," he said, smiling, "and nothing."

I flipped through some of the pages. Astral dimensions. Zodiac signs. Pentagrams. Moon cycles. Ritual introductions. This wasn't going to help me find the Sheet Man.

"You might be interested in page twenty-seven," he said.

I flipped to it and read the heading: "Book of Shadows." It detailed a list of rituals and spells and some specific examples.

"The Summoning of the Far Spirits?" I said. "Why would you need to summon spirits? They're all around us."

"Some would disagree with you," he said.

Well, then, *some* were idiots who knew nothing.

"It's a challenging spell, not something you'd be able to do by any means without years of training behind you."

"Oh. Well, can you do it, then?"

He chuckled, grabbed the pamphlet back, and, in a dramatic, hushed whisper, read:

"Invoked you are
To appear at my side.
Travel through the realms

And journey to my voice,
Which beckons you past the stars,
Through the dust, and into my presence."

Nothing happened.

He frowned. "Still haven't gotten that one to work yet."

"Have you gotten *any* of them to work yet?"

"It's harder than it looks, kid." He sounded insulted. "You try it."

I sighed, knowing full well this was a huge waste of my time, but part of me felt bad I'd wounded his pride. I picked up the pamphlet, smiling earnestly at him, and recited the words.

"Invoked you are
To appear at my side.
Travel through the realms
And journey to my voice . . ."

I'd looked up to make a face that said, *You're right, this is stupidly hard*, and in that moment I learned two semirelated things. The first was that this guy was very much a fraud, in possession of no spiritual gifts whatsoever. The second was that I was very much not a fraud, because when I'd looked up, I'd seen a pair of shimmering red eyes, detached from their owner, hovering just above the skinny Wiccan guy.

I dropped the pamphlet as the eyes pierced my own with their gaze. They squinted at me curiously, as though *I* were some kind of circus freak.

"What's wrong, kid?" the guy asked.

"Look up," I whispered.

He looked right up at the eyes, which looked down at him in an almost pleasant way, and then he turned back to me. "What?"

"I need to leave," I said, hoping the eyes wouldn't follow me out of the store. I actually wanted to look to see if there was an opposite spell—the Unsummoning of the Far Spirits, some kind of Get the Heck Out of Here chant—but I was too afraid to touch the pamphlet again, let alone say any more of the spell, in case the rest of red-eyed entity appeared. Instead I pulled out my lighter, surrounded myself with light, and hyperblasted some positive energy at the big red eyes floating above. They squinted, more annoyed than angry, as if the flames of fire were nothing more than irritating gnats.

"Aw, come on, kid, it's only a dumb spell," the guy said, laughing. "A bunch of hocus-pocus from a dying branch of Wiccan beliefs."

I shook my head. "You need to be more careful

with that stuff." And I walked out the door.

What had just happened? Whatever it was, it didn't feel too menacing . . . it just *looked* menacing, which was almost as bad. I lit my lighter one more time for some reassurance, to make sure nothing negative had attached itself to me. I was fairly certain demons couldn't do anything to me, since Kristina's protections didn't go away simply because she did. At least, I hoped they didn't. I had no real frame of reference to work with.

I debated whether I wanted to continue after having invoked the eyes of a Far Spirit, a phrase I wanted to extinguish from my mind as soon as possible. I thought back to the creation of my talisman, the weird phrases I'd had to recite and the strange ribbons of energy. Wasn't that basically a form of pseudomagic? What else was I capable of? Shaken, but determined I was doing the right thing, I decided to keep going.

The other shop, Madame Nadirah's, was on the other side of the square, past the pumpkin-holding structure and down the main road a little bit. I admired the square again, steering clear of the Plegians and doing my best to ignore the ghosts making requests.

"Please tell my daughter she doesn't need to worry about maintaining my coin collection. I only collected them in the first place because I was so bored all the time, and I don't want her ending up the same way."

"My son's been asking for a sign from me. Go up to him and mention the explosion in Montana, he'll get a kick out of it."

"My sister is right there and needs to know her son has been experimenting with some disgusting substances. Don't walk away from me, young man. I know you can hear me."

"I'm on a mission," I hissed to them. "I don't have time to deliver your messages."

A blinking mom and her daughter looked back at me with concern, and I laughed and waved them off, which I realized only served to reaffirm that I was crazy.

By the time I reached Madame Nadirah's, I must have ignored at least ten ghosts, feeling a pit of guilt grow in my stomach with every rejection, but the good thing was that there were no Brutons or any other sort of demon lingering around the shop. It seemed nice enough. There were no tacky neon signs advertising psychic readings, nor were than any crystal balls or tarot cards in sight. There was just a sign that read MADAME NADIRAH'S MYSTIC SHOPPE, and purple curtains blocked the view inside.

I opened the door, causing a loud bell to ring from somewhere in the back. Crossing the threshold, I was sort of charmed by what I saw. There was a spinning display of books and pamphlets advertising various ways to deepen spiritual connections (DON'T HATE. MEDITATE!); a colorful selection of meditation mats lining one of the walls (A STRONG MIND MAKES A LIFE DEFINED!); posters and plaques inscribed with uplifting platitudes (CUSTOM-MADE TO FIT YOUR SPIRITUAL NEEDS!); and a massive display filled with all kinds of candles (FIND THE SCENT AND HUE THAT'S JUST RIGHT FOR YOU!).

As I was looking at a twenty-dollar candle that had sage-infused wax (BURN THE SAGE TO CLEANSE AND PURGE UNWANTED VISITORS ON THE VERGE!), a short woman with an out-of-control Afro emerged from the back room. She wore a loose-fitting green dress featuring elaborate gold stitching down the sides, and a pair of thick glasses magnified her eyes, making her pupils look twice their normal size.

"I am Madame Nadirah," she said in a breathy, excited voice. "Welcome to my shop. I notice you're looking at the spirit-cleansing candle. Are you experiencing problems in your house?"

"Uh, well, you could say that," I said, shrugging. "I'm actually not here to buy any products. I'm wondering if I could make use of your abilities."

Her eyes lit up. "Ah, you seek guidance from the

spiritual world, do you? I can help you, my child."
She stepped forward, looking me up and down and
clucking her tongue. "You seem tense. Very tense.
There is clearly something bothering you, child."

"You're off to a good start," I said, wondering
why anyone would show up to a shop like this unless
something was bothering them.

"Come, follow me, we'll sort it out together."

She headed for the back door, and we entered a
dark room lit up by black lights, causing everything
white to glow neon blue.

"Oh man." I blinked several times, hoping to make
my eyes adjust to the sudden change in light. "Wasn't
expecting that."

"I feel it's best to channel spirits in a way that can
allow their energy to radiate in a different form, one
that you may even be able to see."

"Right," I said, rolling my eyes. Kristina had told
me repeatedly that most living people couldn't see
ghosts, no matter what they claimed.

"Now, get comfortable," she said, pointing to a
glowing cushion on the floor. I took my seat across
from her, a low table between us. She had her hands
on the table, palms down, fingers spread wide apart.
A soothing song featuring low chants played quietly
from somewhere in the room, and I felt a tingle around

the base of my neck as the energy riled up around me. This woman had some kind of gift. I wasn't sure to what extent, though.

"Tell me your name, child," she said peacefully, like she was starting a mediation.

"Baylor Bosco."

"Now, Baylor, why don't you . . ."

She stopped suddenly, her illuminated eyes flicking up toward my face and zooming all over. She reached up and hit something on the wall.

The black lights went off, and a harsh fluorescent light filled the small room instead. Madame Nadirah's face had transformed from serene to irate.

"Baylor Bosco?" she spit. "Are you kidding me?" Her voice had changed as well. The breathiness had disappeared, replaced by a sharp, sassy tone. "What are you doing in my shop?"

"You've heard of me?"

"Of course I've heard of you! You're only my biggest customer stealer in the state. My shop's been open for fifteen years, and ever since you started delivering messages left and right, my business has gone down by fifty percent."

"I'm sorry," I said. "I had no idea." My hands were sweating.

"You should be sorry," she said. "It's great you've

actually been blessed with a gift and all, but a girl's gotta eat. I'm gonna have to downsize soon, you know, and the real question is how can I downsize from something that's already as tiny as a closet?"

"Wait, what do you mean that I've 'actually been blessed'? Are you saying you're—"

"Not like you," she said. "Mmm, nope. I just give good advice. This is way more fun than having to use my psychology degree."

"Are you really admitting to me you're a fraud?" I asked. "You really sit here and let people pay you for tricking them into thinking you can communicate with their loved ones?"

"I wouldn't go that far," she said. "My gift is more . . . intuitive. I could feel from the second you walked in that there was something different about you, but once you said your name, I wasn't going to sit here and let you embarrass me."

"So you've got intuition," I said. "An empath, right? I could feel that. I could feel the tingle in my neck when you were speaking. That's real, at least."

She raised her eyebrows and let out a laugh after a few seconds. "You playing?"

"No," I said. "I could feel it."

"From the horse's mouth!" she laughed, clapping her hands together. "My auntie was right. She's obsessed with you, by the way, one of those Bay-lievers. Psh. Before you were born, though, she was always saying I was special, that I knew too much. I always just thought I was a good actress."

I thought of that tingle in my neck and wondered if it had maybe been a regular itch. I blocked out that thought. She was the only person in town who could help me. "I need your help, Madame Nadirah."

Madame Nadirah did not like anything I had to say. She didn't like the Sheet Man, she didn't like know-ing my dead twin followed me around, she didn't like hearing that the dead twin had been ghostnapped, and she really, really didn't like knowing that demons were actively floating around the city.

"Those things aren't standing outside my shop, right?"

"No, and that's another reason why I trust you—they wouldn't try to influence a gifted person who had so much positive energy. It wouldn't work. That's why they leave you alone and stick to the frauds."

"Baylor, I just told you fifteen minutes ago I'm a fraud."

"You say that, but you're wrong. You've managed to keep this store open this long." I looked around the room. "You couldn't have done that if there weren't *something* here. I know you're my best bet for entering the dimension where the Sheet Man resides. If you can't help me, no one in this city can. Well, except for my baby sister, Ella, but she can't speak English yet, so for now you're it."

She sighed, twirling a curl around one of her fingers. "Fine," she said. "Fine, I'll help, but if something goes wrong, if one of those little demons swoops in and gobbles you up, don't say I didn't warn you."

"I'm not worried," I said excitedly. I reached into my backpack and pulled out the talisman. "I'm taking this with me."

"What could that be? Looks like a blind carpenter's last try."

"It's a talisman I made to stop the Sheet Man," I said.

"You make talismans?" she asked, nonplussed.

"Not regularly," I said. "This was my first time."

"Oh, Lord." She shook her head, still looking dubiously at the talisman. "Baylor, neither one of us knows what we're doing here. Even if that *thing* can protect you, how do you plan on getting to the dimension where the Sheet Man resides? Do you have a map you forgot to mention?"

I didn't want to admit I wasn't sure about that, either. I had an idea, though. I once asked Aiden what he saw when he shut his eyes, and he said everything was black, but sometimes weird purple and green squiggles and shapes would dance around aimlessly.

But for me, when I close my eyes, I initially see black, and then it's almost as if I mentally walk forward a few feet, and the black dissolves away, letting me see exactly where I am in its pure state, with flowing energies and auras and unfiltered spirits. I assumed if I focused my energy on the Sheet Man and Kristina's energies, I'd be led the right way.

"I just have a feeling," I said, hoping I sounded more confident than I felt.

We spent a few minutes going over the basics and coming up with the necessary protections. Then we got started.

"Lie down, child," she said, her voice losing its edge and taking on that breathy quality. "Get comfortable."

I sprawled out on the floor of the tiny back room and placed my head on the cushion. She flipped the black lights back on.

"Really?"

"Hey, you said I had intuition, and this is where I

feel it the strongest. If you can have a talisman with an egg, I can have a room with some black lights."

"Fine." I shut my eyes.

She placed four sage candles around me, two by my wrists and two by my ankles. As she lit each one, she recited the phrase we came up with: "Let the fire shackle this body to the earth. Let my spirit keep him safe."

With each candle I imagined a fiery handcuff shooting out from the wick and wrapping itself around my wrist or ankle. This ritual was to make sure I wouldn't be trapped in some other dimension while my body lay vulnerable in Madame Nadirah's shop. Otherwise, I'd be easy prey for an insidious, sneaky Insymbio to take over my being.

Once she was done lighting the candles, she placed her hands over my fast-beating heart and recited another phrase: "Let his soul find the path to healing. Let his light expel the darkness."

I felt secure and at peace knowing my body was protected and Madame Nadirah was keeping watch. I let my mind calm down and thought of nothing but Kristina and the Sheet Man.

Kristina, if you're there, if you can hear me, if you can feel me, then lead the way.

It felt daunting. Although I was lying still and

motionless, I was overwhelmed by how tired I suddenly felt. Kristina was so far away. How would I be able to find her?

But slowly the black faded away, and the room materialized back into view. It was quieter, grayer. Madame Nadirah had disappeared, and I could feel an energy lifting my spirit. The feeling of exhaustion had vanished. I pushed myself up and cautiously stepped out of my body and into another dimension, hoping I wasn't making a terrible mistake.

I walked outside the shop, talisman in hand, and saw no one. The only things in this particular dimension were most likely me, the Sheet Man, and Kristina.

Strange shadows floated by me, and I wondered if they were shadows of spirits, somehow reflected into this new dimension. The only question now was where to find the Sheet Man. I felt like there was a good chance that he would come to me if I was exposed for long enough.

I walked up the main road, back to Central Square, and saw the massive structure where the demons had been reclining. The demons were gone, but two large shadows were in their place. I kept my distance. I didn't know if I had any protections from them in this dimension, and I didn't want to test it.

I walked the square once, then headed down the deserted road in the direction where I lived. There was a chance he could be at my house, but it was a real shot in the dark.

"Sheet Man!" I called out. "Kristina!"

Nothing.

Everything around me looked duller and lifeless. It was almost like the city I'd grown up in, but through some bizarre, groggy filter; the spark that made it colorful and lively was gone. It seemed like joy couldn't possibly exist here, like a permanent winter.

"Sheet Man! Alfred! Alfred Parker!" I called out. I had nothing to lose, right? Since I was the only one making noise in this dimension, I figured the sound would carry to wherever he was.

"Kristina!"

A fierce wind picked up, howling in my ears. I looked around, wondering which direction I could expect to see him coming from, when an odd flicker appeared in front of me, as though this dimension offered poor reception.

After several flickers, in and out, Grandpa Bosco burst through in a shower of blue sparks, his body outlined in blue light.

I hadn't seen him since he disappeared with

Kristina to the Beyond more than five years ago, and boy, did he look pissed off to see me.

"What in the Almighty are you doing here, Baylor?" he growled over the wind, grabbing my arm. It was the strangest feeling, like I'd gotten the chills but only in the area of my arm where he was holding on to me.

"Grandpa! What are you doing?"

"Getting you out of here!" He was dragging me back in the direction of the square, his thin hair whipping around in the intensifying wind. "That Tommy told you to come here, didn't he? Darn it, Baylor, just because we're ghosts doesn't mean you can always assume we're right."

"But, Grandpa, Kristina is trapped in here somewhere," I said, trying to pry his hand off my arm, but I couldn't penetrate the blue energy surrounding his body.

"I know that, you dimwit," he said. "But she's dead. She can be here and not be harmed. You, on the other hand, are very much alive, and if something happens to you, you could be stuck in this limbo forever."

"I've got the talisman, Grandpa, I'll be fine."

"Do you think the Sheet Man is the only entity in this dimension?" he said, his eyes wide and grave. "You've got one talisman, but what if another demon attacks you after you've already used it? You can't imagine the kinds of creatures that have been banished to this dimension." His grip tightened as the blue light seemed to intensify. "Bam. You'd be done, Baylor, with no chance of ever entering the Beyond, and frankly, we can't have that."

"If I don't do this, I might never see Kristina again!" I was banging the wooden bowl against his hand, but he didn't seem to notice.

"You'll see her again," he said. "You will. I wouldn't let my granddaughter languish over here otherwise. But it's part of her journey, not yours."

"What? Really?"

"Really," he said. We were nearly back in front of Madame Nadirah's by now. "Baylor, don't you ever come to this dimension again, do you understand me? It takes an enormous amount of energy for a spirit like me to cross that barrier, and I won't be able to rescue you again. Not for a few years at least."

"Okay," I said, only just realizing I was crying. "I'm sorry. I won't. It . . . it was good seeing you, Grandpa. I hope you're doing okay in the Beyond."

His eyes lightened for a moment. "I don't mean to sound so harsh, Baylor. It's a treat to see you, you've gotten so tall!" He half smiled. "I just need to make sure you're safe. I'm learning a lot, buddy boy. I hope to be able to visit you soon."

I could feel his grip loosening, but I didn't want him to let go.

"One more thing, Baylor: Tell your dad to stop worrying. He made the right choice."

Before I could ask what he meant, he tossed me through the door of the shop, and I zoomed back to my body in fast-forward motion, the shop blurring around me as I soared past the books and candles, into the room with the black lights, and onto the cushion, where I suddenly gasped and rocketed up.

Madame Nadirah was standing over me, her palms still over my heart.

"There you are," she said. "You'd gone away for a little while."

I looked around, trying to breathe and swallow at the same time, but instead choking on phlegm.

"Did it work?"

"No," I said, my body shaking and my arm still tingling from where my grandpa had had his iron grip. "Well, yes, it worked, but I didn't do what I wanted to do. My grandpa entered the dimension, yelled at me for being there, and brought me back here. I didn't want to come back yet, but he told me I could get trapped over there forever."

She was massaging my shoulders now and clucking her tongue.

"Child, if there's one thing I know in this life, it's this: When your granddaddy tells you to run, you run."

Clarinets can double as weapons.

AFTER ONE LONG, DAZED BIKE RIDE HOME
I sneaked past the family room, where I could hear
everyone hanging out, and called Aiden from my room.

"I saw my grandpa," I said. "The first time in five
years."

"That's pretty cool."

"Yeah."

"So did you find Kristina?"

"No."

"Oh," he said. A silent moment passed. "J texted
me while you were doing your stuff."

"What did she say?"

"She asked if she could borrow my speech notes tomorrow, she thinks she might have missed something."

I blinked. "That's all she said? I thought you were going to tell me something good about the dance."

"Oh. No."

"It's been two days," I said. "You need to figure something out."

"I'm no good at this stuff, Baylor," he said. "You've got to help me out, man."

"How? Tell me what to do, and I'll do it."

"Ask Cassie out. You're better looking than me."

"Tell me to do anything else, and I'll do it."

"Baylor, dude, come on!" he pleaded. "You've got to do this for me."

I sighed. "Cassie isn't my type. I know she looks innocent, but I have it on good authority she's into some pretty messed-up stuff."

"What? Why didn't you mention this before?"

"It's my burden to know this kind of stuff about girls. It's not fair for me to spoil your life adventures, Aiden."

"It is if she's a devil worshipper or something!" he whispered, petrified.

"It's not that bad."

"Well, it's only going to get worse in my head if you don't tell me anything else."

"One word: taxidermy."

"Oh my . . ."

I'd heard from one of her dead uncles that she was quite good at it too, a skill she'd learned from her family's annual hunting trips.

"I don't do hunting and dead stuffed animals, but that doesn't mean you can't grow to like them."

"I don't want to grow to like anything about Cassie," he said. "The only thing I want to grow to like is J, and I don't even have any more growing to do. I love her, dude."

He sounded so pained, like his heart was being sawed slowly in half.

"We'll think of something," I said. "Don't worry about it."

I wanted to tell Aiden that his problem with J and Cassie was rearing its head at a terribly inconvenient time, and if he could just put everything on hold for a few days, that'd be great. But friends don't do that, so I held my breath and tried to pretend that his problems were as important as mine.

After I hung up with Aiden, I headed downstairs to find my dad. I needed to tell him that I saw Grandpa today, but I was worried he'd react in the same way as when he witnessed my interaction with Aunt Hilda and Marjorie.

I found him playing with Ella on the floor of the family room, which simply meant they were smacking some dolls around, while Jack played a video game. My mom was snuggled up on the couch reading one of her romance novels with a shirtless guy on the cover, a glass of red wine in hand.

I watched the four of them for a minute, thinking about Kristina and feeling lucky I got to be an active part of this family, even if I was permanently grounded. I couldn't imagine always watching from the sidelines.

"Hey, buddy," my dad called to me, his voice giddy. Clearly he was in la-la land with a one-year-old. "Want to show Ella how ladies should be treated?" He reached out for a Barbie and held it next Mr. Potato Head. "With respect and courtesy," he said in a weird, vaguely Irish accent. "Don't put up with anyone who doesn't treat you like the wonderful person you are."

"Dad, I think you're getting to that point of playing with Ella where terrible ideas seem like good ones," I said.

He laughed. "You could be right." He examined my face, pushed himself onto his elbows, and frowned. "You look weird, Baylor. What's up?"

I saw my mom tense ever so slightly on the couch, and I knew she wouldn't flip another page until I was done speaking.

"I have something to tell you," I said slowly, sitting on the ground next to him. "But I need you to brace yourself for it."

My mom's grip on her book tightened until it looked like she was accosting the shirtless guy, and my dad tried to make his face as expressionless as possible.

"What is it, son?" he asked, his voice slightly deeper than normal. For a fleeting second I was sort of amused thinking of all the things they were bracing for me to tell them. How much more trouble could I really get into?

"Okay," I said, drawing it out. "Here goes."

My mom, her entire body clenched, looked like she was about to explode.

"I saw Grandpa Bosco today."

For a moment there was total silence. Even Jack's video game quieted down. Then the reaction from both my parents was instantaneous.

My mom threw her book down and—wineglass still in hand—ran to the kitchen, grabbed an old rutabaga she'd purchased by accident at the farmer's market, and began hacking at it with her chef's knife.

My dad, in that same moment, dropped both Mr. Potato Head and Barbie, grabbed a blanket from the couch, and, my fears coming true, wrapped himself up like a frightened woodland creature.

Jack and I met eyes, and his eyebrows shot up before he returned to his game. Over the rutabaga mutilation occurring in the kitchen—*clang, clang, clang!*—I said, "Dad? Are you all right?"

"Just fine," he said, his voice muffled through the blanket. "Really! I'm *fine*."

"Okay," I said casually, acting along. "Great. So, yeah, I saw your dad, and it only lasted a couple of minutes because, well, it's a long, weird ghost story that you'd really hate, but he looked good." I paused, but he didn't say anything. "He said he's been learning a lot in the Beyond, and that he's going to try to come visit soon."

The chopping grew louder.

"There's one other thing. . . ."

He poked his head out of the blanket and stared up at me like some sort of sad turtle. "What?"

"He said to stop worrying. You made the right choice."

His eyes widened slightly, then he nodded and returned to his hole.

"What does that mean?" I asked.

"I'm just going to stay in here for a little bit."

"Okay," I said, standing back up. "Well, if you want to talk about it any more, I'll be upstairs."

"Uh-huh," he said, sounding just like a five-year-old. I mouthed "Good luck" to Jack before heading to the stairs. As I passed my mom in the kitchen, she whispered, "Baylor!" I turned to see the most finely minced vegetable I'd ever seen sitting in a light-yellow pile on her cutting board. There were even some little pieces stuck in her hair. "What on earth do I do with a rutabaga?"

At school the next morning J took me aside wordlessly, pushed me up against a locker, and crossed her arms.

"What is taking so long, Baylor? I need an answer today."

"I, uh, I . . . you see, a problem arose, J," I said, trying to choose my words carefully. I didn't want to sell out Aiden, but then it occurred to me that it might be the perfect thing to do.

"What sort of problem?"

"Aiden is so bad at life that he accidentally asked Clarinet Cassie to the dance," I said breathlessly, "and now he doesn't know how to break off their date so he can go with you instead."

"Oh," she said, taking a step back and adjusting

her bright-pink glasses. "Okay. Well, maybe I can take care of that."

"Wait, what?" I asked. "What are you going to do?"

She walked away without answering, the brain beneath her bouncing hair obviously filling with ideas, and I wondered if I'd made a huge mistake.

Just before my lunch period I heard whispers from people, and I thought I heard the name Cassie mentioned a couple of times, and it was pretty distinct, because Cassie never gets talked about.

I furrowed my eyebrows, but I didn't ask questions because, frankly, I hoped I'd imagined it.

Sitting down at my normal spot, I took a second to check my phone and saw a text message from Reverend Henry asking me to stop by after school. He almost never texted me, so I was anxious to find out what he wanted, but that thought left my mind as soon as a pair of gruff hands clamped my shoulders and pushed me hard.

"What did you do, Baylor?"

Aiden's face was bright red as he hovered behind me, dropping his backpack to the ground.

"What are you talking about?"

"Haven't you heard? Everyone else has."

I shook my head.

"Apparently, J went up to Cassie between second and third periods and asked if it would be okay if she went with me to the dance," he said, his arms flailing like a madman while he glared at me. "But Cassie said it wouldn't be okay and told J that *she* had a massive crush on me, and no one was going to stop us from going together, which caused J to say that Cassie was being unreasonable, since I'm better friends with J, and that Cassie was just being self-ish, which caused Cassie to slap J in the face *with her clarinet* and tackle her to the ground."

I looked to the side of him but saw nothing. Kristina's absence was all too glaring in this moment. Not only would she have already informed me about the girls' tussle, but she would also have reacted perfectly to Aiden's dramatic telling of it.

"That's insane," I said. "But why are you mad at me?"

"Because you told J about Cassie," he said.

"But I told you about J in the first place."

"So? You're supposed to tell me that because we're bros. But you can't go back to the original girl and tell her about the second girl that I never told the original girl about."

I put a hand up. "This is getting confusing."

"You talked to J when you should have kept your mouth shut!"

"No, she talked to me and said that she needed an answer by today, and since you said you had no idea what to do last night, I seized the opportunity, Aiden. I seized it hard, and apparently J seized some opportunities, and now it looks like all the seizing going on today has failed miserably."

"I'm pissed at you," he said, finally sitting. "None of this would have ever happened if you hadn't said anything. Now Cassie's probably getting suspended, and J's gonna have a bruise on her face in the shape of Cassie's clarinet."

"You're looking at this all wrong," I said, shaking my head in disbelief. "Aiden, two girls were fighting over you today. When has that ever happened to you? When will it ever happen again? You should go find J right now, thank her for fighting over you and getting everyone talking about you, and then kiss her."

His mouth hung open a bit, and he blinked rapidly.

"Oh my God," he said. "You're right."

"I know I'm right."

"I've got to find J."

"You've got to find her right now."

And, leaving his belongings behind, he stood up and half ran, half waddled inside to wherever J was.

* * *

I didn't hear anything about Aiden or J for the rest of the day, and once school ended, the thought of their troubles left my mind, usurped by the curiosity of what Reverend Henry had for me. It wasn't that far of a walk from school, and by the time I got to the church, I had decided that the reason he'd asked me to come by was that Kristina had visited him in a dream and told him of some way to find her.

The reverend was in his office doing paperwork when I knocked. He peered up for a moment, smiled, and said, "Just a second." He was writing furiously onto a sheet of paper and finished by flourishing his signature dramatically.

"I have something for you, Baylor," he said excitedly, reaching into his pocket for a crinkled ball of paper and handing it to me.

"Oh," I said, taking it. "Trash. Thanks."

"Open it up."

It took me a second to wrangle it open, and I smoothed the paper against the edge of his desk. An address—8736 Triumph Lane, Brattleboro, Vermont—was scrawled across the page in crude handwriting.

I glanced from the paper to Reverend Henry's toothy grin. "What is this?"

"We found it in a pocket of a pair of the pants donated by the same person who donated the shoes," he said. "I looked it up online, and it's a nursing home! That explains why 'A. Parker' was written on the shoes."

"A nursing home? That doesn't make sense. I spoke with Alfred's daughter, and she told me his new wife took care of him at home."

Reverend Henry raised an eyebrow. "I say we go find out."

"Mom, I'm spending some time with Reverend Henry this afternoon," I said on the phone a few minutes later as we sailed down the highway.

"Oh, that's great," she said brightly. "I think that's just what you need after the last few days. Tell him I said hi."

"Will do!"

"Are you going to be back in time for dinner?"

"Um, I think so," I said. "Just put any leftovers in the fridge."

"You *think* so?" she said, her voice suddenly edgy. "What are you doing that's going to take so long?"

"Okay, got to go, love you!" I hung up. "Mom says hi."

"Oh, that's wonderful," he said lightly. "I would tell her hi back, but your suspiciously abrupt end to the conversation has rendered that all but impossible."

For the thirty-minute ride I filled him in on the events from the day before, which he listened to in pursed-lip silence.

"I can't believe you would do something so reckless, Baylor," he said once I'd finished, sounding genuinely mad. "I'm glad your grandpa was there to slap some sense back into you."

"I was just trying to do a good thing," I said defensively.

"And cause irreparable damage to your soul in the process."

"You and my grandpa should get together and start a Pessimism Club."

"That's a great idea," he said. "For our first meeting we can talk about how this irresponsible kid we know has made us *pessimistic* about the intelligence of modern youths, since he goes off alone into other spiritual realms with no real protection or plan."

"Well, that doesn't sound like a fun club at all."

"It's a club for pessimists, Baylor. It's not supposed to be fun."

We pulled up in front of a stately brick building adorned with white shutters and white trim and white window boxes. The sign on the fence guarding the property read WHITE FIELDS RETIREMENT HOME.

It wasn't nearly as bad as I'd pictured. I had expected dead weeds everywhere and doors hanging off hinges, and I was surprised to see it actually looked pretty nice. The movies had warped my image of nursing homes.

Inside the lobby a teenage girl manned the reception desk, while several elderly people slowly milled about. I was desperately tuning out the huge throng of ghosts knocking to get through to me; this was no time to deliver messages. Instead I made a mental note to hold a healing session here soon.

"Hello!" said the girl at the front desk. Her name tag read ASHLEE.

"Hi, Ashlee," I said. "I was wondering if you could provide some information about a resident for me."

"I'm sorry, I can't give out resident information unless the resident is accompanying you."

"Right, well, that's sort of impossible, since the resident I'm looking for is dead."

"Oh," she said. "Well, information about any current or past resident is still confidential. I'm sorry."

She frowned like she meant it.

"Excuse me, miss," Reverend Henry said, brushing past me. "I'm sorry to cut off your conversation, but the father of one of my worshippers is near death, and I need to find his room as fast as possible."

"Oh my," she said. "Who is the resident?"

"Ken DeWong," he said. "Please hurry."

Ashlee typed something into her computer, and seconds later she said, "He's in room seventeen G. You're going to need to walk down the hall, turn left, and then go through the door on the right, which will lead you to the G wing of the—"

"I'm much too upset to remember any of what you're saying," he said, talking at an impossibly fast pace. "Can you just lead me there?"

"I'm not supposed to leave my desk unattended, though," she said, eyeing me nervously. "I can call someone to take you there."

"I was just on the phone with Ken's son, and he told me every second counted," Reverend Henry said so earnestly that I almost grabbed his arm to lead him to the room myself. "Please."

She studied his face and sighed. "Okay," she said, getting up. "Follow me." She looked at me and said, "I'm sorry, I'll be right back if you don't mind waiting for a moment."

She touched Reverend Henry's back and guided him forward, and he glanced back to give me a quick but pointed look. Once they turned the corner, I circled around the desk, took her seat, and examined the database she had open on the screen.

In the search bar on the top right she had typed "DeWong," so I deleted it and typed "Parker." I got six results back, and sure enough, one of them was "Parker, Alfred."

I clicked on the name, and the first thing that popped up was all his basic information. I grabbed the notepad on her desk and began scrawling the information as fast as I could. I wasn't sure how much time I had, so I didn't bother looking down, hoping that it would all be legible later.

"Angela Mendoza-Parker," I muttered to myself as I copied the emergency contact information. "There's your phone number. Let's hope it didn't change."

I finished writing, searched for "DeWong" again, and then circled back around the desk and out of the door before Ashlee reappeared.

I ran to the parking lot and found Reverend Henry already in the car.

"How did you beat me here?"

"Ashlee took me to the room, and I told her to leave before I went in, since it was such a somber moment, and when she turned the corner, I walked out of the emergency exit and came right back here."

"Sly move coming up with that story, Reverend," I said. "I didn't know you had it in you."

"Mr. DeWong's son owed me one, so it's all right," he said.

"Well, I got a phone number, among other information," I said.

"Call it!"

"And say what? 'I know you're causing your dead husband to attack me, you gold digger!'?"

"Here, give that to me," he said, taking the paper and pulling out his cell phone. He typed in the numbers and held the phone to his ear.

"Yes, hi, I'm looking for Angela? . . . Oh, this is she, good. Well, Angela, you made a donation to Keene Community Church recently, and we found an item of value in one of the pockets and figured that you might want it back, since it probably wasn't intended as a donation."

My jaw nearly fell into my lap as I watched him lie so effortlessly.

"Oh, what item is it? I'm afraid I'm not permitted to say over the phone; it's something I can discuss only in person, unfortunately. . . . Yes, you're definitely going to want it. I may be a reverend, but I know an expensive thing when I see it." He laughed heartily. "Tomorrow would be ideal, yes. . . . Noon? Is that the only time you're available?"

I shook my head vigorously. I couldn't miss school again.

"Ah, you're traveling tomorrow night. Got it. Okay, well, noon works. Just come inside the church and look for the office that says 'Reverend Henry.' Okay, thanks, Angela. . . . Oh, it's *Ahn*-hell-uh? Great, thanks for letting me know. See you then."

He hung up and looked at me with the strangest expression on his face.

"I keep sinning today," he said. "It's ironic that such behavior is on behalf of the person with the most direct connection to the afterlife that I know of."

"I can't miss school again tomorrow, Reverend Henry!"

"Listen, if I can lie to two separate people in the space of ten minutes, knowing it's for a good intention, then surely you can figure out a way to get to the church tomorrow during your lunch period."

20

Don't cry
at school.

I HAD NEVER BEEN CHALLENGED BY A REVerend before, and I figured if he could bend the rules a little bit, then so could I.

After getting dropped off at home, I debated whether or not I should just tell my mom and ask for a note to leave school early tomorrow, but I knew she would say no, go on a diatribe about the curse that was my gift, remind me that I was supposed to be grounded for all eternity, and then call the school tomorrow to check if I was still there.

I also knew full well that she would be equally mad if

she found out I got caught skipping. It seemed doomed to be a lose-lose situation, and since Kristina wasn't there to offer advice, I chose the side of less confrontation.

Aiden was having confrontation troubles as well. He called me that night to give me the full report on what had happened.

"I found her in the nurse's office," he said.

"And?"

"And that rat-faced, turd-lipped freak Andrew was there."

"What? Why?"

"He didn't hear *why* she'd been attacked, just that some band nerd started beating her with a clarinet."

"So what'd you do?"

"I ran!"

"Aiden!"

"I couldn't help it!" he said, distraught.

"Did she see you?"

"I don't think so. I just saw Andrew there petting her face with his scaly little hands."

"Well," I said, "that's no good."

"What should I do?"

I tried to put myself in J's shoes and imagine what she would do in that situation.

"Aiden, you need to call her right now and tell her you want to go to the dance with her."

"Isn't this sort of thing better in person?"

"Not when you have a cretin like Andrew hovering over her like an alien spaceship, ready to beam her up and away from you. Do it. Now."

Before I'd finished speaking, Aiden started fiddling with some buttons on his phone.

"Aiden?" I said.

No response, more beeps, then ringing.

"Oh no," I muttered. But I couldn't hang up. I should have, but I couldn't.

"Hello?" J said rather reluctantly.

"I love you!" Aiden blurted out. "I've loved you for a whole year and didn't have the courage to say it until today. Until you got beat up . . . for me."

My jaw hit the ground.

"You . . . you love me?"

"Uh, yes," he said, his voice nearly gone, replaced by a high-pitched squeal. "I think I do."

"I got hit in the face today, and you didn't even come see me."

"That's not true," he said. "I did visit, but Andrew was standing there, and I didn't know what to do."

"You should have knocked him out of the way, Aiden," she said, clearly exasperated. "You couldn't man up for five measly seconds?"

"I . . . I . . . that's not what I thought you'd say."

"I'm not trying to be mean," she said, more frantic than I'd ever her sound before. "I'm confused. You *love* me? But you couldn't muster up the courage to come say a simple hello after I got slapped in the face and blindsided by a clarinet for you."

"J, just say you love him back!" I yelled.

Radio silence.

"Baylor?" she said, sounding like she was trying to hold in vomit.

"You're still here?" Aiden shrieked, horrified.

"Uh," I said, panicking. "Yeah. Ha, ha. You didn't disconnect my call."

"And you didn't hang up yourself?"

"This isn't about me, okay? Let's get back to you two."

"Well, I'd *love* to continue this chat," J shouted, "but my mortification quota has been maxed out for the day, so . . . I'm going to go."

"What? No!" Aiden said. "You can't leave me hanging after I just told you . . . all those things."

"I need to process this, Aiden," she said. "I hope you understand. And good night, Baylor." Her voice sounded particularly venomous.

We heard a click, we sat for a moment in suffocating silence, and then Aiden said, "Good advice, dude."

"Sorry, Aiden," I said. "I really thought that was going to work."

"Well, it didn't."

And he hung up too.

School the next morning was somehow more uncomfortable than the phone call. Aiden wasn't talking to me, but then, he wasn't talking to anyone. He sat at his desk with his head pressed into his arms, which were forming a barricade to the outside world.

When I saw J, she tried to avoid making eye contact, but I grabbed her arm and pulled her aside.

"Listen, J, I've got a lot of things on my plate right now, and frankly, the last thing I need is any drama between you, me, and Aiden. Just tell the kid you'll go to the dance with him."

"Seriously, Baylor?" She hiked up her backpack around her shoulders and made herself a few inches taller. "This isn't even about the dance anymore. He told me he loves me. First off, that's crazy. Second, normal people in love usually act like they're, you know, in love."

"Right, J, but in case you haven't noticed, Aiden's never been too concerned with acting normal. He's shy, and an empty bucket has more self-esteem than him. Don't punish him just because he believes he's not good enough for you, okay?"

It was at this moment the tears chose to spill out

as Kristina's words from our big fight spewed out of my mouth.

"He just wants to be with you, J. He just wants to love you and hug you and kiss you, and he really means it when he says he loves you. You can't hurt him, J."

J shushed me and awkwardly smiled at all the people walking by and staring at us. "What's gotten into you, Baylor?"

"I just really miss Kr—"

But I stopped short. J didn't know about Kristina. No one knew about Kristina except for a handful of people. It hit me how totally invisible and forgotten and extraneous she must have felt.

She didn't even have a tombstone in the cemetery as a small reminder that she was a person. She had her own personality and sense of humor and quirks, but no one knew her.

And she was the person I trusted the most out of anyone.

And she was missing in some ghost world and I might never see her again.

The tears weren't stopping, and J was on her tiptoes trying to block my face from everyone passing by.

"Baylor, who's 'Kr—'? Who were you going to say?"

I puffed out my chest and looked her right in the eye.

"Kristina. My twin. My unborn twin, who walks with me through life and helps me manage all the spirits I can communicate with."

J's frozen face told me I should have kept my mouth shut.

"Baylor, you had a twin?"

"I have a twin. Kristina's real, and Aiden is in love with you, and your grandma with crazy hoop earrings thinks you'd be a fool not to pick Aiden, and you're just going to have to deal with it."

"He's such a cutie!" her grandma squealed as she tried in vain to push J's hair back.

I turned and walked away.

"Deal with which one?" she called out, sounding genuinely confused.

"All of it!" I yelled, and a couple of girls next to me jumped in terror.

My eyes were probably still red and wet when Bobby saw me and raised his eyebrows.

"Dude, what happened to you?"

"Allergies," I sniffled. "Really bad allergies."

At quarter past eleven I sneaked out of school and felt my feet propelling me forward to the church. I was clutching the talisman with both hands and muttering about light and positivity under my breath, and to anyone unlucky enough to see me on the street, I probably looked like a ranting lunatic.

The reverend was waiting for me outside the church.

"Oh, good!" he said as I walked through the parking lot to the entrance. "You made it."

"I am so ready for this all to be over," I said.

"Well, she'll be here soon enough," he said. "Hopefully, we'll have our answers."

He eyed the talisman in my hands.

"Expecting a visit from the Sheet Man as well?"

"You never know," I said. "If Angela's the cause of all this evil, then I need to be ready."

He pulled out the cross chain that was hidden below his shirt and smiled. "I'll be ready too."

We walked inside and waited in the office.

At ten past noon Angela Mendoza-Parker strolled into the office. She was a woman in her midthirties, and though it was a Thursday afternoon, she was wearing a hot-pink dress and black heels. Her hair was a nice-looking bundle of curls.

"*Hola!*" she said. "I'm looking for Rrrreverend Henry?"

"That's me," he said, standing up and extending his arms. "Thank you for coming."

She smiled one of those smiles where she scrunched

her eyes and cheeks together, but her mouth didn't move. "You found something espensive?" She saw me glaring at her, and since I also happened to be holding a primitive wooden bowl with an egg resting in it, she immediately assumed I was insane. "Oh, I so sorry to interrupt your time with a . . . a child of God."

"No, it's fine," Reverend Henry said. "Baylor is actually the reason I called you here today."

She blinked, scrunching her eyes up again. "I don't understand. I thought you found something? I was thinking a watch or a necklez?"

Reverend Henry looked at me and raised his eyebrows. I stood up, clutching the talisman tightly, and swallowed hard.

"Angela, my name is Baylor Bosco, and I can communicate with people who have crossed over. Your husband, Alfred, has been haunting me, and now he's taken a ghost hostage in whatever limbo he's trapped in."

Her lips, covered in bright-red lipstick, spread a centimeter apart.

"I know who you are," she said. "You're a devil man. I leaving."

"No!" I yelled as she turned away. "I know what you did!" She froze and looked back, her face finally showing some genuine emotion: fear.

"That's right," I continued, taking a step forward. "I know all about how you married Alfred for his money and then ripped off his kids, making sure they got nothing."

Her reaction was not what I expected. Rather than appearing remorseful or even acting out in rage, her face sank into relief.

"You don't know anything," she said quietly, and she turned and rushed out of the room.

"Wait!" I said, following her out the door and past some pews. "You can't just leave."

"You have no idea what you're talking about," she yelled, picking up her pace. There were a few scattered people sitting in the pews, looking over in shock.

"Then tell me what I need to know so he'll leave me alone!"

"I loved him," she said, practically running to the door. "And it's none of your business."

She had just burst through the doors when I took a running leap forward and grabbed on to her arm. My hand slid down and touched the gold bracelet she wore around her wrist, and suddenly a vision flashed through my head. I saw a hazy, dark room occupied by Angela and another woman.

"This is just the first of many gifts," the other

woman said, holding the same bracelet Angela was
wearing, "if you agree to the terms, of course."

"It's not right," Angela said.

"Alfred's the devil, honey," said the other woman.
"Just think of yourself as a guardian angel making
things right."

Angela was frowning, but she was also hungrily
eyeing the bracelet. She was dressed in baggy clothes,
and her hair looked like black straw.

"He deserves what's coming to him, and we'll all
be better off," the other woman said.

Angela nodded to her, her jaw clenched. "I'll
do it."

And then the most wicked laughter erupted from
the other woman, Rosalie, such terrible, cacophonous
glee that I screwed up my eyes and pressed my hands
to my ears, and suddenly the vision was gone.

"You're a liar!" I yelled as Angela came back into
view in the parking lot. She had clearly just relived
the same memory attached to the bracelet, because
her legs shook violently and her heels seemed in
danger of cracking in half. "You've got to be kidding
me! You and Rosalie plotted against Alfred? She got
you to marry him so that you could steal the money
from his children?"

"It's not like that!" Angela said, tears streaming

down her face. "I was broke, and Rosalie found me and took me under her wing." She wiped away the tears with both hands, her eyes pleading with me. "She got me back on my feet, and then . . . she asked for a favor."

I shook my head. "You are a horrible person. No wonder Alfred's been haunting me."

"No!" she cried. "There's more to it. Once I got to know Alfred, everything changed. He was sweet to me, and he cared about me, and I took care of him."

"No you didn't," I spit. "You put him in a nursing home and told his kids he lived at home!"

"He told me to!" she said, her voice rasping. "He was getting sick in the head, and he didn't want to be a burden. He really loved me." She swallowed hard. "At least, I thought he did. The day he died, a note showed up in my room."

"What did it say?"

She reached into her purse as tears dripped down her nose and onto the pavement. She pulled out an envelope and handed it to me. "I carry it with me everywhere."

On the crinkled front of the envelope Alfred had written "Angie" in neat cursive.

I pulled out the letter, unfolded it, and scanned the page.

Angie,

    We met tonight for the first time, and I plan on marrying you. Why? Because I know Rosalie put you up to this, and since I'm so old and you're so pretty, I thought, why not have some fun in my final years? I know Rosalie is after my money, and the old bag is dim enough to think she can outsmart me. My kids each have a secret trust they'll gain access to when they're 30. I want them to work hard and live normal lives until then.

    As for the rest of my money, you can have it. I've learned a lot about you and know you need it. Help your family out. Do some good with it. All I ask is that you don't share it with Rosalie. That witch would run off with it all and leave our kids penniless if she had her way.

    Thank you, Angie. I hope you're happy with me.

    Al

I looked at Angela in disbelief. "Alfred knew?"

She nodded. "The whole time. And he never said a word."

"So did you keep his promise?"

She bit her lip and nodded. "Yes. After he died, I disappeared, and Rosalie got *nada*. I didn't even go to his funeral because I was so scared I would see her."

I stared in horror. "So if you're not the one who's cursed Alfred into some weird limbo, that means . . ."

"Rosalie." She nodded, wide eyed. "This is my first time back in town since he died, and I'm only here to clear out what's left of Alfred's things. I don't want her to know. She's into awful things that give me heebie-jeebies."

"This all makes sense," I said, a million thoughts rushing through my brain. "You're the only one who knows the truth, and you've been away for years. Alfred needed me to find you so that you could tell me and so that I could . . ." The words sputtered. What was I going to do to Rosalie? Kindly ask her to stop cursing Alfred's name? That probably wouldn't go over well.

"I have to go," I said faintly. "Thank you, Angela. I hope you're spreading the good with his money."

"I have formed a charity in Colombia," she said proudly. "Alfred's memory lives on through the bright eyes of my country's poorest children."

"Yeah, that's great," I said, turning away. "See you!"

But I didn't have to go far, since Reverend Henry was standing outside.

"Well, that was interesting," he said. "What happened with the bracelet? You touched it, and then all of a sudden you both looked shocked and you started yelling about Rosalie."

"There was a memory attached to it," I said, and I quickly explained everything I'd learned. "Can you take me to Winchester? We've got to pay Rosalie a visit."

Reverend Henry looked at me, horrified. "That's a lot to take in, Baylor." He checked his watch, hesitated, and said, "My next appointment is a lost cause anyway. Let's go."

21

Sticks and stones do more than break bones.

"SHOULD WE TELL THE POLICE WHERE we're going, Baylor?" Reverend Henry asked as we sped down the highway. "Is this woman dangerous?"

"She's only dangerous if you're already dead," I said.

My spine was tingling. I knew the Sheet Man mystery was going to be solved today, and I was excited to have Kristina back. I wondered if she would have any good stories to tell me.

"What about your parents?" he asked. "Do they know you're here?"

"Uhh, not exactly," I said breathily.

"Baylor, please do not tell me you cut school and didn't tell your parents."

"I didn't think they would enjoy hearing about this very much."

"You're going to get me in trouble," he said, shaking his head. "I'm going to be cast out of my church because of you."

"Well, hopefully, you'll be rewarded richly in the Beyond for all your efforts."

He side-eyed me and shook his head.

We pulled up outside of Rosalie's charming cottage a little while later, and I found it odd that someone so terrible could inhabit such a nice home. It was the exact same situation with humans, though—sometimes the ugliest souls lived in the best-looking people.

"You can stay here," I said to Reverend Henry. "I can take care of this on my own."

He threw his head back and laughed. "Yeah, right, Baylor," he said, unbuckling his seat belt. "Let's go."

We got out and walked up the brick path to her home. The dogs started barking before we'd even made it up the steps to her porch.

"They don't sound very friendly," the reverend said.

I knocked, but no one answered.

"Doesn't look like she's home," he said.

I knocked once more, and this time the door opened just as my fist collided with it.

I looked over at the reverend, but he was gone. In fact, most of the color from the street was gone. The back of my neck tingled. *This is it.* The talisman was shaking in my hands. I only wished I could blame it on some kind of supernatural power instead of my nerves.

I crossed through the threshold and found myself in a narrow foyer. I could go either left or straight. Something told me to go left.

I turned the corner, and standing in the sparsely decorated living room was Rosalie, dressed in red sweatpants and a tight white shirt. She held in her hand a length of white material, the same as what covered the Sheet Man, who was standing right next to her with the other end of the material around his neck, like a dog on a leash.

My jaw fell open. How was Rosalie in this weird Sheet Man dimension with me?

Then it hit me: She was a medium too!

The worst part of the Sheet Man had been his eyes, and what suddenly struck me was that Rosalie now had the same eyes—black pits of tar piercing into my blue ones. It felt like snakes had invaded my

stomach and slithered through my intestines. I knew
Rosalie was bad, but I hadn't expected this.

"He found us out, dear," Rosalie said quietly,
her voice somehow echoing around the room as she
lightly stroked the Sheet Man's material. "And I'd
been so careful for so long."

The Sheet Man said nothing, and I looked around
for Kristina.

"She's here," Rosalie said, a tight smile forming.
"But I wanted to speak with you alone first."

I saw that whenever her eyes moved, so did the
Sheet Man's, like both sets were controlled by her.

"So Angela told you about our deal," Rosalie said,
"and all about Alfred's last bit of trickery?"

She pulled on the ghost leash, but the Sheet Man
didn't move.

"How on earth did you know that?"

"You have your tricks, Baylor. I have mine." She
tugged on the leash again. "You must look at this
from my point of view," she continued, entirely too
calm for my liking. "You see—"

But I didn't get to see, because I couldn't listen
to this bizarre demon-woman for another moment,
especially not when she had supernatural tricks hidden up her sleeve. I cracked open the egg, grabbed
the stone, and chucked it at the Sheet Man.

The sheet unraveled itself like a tornado of cloth, spinning upward to reveal Alfred and a balled-up Kristina, and then ripping itself into shreds to tie around Rosalie in midsentence. They bound her feet, pinned her arms to her sides, and covered her mouth, making her resemble a very haphazardly assembled mummy.

"You did it!" Kristina yelled, unfolding herself and rising up, her hands balled into fists. "Oh, I knew you would!"

Alfred was beaming at me, and the first thing I noticed was that his eyes were actually a light shade of brown. He looked like a friendly old man, though his nose resembled a small mountain squashed in the middle of his face, and I suddenly thought of his son Will's big nose and laughed. They looked exactly alike.

"This is too funny," I said, feeling slaphappy. "It's so great to see you both."

"Wait." Kristina tensed up and looked through a wall. "We're back in the physical world, and the dogs are coming."

And sure enough, the dogs came bounding from the front door—where they'd been barking at Reverend Henry, who was still outside—and leaped at me, their sharp teeth bared.

Alfred laughed, and a fusion bomb of blue

energy flew from his hand and hit the dogs with a force so great that they were blasted out the window in a disharmonious concert of broken glass and pathetic yelps.

"So not fair," Kristina said, shaking her head with admiration at his blasting abilities.

"I've wanted to do that for years," he said, flexing his still-glowing fingers.

Reverend Henry rushed to the broken window and looked in to find me there with Rosalie all tied up.

"Baylor, where did you go?!" he yelled. "You just disappeared!"

"I was transported to that limbo realm," I said. "Everything's fine now."

"That's great to know *now*," he said while bending over and huffing, "but I panicked and called your mom. She's on her way here, and she is *not* happy with us."

"What?" I moaned. "No!"

"Who cares, Baylor!" Kristina said. "We need to deal with this whole situation first."

She motioned to Rosalie and Alfred. Their eyes were back to normal, and I was so relieved never to have to look at those beady black eyes ever again.

"Thank you so much, Baylor," Alfred said, practically dancing around the room in celebration of his freedom. "My lovely ex-wife had been using some voodoo magic for years before I died, and I was trapped in that gray landscape the second I crossed over."

Rosalie tried to say something, but her mouth was tightly gagged.

"It's not so great being bound up, is it, dear?" he said.

She glared at him, but her now unremarkable eyes affected no one.

Reverend Henry, unaware of the two ghosts present, kept looking from me to the bound-and-gagged Rosalie in shock. "What? Bay—wha—how—are you serious? What is this?"

"Just settling some grisly ghost business, Reverend," I said, grinning dreamily.

"I'll ask you for just one favor, Baylor," Alfred said, turning back to me. "If you wouldn't mind going downstairs to the basement and destroying her hate shrine dedicated to me?"

I looked at Kristina, who was also grinning like a fool, and she nodded.

"Okay," I said, and he led the way down the hall and into the kitchen.

"It's just down there, in the far left corner," he said, pointing to a door next to the refrigerator. "I'd

go with you, but you'll forgive me for being a bit
paranoid about being so close to evil so soon. I can
still feel it lingering all over me."

"I'll come with you," Kristina said, and she flicked
something in my mind to tune me into the spirits.

I frowned at her, wondering why she wanted me
tuned in, and we walked down the stairs. I found
the light switch, and the air was sucked out of my
lungs.

Rosalie had erected a table in the corner covered
in all kinds of paraphernalia: an ancient, thick book,
tarot cards, a cracked mirror, dark prisms, and a
small voodoo doll covered in a white sheet, with pins
sticking into all parts of the body.

Standing guard over the table was a Bruton, its
black, jagged wings spread apart like a massive bat's,
taking up nearly the entire width of the basement.
The fire in its eyes burned mercilessly.

"Kristina," I said under my breath. "Back up. Go
back up."

"No. Walk over with confidence and destroy the
relics," she said, defiant.

I started walking slowly again, and with every step
the fire in the Bruton's eyes glowed more sinisterly.

"Good demon," I said breathlessly. "Good boy.
Please don't attack me."

Its head followed me and shifted violently around, like black smoke escaping into the air.

I focused on my breathing, trying to keep it steady, in and out.

It can't hurt you, I reminded myself. *It can't touch you.*

I collected the tarot cards as the Bruton hovered over me, maybe three feet away. I ripped them up, trying to stifle a horrified gasp as wisps of black energy slithered into the air from the paper shreds and circled my hands, as if trying to invade me, before ultimately returning to the demon. Then I threw the book onto the floor and chucked the mirror at it, a thousand pieces of glass stabbing into its cover and scattering all over the bare gray concrete; the prisms met the same fate a few seconds later

Finally, the doll. With each needle I removed, more black energy returned to the Bruton, like he was vacuuming it up. I shredded the miniature sheet, then ripped the head off the ragged voodoo doll, threw the pieces down, and stomped on them.

The table empty, I smiled at Kristina and said, "That wasn't so bad."

The Bruton, which had been eerily watching me, suddenly screeched, and it was like an airplane had just crashed into the house. The fire in its eyes exploded out at me, and it started beating its wings back and forth to direct the flames all around me.

"Run, Baylor!" Kristina yelled.

"Where?" I shouted back, seeing only fire, which seemed to take alternating shapes of people writhing in pain.

Kristina looked around, then stuck her hand out and tried to blast a spot through the wall of fire, but it was like water evaporating in the heat of the flames.

The wall started closing in, eviscerating the table and chairs, and before I knew it, the intense heat was just a few feet away, the hairs on my arms burning, the skin practically melting off me. The terror etched in Kristina's face was sinking in, and I closed my eyes and simply thought, *Help*.

A white flash lit up the circle of fire, and Colonel Fleetwood dropped down from nowhere, wielding his silver battle sword. He cut through the flames and thrust the sword forward into the body of the Bruton.

The fire instantly vanished, reabsorbed into the shrieking Bruton. With one final fiery gaze, it tilted its head at me—at least, I think it did—and, wings beating furiously, flew off to terrorize someone else.

"Demon dung," Kristina and I said in unison. We looked at each other and laughed nervously.

"Thank you, Colonel Fleetwood," I said.

"The pleasure was all mine, Baylor, now that I can freely travel between sides again," he said. He looked Kristina up and down. She was the closest to crying I'd ever seen.

"I don't know what happened," she said.

"The protections are currently dismal at best," the colonel said. "We'll need to reinforce them later today."

"Baylor was almost taken by a Bruton," Kristina shrieked. "We should do it right now."

Before the colonel could say anything else, though, Reverend Henry's bloodcurdling scream bellowed from upstairs.

22

Seriously, avoid Brutons at all costs.

"WHAT HAPPENED?" I YELLED, SPRINTING up the stairs to the kitchen. "Can either of you see?"

Colonel Fleetwood disappeared, but Kristina stuck with me. I sprinted down the hall to the living room, where Rosalie was standing behind Reverend Henry, holding a sharp dagger to his neck. Alfred and the colonel hovered near them.

"Blast her!" I yelled.

"The knife is right against his throat," Kristina said. "The force would cut his head off."

"How did she get out?"

"The dark energy of that demon slashed her bind-ings off," Alfred said.

"The Bruton!" Anger detonated inside of me. "I'm going to hunt it down and banish it."

"Baylor, let's focus on the situation at hand," Kristina said warily.

"Right," I said, looking at the reverend's distraught and very confused face. "Rosalie, you insane witch of a person, drop the knife right now."

"Baylor Bosco, I knew the second you showed up on my doorstep that you'd be a thorn in my side," she said. "Although I should have realized that the first time my dear Alfred escaped to visit you."

"You escaped her to see me?" I said to Alfred.

"I did, though it didn't accomplish anything except to terrify you," he said. "Sorry about that. I needed to pass on a message to you somehow but couldn't find a way."

"Why did you almost kill me on Halloween, then?"

"That was me," Rosalie said brightly. "Once I realized what he'd done, I decided to send my own message."

"And then you showed me the shoes," I said to Alfred, "knowing Angela was back in town and had dropped them off."

"He certainly did," Rosalie hissed.

"I can't believe you can communicate with ghosts," I said, shaking my head. If my purpose in life was to help people, surely hers couldn't have been much different. "How could you treat someone this way?"

"Unlike you, dear," she spit, "this curse is not something I'm proud of."

"Clearly, since you're holding a reverend hostage with a knife at the moment."

"He's my insurance," she said. "With him as my hostage, you'll do whatever I demand."

"You can't go five minutes without terrorizing someone, you psychopath," Alfred said, sounding amused.

"Now that you're dead, *dear*, your opinion is worth even less to me than it was when you were alive," she said.

"Fantastic," he said. "Then it certainly won't interest you to know that Baylor's mother is almost here with a police cruiser close behind."

Her eyes flashed in shock, and she bit her lip. "Well, it looks like this will have to be fast, then. Baylor, now that you've taken away my puppet, you're going to help me get the money Angela owes me."

"That's not going to happen," I said.

"It is," she said, "because if you don't, I'll find you, and I will hurt your family." She smiled. "And I know you wouldn't want that."

"Are you insane?" I asked.

"The answer is clearly yes," Kristina said.

"Be quiet, you dumb girl," Rosalie spit. "I thought once I had you out of the way, Baylor would be too stupid to figure any of this out. I was wrong about that, but since I know he was so dedicated to finding his dead sister, it's not too big of a leap to guess he'll be just as dedicated to keeping his family alive."

She grinned horribly, revealing her straight, coffee-stained teeth, while Reverend Henry's hands gestured by his sides. He had remained silent the whole time, since he couldn't totally follow the conversation taking place with the ghosts, but he now started to give me a strange look with exaggerated wide eyes, his lips clenched together in a white line.

"What?" I asked slowly, trying to pick up his clues. "If I don't help, you're going to kill Reverend Henry? Or are you going to keep him alive and hurt my family? Which is it?"

That's when the reverend smiled. That was it! Of all people, he was the one most familiar with the ramblings of lunatics, and he could recognize a crazy woman without a plan from a mile away. Without wasting another second, I took off through the door and ran as fast as I could down the street.

"Stop!" she screamed.

I sprinted around the corner and down Main Street. Kristina was gliding next to me a second later.

"She's getting in her car," she said. "She's going to chase you down."

"The police will be here any minute," I said, panting. "She should leave town before she gets arrested for attempted murder of a holy man!"

"She's not thinking clearly," she said. "She wants that money, and she doesn't want her kids to know what she's done."

I veered into the tackle shop I'd visited with my dad on Sunday. "Call the police!" I yelled to the cashier. "A crazy lady with a knife is chasing me."

"I knew I should have stayed in bed this morning!" said the cashier, lifting up the phone and dialing 911.

"Keep running, Baylor," Kristina said suddenly.

"Do you have another exit?" I asked. The cashier nodded furiously, pointing to a door in the back of the store. "Lock your doors!" I yelled, and took off running.

I passed through a small office and clambered out the door, where there was a squat-looking ghost with hair twisted into a tight bun standing in the back alley. She looked sort of familiar, and my face must have tipped her off that I recognized her, because she sneered at me.

"You should have helped me when I asked," she said. Then it clicked—she was the ghost Kristina vanquished when I woke up in the hospital. Before I could say anything, she yelled out, "They're back here!" her voice amplified like she was talking into a megaphone.

"Argh!" Kristina yelled, stretching out both hands and blasting the ghost with blue energy; the woman flitted her fingers sarcastically as she faded away. "*Now* it decides to work," she mumbled, clearly still bitter about the Bruton. "Run faster, Baylor."

I took off again and tried my best to sprint, but I didn't know the area well and wasn't sure which way would be the best route.

"Left or right?" I said, as the road I was on was about to dead-end.

"Right! Stay hidden, but stay close to the crowded areas!"

I circled back to Main Street, wondering where Rosalie was. I was sprinting down the street, in the opposite direction from her house, when her car came screeching from a side street and stopped a foot short of hitting me.

"Stop, Baylor," she hissed, exiting the car. "Listen to me. You will help me, or you will never be free of me. Ever."

"He'll be fine," Kristina said. "You don't stand a chance against me and my spirit guides."

"Tell that to the Bruton who nearly burned your brother to a crisp," she said.

Kristina's mouth dropped open a little, but she kept her cool. "I'd be happy to."

Alfred appeared next to us.

"Leave the child alone, you monster," he said, getting in Rosalie's face. "Haven't you done enough damage?"

"Get out of here, Alfred," she said, her eyes hungry for me. "This no longer concerns you. You can cross over to the Beyond now."

"Rosalie, you idiot, I knew the whole time Angela was working with you, and I liked it," he said. "I liked having a young, beautiful girl fawning over me in my last years."

Rosalie's face was motionless. "What?"

"You think I didn't have anyone watching you after you didn't get any of my money in the divorce? I knew what you were up to the whole time. I asked Angela not to split the money with you as my dying wish."

"You knew? And you left me and your children with nothing?"

"Of course not. The children have trusts," he said. "They'll be granted access on their thirtieth birthdays."

Rosalie swallowed hard. "You left the kids money?"

"Yes, and do you know what?" He took a step forward, like he was threatening her. "They probably would have been more than happy to share it with you. But not after they find out everything you've done."

Her eyes targeted me, and the crazy rage had grown manic. "You can't tell them."

"Oh? Is that how this is going to work now?" I said. "And you're going to stop me how, exactly? Both the reverend and I know about what you did. Are you going to kill us both?"

She was silent for a moment, her eyes never leaving mine. Then, originating from somewhere deep within her, somewhere infernal, a shrill, inhuman scream erupted from her mouth, and black energy shot out of her hands and straight at my chest. Alfred leaped in front of it, and he screamed in agony and dropped to the asphalt as the Bruton descended to Rosalie's side.

That was my cue to run.

"It's time for this to end, Baylor," she growled from somewhere too close behind.

Kristina tried to blast her back, but the Bruton effortlessly absorbed the energy, fanning the flames in its eyes.

"Fleetwood, we need your help!" Kristina yelled.

I looked back to see Rosalie chasing me with the knife, her arm stretched out and slashing wildly just a few feet behind. I wondered if anyone could see this, if anyone else thought this looked as absolutely insane as I did. Where were the police? Where were the people to help? Had Rosalie's evil power distracted them? Had she utilized the Bruton to do her bidding without us realizing it?

I sprinted past the last of the shops and turned down a busy road, Rosalie hot on my heels.

"You can't win, Baylor!" she said.

I didn't say anything but heard a grunt a moment later. I looked back to find the knife hurtling at my head, but Fleetwood appeared and swatted it down with a flash of his sword.

"You British maggot!" she said, picking the knife up off the road.

Kristina gasped, looking into the distance ahead.

"What is it?" I said.

"Run as fast as you can, Baylor!"

"What is it, Kristina?"

But she was gone. Where did she go? What did she mean? What on earth was I running from now?

Rosalie continued chasing me down the empty street, flanked by Alfred, Fleetwood, and the Bruton, a flurry of black, blue, and white energy passing back and forth between them, and we traversed another twenty yards before the first car I'd seen the whole time finally appeared from behind a hill up ahead.

It was my mom's SUV. I had no idea what Kristina had planned, but I remembered her words and commanded my legs to pump harder and faster than they'd ever worked before, rocketing me forward, away from Rosalie.

Fifty feet.

Thirty feet.

Ten feet.

A half second later I closed my eyes and leaped forward as my mom's car swerved left, cutting just behind me. I could feel the wind from her car pushing me forward, and then a piercing scream hit my ears, followed by a terrible thud.

My mom scrambled out of the car, not sure whether to run to me or to check out the scene on the other side of her car.

"Oh my God! Oh my God!" she screamed over and over as she decided to run to me first. "I don't know what happened."

"Connie Bosco, you need to calm down and get back in the car," I said. Rosalie could be creeping around the corner to attack us at any moment. I grabbed her arm and threw her into the backseat. I lunged in behind her, locked the doors, and crawled past her to the other side to survey the scene.

Rosalie was slowly getting up and looking around. It was a brutal sight. Her face was covered in blood, and her expression was more savage than ever.

"We need to call for help! She's probably hurt," my mom said.

"Mom, she was chasing me with a knife," I said. "She's not the one who needs help."

"It's still not safe for you," Kristina said, appearing in the car. "Tell Mom to hit the gas!"

"You don't need to tell me twice," I said. "Mom, get in the driver's seat and get us outta here."

She started to protest and motioned to Rosalie, who was now reaching for the knife. "But what about that—"

"Kristina just said we're in danger and need to go!"

I'd said the magic words. She crawled into the front seat and shifted gears. We'd made it about three feet when Kristina and I both gasped simultaneously.

My mom slammed on the brakes. "What's going on?"

She couldn't see it, but the Bruton had glided over and latched on to Rosalie with its fingers, if you could call those black, talonlike appendages fingers.

"What are you doing?" Rosalie screamed as black

smoke rose from the point where the fingers were touching her. "Stop it!"

"What's happening to her? What's that smoke coming from her arm?" my mom whispered in fright.

"The time has come for you to repay your debts," the Bruton said with a crackly, deep voice, like a blazing fire pit come to life.

"But I'm not finished here!" Rosalie screamed, her voice earsplitting.

"We say otherwise." Its wings beating vigorously, the demon ascended toward the sky with Rosalie in its clutches, like a squiggling mouse caught in the talons of an owl, away from both the physical world and the Beyond, to a place Kristina and I knew little about. The last thing we heard from her was one long, anguished scream.

"How is that woman flying?" Mom yelped. She looked at me in horror. "You can't fly, right, Baylor? Please tell me you can't fly."

I shook my head. "Definitely not."

The police arrived shortly after, and I felt justified in my thinking that the Bruton had kept them from getting there faster when they mentioned how their sirens had caused three different car accidents, delaying their journey into town.

"Hey, you're that ghost kid!" one of the officers said, a goofy smile on his face.

"Uh, yeah, I am," I said.

"See any ghosts around now?" he asked excitedly, looking from left to right as though he might be able to spot one passing by.

His grandmother swatted him on the hand. "Tell Patty-cakes to shut up and do his job."

"Your grandmother would like me to say, 'Patty-cakes, shut up and do your job.'"

The color drained from his face. He pulled out a notepad and coughed a little. "All right, sir, let's get your statement."

And most importantly: Be brave.

THE NEXT FEW DAYS WERE INTERESTING, to say the least.

Mom was featured in the local news as a hero who saved her baby boy from a crazy woman who had somehow evaded capture and was on the loose, and the story made national news when they realized the baby boy was none other than yours truly, Baylor Bosco, the weirdo extraordinaire who could speak to ghosts.

Once that happened, reporters camped outside my house, looking for me to give them any sort of material. They wanted the wondrous boy medium to deliver healing messages on camera, which I politely declined. They asked if I was nervous that Rosalie Parker—or as she'd been known since the divorce, Rosalie Timmons—might come out of hiding and attack me, but when I told them that a demon had taken her away, they laughed like I was joking.

There were long days filled with police questioning for me, my mom, and Reverend Henry, but in the end there was nothing to be done. Rosalie was gone. My mom felt indirectly responsible for Rosalie's disappearance, since she'd swerved in front of Rosalie and precipitated her capture by the Bruton, but I reminded her that Rosalie had been chasing me down the street and trying to kill me. I asked Kristina why the Bruton had taken Rosalie away so suddenly, but she shrugged and said, "The evil play by a different set of rules."

The best part was getting to talk to Will and Isabella Parker. They came to Keene devastated and distraught, but with Alfred's assistance I got to tell them the truth they'd been waiting years to hear.

In a matter of minutes they went from destroyed over their mother's disappearance, to horrified by the news of what she'd been doing, to overwhelmed with joy over the revelation that their father had known exactly what he was doing.

"Tell Isabella she can finally move back home,"

Alfred said, gazing affectionately at his sobbing daughter. He was still battered from Rosalie's black-energy attack, but Kristina said he'd be fine eventually. "She has nothing to run from anymore."

He also gave me permission to spoil the news of their trusts. They were going to get a special letter on their thirtieth birthdays, but he decided that now would be as good a time as ever to reveal the news. That led to more crying and joyous outbursts, followed by one more message from Alfred.

"Find Angela," I said to them. "She made your dad very happy, and he'd like for you to have a relationship."

Their faces tightened, but they didn't protest.

Keene High School's homecoming game was that weekend, and since my dad was a teacher there, he liked for the whole family to attend. My parents, unfortunately, hadn't forgotten about my disaster with Aunt Hilda, so this year they invited her to come along with my grandparents as a gesture of goodwill. It was a cold night, the first time we had to break out the winter gear and bundle up, and I hoped Aunt Hilda would be wearing too many layers to be able to speak.

The night was going smoothly until some freshman

girls spotted me in the stands after the band's half-time show and started clamoring for messages. Since I'd been on the news so much, the number of Bay-lievers had skyrocketed. Meanwhile, Aunt Hilda sat there with a big frown plastered on her wrinkly face, suddenly fascinated with the gum stuck to the metal bleachers by her feet.

I had delivered a few messages when a woman with the same attitude as Aunt Hilda spoke up. She had blond hair that was cut short above her shoulders, and she turned around to look at me down her nose.

"Honey, I have a close relationship with my maker," she said with a condescending grin, "and I know where you'll be going if you keep up this spirit nonsense." She pointed down to the ground.

"Hey, now," my dad said, "there's no need to be rude, Mrs. Jalasky."

"I'm just stating my beliefs, sir," she said, turning back around.

My dad was about to say something else, but I put my hand on his shoulder and tried not to laugh out loud. The woman's father was standing next to her, rolling his eyes and saying, "Do you hear this girl? Can you believe I raised someone so closed-minded?"

"Give him something specific to say to her," Kristina said, nudging him.

"Tell Tammie she shouldn't be judging you when *she's* the one who's been buying five bottles of wine every weekend instead of donating that money to people who actually need it."

"I can't say that," I murmured, blushing.

"And one more thing, Mr. Bosco," Tammie said, turning around yet again. "Now that I know the beliefs you instill in your children, I can't say I'm too thrilled about my son having you for his teacher."

My dad's eyes flickered in shock, and I knew he was thinking of his dad. He'd finally confessed to me that Grandpa's message was about his insecurity over changing jobs. I guess he'd been worried about the fact that he wasn't making as much money working as a teacher, but it made him happier than working as an accountant.

Seeing the pain in my dad's eyes, I was suddenly furious with the woman. "Hey, Tammie," I said, enunciating every syllable, "your dad says to lay off the weekend wine and donate the money to people who need it instead."

The woman's jaw dropped dramatically, and Kristina, giggling, let me see her red, embarrassed aura.

"How dare you!" she said, looking around at the

other moms, who were staring at her awkwardly, her blond hair smacking her face. "I should sue you for slander."

"Ask her to let you sniff her 'water bottle,'" her dad said, making air quotations with his fingers.

"Tammie, your dad thinks you should let me smell your water bottle," I said quietly. "Any reason why?"

The muscles in her neck flared, and she got up, grabbed her purse, and stomped away as the football players ran back onto the field to start the third quarter.

"Well," my dad said, a little smile on his face, "that was embarrassing."

After the game ended, I was holding Ella and walking next to Aunt Hilda, who was hobbling along with her walker. The only sound was Ella's gurgling.

"Did you have fun, Aunt Hilda?" I finally asked.

"Sure," she scoffed. "I especially enjoyed the half-time entertainment."

My cheeks flushed, and I was fed up. "Is there a reason you don't like me, Aunt Hilda?"

Her eyebrows shot up, and almost as soon as I finished speaking, she blurted out, "Why haven't you ever delivered a message from Marvy?" She nervously caressed her half-heart necklace, and for the first time I noticed the letters *MAR* lightly etched onto the pendant.

"Her husband, Uncle Marvin," Kristina said, wafting back from eavesdropping on a conversation Jack was having with my dad. Her voice was ominous. "I've never seen him before. I don't think he's in the Beyond, Baylor. . . ."

"Uh, I'm sorry, Aunt Hilda, but he's never appeared to me," I said. "I can't make him deliver a message if he doesn't want to." I paused. "Or maybe he can't deliver one."

She stopped walking and reached into her pocket for her handkerchief. "I wish he would."

She blew her nose while Kristina and I exchanged awkward glances. If Uncle Marvin wasn't in the Beyond, then he was somewhere else . . . somewhere bad. Maybe even with Rosalie.

"Sorry," I said quietly.

Then we kept walking like nothing had happened.

The Fall Ball was less than a week away, and Aiden and J had successfully avoided talking to each other for several days. But no longer could they avoid the subject.

As far as I knew, J had said no to Andrew but still hadn't said yes to Aiden. Aiden had gotten out of his mess by telling Cassie he could never be with someone who would attack one of his friends.

But even though they had no attachments precluding them from getting together, they still weren't together.

"This is getting pathetic," Kristina said as she sat with us at lunch and watched Aiden eat his pepperoni sandwich in sad silence. "It's even worse than listening to Napoléon perform his speeches over and over again." She shook her head. "And nothing has ever been worse than that."

"Well, what are we going to do?" I muttered. She did a double take. She wasn't used to me responding to her questions at school.

"We've got to make him man up, like you said J wanted."

We watched him use a pepperoni to wipe mustard off his lip and then eat it.

I tried to hide my disgust. Kristina didn't have to worry about that and looked at him as though he'd just sneezed in her face.

"You're going to have to help him again," she said. "I'm sorry, but it's just the way it is. Remember last year's jazz concert, when you all performed with that soloist?"

"Yeah?"

"Well, you should perform it, and Aiden can be the soloist," she said with a devilish grin.

And the image bloomed so clearly in my mind that I thought it just might work. I ran to the band room, grabbed my tuba, and brought it back to the table.

"What are you doing with that?" Aiden asked.

"Aiden, I'm helping you redeem yourself with J," I said.

"What's going on? What are you talking about?" he asked, panicked.

"Remember that jazz concert from last year? That funny love song we did?"

"Yeah," he said slowly, "we had that pretty singer from the high school perform with us."

"Well, you get to be a pretty singer for a few minutes."

"What?" he squeaked, and I thought I saw tears spring to his eyes. "Baylor, no, you can't do this to me!"

But the bell rang, and I already had my tuba, and Kristina was goading me on, and J was walking in our direction.

"Sorry, buddy!" I said sincerely. "In three, two, one."

And I began playing the notes, while a couple of our band friends pushed him to stand on the table.

"Oh my God," he said, his legs suffering from an earthquake only he could feel.

J was looking at Aiden with alarmed intrigue, which I took as a good sign.

"Now!" I said to Aiden between breaths.

"I'm wise to you baby," Aiden croaked, completely out of tune and speaking instead of singing, his arms stiff at his sides. "Think that I'm going away."

J walked slowly our way, and I played my tuba with gusto. Bobby ran over, laughing, and starting drumming the beat on a textbook.

"People call me craaazy, at least for today."

She smiled, and miraculously Aiden smiled and started singing with an air of confidence, looking only at J while everyone around us snickered.

"When you say you don't waaaant me, it makes me feel bluuuue."

Kristina jumped up as J stopped a few feet from us. "It's working!"

"If you don't believe I looooove you, look what a fool I've beeeen! If you don't think I'm siiiiinking, look whaaat a hole I'm in!"

Aiden climbed down from the table and grabbed her hands.

"Before I met you, I had a good pair of shooooes, but take a look at me now!" He let go of J, stepped back, and kicked off his shoes, falling to his knees dramatically. "I've got the barefooted bluuuues!"

Everyone around us was cheering and whooping, and Aiden reached up for J's hands again and pulled her down to the ground with him. Kristina touched my shoulder and told me to stop playing, and I motioned for Bobby to stop too.

Looking her right in the eyes, a small smile on his face, Aiden sang the last line: "If you don't believe I love you . . ."—he swallowed, trying to keep his voice from cracking—"look what a fool I've been."

There was a moment of silence where J and Aiden stared at each other, and everyone else stared at them in jealousy, and everyone was wondering what was going to happen next. Then J smiled, leaned in, and kissed Aiden on the cheek, and the crowd exploded.

A bunch of girls came up and started gushing to me.

"That was the most romantic thing I've ever seen."

"You're so talented, Baylor!"

"You're just so blessed!"

"Do you have a date for the dance this weekend?"

I looked at Kristina, who was grimacing next to me, grossed out I was getting attention from girls. She nodded at me to talk to them, so I smiled, embarrassed, and tried to answer them politely. Bobby sauntered over and said, "This fine gentleman is up for grabs, and Baylor is too. Any takers?" The girls giggled, and I blushed almost as bad as Aiden.

The truth was, I didn't have a date. I'd been so distracted by the Sheet Man escapades that I was planning on going alone, or possibly with Aiden if he and J hadn't made up by then. But really, I wasn't going alone. I'd be going with Kristina.

Except . . . she was my sister, and dead or alive, that was still weird.

"Don't feel bad for me," she said, as though she could read my mind. "I can ask Colonel Fleetwood to accompany me that night."

I smiled at her and turned back to the girls.

If I could get a date out of it, why not?

The night of the dance, before my mom took me to J's house, where a bunch of us were meeting to take pictures, I gathered my family in our backyard, much to their chagrin. It hadn't snowed yet, but the temperature was so low that we were one spilled cup of water away from having snow.

We huddled together by one of the bushes, and for once Kristina had no idea what I was about to do. I had secretly recruited Madame Nadirah to help me.

"What's this about, Baylor?" my mom asked as she clung on to my dad for warmth.

"So, family, as you all know, I can see and speak to Kristina," I said, holding something heavy and wrapped in a towel, "and even though you can't see or hear her, she's constantly around and very much a part of our lives."

"Baylor, what are you doing?" Kristina asked, sounding embarrassed.

"And I thought it was sad that there wasn't a tangible reminder of her in our house, so I decided to change that."

I put the object down on some mulch and took the towel off to reveal a flat rock with an inscription: FOR KRISTINA, OUR BELOVED DAUGHTER AND SISTER, WHOSE LOVE LIVES ON IN OUR HEARTS.

"There," I said. "Now no one can ever forget you."

Kristina, looking grateful that ghosts can't cry, walked over and melted into me, sending chills all throughout my body.

"I hate when you do that!" I said, backing away.

Ella laughed. "Kristi hug!" she screamed in my brother's arms, and I ran my fingers through her curly hair.

"That's right!" I said. "Kristina gave me a hug."

I looked over at my mom, who was breathing deeply and nodding.

"That was so nice, Baylor," she said softly as we walked back inside. "After all she's done for us, I can't believe we didn't have anything like it before."

"I sort of can," my dad said, wrapping his arm around her waist, "if only because we were too sad to create one."

"Well, this surprise was mainly for her," I said, my voice barely containing my excitement. "I've got one more for you two."

My parents glanced at each other, worried, as I opened the hall closet and handed them a wrapped box. "Open it!"

My mom tore off the wrapping paper slowly, my dad at her side. The paper floated to the ground as they stared in shock at the framed portrait of Kristina.

I had made some friends at the police station, which is to say I charmed them by delivering end-less messages from their loved ones, and one of them knew a sketch artist, who agreed to help me draw Kristina. However, it turned out that I wasn't very good at describing Kristina's features, so the frus-trated artist left me alone in a back room to search through a database to find the facial features that looked most like Kristina's. It was boring at first, but as I scrolled through pages and pages of noses, I got to ask Kristina over and over about a lot of the things that'd been bugging me about her world.

"But what can you *do*? Tommy specifically said you weren't an average ghost," I said, flipping through nose after nose on the computer, trying to find one that matched hers. "It's not fair. You know I can talk to ghosts, so I should get to know whatever makes you special in the Beyond."

"Tommy needs to learn to keep his mouth shut," Kristina snapped. She still hadn't gotten over him advising me to venture into that weird limbo by myself. "All I can say is that I get to learn lessons in the Beyond."

"But everyone learns lessons in the Beyond. You say that all the time."

She shrugged.

"Do you go into a classroom and listen to someone talk and take notes? Who's the teacher? Is it Gandhi? It's totally Gandhi, isn't it?"

"Baylor, stop."

"And Grandpa Bosco said that being ghostnapped by the Sheet Man was part of your journey. What does that mean? How was being trapped in a bunch of sheets for a week beneficial to you at all?"

"Baylor," she finally said after the fiftieth time I'd asked, "listen to me."

I looked up from all the noses and smiled politely as she walked over and crouched down next to me. "Yes, ma'am."

"I truly don't know that much more than you, but I

promise we'll both find out more as we walk through this life together," she said, smiling widely, like she was looking forward to it or something. "We're a duo, Baylor. The undead duo! And this really is just the beginning. We have so, *so* much more to learn."

In the end the sketch artist and I had finally come up with a pretty accurate depiction of Kristina. The long hair, the skinny face that matched my mother's, the kind eyes that so resembled Ella's, Jack's funny nose, the flat mouth of my father, and my round chin.

"This . . . this can't be . . . ," my mom said, shaking her head, tears streaming freely down her face. It's a good thing we weren't outside, or else they'd have turned into icicles. "Kristina?"

I nodded. The cold weather must have really dried my eyes out, because they were suddenly flooded with water too.

My dad studied the portrait in silence, his eyes moving rapidly, his head nodding to a fast beat only he could hear.

Kristina stood off to the side, staring happily. She had been embarrassed at first about the idea, but the more she thought about it, the more she wanted them to have it. In fact, it was supposed to be their Christmas present, but she was so pleased with how it turned out and so eager for them to finally see her, she said she'd help me find something even better. Watching my parents' reactions, I realized I'd been duped.

"She's beautiful," my mom whispered.

We stared at the picture for a few more minutes, until my mom shook her head fast and said, "It's time to go, Baylor! You're going to be late for pictures!" She sounded giddy and ran to clean up her mascara so she could look nice for all the other parents. "We still have to pick up the corsage, too!"

At the florist's shop my mom and I watched as the woman behind the counter bounced with excitement.

"I just love all these dances the school puts on!" she said as she wrapped up the corsage. "It's so cute to see the kids get all dressed up and pick up flowers and act all nervous."

"I'm not nervous!" I said, and my voice picked that exact moment to crack. She winked me, and I blushed.

Just as we were leaving, a nice grandma ghost tapped my shoulder.

"I'm sorry, young man, I know you're busy," she said, smiling in a sheepish way. "But I was hoping you might tell my daughter how proud I am of her for chasing her dreams and owning her own flower shop." She looked down at some lush yellow roses and smiled sadly. "I so wish I could smell these. They've always been my favorite."

I looked at my watch, and Kristina smiled and said, "It'll only take a minute."

"Hold on, Mom," I said. "Duty calls."

I turned back to the counter and smiled at the florist. "One more thing, ma'am," I said. "My name is Baylor Bosco, and I can communicate with people who have crossed over."

Acknowledgments

TO MY WONDERFUL PARENTS—I ALREADY dedicated this book to you. What more do you want?! I'm kidding. Thanks for your endless love and support. I'm not sure how I got so lucky to deserve such a great mom and dad, but I'm not going to question it. Ben and Jenny, my dear siblings, thank you for the many years of fighting and yelling and emotional scarring from when we were growing up. You've provided *plenty* of material for future books. (Just kidding again! I'm on a roll. Love ya.)

All my thanks and gratitude to my agent, Dan Lazar—the best in the biz—for being generally awesome, relentlessly tenacious, and totally game to answer my e-mails at all times of day. Thanks to everyone else at Writers House, especially Torie Doherty-Munro, Cecilia de la Campa, and Angharad Kowal.

To my editor, Michael Strother—thanks so much for all your hard work. Where would I be without your fantastic, insightful notes? Well, we're about to find out, since your talents have taken you elsewhere! However, I'm thrilled Amy Cloud has taken over editorial duties and I look forward to working with someone so delightfully warmhearted and smart. Thanks to everyone else at S&S/Aladdin, especially Mara Anastas, Audrey Gibbons, Jodie Hockensmith, Mary Marotta, and Carolyn Swerdloff. Oh, and of course, thanks to Hugh D'Andrade, for creating a cover that perfectly captures the spirit of the book.

Thanks to my family, friends, teachers, coworkers, and countless other people for all your support and kind words of encouragement. Huge thanks to Sue Davis, Seema Mahanian, and Lauren Vallario for your invaluable input and guidance.

I'd be remiss not to acknowledge anything and everything that's helped me along from, well, the other side. My long-lost twin, wherever you are, thanks for the inspiration. Theresa Caputo, my other vital source of inspiration—you are a gem. And, finally, a special shout-out to Grandpa Erv, Uncle Moose, and Mr. Senior—thanks for keeping watch over me.

READ ON
FOR A SNEAK PEEK AT

BAYLOR'S
Guide
to
Dreadful
Dreams

1

Keep your electronics away from ghosts.

BOY MEDIUM BAYLOR BOSCO: BEWITCHED OR BEDEVILED?

Keene, New Hampshire. A small town with a big claim to fame. Just last year, the annual Keene Pumpkin Festival achieved a Guinness world record for most jack-o'-lanterns gathered in one place—that's 30,581 pumpkins carved and lit up with candles.

In the last few weeks, however, the city has captured national attention for a *very* different reason. Baylor Bosco, 13, claims to be a medium. A boy who, yes, talks to dead people.

Bosco first caught people's attention when he seriously injured a 68-year-old woman at a local Italian restaurant in early November.

"He was walking right toward her and sped up," said Michael Lindberg, who witnessed the incident. "She went flying to the ground. That little punk did it on purpose."

The paramedics were called, but strangely, no charges were filed. Witnesses reported that Bosco then held a group séance and communicated messages from patrons' "loved ones" for close to 30 minutes.

Less than a week later, Bosco was plastered all over the news again for his involvement in the disappearance of Winchester, NH, resident Rosalie Timmons. Ms. Timmons seriously injured herself after running full-speed into a vehicle that had blocked her path, according to the police report. And the driver of that vehicle? None other than Constance Bosco, the mother of the boy medium.

When asked about her role in Timmons's disappearance, Ms. Bosco emphatically uttered "No comment" no less than eight times while virtually running away from this intrepid reporter.

Baylor himself was a little more forthcoming. I was able to ask him questions during a recent walk home from school. The 13-year-old seems rather short for a boy his age; he has unstyled dirty blond hair, eyes the color of dirty lake water, and a permanent scowl stretched across his face.

"That woman was evil!" he screeched about Timmons, who had long been known in the Winchester community for her philanthropic efforts. "She tried to kill me!"

Then he appeared to have a spasm, as he grimaced at the air next to him and said, to no one, "No, Kristina, I'm not doing that." His clear affinity for inflicting pain onto others reared its ugly head when, a few moments later, he spouted off some deeply personal information about this reporter; information he'd clearly thoroughly researched before our meeting.

Whether Baylor Bosco does more good than harm with his supposed gift remains to be seen. Regardless, it looks as though Keene has another eccentric attraction here to stay.

—Carla Clunders, editor-at-large,

NewEnglandRealNews.net

I finished reading the article on my phone and sat dumbfounded on my bed. Rage tingled across my skin.

"Baylor, it's one bad article written by one terrible person," Kristina said, hovering over my shoulder. "Ignore it."

"Easy for you to say!" I scrolled through it again, trying to figure out which part was the worst.

"Isn't this the same website that picked a fight with the mayor and called him a 'really big doo-doo head'?"

"What's your point?"

"It's not exactly reputable. Think of all the nice articles about you that were posted on legitimate news sites. This woman is a fraud."

"I'm not short, Kristina, okay? I'm, like, five foot four. With shoes on, definitely five foot five."

"I didn't say you were short," she said slowly.

"Well, you didn't say I was tall, either," I said, glaring at her.

"I'm sorry, I didn't think I needed to considering how I've been saying for ten minutes that this woman is a moron," she said, her hands forming fists. "She's clearly a nonbeliever bent on making you look bad. Why are you wasting any energy on her?"

Somewhere deep down inside, I knew she was right. I mean, what kind of real journalist would compare someone's eyes to dirty lake water? (*Especially* when other people have compared those same eyes to a majestic spring sky, but that's beside the point.)

How could this woman sit there and write such negative things about me? What had I ever done to her? Well, aside from delivering her dead sister's message about constipation solutions, but that was hardly my fault. It was, in the most literal sense, a healing message, and it was my life's purpose to deliver as many of them as possible.

I reread the line about spouting off some deeply personal information I'd researched before meeting her. Ha! She made it sound like we'd agreed to an interview when, in reality, she'd hopped out from behind a tree and ambushed me on my way home from school two days ago.

"Carla Clunders. What kind of stupid name is that anyway?"

"That's it, Baylor," Kristina said, her hand outlined

in blue. "No more." She wrapped her fingers around my phone and squeezed hard, emitting a pulse of blue energy; the screen went haywire.

"Did . . . did you just break my phone?"

She frowned, releasing her grip. "I really hope not, but I'm still getting used to this." She'd never been able to use any sort of energy before, but after my recent escapades battling some uninvited demon visitors, she'd finally gotten the go-ahead from . . . someone.

I still wasn't exactly sure how it worked with Kristina, my twin sister. She was miscarried in the womb, but somehow she grew up with me and hung around on the other side. She split her time between hanging with me and mingling with other ghosts in the Beyond, the place where all ghosts eventually wind up. The Beyond is sort of like an exclusive club on the other side, and only decent ghosts get admitted. There are other places and dimensions on the other side too, but unless you're a big fan of hordes of fiery-eyed demons, it's best to avoid those bad neighborhoods and stick to the Beyond.

She claims to go to the Beyond to learn lessons and get advice from spirit guides, but in my head, the Beyond was nothing more than one giant party, with a few billion ghosts just hanging out, sipping on some ghostly soda, eating some ghostly chips, for all of eternity. She always mentions chatting with all these iconic people, like Napoléon or Washington, but the only people I ever got to talk to were random dead people who wanted to tell their loved ones they needed to hit the gym. I wasn't jealous, per se—I like being alive, after all—but sometimes it felt like I was getting the short end of the stick.

Her long golden hair whipped around her face as she flexed her hand for a few seconds, wiggling her fingers. "I wonder if this is what it feels like, Baylor, when you lie on the couch for an hour watching TV and then your arm falls asleep and you whine about how much it tingles."

"You're not being helpful."

I glanced at the clock and sighed. I was going to be late for school if I didn't leave in exactly four minutes and speed walk the entire way. My day was already off to a bad start, and the last thing I needed was a detention on top of everything else.

I rushed through my morning routine—the usual stuff like brushing my teeth, combing my hair, and lighting candles to ward off evil spirits—and headed out the front door as Kristina chattered away in my ear.

"Think of all the positive news stories about you after the Rosalie incident. Why focus on the negative one?"

"It's just weird. It's almost like she's on a mission

to make me look bad. Isn't there some sort of law to protect me against creeps like her? I'm only thirteen, after all. She's endangering a child."

"You're acting a tad dramatic about this, don't you think?"

"No, I don't," I said. "In fact, I think I ought to sue Carla Clunders for libel."

Kristina rolled her eyes and muttered, "She wasn't wrong about the height thing."

I pretended like I didn't hear her and sped up. It was mid-November, and Keene was already experiencing frigid winter temperatures. I tried to convince my mom to drive me to school yesterday morning, but she laughed and said that the cold built character. I disagreed and told her walking a mile through freezing temperatures would only make me a bitter, unhappy person for the rest of my life, but she didn't seem too concerned about that.

By the time I got to school, my teeth were chattering like broken wind chimes.

"You look rough," Aiden said as I took my seat next to him. "Oversleep?"

"No," I said shortly. "I woke up to some stupid article written about me."

"Oh," he said, chuckling. "Another Bayliever blog post rambling on about how cute you are?"

My cheeks burned, but no longer because of the cold. "That was one time."

He shrugged. "Still. She had two hundred comments all agreeing with her. Another one's bound to pop up sooner or later."

"Well, this new one is the opposite of that. For some reason this woman is determined to make me look bad."

"Make you look bad?" J. said, sitting in the desk in front of Aiden. "That's not exactly hard to do, Baylor." She winked at me through her neon-green glasses. J. was so smart that if she didn't become one of the youngest astronauts ever, it'd only be because she was probably busy studying for medical and law degrees at the same time.

"Good morning to you, too, J.," I said, scowling.

She turned to Aiden and smiled. "Morning!"

Aiden sputtered and choked on his own breath. Kristina and I looked at each other and shook our heads. They'd been going out for maybe ten days now—after Aiden finally got the nerve to tell her he liked her in a musical blaze of glory prompted by yours truly—but he somehow acted more nervous than ever around J.

"Anyway," J. said, her eyes framed by the bright green glasses. "Are you guys ready for tomorrow?"

The band was marching in Keene's Thanksgiving Day Parade. I played the tuba; Aiden rocked the flute. The parade always takes place the Saturday before Thanksgiving because most of the residents head out of town for the holiday. Keene learned that lesson the hard way during its inaugural parade a few years ago, when it was held on Thursday morning and only, like, twenty people showed up to watch it.

"I think so," I said. "Now that Mr. G. finally dropped that weird "Silent Night/All I Want for Christmas Is You" mash-up, I think we're in pretty good shape."

She chuckled. "I'm bummed I never got to hear it."

Kristina groaned from behind. "She should consider herself lucky."

I agreed with Kristina. If I never heard any of those songs again, I'd be a happy guy. It wasn't just because the mash-up sounded like a chorus of dying parrots, though. It also brought up some bad memories from the last few weeks.

Right around Halloween, I'd been plagued by a demon wearing a sheet, whom I endearingly referred to as the Sheet Man. It turned out the demon was this poor dead guy named Alfred who was being controlled by his ex-wife, Rosalie. That wasn't so easy to figure out, though. At one point, I'd wound up in the hospital after the Sheet Man visited me during band practice. We'd been rehearsing the mash-up when he just showed up out of nowhere and, next thing I knew, I woke up in hospital, nearly concussed after my tuba had fallen on my head.

All's well that ends well, though, and that whole situation ended when Rosalie was suddenly picked off by a horribly evil spirit called a Bruton, one of the worst kinds of demons around, and taken to some place far, far away.

Okay, so maybe it didn't end well for Rosalie, but that's what happens when you involve yourself in evil activities.

After school, during the last rehearsal before the parade, Mr. G. made us run through the songs and practice our marching about a million times. By the time I got home, I was ready for a nap before dinner.

"Well, before you nap, I just want to warn you," Kristina said, her voice sounding a bit thin.

I turned to her slowly. Warnings from Kristina were just about my least favorite things in life. "What is it?"

"Well, it's nothing bad," she said quickly, looking sort of embarrassed, "but tonight we'll be having some company."

I glared. "Are you saying—?"

"Kristina! Baylor!" rang a British voice from behind me. "How are you this fine evening?"